C IS FOR CADAVER

Alex, regretting his good flannel trousers and cursing practical jokesters in general and medical students in particular, climbed up over the row of shields. Cautiously, his feet slipping on the wet ice, hanging on to the gunwales, he made his way forward in the ice sculpture to what might have been a hatchway. Here, well in the shadow of the rising sides of the Viking ship, was a small raised rectangle, and under a layer of melting ice, Alex could easily make out a human shape: coat, stockings, boots, dark mittened hands, a dark cap fitted around a pale oval face, and around its neck, taking several turns, a long dark school scarf....

"Sarah," Alex called. "It's not a med student's prank. At least I don't think so. Will you call the ambulance, and"—it wasn't really an afterthought—"the police."

"BORTHWICK WRITES BRIGHTLY WITH A NICE TWIST OF WRY HUMOR."
—*The Washington Post Book World*

THE
STUDENT
BODY

J.S. BORTHWICK

SMP
ST. MARTIN'S PAPERBACKS

Bowmouth College, its faculty, and all the other characters in this book are fictitious.

THE STUDENT BODY

Copyright © 1986 by J. S. Borthwick.

Cover illustration by Jeff Walker.
Text illustrations by Alex Creighton.
Map by Margaret S. Creighton.

Library of Congress Catalog Card Number: 86-13797

ISBN: 0-312-92605-7

Printed in the United States of America

St. Martin's Press hardcover edition published 1986
St. Martin's Paperbacks edition/August 1987

10 9 8 7 6 5 4 3 2

For Mac and J. Ashley C.

Cast of Principal Characters

SARAH DEANE . . . . Teaching Fellow, Bowmouth College

ALEX McKENZIE, M.D. . . . . Internal Medicine, Mary Starbox Memorial Hospital

HOWARD BELLO . . . . Associate Professor, Chairman English Department

PATRICK FLETCHER . . . Professor: Old English, Medieval literature

CONSTANCE GARVEY . . . . Associate Professor: The novel

JOSEPH GREENBERG . . . Professor: The novel, contemporary literature

JAKOB HORST . . . . Associate Professor: Poetry, Poetics

IVAN LACEY . . . . Associate Professor: Sixteenth century, Shakespeare

AMOS LARKIN . . . . Associate Professor: Eighteenth-century literature

EUSTACE MERLIN-SMITH . . . . . Associate Professor: Seventeenth century

VERA PRUCZAK . . . . Associate Professor: Drama; as Olivia Macbeth, novelist

MARY DONELLI . . . . Teaching Fellow

DRAGO COLLINS . . . . Teaching Fellow

ALICE MARMOTT . . . . Undergraduate student

ROSALIND PARKER . . . . Secretary to the English Department

ARLENE BURR . . . . Clerk to the English Department

LINDA LACROIX . . . . Clerk to the English Department

GEORGE FITTS . . . . Sergeant, CID, Maine State Police

MIKE LAAKA . . . . Sheriff's Deputy Investigator

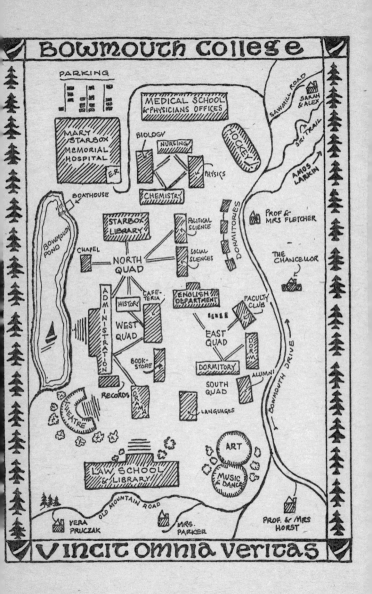

ONE

"...The Mock Turtle went on.
'We had the best of educations.
... Reeling and Writhing, of
course, to begin with ... and then
the different branches of
Arithmetic—Ambition, Distraction,
Uglification, and Derision.'"

—*Alice's Adventures in Wonderland*

There was only a day left before the beginning of the winter term, and except for the usual flaring of tempers that always accompanied the registration process, things went on pretty much as usual in the Bowmouth College English Department.

Professor Constance Garvey sat in her cramped half-size office and scowled at a memo from a mush-headed (her words) faculty adviser urging that two students be given incompletes instead of failures for their fall semester's work. Without missing a beat, Professor Garvey crumpled the memo and wrote large *F*'s on two grade sheets and then picked up her briefcase and headed for the Faculty Common Room. Time for her morning cup of cocoa.

Across the hall in a commodious corner office, Professor

Patrick Fletcher turned on his desk tape deck to a recording of Gregorian chants and addressed himself to the agreeable task of signing a stack of presentation volumes—*The Seafarer and the Wanderer: A New Translation From the Old English.* Two doors down, in an office with a fine view of the second-floor ladies' lavatory window of the Social Science Building, Professor Ivan Lacey lifted graduate student Tammy Finworth from his lap and, with a final nuzzle in the back of her neck, pleaded the need to prepare for tomorrow's Shakespeare seminar. One office beyond, Professor Eustace Merlin-Smith (né Schmidt) stared with a moist eye at a framed needlepoint motto his wife had given him for Christmas. What was the use of it all, he thought. Life, work, everything on this godforsaken campus seemed to be going up in smoke, and the needlepoint words—worked in the Bowmouth colors of crimson and blue—*Vincit omnia veritas*—Truth conquers all—gave no comfort.

For Professor Amos Larkin, directly opposite, comfort was no problem. A bottle of Jim Beam had taken care of the matter, and now the professor found that all the books and papers in his piled-up office had melted together into a hazy indeterminate mass. Diagonally across the way from Amos Larkin, Professor Jakob Horst closed his door on a student who for the third time that week had arrived to demand the return of last semester's term paper and then settled himself down to a dissection of Andrew Marvell's poem "The Nymph Complaining for the Death of Her Fawn."

Meanwhile, the chairman of the English Department, Howard Bello, in his large center office facing the corridor, hearing the clarion voice of resident drama professor Vera Pruczak sounding in the distance, rose in distress, switched off his light, and ducked behind his coat rack. Shortly after Professor Bello had gone into hiding, Professor Joe Greenberg found himself besieged by several students that Professor Bello had earlier refused to see and so spent a frustrating hour trying to find out why the students had found themselves in classes for which they were not registered and not in those for which they had.

In the center of the hallway, in an office that served as the nerve center of the English Department, Mrs. Rosalind

Parker, Secretary, sorted and discarded, commanded and dispatched. In the space of four morning hours she had spoken her mind at a faculty meeting, gone on the warpath with the bookstore, which had garbled a textbook order, brought the two English Department clerks, Linda and Arlene, into line, unscrambled the registration computer card mess, and assured Professor Bello by telephone that he had the rest of the day free and she would deal with his student appointments "just as I have done before, Howard. You know I have never let you down."

So far, so good, thought Sarah Deane. New snow, a fine clear January day, and signs of welcome. The wrought-iron gates marking the entrance to the North Quadrangle stood open, the bottom row of scrolls and ogees heaped with clean shoveled snow. Two snow-capped griffins (gift of the Class of 1913) stood at each side atop a stone pillar, and both animals, by the sculptor's intent or a from a trick of lighting, seemed to smile on the visitor and cry welcome.

Sarah, newly appointed teaching fellow of the college, hurried through the gates and along the walk that led to a long row of academic buildings. She had from a rush of nerves arrived some forty minutes early for her appointment with Professor Bello, but now, encouraged by the welcoming griffins and the open gate, she felt a slight relaxing of the death grip she had taken on the handle of her new briefcase. She slowed her step and took time to note the eminence of the rotunda-crowned library on her right and then the three brick Georgian buildings housing classrooms and the departments of social and political science that stood on her left, just ahead of her present goal, Malcolm Adam Hall, home of the English Department and senior English faculty. This reached, she opened the door and, as directed, mounted the worn stone steps to the second floor and found herself looking down a long hall covered in a buff and black diamond-pattern linoleum.

Some ten minutes later, Sarah decided that the welcome mat had ended with the griffins and the open gate. She had advanced first to a mid-corridor door marked ENGLISH OFFICE to find its glass top covered in a depressing fall of purple macramé on which was hung a sign: LUNCH PERIOD. COME BACK AT 1 P.M. Sarah checked her watch. Ten of twelve. Well, her appointment wasn't until twelve-twenty, so she could look around, get the feel of the place. The door opposite the English Office showed clear glass and the painted information that this belonged to Mrs. Rosalind Parker, Secretary; beneath, a neatly printed notice advised that Mrs. Parker was at a meeting and would—like General MacArthur—return. Sarah retreated and saw standing ajar a solid oak door with a brass plaque identifying the Professor Moses Shelldrake Faculty Common Room. But she had hardly moved three steps inside when a large and hostile-looking female with the brow of Mussolini—it was Professor Garvey—entrenched in a leather chair looked over her glasses and said, "Only faculty here. You want the student waiting room. Kindly close the door."

Rather daunted, Sarah retreated to the department entrance and a chamber opposite the waiting room marked FELLOWS' ROOM. Well, that's what she was now, a fellow of Bowmouth College, but judging from the typing rattle and occasional muffled expletive coming through the door, this was an already established center of work. She hesitated, not wanting to break in. After all, she was arriving midterm, when all office space for the year would have been pretty well set. In fact, she had been taken on at Bowmouth only when one of the fellows had abandoned academe for the greater glory of the giant slalom competition.

Having run out of options, Sarah turned and opened the door to the the student waiting room. Here, settled in an imitation Danish modern chair by the window some distance away from three students who were restlessly moving from chair to chair and slamming their textbooks open and closed, she looked out over the quadrangle and heard the first notes of the hour sound.

There is something reassuring about bells rung out over a campus, especially the sixteen-note sequence of the Westminster chimes followed by the steady *bong, bong* of the hour. From her listening post, Sarah reflected that even the most harried teacher, the most forgetful student, the most overworked clerical drone must hear the sounds with a reassuring sense that all was well and the college world was turning in its proper orbit. She leaned back in her chair and indulged herself in the pleasant fancy that all the love and loathing that boil behind the academic facade, the struggles for tenure, for precedence, for professional acclaim, for the B average, for the perfect term paper, were, for this short space of measured time, on hold.

The bells from the Starbox Administration Building tower tolled twelve times for noon, and from the chapel side of the campus, chimes, sounding brittle and faint in the cold air, gave out with "Love Divine, All Loves Excelling." The three students looked up at each other, picked up their bags and sacks, and, perhaps in search of lunch, banged out of the room and down the stone steps.

Left now to peace and quiet, Sarah found that she had nothing more to do than wonder how college freshmen differed in kind from the high-school students she had been teaching at a Boston country day school. One thing sure, she could hardly threaten to notify their parents if she found them delinquent. And how much authority did a lowly teaching fellow have anyway? The absent Mrs. Parker, despite a masterful display of circumlocution, had made it clear in her correspondence that teaching fellows functioned somewhere on a par with sweepers, sophomores, and delivery people.

She leaned back, letting the last notes of "Love Divine" wash over her. Well, it was going to be peaceful. A settled life at last. The slow and certain pace of the academic world on a campus that even in the sixties had not seen much in the way of protest: only a few faculty members burned in effigy and the president's office occupied just once in a halfhearted two-day stay. Bowmouth, nestled cozily as it was into the Camden Hills, was almost the prototype of a tranquil New England college. It sat in the middle of a town of white steepled churches and clapboarded houses, looking over a tree-lined mall with a Civil War statue and two World War monuments. There would be a country store, Sarah told herself, with a potbellied stove, selling rubber boots, yellow-eyed beans, and backhouse lime, and a stationer's store with daily papers and licorice in long black twists. Of course, since there are flies in every ointment, there would also be classes. Naturally, there had to be classes. Classes to teach, graduate seminars to take. But these intruded only briefly on her happy picture, and she began inventing scenes of cross-country skiing on the snow trails of nearby hills and summer moments swimming in pine-shaded ponds. There would be bird-watching for Alex; perhaps she would take piano lessons. And there would be town meetings. She and Alex would be model small-town residents. They would pull on their boots and their woolen jackets and trudge through the snow to the firehouse and sit on folding metal chairs to hear about the problems of the yearly burning over of the blueberry fields, the taking of undersize lobsters, and the trespassing of clam diggers.

The tower clock sounding the quarter hour jolted Sarah back to the waiting room. Almost time for her appointment. Reminding herself that she was now a serious scholar, she picked up a copy of *PMLA*, the publication of the Modern Language Association, and turned the pages. She supposed she would have to be trying to write essays like this one on the "Ethical Problems of Moral Sanction Independent of Morality in *Jude the Obscure*" or "The Dialectics of Movement in Keats's 'To Autumn.' " Sarah, who had barely recovered from the rigors of writing her master's thesis, felt slightly ill.

"Amanda Tibbs. There you are. C'mon back my office."

Sarah looked up and inhaled a cloud of pure bourbon. A tousled red-haired man in an unbuttoned tweed jacket and a loosened red tie leaned over her.

" 'Kay, Miss Tibbs, my office," he repeated. He seemed to Sarah to be trying to focus on the top of her head. "Just have talk 'bout that *F* your last paper. Deserved it, Miss Tibbs. Know why? Never bothered finishing *Gulliver*. Thought you could get away with *Monarch notes*. Skipped the Houyhnhnms. Can't write paper on *Gulliver* and leave out the horses. Point of the book."

"But I'm not Amanda Tibbs," said Sarah, rearing back from the bourbon.

"Sure you are. Gave you *F. F* as in . . ."—then with a great effort at articulation—"*F* as in fail, *F* as in fruitless, *F* as in foolish. So come 'long. Haven't got all day."

Sarah swiveled around in her chair, thinking that perhaps the real Amanda Tibbs might be cringing in a corner of the room, and then the waiting-room door opened and was filled with a statuesque rose and pink figure. "Sarah Deane?" it said.

"Amanda Tibbs," said the man. "Gave her *F*."

"No, Professor Larkin. Amanda Tibbs came into my office just now looking for you. I've sent her along and made another appointment. I've called your brother at the medical school, and he'll be here in a few minutes to drive you home."

"Not going home. Home is where heart is and who's got one? Rhetorical question. Not you, nursemaid Parker." He turned to Sarah. "So don't want see me, so go away, get thee to . . ." Here Professor Larkin seemed to pull himself together. "Thanks for coming, Miss Tibbs. See you, 'nother appointment." This as Sarah stood up and backed away toward the door.

"Just come with me, Miss Deane," said the woman. "I've been looking for you. I'm Mrs. Parker, the English Department secretary."

"Don' be modest, Parker baby." Professor Larkin collapsed in Sarah's chair. "Tha's number one sec'tary. Executive sec'tary. Sec'tary of interior, treasury, sec'tary of war. Sweetheart of Bowmouth College who if laid end to end wouldn't be surprised—"

"Here's your brother now, Professor Larkin." Mrs. Parker smiled, floated a queenly pink cashmere arm in the direction of the door, and then, indicating to Sarah that she was to follow, stepped smartly down the hall, her coiled and lacquered auburn head inclined forward, her pointed lizard shoes tapping, her gold bracelets gently clinking. She stopped at the glass-windowed door and waved Sarah in.

"Professor Bello is tied up today, so I'll take care of you, Miss Deane. I think you'll find we have everything in hand except a few details, a few loose ends." Mrs. Parker settled herself in a chair, pointed to another, pulled out a file marked *Teaching Fellows—Winter Term*, and began rapidly turning pages.

Quite a spread, thought Sarah, as she waited. A bright office with a window, albeit with a view of the parking lot, handsome colored photographs of Bowmouth College in spring and autumn dress, a typing and switchboard center, a shelf of texts and reference books, two ranks of file cabinets, and a framed certificate proclaiming Rosalind Parker recipient of the Bowmouth Special Service Award three years back.

Mrs. Parker followed Sarah's glance and smiled graciously. "Really an administrative staff award. I was quite honored. And now, Miss Deane, we have serious gaps. Professor Bello has pointed out that if you expect to do your doctoral work in the field of English literature—nineteenth-century novel, I see—you must start filling in. We have you down for Anglo-Saxon seminar—that's Old English—with Professor Fletcher, Shakespeare with Professor Lacey, and Eighteenth Century with Professor Larkin."

"*That* Professor Larkin?" said Sarah, remembering the bourbon.

Mrs. Parker nodded and pressed on as if preferring not to acknowledge a flawed faculty member. "And we hope you will try to audit classes in Poetics—that's Professor Horst—and Professor Merlin-Smith's lectures on Milton and the Seventeenth Century. Then there are your own teaching classes: a section of freshman composition and a class in introductory literature. Since you are taking over Mr. Wellbeck's classes, you will have to use the texts he ordered."

Twenty minutes later Sarah found herself encumbered with class lists, registration cards, and stipend information. "Regarding stipend," said Mrs. Parker, "we hope you understand that your appointment as a Bowmouth Teaching Fellow can never be used as a credit reference. You—and the adjuncts, of course—are outside of the college benefit umbrella." Here Mrs. Parker smiled again and showed her fine, even set of teeth. "And here, "she continued, producing a mimeographed folder, "is a description of department functions, the semester's calendar, and a list of faculty. To make sure you quite understand your position here at Bowmouth, I will explain. First we have the senior faculty, those with tenure who have the appointment of full professor or associate professor. Then comes the junior faculty—assistant professors, instructors—who may or may not be in line for tenure. These, unless they have written something quite unusual, have their doctorates. Do you follow me?"

Sarah sighed and nodded. She could hear it coming.

Teaching fellows down somewhere in the faculty basement.

Mrs. Parker was warming to her work. "Then—on a separate list in the back pages of your folder—the Fellows, Research and Teaching. Fellows are, indeed, part of our department family since they are doctoral candidates, though as the Bible so aptly puts it, many are called, few are chosen. Last we have the adjuncts." Mrs. Parker's voice took on a note of contempt. "Admirable people, many of them. They fill in our holes, teach extra sections of freshman composition, that sort of thing. They're given the title of 'Lecturer,' but since few of them have their doctorates they are quite expendable—not really a part of the college. Fellows and adjuncts never attend regular faculty meetings, but we all pull together to make the department work. Now come along and I'll show you the Fellows' Room. You'll have a locker for your personal things and a carrel in the library. Any difficulties, come straight to me. Professor Bello is so very busy that I try to take care of the routine problems. And remember we like to have copies of your exams ten days in advance for departmental approval."

Sarah wondered whether Mrs. Parker always used a royal "we" or thought of herself in the plural, but, holding her folders and cards, she followed Mrs. Parker down the hall. It was all exactly like her first day in high school.

"We are not as informal as some colleges," said Mrs. Parker, over her shoulder. " 'Professor' is the preferred title if the appointment is such. No first names for your students. Mister, Miss, Mrs., or Ms.—if they insist. I detest Ms., but we must swim with the times."

Sarah nodded again, thinking of the faculty she had left behind her, known as Ellie, Ira, Soapy, and Liz.

"Use this building for your headquarters," went on Mrs. Parker, stopping before the door marked FELLOWS' ROOM. "We do have a large number of faculty housed in the West Quad, but they are junior faculty or those who have special chairs: The Enos Starbox Chair of Poetry, for instance. Naturally, we do not give the adjuncts offices."

"Naturally," said Sarah.

"All the *senior* English faculty are here in Malcolm Adam Hall, along with the department clerks, and of course I am here and am always available." Another smile. Sarah could tell that for the secretary the senior faculty was the power and glory and she, Mrs. Parker, was at its center with her hand on the controls.

The secretary knocked at the Fellows' Room door and, without waiting for an answer, pushed it open. Two people sitting at a table heaped with papers, coffee mugs, and open books looked up.

Sarah saw that the room, painted in what she had learned to call academic beige, harbored a scatter of unmatching chairs, a line of metal lockers, a steaming kettle, a tin of coffee, and a jam jar labeled *Tea bags*. Taped to the wall was an old poster of the Rolling Stones, a black-and-white portrait of George Eliot to which someone had added sideburns, an enlarged photograph of John Keats's epitaph, and, over the lockers on an angle, a strongly tinted copy of Gilbert Stuart's portrait of Bowmouth College's first chancellor, Leander Starbox.

A hefty-looking black-haired youth with a snub nose and a wide comic mouth looked up. "Mrs. Parker, did you get my ten o'clock lit section changed?"

"Not yet, but I'm doing everything I can, Mr. Collins. Now here is Sarah Deane."

Mr. Collins grinned at Sarah and turned back to the secretary. "Look," he said, "there's no way thirty-four students can fit in a classroom meant for twenty. I've got 'em all over the floor. I don't care, but they can't take notes."

This," repeated Mrs. Parker in a louder voice, as if she were demonstrating a new and promising piece of equipment, "is Sarah Deane. From Boston University. She'll be taking over Mr. Wellbeck's freshman sections."

"Hi there, Sarah Deane," said the young man. "I'm Drago Collins, and that's Mary Donelli. Join the proletariat" —and, as the door shut behind Mrs. Parker—"I see the hand of our brigadier general, Rosalind Parker, has been laid upon you. Keep on her good side, and you may get a classroom with a window that opens."

"And after a year or so," said Mary, a round-faced, dark-haired, brown-eyed person with a crooked smile and a wry expression, "you might be scheduled to teach classes later than seven-thirty A.M. Don't tell anyone if you have children, because they're out to get working mothers—you know, early-morning classes and evening conferences."

"No children," said Sarah.

"Well, if you're thinking about it, have them in the summer session. This is still a male enclave."

Drago Collins, who was stuffing papers into a battered briefcase, looked up. "Come off it, Mary. Bowmouth has had women students for eight years."

"But females are still treated like fugitives from the kitchen sink. Of course some, like so-called Professor Connie Garvey, are men in drag. And no ladies' loo in half the buildings, only scattered little cement cells painted pink in the basement. Not only do we have to try harder, our bladders have to last longer. Are you going to the thing tonight?"

"What's that?" said Sarah.

"Professor Bello," said Drago Collins. "You've got the invite there with all those class cards. At eight o'clock our invisible chairman opens up the Faculty Club and passes among us with stewed wine, dry cheese, and unspeakable crackers, while the English faculty, the proper faculty, that is —mill around and act like all of us fellows and adjuncts are colleagues and equals, which is a lot of shit. They're really only interested in snapping at each other's heels and carving up each other's articles."

"Oh, there are a few humans here and there," said Mary. "Joe Greenberg is decent, really sharp. He's nineteenth- and twentieth-century novel," she added for Sarah's benefit. "And Fletcher is pretty hot stuff—he's Old English and Anglo-Saxon culture and medieval—and Amos Larkin is good even when he's sloshed, which is about half the time. He's eighteenth century: Swift, Johnson, Pope, and the rest."

"I ran into him. He thought I was someone else."

"Yeah," said Mary. "He was a little gone today. I saw him leaving the building. I'd guess Parker saved his ass. Once again. I'm doing my dissertation on Swift's poetry, and he's been sitting on the first four chapters for a month." She stood up and pulled on a blue parka hanging on the back of the chair. "See you at the party, Sarah. Have you got a buffer, a friend or husband or any live body?"

"I'm living with Alex McKenzie. He's practicing here and teaching at the med school. I'll try and convince him that an English faculty reception is just what he needs for relaxation."

"Well," said Mary, "the department certainly has its share of weirdos, if that's what he likes. Is he a psychiatrist?"

"Internal medicine," said Sarah. "And we haven't even unpacked. The moving van just came yesterday and everything's a mess. We're renting this falling-apart double house on Sawmill Road, and I'm not sure there's even any hot water. Anyway, Alex is probably on call."

TWO

"Whew," said Sarah, dumping her briefcase on top of a stack of cartons in what someday might be a living room, "what a day! And I thought Boston was a pressure tank. I suppose you're on call."

"Of course," said Alex. "Penalty of being the new boy. And my office; it's the size of a refrigerator and the same temperature. I have to stand in the hall while the patient puts on an examining gown. If one of them weighs over two hundred pounds, we'll both have to go out in the hall."

"So much for prestigious teaching hospitals," said Sarah. "But at least you have an office. I have a communal cage."

"So are you all set? The English Department put out the welcome mat?"

"Well, I never did meet the chairman, but the secretary did the honors. A Mrs. Parker, who seems to run the place. A sort of combo colonel-in-chief and Jewish mother."

"Most good secretaries run things. The faculty is just there for decoration."

"And there's wine and cheese at eight o'clock courtesy of the Department. I'm allowed an escort."

"I'll drop you off and pick you up, but I have to go to the hospital and check some orders. Four new admissions this afternoon, and the resident has just come on service. But the hot water is on and you can have a bath. And I've put the bed together. As soon as I got the comforter in place, Patsy staked out his place. It's time that dog had a bed of his own. I'm tired of sharing." This as a gray-bearded Irish wolfhound strolled into the room wagging his tail and sweeping a saucepan from the kitchen table.

"Of course," said Sarah, rescuing a mixing bowl. "He's feeling displaced. He's very sensitive. And who on earth is in the other half of the house? I heard a noise like a machine gun as I came in."

"Medical students."

"Oh, Lord."

"Best we could do. Near your job and mine. Sawmill Road is considered a top location."

"For sawmills, you mean. The house is held up by hairpins. And no rest for the eternal student. I've got to do the complete Shakespeare as well as learn Old English and read Anglo-Saxon lit. *And* take a course from the department drunk and audit two other courses and teach my own classes. Right now, Boston's looking pretty good."

"Forget Boston. We've come to the land of peace and quiet. Quilting bees and blueberry picking. I saw a Snowy Owl today on the hospital roof. Now come here. Never mind the complete Shakespeare. I want the complete Sarah. I love you, and I haven't been able to get my hands on you in weeks." Alex stood up, stretched out his hands, took a step, and fell over a large carton.

"Look out. Those are the wineglasses." Sarah reached over and gave Alex a quick kiss on the nose. "Look, can you pick up a pizza somewhere for us? I have to feed Patsy, go over my teaching class stuff, take that bath, dig out a dress, and prepare to meet the elusive Professor Bello, although I suppose making time with La Parker would be more to the point."

"Well, she'll hardly be at the faculty wingding. You may have to make do with Professor Bello."

But here Alex was wrong. The first person Sarah saw as she opened the door to the Faculty Club reception room was the well-corseted figure of Rosalind Parker, her upswept hair sparkling with a fan-shaped ornament, her body swathed in a layered dress of cloudy blue. She was moving slowly, nodding graciously, through the center of the room.

Sarah took a deep breath and plunged in, saw Mary Donelli free, and joined her. "Is Mrs. Parker faculty?" she asked.

"Better than," said Mary, flourishing an empty wineglass. "Without her there'd *be* no faculty. I wouldn't be surprised if they gave her tenure."

"So who's who?" said Sarah. "For instance," she pointed to a gesturing woman with electric-gray hair and the face of a Medici standing by the punch bowl. She seemed to be constructed entirely of capes, scarves, belts, and boots.

"That's a live one," said Mary. "Miss Vera Pruczak. Teaches drama and directs the community theater productions. Bowmouth lets her use its stage, and she usually ropes in half the college people."

"She looks like something out of a gothic novel," said Sarah, as Miss Pruczak raised a hand to her throat and rolled her eyes at the ceiling.

"On the button. She writes them as Olivia Macbeth. Forty-five published novels."

"Good Lord," said Sarah. "That's Olivia Macbeth? Why, she takes up two whole rows on the bookstore paperback shelf."

"A hot new one every fall just in time for Christmas. This year it's *Lady Daphne's Revenge*. They're really sort of fun. And Literary Guild every time, so pots of money. And over there, tall, handsome, and distinguished Patrick Fletcher, with his equally handsome but not quite as distinguished wife." Mary indicated a man with a splendidly classic profile, a fine head of graying hair, strong-looking shoulders, and an erect posture. He stood next to a woman whose tawny hair was pulled back into a single fall down her back. She in her deep crimson dress with black sleeves and he in his well-cut flannel suit lent flair to the entire room. "And that one," said Mary, pointing to one side, "the one shaped like a jam jar with his bald spot combed over, is the chairman."

"So that's Howard Bello," said Sarah. "I've been wondering. Do you think I should go over and say hello?"

"Don't rush it," said Mary, but then she added reluctantly, "I guess he knows a hell of a lot about Emerson and all those Concord types, though he mumbles when he lectures. Here comes Parker. She'll take you around."

Sarah looked up to find Rosalind Parker, all smiles and bracelets, bearing down on her. "Miss Deane, Professor Bello wants very much to meet you." So rather in the role of a child being taken to meet her parents' friends, Sarah found herself propelled forward.

Professor Bello was wistfully confronting a large tray of sausages with toothpicks while a tall woman in a black satin blouse hung with amber beads was saying, "Absolutely not, Howard. They're loaded with salt. Haven't you any sense? Oh, hello, Rosalind. The new recruit?"

Miss Parker performed the introductions and moved off to a corner with the woman, who proved to be Professor Bello's wife. Sarah thought she offered a noticeable contrast to her husband, who to anyone's eyes must be thought rather seedy. The department chairman's corduroy jacket looked slept in, his wool tie was poorly aligned, and his shoes scuffed. His face, features pulling to the center toward a flat nose and buck teeth, reminded Sarah of a badly maintained guinea pig. The professor, for his part, seemed unsure of where to begin, finally coughing and saying, "Everything in order? Mrs. Parker's taken care of you all right? Classes all set?"

"Yes," said Sarah. "I think she's done everything."

"You're not doing nineteenth-century American lit, are you?"

"That was my master's program," said Sarah. "And I've read quite a few of your articles—the series on Poets and Philosophers where you point out how Emerson could never be logical for more than a paragraph, and how contradictory he was when he said that genius was the enemy of genius through overinfluence."

Professor Bello moved his shoulders in a hopeless gesture. "Oh, that. That was a long time ago. I've got a whole new slant now."

"Oh," said Sarah, rather dismayed. Her master's thesis had leaned heavily on Howard Bello's view of Emerson.

"It doesn't matter," said the professor, fumbling with his buttons. "Have you found a place to live?" As he asked this he looked over Sarah's head in the direction of Mrs. Parker with a hint of desperation.

Sarah, seeing herself dismissed, said, "Yes, on Sawmill Road." She shook the professor's hand and headed back toward Mary Donelli, who had settled herself comfortably in a large leather armchair.

"Come this way, Miss Deane." There was Mrs. Parker right on her heels. "You've got to meet the rest."

So Sarah found herself circling the room. First she shook the hands of Patrick Fletcher and his wife, who both smiled pleasantly and mentioned the weather. "So lucky to have Professor Fletcher here at Bowmouth," hissed Mrs. Parker in Sarah's ear as they moved on to their next introduction. "He did his graduate work at Yale and has published some really distinguished studies in Old English. Now here is Professor Horst. He was with the Mathematics Department and switched to English, where he has done original work."

Sarah found Professor Jakob Horst a rather intimidating figure with large hands and a red face that suggested a rare side of beef. He nodded briefly to her and returned to his conversation.

"That's Professor Pruczak, I mean Olivia Macbeth, isn't it?" asked Sarah, hoping to be steered next in that direction.

"*Miss* Pruczak, really," said Mrs. Parker. "She's ABD—all but dissertation—but with those novels the department waived the Ph.D. requirement and gave her the appointment. The dean believed it helped the college to have a novelist on the faculty—from a publicity point of view. Not that she writes what anyone in the department calls literature."

"She certainly sells," said Sarah. "When I'm tired or have a cold, I read them. They just roll you along."

Mrs. Parker's mouth contracted. "They don't roll me anywhere, I'm sure. Well, here she comes."

"Rosalind. That dress. Quite marvelous, though I'd look like a piece of blue cheese in it. And don't tell me because I do read my mail, this wisp of a thing must be Sarah Deane filling in for that no-good Wellbeck boy who went off skiing, and after I'd cast him as Edgar. We're doing *Lear* in the spring," she said to Sarah. "Though I don't blame him," she added. "I'd take off for the ski circuit too if I could." Miss

Pruczak made a wide gesture so that her layers of scarves and capes fluttered. She stepped back from Sarah and gave her a thorough up-and-down and then said, "Good bones, not a sense of assertion but a good set to your head. Can you read?"

"Yes," said Sarah, startled.

"Music and a part, I mean. We're doing *The Mikado* for carnival weekend, and I'm still looking for a Goneril for *Lear*. How do you feel about Goneril?"

"Well," said Sarah doubtfully. Was there any question about how one should feel about one of the nastiest females in all Shakespeare?

"Never mind. You may be a bit slight for Goneril. We need a real presence there. Just come and sing for us. *The Mikado* cast is coming apart. Now don't let the senior faculty intimidate you. Go your own way. That's what I do." And with a flip of her cape, Miss Pruczak swept across the room, leaving Sarah to wonder whether not being enough of a presence for Goneril was a good or bad thing. She turned back to Mrs. Parker to find that lady a study in distress, staring at the entrance of the room. The cause was clear. Professor Amos Larkin, listing noticeably to starboard, filled the doorway. Sarah decided that the professor's brother must have let him slip from his grasp.

Professor Larkin now advanced into the room and reached for the back of a chair for support. Mrs. Parker left Sarah's side and moved into position, ready perhaps for another rescue.

"Hah!" said the professor loudly. He stood there swaying slightly, his red hair on end. "If it isn't all the little loaves and fishes going to eat each other up. Whazza matter, Howard," he said, reaching out for the chairman's corduroy arm, "didn't expect me to come to your party? Howard the coward's got the whole tribe. Brotherly love thick as thieves. That you, Rosie O'Grady O'Parker? Thought I'd gone home. Fooled you. 'For he on honey-dew hath fed,/And drunk the milk of Paradise.' " Here Professor Larkin straightened with an effort and held up his hand.

"Methinks, I hear 'em speak;
See, how the Dean begins to break:

Poor Gentleman, he droops apace,
You plainly find it in his Face:
That old Vertigo in his Head
Will never leave him, till he's dead:
Besides, his Memory decays,
He recollects not what he says. . . .

"Know that one, Howard? S'matter, all you Yahoos?" Professor Larkin leaned forward and fixed the silent room with a baleful eye. He began to recite again, and now the voice —an impressive baritone—was clear, the enunciation much improved. It was, Sarah thought, almost a dying effort.

"My good Companions, never fear,
For though you may mistake a Year;
Though your Prognosticks run too fast,
They must be verify'd at last."

Amos Larkin sank back into a chair, and as a group gathered about the professor, Sarah retreated and joined Mary Donelli, who had her coat on.

"Just leaving. I've earned my Brownie points. He's something, isn't he?" Mary indicated the crumpled professor. "I mean, even if he's about to go into D.T.'s, he's still good."

"What's that about the Dean?" asked Sarah.

"Jonathan Swift—one of Swift's poems. Sometimes Amos thinks he's Swift. Like now."

"I'm supposed be taking his eighteenth-century seminar," said Sarah. "Maybe I shouldn't."

"Oh, stick with it. You could do a lot worse. The dragon, for instance." Mary pointed to a stout woman in burgundy at the end of the room, whom Sarah recognized as the angry female of the Faculty Common Room. "That's Professor Constance Garvey. She wears breastplates and uses a pointer. Hey, who's that man over there, at the other door waving at you? Not bad. Brontë type, tall, dark, and brooding."

"Oh," said Sarah, looking up with relief. "That's Alex, for me. He doesn't really brood."

"Lucky you. My men are all short and going bald."

Sarah looked across the room. Yes, there was something

rather dark and piratical about Alex, with that slash of a mouth and black hair. She waved back at him—a gesture that seemed to arouse Amos Larkin.

"Amanda Tibbs. Gave her *F*. Foul fiend flibbertigibbet gave Amanda *F*. Deserved it. . . . Lady Parker, I presume." This as the secretary, a stern figure armed with the chairman, stepped in front of the professor's chair.

"Now, Amos, I think it's time you went home," said Professor Bello without much conviction.

"Hail, fair Rosalind," said Amos Larkin, ignoring the chairman. "Fair foul fiend Rosalind, if there be truth in sight, you are my Rosalind."

Sarah crossed the room and seized Alex by the arm. "Save me."

"So," said Alex as they made their way through the paneled and portrait-hung halls of the Faculty Club, "from my quick once-over, the members of your department don't look any worse or any better than any other department."

"I suppose so," said Sarah, "though Professor Larkin is certainly a standout."

"There's a drunk on every faculty."

"Like the king's jester, to remind them they're all human." Sarah walked ahead through the arched door leading to the North Quad. On a weekday evening at nine o'clock, the square should have been emptied out—small groups, a few singles, hurrying across the frozen diagonals to the libraries, to the auditoriums for a rehearsal, or back to their houses and dormitories. But tonight the square was alive with students, holding extra lights on extension cords, standing on stepladders, plying shovels, and heaping up snow. "What's going on?" she asked Alex.

"Winter carnival. Annual gala. Not for two weeks, but don't expect any of your students to concentrate on proper paragraphing until it's over."

"Feel that wind," said Sarah, pulling up her coat collar. "I remember going up to Dartmouth for their carnival. Once was enough. A four-day drunk and sleep-in. I don't know how anyone managed to stay upright on skis."

"I don't think Bowmouth is quite that bad."

"Nothing could be," said Sarah. "My brother, Tony, was

there then, and my parents blame things like the winter carnival for the fact that Tony's still bombing around with a banjo."

"Here's the car," said Alex. "I can't tell you, Sarah, my love, what a joy it is to be going home with no more of that damn Boston traffic to claw through. Just one beautiful dilapidated half of a house with you to myself."

"And only a pack of medical students on the other side of the world's thinnest walls," said Sarah, "but I'm not complaining. We can put down roots and start growing moss."

"Sounds good," said Alex, starting the car. "Get old and stooped in the service of Bowmouth College. . . . Which reminds me, I've got to stop at the hospital and write some orders. So much for growing moss."

"Damn," said Sarah.

THREE

The founding fathers of Bowmouth College had in 1804 two publicly expressed aims: to provide higher education and training to the youth of mid-coast Maine and to present the nearby towns with a steady trickle of educated persons who could minister to the needs of these communities. Another purpose, not generally aired, was to contain for a few more years the ambitious young sprigs of the local shipowners, sea captains, merchants, and farmers so that their fathers, uncles, and grandfathers could rest secure in the saddle for at least four more years.

In the early part of the nineteenth century, Maine was already involved in shipbuilding and coastal trade so that property in easy distance of the ocean came high. Fortunately, back in the forested footlands of the Camden Hills, surrounded by the blueberry barrens of the townships of Union and Appleton in a natural series of hollows and pinnacles, lay land of sufficient agricultural poverty to suggest a site for the four buildings that would comprise the newly conceived college.

In the fullness of time, these four buildings dedicated to the arts and sciences, handsome in Georgian red-brick style, expanded, grew appendages, and fathered schools of medicine, law, and music, thus becoming, in fact if not in name, a university. Later in the century, ignoring the sensible proportions of the earlier architecture, additions sprouted in Gothic Revival and Italian Villa, and these were followed by depressing variations on the Romanesque, the Bauhaus, the Frank Lloyd Wright prairie style, and, still later, by what some Bowmouth critics called "mansard monster" and "fortress modern."

Once the visitor had penetrated all the way to the original campus, however, the college revealed a certain antique charm. Rosy red-brick ivy-hung buildings, here and there interrupted by ones of cut granite or white clapboard, had all been built in a series of interconnecting squares so that each set of buildings had its own quadrangle and every archway entrance presented the viewer with a varied prospect. To the front and center of all these interlocking squares, situated at the top of a long incline, stood the three-story Starbox Administration Building, topped by an imposing clock tower. This double-winged structure, reached by a discouraging flight of granite stairs, presided over two avenues of red maples, which in turn split off and circled Bowmouth Pond. On this stretch of water, running the length of the campus, the Bowmouth crews plied their oars and raced their sailing dinghies.

Sarah, flanked by the two Paul Manship bronze elk, stood at the top of the Administration Building stairs and thought that this was one of those moments when the trivial and dingy moments of academic life melted away and were replaced by a kind of awe. She supposed it was the sort of feeling that overwhelmed old graduates when they met at reunion to sing "We salute thee, Bowmouth College, hail the red and blue," and then with tears in their eyes coughed up contributions to the endowment fund.

Today a freeze, a thaw, and a second freeze had turned the whole college into an illustration for the hall of the Snow Queen. Trees, branches, twigs, each in a sheath of ice, glittered in the pale morning sun, and a gleaming sheet of snow turned the pond surface into a table of unbroken white.

Yes, Sarah thought, just for this moment, to be standing here on these steps, a part of this timeless glacial scene, might be thought worth a good deal. Then the clock in the tower struck the quarter hour, and Sarah came to and remembered her own freshman sections at eight-thirty and her upcoming graduate seminar with the questionable Professor Larkin. All that, plus the day ahead shrill with class lists, new textbooks, her ID photograph and parking lot sticker. She shook herself, loosened her glove from its frozen grip on the railing, and hurried down the steps.

The next few days went by for Sarah in a jumble of her own teaching classes—row on row of strange faces and names to be learned, dropouts to be reported, new students added —all this interlaced with the graduate seminars necessary for her doctoral program. The one in eighteenth-century literature, held the day after the faculty party, presented Professor Amos Larkin in a caustic vein. He was obviously suffering from his recent binge and handed out enormous assignments seasoned with remarks like "I assume you're all up on your Latin because you won't get through this course without it" and "If you missed last semester on Pope, you'd better make it up because Pope will be on the exam." Sarah, sitting, she had thought, inconspicuously in the back of the room, suddenly found herself held up as the delinquent Amanda Tibbs, an undergraduate student who had not bothered to finish *Gulliver's Travels.* "And what," said Amos Larkin, fixing her with a bloodshot eye, "are you doing in a graduate seminar?" Just as Sarah was trying to decide how best to establish her true identity, Professor Larkin pounced on another victim. "You." He pointed at a small person with fair hair braided around her head who seemed to Sarah's eyes to be about twelve years old. "You, have you a class card? You know," he said fiercely, addressing the whole seminar, "this isn't an introductory class. If you don't have a comprehensive idea of the entire period—and I mean comprehensive—and a good working knowledge of European and Anglo-Irish history, then go." He turned back to the fair-haired person. "What's your name—Alice Marmott? Are you a graduate student, Miss Marmott? No? Then what do you have to say for yourself?"

Sarah watched as Alice Marmott quietly put down her pencil, closed her notebook, and, rather flushed, but shoulders straight and head erect, addressed a few softly spoken words to the professor. At the first phrase, Professor Larkin cocked his head and listened with great attention. When she had finished, he nodded. "Stay put, Miss Marmott." He swiveled toward Sarah. "Now, Miss Tibbs, why are you here?" Sarah had just opened her mouth to speak when the bell marking the end of the period clanged and the students rose and pushed toward the door. Seeing several students, including Mary Donelli, crowd around Professor Larkin's desk, Sarah decided to put off assuming her own name until next week's session. After all, her acquaintance with eighteenth-century England, except for *Tom Jones*, *Tristram Shandy*, and *Moll Flanders*, was barely a nodding one, and even in justifying her presence in the seminar as a legitimate doctoral candidate, she could hardly hope to come off as well as Alice Marmott. That young woman had explained herself entirely in Latin.

FOUR

Her eighteenth-century seminar notwithstanding, Sarah withheld judgment on graduate life at Bowmouth College. Taken all in all, however, it added up to an extraordinary amount of library research, essays to be written, and, of course, her Latin to be refurbished. How, she thought, do you revive Latin when you have a competing course in Anglo-Saxon with its Germanic throat noises, its varied spelling, and at least three strange alphabet letters? It was no comfort to discover that the miraculous Miss Marmott had turned up in this class too and was reading and reciting as if she had been born during the rule of Alfred the Great.

Every now and then Sarah met Alex for lunch at the hospital cafeteria, and once they found half an hour in which to wander from one quadrangle to another to inspect the progress of the competing ice sculptures. The theme chosen that year was Early Explorations, and already the squares were decorated with recognizable snow-packed shapes: frigid figures in canoes, pathfinders in ice-fringed shirts, a frozen admiral on a frozen poop deck, and, most impressive, a huge Viking ship.

Alex, thought Sarah, examining him critically, looked less pale than he had in Boston—windburn, perhaps—but just as haggard. In fact, she decided, as they inspected one of the canoe groups, he looked rather like one of those Canadian voyageurs after a particularly hard passage. His face seemed thinner, and his dark hair, now in need of professional attention, hung low over his forehead. And I'm about in the same shape, she added to herself: tired, edgy, and too pressured.

"We need a day off," Sarah announced. "Either that or a sunlamp."

"How about cod liver oil?" said Alex, as he took himself off to the hospital.

In the week that followed, Alex buried himself in his new practice and his teaching at the medical school, and Sarah was swept into the double life of teacher and graduate student. She had begun to sort out the students in her own teaching classes—two Michaels, three Jessicas, and four Rebeccas in her Introductory Lit sections and three Benjamins and two Aarons in her freshman composition class. Happily, it was not necessary to know the names of the fellow sufferers in her graduate seminars—enough to struggle with the finer points of the *Tale of a Tub* and, in her Old English class, discover the difference between Alcuin's *Life of St. Willibrord* and the *Hodoeporion of St. Willibad* written down by a nun of Hedenheim, while at the same time going about declining Anglo-Saxon verbs to herself—bēodan, bēad, budon, geboden; brēotan, brēat, bruton, gebroten.

The only breathing space in Sarah's academic day came from Ivan Lacey's course in Shakespeare. Professor Lacey neither drank like Professor Larkin nor was distinguished and scholarly like Professor Patrick Fletcher, who taught Old English. Ivan Lacey, according to Mary Donelli, who had turned up to audit the class, was a sex fiend on an ego trip. He fancied his mastery of Elizabethan cadences, and often at the end of a period in which the students discussed and read aloud the more notable passages of a play, he took over most of the parts; once, during *Othello*, after grabbing Iago, Cassio, and Othello, he added Desdemona. He had the face, Sarah thought, of an overbred horse, complete with black mane, which he tossed while widening his nostrils. He had wicked little dark eyes, alert for a lowered neckline, a braless student, or a too-short too-open skirt. However, perhaps because of these outside interests and an obvious aversion to hard work, his assignments were light, for which Sarah, gasping for breathing space, was grateful.

One recurring figure in those early days was Alice Marmott. She did not become a friend. In fact, she seemed to Sarah to walk always alone, and the few times Sarah spoke to her after class or going across the campus yielded nothing more than the sense of a student who was so absorbed in her own thoughts, her own studies, that there was barely time for her to look up and respond to Sarah's greetings. Sometimes she appeared to be looking at Sarah as if she wondered where on earth she had seen her before. Alice's clothes certainly set her apart from other undergraduates. With her navy-blue wool coat, her navy beret pulled tight over her light hair, her neatly tucked-in tan wool scarf, her brown woolen stockings and her overshoes—overshoes!—she looked like a student from some foreign university, Estonia or Latvia perhaps, who had mysteriously dropped into the heart of this very New England college. In her never-varying costume, Alice was easy to pick out from the stream of quilted coats, red, blue, yellow, and green parkas, knitted hats, and corduroy trousers, or the long skirts and high boots favored by the other women.

"Are you from Maine?" asked Sarah of Alice, meeting her in the student union cafeteria line.

"No," said Alice. "Ohio." She selected a tuna fish sandwich and moved ahead.

"Are you taking all graduate courses?" persisted Sarah.

"Oh, no. They won't let me. I have to take my B.A. first, but I don't need to take all my courses on an elementary level."

"Well, you've certainly got the rest of us bug-eyed," said Sarah. "You must be a whiz at languages."

"Languages aren't difficult for me," said Alice in her mild voice, "but I'm having trouble with Professor Fletcher. he wants to limit the course to Old English and its literature."

"That's certainly enough for me," said Sarah, sliding a bowl of beef stew onto her tray.

"The critical material is very important," said Alice seriously. "I'd like a discussion of it in class and an attempt on our part to come to terms with the different interpretations of the major works. Anyway, I've been examining the periodical literature, and I'm going to write a paper."

"Even if it's not assigned?" said Sarah, appalled.

"As evidence of scholarship," said Alice. "I've sent Professor Fletcher a note saying that I think we should all try and do just a little original research."

"Good grief," said Sarah. "It's all I can do to learn the first declension. I hope he turns you down flat." She smiled to indicate goodwill, but Alice's habitual frown deepened and she excused herself.

"I always eat alone because it gives me a chance to review the morning lectures."

"Hey, Sarah," said Drago Collins, the teaching fellow Sarah had met on her first day. He slid his loaded tray in behind her in the line. "Isn't that the one Mary Donelli's always talking about—Alice somebody? Because now she's started auditing my poetics grad class and she knows more about poetry than old Horst. She told him in detail about Keats's revision of "The Eve of St. Agnes," and I thought Horst would bust a gut. She wasn't mean about it, just corrected his analysis because it left out the early versions, and then had a word to say about the metrics. I think she's some kind of faculty KGB agent. Here's Mary. Let's find a table. Why in God's name are fellows and adjuncts condemned to eat in the student cafeteria? Couldn't they have found some dark corner of the hockey rink or the laundry for us, because, I mean what's the point of a B.A. if you have to sit down with all these children yelling and playing their tapes?" Here Drago, a world-weary twenty-four-year-old, looked disdainfully around at the writhing mass of parkas, trays, book bags.

"Some of the older folk go out to one of the tourist bins in Camden to grab lunch," said Mary, pushing her way to a table. "But Camden costs a mint just for a veggie sandwich."

"That's me," said Sarah in bed that night to Alex. "One of the older folk—twenty-six going on fifty."

"An Infant Phenomenon?" said Alex.

"Speaking of which, we have a real one." And Sarah told Alex about Alice Marmott. "One of the fellows suggested that she's a faculty spy, but I'd say it's more likely she's here from one of the Eastern bloc countries to scout gymnastics or the ice-skating competition, and all the academic know-how is cover. She is so bloody *serious*.''

"Serious wins gold medals or scholarships," said Alex. "I'm glad to hear there's one undergraduate who isn't going ape over the ice sculpture and a weekend of binging. The med students pretend they're above it all, but they're all cranked up.''

"It's cabin fever or campus fever. We should take that day off.''

"Not me for a while. Yours truly has a new job—medical examiner for the county—one of two. I'll have to study up.''

"Medical examiner? What does that mean? Dead bodies?''

"Since you put it that way. It's nothing I was looking for, but I said yes as a favor.''

"You mean you just do those people who turn up dead in cars or who fall off Mount Megunticook? It sounds ghoulish.''

"Somebody's got to do it. We just rule on cause in what they call an 'unattended' death. We find out if the person has a doctor, what the past medical history is, and whether something untoward had happened. If it has, then the state medical examiner, who's a proper forensic pathologist, takes over, does the autopsy, and works with the State Police.''

"Were you asked because of your great credentials?''

"If you're referring to my career as your assistant investigator galloping through the swamps in Texas, forget it.''

"I think you have great credentials. You saved my sanity in Texas and my neck on Weymouth Island last summer. But don't take this new job too seriously. You've bumped into enough bodies.''

"I'm through with crime and so are you.''

"Well, knock on wood," said Sarah, reaching over and banging the headboard of the bed.

"I never knock on wood. It's asking for trouble.''

It was a remark that Sarah was to remind him of in the future weeks.

* * *

In the days that followed, Alice Marmott cut a wider and wider swath through the English Department regulars. Soft-voiced, relentless, accurate, Alice brought instructor after instructor to the boil. Even Professor Lacey, a man who could fence in a dashing way with student ideas, found himself on the defensive. The class had advanced to *Hamlet,* and the professor had been holding forth on Polonius as a man so focused in one direction that when it came to practical action, such as spying on Hamlet, the results were disastrous. "I like to compare Polonius," said Professor Lacey, smiling at a line of graduate-student bosoms in the front row, "to a sort of Cyclops—a man with one eye and that in the back of his head."

There was an appreciative rustle, the movement of a few pens, and Alice Marmott's hand went up.

"Yes, Miss Marmott?" said Professor Lacey, sighing. He had already sustained damage from his encounters with Alice.

"The comparison to Cyclops," said Alice, "is taken from Coleridge's criticism of *Hamlet.* From *Table Talk, 1827.*"

To Sarah's distress, Professor Lacey began to waffle, citing the number of people who could have used the Cyclops image, the commonness of "cyclops" as a reference point, and even, with a laugh, the suggestion that great minds run in the same stream. Fortunately, the period bell cut him short before he had completely disgraced himself.

"Why can't people just admit they're wrong or that they're borrowing?" said Alice to Sarah, as they filed out of class. "I've been reading the *Hamlet* criticism, and Coleridge's is very well known. Professor Lacey is treating us like children."

Sarah nodded and made a note that when she had a spare five minutes she would look up Coleridge.

Alice struck again during the class in eighteenth-century literature. Professor Larkin, who had obviously had a couple of belts before class but was still very much in possession of his wits, had chosen to illustrate Swift's satiric poetry with an examination of "A Beautiful Young Nymph Going to Bed." He cited the taking off of the artificial hair, the eyebrows made from "a Mouse's Hyde," the removal of "Plumpers" from hollow jaws, the rags that propped her "flabby Dugs . . . the

Bolsters that supply her Hips . . . Her shankers, Issues, running Sores. . . .''

Sarah closed her eyes and tried to think of something else, and even that great admirer of Swift and Professor Larkin, Mary Donelli, winced, but the Professor, in full flight, bore relentlessly to the end: " 'The Nymph, tho' in this mangled Plight,/Must ev'ry Morn her Limbs unite.' " Professor Larkin slapped his book on the desk. "Swift ends the poem by saying, '*Corinna* in the Morning dizen'd,/Who sees, will spew; who smells, be poison'd.' Now, did he mean his readers to spew? What is the purpose—if any—of such verse? Can we consider this simply run-of-the-mill satiric verse in the *Hudibras* tradition? Invective in the Juvenal mode?"

Alice Marmott was ready. "I don't think you can judge these poems, the ones about the physical decay and falsity of fashionable women, unless you read the Stella poems at the same time. For balance. To see that Swift wrote a kinder sort of satiric poetry."

Professor Larkin shook his head, a movement that obviously cost him dear, thought Sarah, seeing him blink with pain. "Miss Whatever-your-name-is, please remember I have not yet assigned the Stella poems. Perhaps you may find the balance, the kindness, in these lines—which *were* assigned.

> " 'Tis sung; wherever Celia treeds
> The Vi'lets ope their purple heads,
> The Roses blow, the Cowslip springs;
> 'Tis sung. But we know better things.
> 'Tis true; a Woman on her mettle
> Will often p———s upon a nettle;
> Yet, though we grant she makes it wetter,
> The nettle never thrives the better."

Sarah, gathering her books together after class, told Mary Donelli that she thought it was a draw, but Mary shook her head. "Amos wins. He can always zap the Marmott with a quote, because even she can't have memorized all of Swift. I'll bet on Amos anytime unless he's too far gone. Besides, I prefer him to Alice."

"Watch it, Mary," said Sarah. "You'll be thinking you can reform him, and you know where that leads."

"Yes," said Mary with a little chuckle. "I know, and it might be fun."

"It would not," said Sarah. "He's a sodden bastard, and he hates women."

"He's afraid of them," said Mary. "I can wait."

Nothing daunted, Alice Marmott took on Professor Patrick Fletcher to the point where she caused him to grind to a halt in the middle of an explanation of Old English patterns of stress and alliteration and redefine the limits of the class. It was, thought Sarah, listening to an exasperated Professor Fletcher, as if a small terrier had caught hold of his trouser cuff and would not let go.

Professor Fletcher spoke in a resonant and cultivated voice and had a flair for explicating the duller parts of grammar. He had up until now worked patiently with his students' halting efforts at oral translation. But today it was clear that Alice Marmott was driving him up the wall. He pressed his hands down on his lectern and spoke directly to her. "The students in this class are still facing the problem of *learning* the language and making themselves familiar with some *fragment* of the literature."

"If we all worked on an original piece of research and criticism," repeated Alice in her quiet insistent voice, "we could get to the heart of some of the questions facing the Old English scholar."

Professor Fletcher exploded. "You, Miss Marmott, are here with my permission. You are an undergraduate student and this is a graduate class. I don't care if you read ahead and finish *Beowulf*—a poem we will not even discuss until after the spring break—but you must adjust yourself to the pace of this class or I will withdraw that permission. Otherwise, take a suggestion. Leave Bowmouth. Go somewhere else. Find some enormous university with an enormous library and dig in. We are a small college. Our Old English library is limited. This course merely meets a graduate requirement, and it is no place for someone of your obvious learning. And now, all of you." Professor Fletcher straightened and faced the class. "No research papers, no critical papers. I will not read them. Learn to walk before you try to run. You, Miss Marmott, may accept my terms and stay—otherwise, be off."

And Miss Marmott, showing no expression on her face, stayed in her seat.

A clear victory for Patrick Fletcher, thought Sarah. Alice was having a hard week. Two down and only Professor Lacey brought to heel, though the memory of that man being made a fool of was not pleasant. The class ended, and Sarah saw Alice rise and go up to the professor, saw him nod and indicate a chair by his desk. Reconciliation, she thought. That's better.

FIVE

The weather remained clear and well below 32 degrees, so that by Friday the snow sculptures were finished and ready for a last smoothing and spraying that would transform each into a massive form of ice. Alex and Sarah met after an early dinner and did the tour. Lights had been strung on the trees in the quadrangles so that the figures glittered against the dark.

"Is there a prize?" asked Sarah, as they inspected an outsize Daniel Boone.

"Of course," said Alex. "Bowmouth was founded by mercenary types. Each school or college division, each quad competing. Even the med and law schools. Everyone votes, and the winner is announced next week. I think I'll go for the voyageurs. But tonight we've got the hockey game."

"There's a hockey game?"

"Naturally. I've got our tickets. Bowmouth versus Colby. Big rivals. Tomorrow ski races, dogsled races, cross-country, the whole bit, and then everyone jams into a small space and starts drinking. An operetta Saturday night with one of your faculty directing."

"That's Vera Pruczak," said Sarah. "Or Olivia Macbeth. I've been hearing chunks of the *Mikado* all week. She wanted me to sing for her, but I never had the time—or the desire. And look, there she is, coming right across at us."

Vera Pruczak floated into their company trailing a long wool cape trimmed with what appeared in the dimly lighted North Quad to be the fur of a collie. "It's Sarah, the new English Department drudge," said Miss Pruczak. "You never sang for me. *Can* you sing? I mean at all."

"A little," said Sarah. "But not seriously."

"I only want a little. My dear, I'm desperate. Three members of the chorus down with strep throats, Pitti-Sing with the flu, and her understudy is pregnant and gone all sick on me. Can you fill in? Say yes."

"We're going to the hockey game," said Alex.

"Can *you* sing? I'm short of baritones."

"No," said Alex. "Absolutely not."

"Well, it won't interfere with the hockey game. Nothing," continued Miss Pruczak in a bitter voice, "could interfere with that. No one has a sense of priorities. Rehearsal tomorrow, Sarah, nine o'clock A.M. sharp and again at four. I'll have a costume for you, though it will need taking in. Pitti-Sing was bust heavy. Now go right over to the English Department, the script is on my desk. Run over Pitti-Sing and the chorus entrances. Mrs. Parker is working late, and she'll let you in my office. Darling, you are sent from heaven. I'll give you a copy of my new book, all autographed, rubbish though it is." She turned to Alex. "You have a face, sinister in a *good* way. I could use you for Dracula with not too much makeup. And now I must run. I'm voting for that marvelous Viking ship. I always vote for the biggest sculpture." And Vera Pruczak was off into the night, her cape rising up behind her.

"Dr. Dracula, at your service," said Alex. "Shall we find some quiet corner where I can drink some blood . . . maybe that woman's?"

"I think I like her, except she never lets you say no, and now here I'm stuck with *The Mikado.*"

"And I've lost my date for tomorrow night."

"I'll bet you could have sung, I've heard you warbling in the tub."

"Nothing on God's earth would put me on a stage in a kimono," said Alex.

"I've got to run over to the English Department and pick

up the *Mikado* part so I can study if the hockey is too boring."

"Hockey is never boring," said Alex. "At least not to an old defenseman like me."

The English Department, if the lights from the various office windows were taken as evidence, had attracted several night owls. The Faculty Common Room door was open, and Sarah, walking past, could see that the room was in some disorder, periodicals sprayed about and at least four lamps lit. Under one of them Professor Larkin sprawled in a leather chair, his sheepskin coat open. Farther down the hall the clatter of the computer printer told Sarah that in the English Office at least one of the clerks was working late, and across the way, in the opposite office, she found Mrs. Parker bent over her typewriter. The secretary looked up. "Oh, yes, Miss Deane. Miss Pruczak said I was to let you in. Come along. I'm trying to finish the final class lists with all the drop-and-add changes. Quite a job, I assure you."

"Adding and dropping is miserable," said Sarah, keeping step with Mrs. Parker as she stepped down the hall, her ring of keys chinking with every step. Sarah saw that a light showed from under Professor Fletcher's office door. The upper half was covered by a square piece of green stained glass that gave the interior an aquariumlike ambience and showed the professor's indistinct form standing over a bookcase.

"Here you are," said Mrs. Parker, opening a door and flipping the wall switch. "Right on her desk."

Sarah picked up the folder, Mrs. Parker relocked the door, and together they retreated down the hall. "You aren't going to the hockey game?" asked Sarah.

"I'll be along later," said Mrs. Parker, "but I've got Professor Garvey coming in with an undergraduate reading list, and then I have a student to see. How are you getting along, Miss Deane? As Professor Bello might say, I feel *in loco parentis* with all our students."

"My nose is just above water," said Sarah. "I shouldn't be doing *The Mikado* and certainly not going to the hockey game."

"All work and no play," said Mrs. Parker, suddenly kittenish. She smiled and patted Sarah's shoulder. "Winter carnival at Bowmouth is quite special. It brings us all together."

Making her way through the North Quad toward the hockey rink, Sarah reflected that Mrs. Parker seemed to be the victim of some fond delusion and that it would take more than a winter carnival to bring the members of the English Department together. Halfway across the square she paused to look up at the completed Viking ship, which showed an impressive attention to detail. A long row of round shields overhung the gunwales, and the bow rose up in a reverse curve and was finished with some kind of mythical beast's head. Two bearded, horn-helmeted ice figures stood waist high above the deck, targs and swords held at the ready. "Yes, I think I'll vote for that one," Sarah said aloud, and then realized she had been joined by a silent figure holding a briefcase.

"It's not really authentic," said Alice Marmott. "I'd say that they only used a popular encyclopedia. After all, there are Scandinavian remains available—the *Gokstad* vessel in Oslo and even a pre-Viking Anglo-Saxon burial ship at Sutton Hoo in Suffolk. I've been reading ahead and doing some research." She looked up again at the ship. "Oh, well, I don't suppose they could do too much more with snow and ice."

Quite a concession for Alice, thought Sarah. And then she remembered that Alice never seemed to be with a friend, never walked with a group of students, but trudged always alone, her black briefcase—the kind Sarah had seen nuns carry to class—held to her side. "Would you like to come to the hockey game and sit with us? We could see if there are any tickets left."

Alice appeared to be astonished by the question. "Oh, no. I have an appointment; and besides, I never go to those things. They're an awful waste of time when I've got so much to do." Alice's face, framed by its dark beret, was a pale oval under the ice sculpture lights. She paused as if she had an unusual scholarly question to puzzle over. Finally she said, "Thank you for asking me. People usually don't. But then," she added, "I don't encourage them. There are just so many hours in every day, and I try to account for them."

Sarah had a thought. "You're not a Quaker, are you, or a Mennonite, or"—this now seemed possible—"a nun who doesn't wear a habit?" Surely only some severe sect or religious commitment could account for such extreme devotion to study.

"No," said Alice. "I'm not satisfied with the established religions. Most of the popular ones are based on logical fallacies even a grade-school child should see through. But thanks again for asking me to the hockey. It was kind of you."

Honestly, thought Sarah as Alice passed her, what an oddball. Or perhaps Alice was actually what was rarer on any campus than rubies, a true scholar. Then she remembered Alex waiting at the hockey arena door on the other side of the North Quad and broke into a run.

After she had reached the age of refusal, Sarah had avoided hockey games. She thought of them as poorly regulated scenes of mayhem, thick with curses, flying gloves, shattered teeth, and bloodied faces. But growing up with a hockey-playing brother and parents who were fans, she had endured her share of games and certainly knew a forward from a goalie and the rules about blue lines and icing. So, through the first period, to please Alex and in deference to her new association with Bowmouth, she tried valiantly to pay attention. Colby College seemed to be wiping the ice with Bowmouth, and that fact stimulated wild shrieks, hootings, and horns from the Bowmouth students, who, arriving with cans of beer in their mittens, were already too well stimulated.

During the second period, in which the home team came to life, Sarah took up her score and the libretto of *The Mikado* and, humming to herself, tried to get a grip on the operetta. Was she to be Pitti-Sing or just in the chorus? Was the pregnant understudy likely to recover? Let's see, two flats. "Life is a joke that's just begun!/Three little maids from school!/Three little maids who, all unwary,/Come from a ladies' seminary,/Freed from its genius tutelary," sang Sarah inside her head.

Alex disappeared at the end of the second period to see what could be done about hot dogs and root beer, and Sarah put down the score and looked about. Vintage winter college scene. Long woolen scarves, the padded coat brigade, couples with rugs around their knees—the rink was an ice chest with the damp cold air sinking into one's every bone. There was the so-called sexpot, Professor Lacey, on an opposite bleacher in a domestic arrangement with three teenage children and a woman in tortoiseshell glasses, her gray hair pulled back into a bun in the style known as the faculty knot. Seven or eight seats away sat the estimable Mrs. Parker, smartly muffled in a black fur number and a red wool toque. She was seated next to a blue-haired woman whom Sarah had come to recognize as one of the real powers at Bowmouth, the registrar. Farther along the bench sat Professor Jakob Horst, red-faced and stolid, puffing on a pipe and sharing a rug with a equally stolid blond woman, the pair looking like illustrations for *Hans Brinker or The Silver Skates*. And over in the corner at ice level—she might have guessed it—supported by the rink entrance gate was Professor Amos Larkin. He was hatless and his sheepskin coat was buttoned crookedly. His mouth was moving, and judging from his wide gestures, he was reciting, although there was no one near who appeared to be listening. Sarah looked over and saw that Mrs. Parker had seen him too and was pointing him out to the registrar. Tattletale, she thought, but then told herself that Professor Larkin's state was hardly a secret and the registrar must have known all about him. In fact, Sarah felt that if things went on as they were, in spite of periodic classroom performances of brilliance, the overall condition of the man must be heading him for the ash heap—a leave of absence from which he would never return. He was the sort of person who would from time to time turn up in ever lower, ever less selective university circles and perhaps end up as an all-purpose English teacher in some benighted public high school noted for absentee students, razor blades, and drug deals. Sad, Sarah thought, because the man had a brain, an organ that seemed missing, in whole or in part, from so many tenured members of colleges and schools. She reopened her score. Three flats in this one. Pitti-Sing, gracefully, a tempo, "For he's going to marry Yum-Yum . . . your anger pray bury, for all will be merry, I think you had better succumb. . . ."

"Your hot dog, madam." Alex sat down and handed over a mustard-dripping roll. "Okay, this should be one terrific period."

"Why?" said Sarah, accepting a paper cup of root beer.

"Idiot. The third period. We've almost tied it up. Where were you?"

"Up to my neck in *The Mikado*. Wishing I had the guts to say no. And I've been checking the house. Quite a few English faculty supporters plus Madam Parker."

"So watch this period. It's five to four and Colby's been picking up penalties." Here Alex began an enthusiastic and unnecessary explanation of penalty killing, cross-checking, and high-sticking. "And watch number five. He's only a sophomore, but can he skate! From Montreal."

"Athletic scholarship?" said Sarah darkly.

"Don't know, don't care," said Alex. "No time for ethical discussion."

"I didn't know you were such a jock."

"Be quiet. Here's the face-off."

Sarah pulled her quilted coat tighter about her and settled back. She wished she cared who high-sticked whom, who had a hat trick. Something lacking. She tried to run over her experiences in the sporting world and decided that the last time she had been truly excited over such an event was the night before the Camp Merrilark jacks tournament when she had thrown up from an excess of nerves. For a while she returned to the trials of Yum-Yum, and then, judging from the increase of shouting that the period was almost over, she let her eyes wander again, picking out here a student, there a teaching fellow, a faculty member. Across the way, her back to the rink, Vera Pruczak in her cape, a knitted balaklava, and warm-up stockings was buttonholing a black-bearded young man, probably signing him up for Dracula, and beyond stood Professor Fletcher by the hot dogs with his wife, striking in a green wool poncho. Professor Larkin had disappeared or perhaps had just slid to the floor and been swept up by the ice-cleaning machine. And then Sarah suddenly woke to the fact that the whole arena had exploded, waving hands, stamping feet, and yelling, "Bowmouth, Bowmouth, Bowmouth!"

"Terrific," said Alex, pulling Sarah to her feet.

"It's over?"

"You're hopeless. We won, six to five. A good beginning for the carnival. Come on, we can duck out the side entrance.

Let's take one last tour of the ice sculptures and then vote. The ballot box is over by the bookstore."

But their tour stopped short in the North Quad just at a large ash tree midway between the Viking ship and the archway separating that quadrangle from the path leading to the hockey arena. On every side streamed students, shouting, waving banners, beer cans, and bottles, but as Sarah and Alex left the throng to circle the sculpture, there in the shadow, inconspicuous, on his face, lay the coatless, shirtless, shoeless, hatless figure of Professor Larkin. He lay, hands at his side, chin against a frozen snow-crusted tree root, stocking feet splayed out behind him.

"Oh, my God," said Sarah. "He's passed out."

Alex knelt beside him. "I hope that's all he's done. I'm just getting a shallow respiration. We'll get him over to the emergency room fast. Hypothermia if he's lucky."

Sarah found a seat on a bench beside the emergency room and waited for Alex. She hadn't liked Amos Larkin—even at his most sober he hadn't offered much of himself to like—but she had never wished him to come to this: lying half frozen in the snow while the entire college went berserk at a hockey game. He must have wandered outside sometime after the second period and been so tanked up that he didn't even notice the cold, just stumbled about shedding clothes, losing his shoes until he tripped or passed out. Sarah looked about and found little to reassure her in the waiting room. An anxious-looking woman with an arm around a man with a gray face, a drunken student holding a bleeding hand in the air, teenage girl whose ankle was wrapped in a makeshift bandage. Sarah picked up a glossy magazine titled *Emergency Medicine* and flipped the pages. What a periodical to leave around for worried parents and relatives. Trauma, anatomical drawings of shattered limbs, blocked blood vessels, and damaged cerebellums. She put the magazine back on the table and then with relief saw Alex coming out of the swinging doors to the examining rooms. He had changed his jacket for a blue scrub shirt, and his stethoscope still dangled around his neck.

"We've been working him over and I think he'll make it. His blood-alcohol content is a wonder to behold, over .352.

I'm surprised he made it as far as the North Quad. Anyway, he's being admitted here. They'll warm him up gradually, hold him quiet on a tranquilizer, and dry him out. I gather he's pretty well known in local medical circles . . . fell out of a boat last summer and dislocated a shoulder and went through a pair of French doors this fall, which allowed the med student on the service plenty of suture practice."

"Doesn't he have a regular doctor?"

"I've called around and apparently not. Alcoholics usually leave a trail of physicians behind them because they don't like the advice about quitting drinking. Anyway, until he fires me, I'll take the job. For the short haul, I think he's safe, but in the long run, who knows. You never can tell with these birds."

Saturday passed for Sarah in a maze of *Mikado* rehearsals broken only by trips to the library to prepare for her Monday classes. She was dimly aware of the pervading carnival clamor, loudspeakers set in the trees blasting the air with rock music and announcements, people with skis shouting to one another, waving paper cups and beer cans, and twice, at great hazard to pedestrian life, three teams of huskies careening over the campus, their drivers yelling "Hike!"

At three that afternoon Sarah found herself sitting in a darkened basement braced for dress rehearsal while Vera Pruczak did things to her short dark hair with bolsters and a black wig. "It's too bad that you're stuck with Pitti-Sing, but I've combed the college," said Vera. "You'll have to do your best. You have a nice voice, but it's a little light, so open your mouth and sing right out. And practice with your fan. You and Peep-Bo and Yum-Yum have to use them together. Delicately. It's an art."

"Do you know how Professor Larkin is?" asked Sarah when she could get in a word. "I haven't heard from Alex."

"I went to the hospital at noon and marched right into his room. 'No Visitors' signs apply only to visitors, and I've known Amos for a coon's age. He looks absolutely ghastly, but he's alive and as nasty as you please, which is always a good sign. I told him to shape up or they'll ship him out. Even Howard Bello, who puts up with anything, won't stand for it much longer, and of course Mrs. Parker has had it—missed appointments, meetings, late book orders, students' papers not handed back—for all of which she takes a lot of flak. I'm afraid she'll persuade Howard to dump him even before spring break. Now, my dear, don't shake your head when you sing, this hairdo is precarious, and hold your elbows in to your sides—stereotyped gestures, very formal—like a doll that's been wound up, and if you see any of Amos's students around, tell them that his classes will be canceled because of an accident. No one will read notices this weekend. Try and build up some sympathy for the beast, because otherwise the students will be in with petitions asking for his head. Student power is something to reckon with these days."

"Yes," said Sarah, her mind trying to arrange these instructions in order of importance.

"You see," said Miss Pruczak, turning Sarah around and adjusting her cherry-colored obi, "Amos did me a favor once —he's not a snob about women who write gothics—so I'd like to even the score. After that he's on his own. There's your music cue. Don't let Yum-Yum drown you and Peep-Bo out *completely*, which she very much wants to do."

Somehow the *Mikado* cast, even with half its original members missing with flu or hung-over from Friday night's celebration, survived the dress rehearsal and, gathering a new head of steam, managed to come up with a fairly creditable rendition of Mr. Gilbert and Mr. Sullivan's classic.

Alex, sitting midway in the audience, saw Sarah with new appreciation. She was, he decided, in her cream kimono and cherry obi, her rolled black hair and eye makeup, a very taking presence, and her voice, though tremulous and breathy in her opening scene, gathered resonance as she went along, and she delivered the "going to marry Yum-Yum" with vigor.

"I think I'll buy you a white kimono," said Alex, as they drove home, Sarah flushed with triumph and an energetic rubbing with cold cream. "When's your next appearance?"

"Once more, tomorrow night, and then the coach turns back into a pumpkin. But Miss Pruczak wants me to try out for something in the spring, so I may cash in the English Department and go with drama. Which reminds me, how's Professor Larkin?"

"Doing well, somewhat sober. Has some of the usual problems we associate with alcoholism. Malnutrition, a touch of jaundice, the shakes, the wobblies."

"Can he remember how he got outside to the Quad?"

"He doesn't even remember going to the hockey game, never mind how he lost half his clothes and ended up outside. Maybe this will be just the sort of jolt he needs to try and clean up the mess he's made of himself."

"I'd hate to be the one who tells him that," said Sarah. "And now I've got forty papers to correct for my Monday students."

"You probably won't have that many. The Monday after carnival weekend is pretty thin."

This was an accurate guess. Sarah's classes were sparsely attended by a few unwholesome-looking freshmen. And the winter carnival had decimated even the graduate seminars. "I thought grad students were above these high jinks," said Sarah to Mary Donelli as they went into their Shakespeare seminar.

"Don't you believe it," said Mary. "They pretend they are, but give them a chance to break loose, and pow! Drago Collins really tied one on. I saw him doing a war dance around Daniel Boone last night."

"Even Alice Marmott's missing," said Sarah, twisting around and counting the house. "She said she never went near student fun and games, but maybe she gave in to temptation. That sort always falls hardest."

"Wine, women—or men—and song," said Mary, "or more likely the flu. Half the campus is sick."

Professor Lacey was in fine fettle. The absence of Alice Marmott seemed to act as a stimulant. He tossed his mane, paced the room, and expounded with broad gestures, rolled up the critics, tossed them in the air or out the window, and even listened to the ideas offered by the shrunken class. As a final proof of geniality, he allowed Mary to discuss and then read Gertrude in the closet scene with himself as Hamlet and let Sarah take on Ophelia's last mad scene.

"Winter carnival suits Lacey," said Mary, as they filed out of the classroom. "He can be grandiose and no one notices, what with all the jamboree."

"Who won the ice sculpture thing?" asked Sarah.

"They'll announce it tomorrow—Founder's Day."

"Not another holiday?"

"No. Morning classes and then special symposiums, which are absolute yawn. You know, 'Has the vision of Leander Starbox to provide higher education for mid-coast Maine borne fruit?' or 'Is Business Management a legitimate discipline?' Stuff like that. Then there's a big bonfire in the quad that has the winning sculpture, which naturally almost melts it down, and a hunk of cash and a banner is handed over to the winning group."

"Banner proudly displayed through the year?"

"Until spring, when someone tries to steal it during June week. How about lunch?"

"I'm meeting Alex at the hospital cafeteria. Want to come?"

"As a matter of fact, yes. I'll send a funny card up to what's left of Amos. Don't want him to think he's been abandoned by all."

"Do you call him Amos to his face?"

"God, no. He'd probably slice me up. I don't know much about him, how old or anything. With all that booze he could be ninety."

"Alex told me when they admitted him that he turned out to be just forty—only five years older than Alex himself, which is unbelievable."

"Well, you could have fooled me. Say forty going on ninety. What a wreck."

SIX

"We won't need a bonfire," said Alex to Sarah Tuesday night. "This thaw is going to melt everything into mush—it must be almost up to fifty." They were hurrying along with a stream of students and faculty and a collection of townspeople who were drawn by the spectacle of the college at play and the possibility of free beer.

"Just why are we getting trapped into all these undergraduate affairs?" said Sarah crossly. "I have an Old English translation and about thirty student essays on 'The Death of Ivan Ilyich' to go over."

"Serious stuff for carnival weekend."

"I know. I should have assigned *The Bacchae*. And I haven't even begun to get a grip on Aelfric's 'Preface to the Homilies.' How does this sound? 'Ic Ælfrīc munuc and mæsse-prēost, swā þēah wāccre þonne swilcum hādum gebyrige.'"

"What a terrible noise. Is that a language?"

"Probably not the way I say it. Okay, we'll see if your voyageurs won and watch the bonfire."

The announcement of the winner took place on the steps of Starbox Administration Building. A figure in full academic regalia, including impressive white fur panels and a gold chain, held up his black-winged arms for silence. Sarah, remembering the Bowmouth catalog, recognized the silver head and beard as belonging to the chancellor, a personage of almost mythic proportions, never seen except in the blur of a student newspaper photograph or as a distant escort of possible financial godfathers.

"The winner," called the chancellor into the public address system, his words echoing down through the avenue of maples and across Bowmouth Pond to the hills beyond, "the winner this year, by two hundred and fifty-nine votes, is North Quad's ice replica of a Viking ship"—he waited for a cheer to rise, boom, and echo—"and I hereby award the banner to that quad to be hung there until winter carnival week of next year. The bonfire committee is now laying the traditional bonfire material in North Quad and will welcome you there in half an hour's time." Here more cheers, beer cans lofted, and a few hats sprinkled with foam. "Honorable mention this year," shouted the chancellor, his microphone fading, "goes to the medical students' representation of 'The Anatomy Lesson.'"

"That's playing fast and loose with the theme," said Sarah. "Early Explorations, my eye. And besides, it's horrible."

"It's Rembrandt, which gives it class. They were going to use a real cadaver and freeze it in until they were found out."

"I will never understand medical humor," said Sarah.

"You laugh at *M.A.S.H.*"

"That's different—I think."

"You're on your way. Next year you'll laugh at cadavers in ice sculptures."

"Never, never, never, never. Never."

"Okay, never. Come on, we'll do the bonfire and I'll take you home to Aelfric's homilies."

It was quite a sight. A huge six-deep ring of students circled the North Quad. Arms linked, swaying from side to side, they sang—songs that everyone, students, faculty, townspeople, had grown up with, songs that were part of their blood and bone: *There is a tavern in the town, and there my true love sits him down. . . . From this valley they say you are going. . . . Jimmie crack corn and I don't care. . . . What shall we do with a drunken sailor. . . . Waltzing Matilda, waltzing Matilda, you'll come a-waltzing, Matilda, with me. . . . And here's a hand, my trusty frien' and gie's a hand o' thine; We'll tak' a cup o' kindness yet, For auld lang syne.*"

"Is that moisture on the cheek of the great cynic?" said Alex, looking down at Sarah.

"People singing always get to me. And everyone looks so young in the firelight. Even you, Alex."

"For those kind words I shall stay firelit forever. Hush, now, they're doing the college song. It may sound familiar, but the Old Bowmouthites claim they used it first."

This anthem did bear a remarkable resemblance to "Far Above Cayuga's Waters." *Noble walls o'ergrown with ivy*, sang the swaying crowds,

> *Halls of learning true,*
> *We salute, thee Bowmouth College,*
> *Hail the red and blue.*

The three following verses, because they were progressively less familiar, ended with only a few wavering voices accompanied by a kind of communal drone. Sarah, as the anthem wound down, watched with interest a loyal son of Bowmouth struggling with a ladder toward the Viking ship. This he placed at a precarious angle against the frozen side of the boat, and now Sarah saw that it was Drago Collins, an undergraduate at heart. He clutched to his chest the winning crimson and blue banner and began working his way along the glassy gunwales and shield row and up to the prow, which curved dangerously high over frozen snow that had been carved into a series of knifelike triangles to simulate waves. Hatless, his black curly hair and red jacket illuminated from the overhead string of lights, his stretched-out body and the dragon's head seeming to pulse in the moving glow of the bonfire, Drago inched himself along. Then, climbing astride the dragon's neck, he pulled himself from one icy scale on the dragon's neck to the next. Sarah saw that his intention was to hang the banner from the dragon's mouth, but it seemed a horrible risk. Twice Drago reached out over the animal's carved and protruding eye, and twice he slipped back down the neck.

The crowd was now entirely silent, focused on the slipping, struggling figure. "He's going to fall," whispered Sarah, and she saw that Alex's gloved hands were clenched. Once again, Drago, crouched like a jockey, pulled himself up to the neck, to the crown, and reached over the eye, past the funnel-like nostril and to the tusks that stuck up from the lower jaw. The banner unwound and floated down. Drago lifted both hands in a victory salute and in that single moment was sent hurtling back down the neck between the scales, like someone practicing a backward luge, to disappear head first into the center of the vessel. There was a gasp, a roar of laughter, and then a great rising cheer. The crowd broke from their circle and surged forward, yelling.

"Is he all right?" said Sarah. "What's down in the boat, anything sharp?"

"I hope not," said Alex. "But I didn't enjoy that. Those waves could have cut him in half."

"Well, if he's all right, where is he?" Sarah liked Drago, who, though often unprepared in his seminars and the butt of faculty sarcasm, remained cheerful.

"Here he comes." Alex pointed to a face rising over the gunwale.

"Something's wrong," said Sarah. "He's yelling." But Alex had broken into a run and was already at the foot of the ladder and, helped by many hands, was hoisting himself up.

Drago leaned forward and forcing his voice above the clamor gave the urgent, terrible information. "A body. Someone's body. It's frozen in—it's frozen right into the ice—into the boat."

"Goddamn," said Alex. He let out his breath in one long exasperated expiration. "Those blasted medical students."

Sarah, moving forward, saw Alex turn to Drago and point in the direction of the medical school. She remembered the cadaver meant for "The Anatomy Lesson" and in her turn said "Damn."

Alex climbed partway up the ladder and shouted into the crowd, "Any med students there? Any one from the medical school? Get up here, on the double. We'll need a pick and a shovel."

The last thing Sarah wanted to do was stand around for

an hour or so by the expiring bonfire and watch while Alex and some medical school ghouls cracked the body out of the ice and brought it down the ladder—probably naked and frozen solid. But she and Alex had come to the campus that day in one car, and even the libraries were closed by now. Well, at least it wasn't snowing. Swearing not to look at the ice ship until the cadaver was safely away, she took herself off to a bench under a lamp in a far corner of the quad and opened Aelfric's "Preface to the Homilies."

Alex, regretting his good flannel trousers and cursing practical jokesters in general and medical students in particular, climbed up over the row of shields. The fact that he himself had participated in a very similar affair as a student did nothing to soften his displeasure.

Drago seemed much relieved. "God, I thought I was seeing things. I've read about how the Norsemen buried their warriors in ships, and then, Christ, I saw this body under the ice, all in dark clothes."

"At least the med students dressed it," said Alex. "It's not like them to be so civilized."

"I went spinning down from the bowsprit ass over teakettle. Christ, I guess—I guess it was the beer, because I'm afraid of heights. I went down between those two Vikings." Drago indicated two ice warriors, their horned helmets, beards, and swords now molten and dripping. "I slid right down into the middle of the damn boat, and when I tried to stand up I fell again toward the bow—it slopes into a sort of hollow—and God, there it was. Come and look."

Alex grimaced and nodded. Cautiously, his feet slipping on the wet ice, hanging on to the gunwales, he made his way forward to what in a modern boat might have been a hatchway. Here, well in the shadow of the rising sides of the ship, was a small raised rectangle, and under a layer of melting ice, Alex could easily make out a human shape: coat, stockings, boots, dark mittened hands, a dark cap fitted around a pale oval face, and around its neck, taking several turns, a long dark school scarf. . . .

"Sarah." Alex stood beside her, minutes only, it seemed, from the time she had beaten a retreat. "It's not someone from the medical school. At least I don't think so. Will you call the ambulance, and"—it wasn't really an afterthought—"the police."

Half an hour later, with the assistance of the ambulance medics and several medical students—Drago Collins having taken himself off to be sick—the body was released from its ice coffin, covered with a blanket, and driven to the hospital morgue with a police escort.

"I'll drop you off home," said Alex to Sarah, "and then go on to the hospital."

"Why? There's nothing you can do, is there?"

"I'm one of the medical examiners, remember, and the man on the spot, so I suppose this is my first job—though God knows I wish it weren't."

"You said it was a woman. Are you sure she doesn't belong to the med school and the students dressed up the body?"

"I thought so at first, but with that scarf around the neck I took a second look. Besides, the police have called the med school and no cadavers are missing. No ID. Just that she's young and wears dark clothes."

"What sort of clothes?" said Sarah, with a terrible feeling of apprehension.

"Oh, a dark coat, the kind an older woman might wear. Not funky, something a respectable housekeeper might buy. And rubber overshoes. No one wears those things. I'm not a fashion nut, but even I know that. And a sort of beret."

"It's Alice Marmott," said Sarah in a desolate voice.

"Who? You know who it is?"

"She hasn't been in class lately, and she's not the kind to skip. She dresses just like a nun. Dark and plain. Was this one —I mean was she very fair, hair in a braid around her head?"

"Yes, I'm afraid so."

"Alice Marmott," repeated Sarah. "Oh, damn it, damn it. Why, I just saw her before the hockey game. I asked her to come with us because she was always alone, but she said she had an appointment, that hockey games were a waste of time."

"If you really think she might be Alice, do you think you could come along to the hospital and identify her for the police? Only if you want to, because I'm sure we could find someone from the college, though the sooner the better."

"Yes, you'll have to get hold of her family." Sarah gritted her teeth, remembering how she had wanted to hide from the sight of the body being brought down from the Viking ship. "Okay, I'll do it. Was she—I mean, do you think she just climbed up there and froze to death—sort of a prank—or to meet someone, to make love? Or suicide?"

Even as she said it, Sarah felt that by no wild flight of imagination could Alice Marmott be thought to have been capable of any such aberrant act.

"It was murder then," she said.

"I'd say so," said Alex. "I think she was strangled by that scarf. One of those long ones you trip on."

"I never saw Alice in anything like that. Just a little tan woolen thing tucked into the top of her coat."

"That was stuffed in her pocket. Come on, let's get this over with. The police are waiting at the hospital."

It was all very well for Alex to talk about "getting it over," thought Sarah after her visit to the morgue. He's done this before. But what one doesn't get over is going in and seeing someone—someone who though not really a friend had certain singular human qualities, certain excellences—on a table under the cold glare of a low-hanging fluorescent light. The police had taken Alice's clothes, and now she was protected only by a sheet. Alex had turned down the corner to expose Alice's face and covered it almost immediately. Sarah was shocked into silence. Was it even Alice, this swollen bruised face with the tongue blocking its mouth? Sarah jerked her head away.

"I'm sorry," said Alex. "It's because she was strangled. Is it Alice?" He turned down the sheet again.

This time Sarah really looked. She saw the tilted nose, the very fair hair like corn silk pulled away from the high forehead and circling in a now disordered braid around the tiny ears. She tried not to see the gasping mouth, the half-open eyes, and knew at the same time she would never forget them.

"Okay," said Alex. "That's that. I should have prepared you."

"I'm all right," said Sarah in a shaking voice. "It just took me by surprise, and it was worse than I thought."

"It's always bad. Disease, violence. You never get used to it."

"I thought doctors, nurses—"

"You thought wrong. To quote you—and King Lear—never, never, never. Oh, there's a lot of tough bluff and bluster, jokes and hamming it up, but I don't think many medical people ever get used to seeing people turned into cold meat. They just hide it. Now let's go home."

SEVEN

S arah spent a fretful night half between sleeping and waking. Alice Marmott, both alive and frozen, figured in dreary cameo appearances, scenes in which students, faculty, Alex, her own mother and father, and a brigade of unnamed morgue attendants came, admonished, and cautioned like a disorderly chorus from *Oedipus*. Now she sat up in bed heavy-eyed and listened to the whirring of Alex's electric shaver from the bathroom.

"Alex," she called, "what happens now? About Alice. Do you do anything more?"

Alex came into the room, barefoot, his hair on end, his shirt open at the neck. "I'm just about finished. I only have to make a complete statement about finding the body. The police will call the chief medical examiner and start in with questions for her classmates, her teachers, and her family. Try to find something out about the girl. You may be asked for anything you might have noticed."

"Like the fact that Alice was very, very bright. I think she remembered everything she'd ever read and then wrote corrective commentaries. Did they find her briefcase?"

"I don't know, but George Fitts will be vacuuming the whole quad. You remember George from last summer. He's still assigned to the Knox County State Police CID, a genuine walking machine."

"Unforgettable George. Head like a lightbulb, on the glacial side, very efficient, and hardly ever smiles."

"We need glacial efficiency for this case, not smiles."

Making her way to the student cafeteria for a quick cup of coffee, Sarah found that the North Quad was already roped off except for a narrow path at the edge of the square. She watched for a minute as a team of plainclothesmen pawed through layers of melted snow and uncovered a clutch of gloves, a knitted hat, a textbook, and three beer cans, all of which they added to a growing pile of detritus. Then she was sternly moved on by a watching policeman in a black windbreaker. "Nothing for you here, lady. Take a walk."

The cafeteria was humming with the news of a body in the Viking ship. Mary Donelli waved to her from a nearby table. "God, what a night. Drago told me all about it. I heard it's Alice Marmott. Drago said he almost barfed all over the sculpture."

"How does everyone know so soon?" said Sarah.

"Drago's got a friend who's a nurse in the ER. I ran into one of my freshmen comp class students, and she said that Alice lives on her floor and no one's seen her for—well, for days. But Alice rooms alone, and what with the winter weekend follies, no one paid much attention. She said Alice wasn't very noticeable in the first place. God, it's enough to put you off winter carnivals for life."

"What's so horrible is that she may have been frozen into that sculpture for days." Sarah put down her coffee, trying not to see Alice under the morgue sheet. "She was really almost a child."

"A child with a very adult brain," said Mary. "Poor thing."

"That's all," said Miss Heidi Toner at the end of an hour's interrogation. Sergeant George Fitts tapped his desk with the end of his pencil. He had set up a field office in a seldom-used classroom in the North Quad and was engaged in helping move telephones, a typewriter, a computer, and boxes of recording equipment into the room. Alex, persuaded by George to shift his morning patient appointments, nodded to him without speaking. George had little time for pointless remarks, and Alex had grown used to the sergeant during a particularly aggravating case last summer on Weymouth Island. George was smooth-shaven and smooth-headed—the Yul Brynner look—and wore his plain gray windbreaker and navy pants in such a manner that one could almost see uniform tabs and stripes and regulation buttons. A car driver seeing George standing at the edge of the street would immediately temper his speed and reach for his driver's license.

Nothing had come of the first students to file in review past George's desk that morning. Miss Toner was the last of those who lived on Alice's dormitory corridor and had even less to say than her predecessors.

"Are you an English major?" asked Alex finally, thinking that the academic, not the social, route was the way to go.

"Yes, but that doesn't mean I saw anything of Alice. She's a transfer student—from Ohio State, I think, so I didn't get to know her as a freshman. Those freshman English comp and lit classes are smaller than the other big lectures and you usually find out something about each other. You know, those essays on my early life and how no one understood me. Everyone writes personal junk when they first come to college."

"But last year and this, did you have any classes with Miss Marmott?" said George, bringing the subject back on track.

"Well, she's a junior like me, and I did have some English classes with her. Let's see. Last year American Lit and the Contemporary Novel, and this year English Nineteenth-Century Novel, Poetry, and Shakespeare. But then she started taking those grad courses and left the Shakespeare undergrad one. God, I don't know how she did it. I haven't time to brush my teeth."

"Of course," said Alex, after Miss Toner had been thanked and sent on her way, "that's all Alice Marmott did. No fun and games. If you skip all the college distractions, don't fool around in the dorms, don't go out on dates or hang out with a group, I suppose there's time to take double the number of courses—especially if you've one of those super-retentive brains. Sarah told me she always wanted to know more than was being offered."

"We'll talk to the students in all her classes and then try and get a handle on this past weekend. Winter Carnival, I know."

"I'll bet you know," said Alex.

"Yes. Triple the number of OUIs—Operating Under the Influence—and the town police working double shifts. Things tapered off by Sunday night so we didn't expect violence three days *after* the carnival weekend, let alone an in-house homicide."

"What makes you think it's an in-house affair?"

"The college-type scarf, the use of the sculpture as a hiding place, plus probably a knowledge of the campus layout and activity schedule."

"It could perfectly well have been a stranger, a prowler, who found Alice walking across the campus and got her up into the boat when he heard someone coming."

"But he used the ladder, which I gather was well hidden behind the bushes next to the political science building. We think the murderer carried Alice up into the boat using the ladder—we've found a piece of navy blue material on a rung that looks like it came from her coat. The murderer replaced the ladder, so no one thought that anything was amiss with the sculpture. The ladder was used only when the students were working on the sculpture and was put away every night, then put away for good after the sculpture was finished several days before the hockey game. The students did some spraying with a hose from the ground level every night until the thaw, just to build up the ice. We believe someone would have to have been around to notice where the ladder was stowed."

"Okay, so a stranger is not likely . . . but possible. Have they finished with the autopsy? Was Alice raped?"

"Report's not in. Right now we're setting up interviews with the English faculty, starting with the chairman. Professor Howard Bello."

"You'd better include the department secretary, Mrs. Parker. Sarah says she runs the whole ship."

George inclined his head and made a tidy little note. "I'll need Miss Deane—Sarah—for something else." He pronounced Sarah's first name with reluctance. George Fitts, even though well acquainted with her, was not at home with first names; they suggested softness and informality. "We've found the victim's briefcase. It was shoved in past the body, into a hollow. The water from the hose collected there and froze over it. Since Sarah is a graduate student here, we'd like her to look over the papers and notebooks and tell us if anything seems out of place. Of course, we'll be asking one of the regular English faculty to do the same."

"Any idea of the exact time of death? I certainly couldn't tell," said Alex. "She was still partly frozen. But, as I've told you, Sarah says she was alive and well just before the hockey game."

"It's a problem, but the lab will check stomach contents and try and make allowance for the gastric tissue freezing. The temperature stayed below freezing until late Monday."

"So you're guessing she was put in the ship anytime from the beginning of the hockey game until the thaw on Monday. You couldn't have her frozen in like that after the thaw set in."

"That's right. And the repeated spraying accounts for the heavy ice layer. Unfortunately for us, no one is known to have climbed into the boat until Mr. Collins tried to hang his banner. I suppose most of the students were too drunk on Friday night and Saturday to notice whether Alice Marmott was around." George snapped out his words in a way that told Alex exactly what the sergeant thought of students.

"Things were certainly hopping," admitted Alex, "but I'm sure there were a few sober souls around: the operetta people, the grinds, and students with loftier things on their minds than winter games. But you'll have a hell of a lot of out-of-town guests to hunt up. Girlfriends, boyfriends, visiting bedfellows."

"I've asked for extra men to chase them down. And the sheriff's investigator will give us a hand. You remember Mike Laaka?"

"I grew up with him, and then last summer—"

George with a slight shrug dismissed last summer. "The trouble with Mike is that he's still more interested in the fifth race at Aqueduct than in his proper job. Fortunately for us, it isn't Kentucky Derby season yet."

Alex stood up and grinned. "If there's a derby anywhere in the country, Mike will find it."

"Probably," said George gloomily. "One more thing. That blue scarf—navy blue with purplish lines, the one around the victim's neck. It didn't belong to Alice Marmott, it's not a Bowmouth one, and it's been identified as exactly like one usually worn by Amos Larkin."

"The hell it has."

"Who, I understand, is your patient in the hospital. May we interrogate him today?"

"I suppose so," said Alex. "We're letting him go this afternoon. He's not in the best of shape, but he wants out."

"Write down an exact description of his condition and his location in the North Quad."

"I think he was way too far gone to do anything so athletic as prop up a ladder and carry a girl into that ice ship."

"Possibly. But he may not have been too drunk to strangle her."

Alex caught up with Sarah after five that afternoon about a mile from their frame house on Sawmill Road. She was jogging along in the dark by the side of the road, orange reflective tape crisscrossed on her sweatshirt and accompanied by Patsy in his reflective collar.

"Are you trying to turn into a pedestrian incident?" he said, opening the car door. "The kind where the driver isn't held because of bad atmospheric conditions?"

Sarah pulled Patsy into the rear seat and settled herself beside Alex. "I know it's starting to rain, but I don't want to turn into complete mush. My eighteenth-century seminar—that's Professor Larkin—is still canceled so I had some extra time. Besides, I'm trying to run off some of the misery about Alice Marmott. It's really getting to me. I'll bet she wasn't over seventeen."

"Just eighteen according to George Fitts's records. She finished high school early. I've asked at the Administration Office about her family. Own mother and father dead. Lived with her father's second wife, who's flying in from Ohio. Now tell me, did Amos Larkin wear a scarf?"

"Oh, yes, a great long thing. Do you mean—oh, how horrible."

"Yes."

"It's bad enough to know the victim, but to know the murderer—or someone who might be—it's sort of a double horrible."

"I agree. And so Larkin had a long scarf. What color?"

"Dark blue, I think. With thin magenta stripes. Something like that. The undergraduate look, though Professor Larkin hasn't an undergraduate hair on his head."

"Well, George Fitts wants you to look through Alice's briefcase for any oddities."

"You'd better get a senior faculty member on that."

"He will, but you're to give the graduate student slant— see if Alice was true blue or into some nefarious student sideline."

"But Professor Larkin killing Alice?" Sarah closed her eyes and the picture of Amos Larkin rose before her: Amos at the faculty party, drunk, loud-voiced, self-pitying, reciting and hectoring; then Amos, sober, hung over, caustic, going on about Amanda Tibbs's failing grade. "He's certainly nasty enough even when he's sober, but he's aggressive with his tongue—a real razor blade. I don't see him as the hands-on type."

"A nasty tongue can lead to nasty hands. I think you know that."

"Yes, but Alice got under every professor's skin. Even the students in her classes must have been ready to throttle her themselves. She probably caused extra assignments and by contrast made them all seem like grade-schoolers. And yet she was perfectly courteous—just relentless. And single-minded, no humor. I doubt if she had much imagination; it may not have occurred to her that other students didn't have her capacity for work or that the graduate fellows had two or three sections of freshman English to teach plus their own seminars and orals and a dissertation to worry about, and that many of them held outside jobs and had families. They simply didn't have time for a massive assault on each class. Look at me, up to my gills in work and with no outside jobs, no children, no domestic duties. Anyway, Alice was one of a kind."

"Do you think that fact did her in?"

Sarah spread her gloved hands helplessly. "I think you'll have to find out more than I can even guess at about Alice, but I'd begin with the overkill study syndrome. She said she had to account for everything she did."

"Account to whom?"

"Her conscience, I suppose. Or to some master plan."

"Trying for sainthood?"

"That's what I thought, that she'd taken a sort of vow or belonged to some ferocious sect—you know, everything forbidden except good works and being saved—except, of course, she said she wasn't satisfied with established religions."

"So maybe she was into a nonestablished one, a closet postulate, or her studies were her religion. She wouldn't be the first, even at Bowmouth. When you saw her before the hockey game, did she say where she was going or did you see her head off in a particular direction?"

"Something about an appointment. I wasn't paying much attention because I was trying to get back to the hockey rink."

"George would love some solid facts to fool around with."

"He and Mrs. Parker would make a great pair," said Sarah. "I can just hear the whirring of disk drives, the tapping of keys and space bars. Except Mrs. Parker hasn't cottoned to the computer yet. She's got a vintage IBM machine in her office. The computer ladies are the two clerks across the hall. But Parker calls all the shots; they just come up with the data she needs to run the place. Now what about dinner? We haven't a thing in the house."

"You're sitting on some beef and mushrooms I picked up. We can throw some curry on it. As the blood transfusion team says, curry is the universal donor. And we won't once say 'Alice' or 'murder.' "

Which remark ensured that Alice and murder were the main ingredients of the evening meal.

The next day was Thursday, and Sarah, going from class to class, slipping on patches of melting ice and wading through lumps of dirty snow, thought dark thoughts about winter carnivals and murder. These events had shortened her freshman students' already truncated attention span to something under five minutes. Even in the graduate seminars, everyone, faculty included, seemed afflicted with the general blight. Coughs and sneezes, dropped notebooks, lost papers, and wandering and interrupted lectures became the order of the day. Sitting through a bronchial-sounding Professor Lacey's rambling exegesis of *Coriolanus*, Sarah found herself alternately lamenting the loss of Alice Marmott, who would have surely made the professor toe the mark, and wondering how George Fitts was faring with the redoubtable Mrs. Parker. It occurred to Sarah that the secretary shared many of the characteristics of Coriolanus's mother, Volumnia.

You had to admire George Fitts, thought Alex, listening to the sergeant question Mrs. Parker—a soft pedal, his low expressionless voice, the formal deference due a lady of importance. Mrs. Parker, smartly gotten up in two-tone beige wool and holding matching gloves, seemed to be enjoying the attention, unaware that George was quietly taking her away from green pastures and still waters toward dangerous bogs and sinkholes. Now he was saying what a burden it must always be to have the weight of an important college department on her shoulders.

Mrs. Parker agreed. "You have no idea, officer. It isn't just the class schedules and seeing that everyone's satisfied with their room assignments—the fellows and the adjuncts can be so difficult, though I try to make every allowance—it's things like keeping the bookstore up to the mark, typing manuscripts, and checking up on all the English majors. The chairman, that's Professor Bello, is so occupied that I try to be a stand-in. I've been here long enough to know the undergraduate and the graduate English requirements. Then there are the book lists and the periodical subscriptions and—"

"So," said George, stepping in, "you must have helped Alice Marmott with her schedule." Here he paused, allowing

Mrs. Parker an appropriate expression of distress. She did it nicely, Alex thought. The gentle shake of the auburn head, the purse of the lipsticked mouth, the clasp of the manicured fingers. "So tragic, one of our own students," she said. "And so gifted—not that she should have ever been allowed to take those graduate courses. We advised against it." ("We"? thought Alex, as Sarah had before him. Royalty?) Mrs. Parker made a negative gesture with one beige glove. "Some of the undergraduate advisers and the dean—well, they're just a little softhearted when it comes to special students like Alice. They allowed her to register for three graduate seminars. The senior faculty didn't care for it, I can assure you, but no one wanted to make an issue. Well, you can see what it's all come to."

"A real problem for you, Mrs. Parker," said George quietly. "Exceptions to rules make it very difficult for the staff."

"My words exactly, officer," Mrs. Parker said in a pleased voice. "Both Professor Lacey and Professor Fletcher came to me after Miss Marmott turned up in their seminars and suggested that she would be happier in an undergraduate section. They felt that her comments were not always to the point and disturbed the graduate students who were properly registered for the courses. But Alice was quite stubborn, a difficult personality, and since she'd done nothing in a real way to disturb the classes—well, she was allowed to remain. Of course, the semester was young and who is to say that she wouldn't have found herself beyond her depth before long."

"And Professor Larkin. Did he complain about Miss Marmott? She was in his graduate seminar too, I think," said George, flipping open a folder.

"Oh, my. Poor Professor Larkin. Dr. McKenzie, how is Professor Larkin?" Mrs. Parker, all solicitude, inclined to Alex. "We've been expecting something like this. He hasn't been at all well this past term."

"You mean," said Alex, "that he's been drinking. Like a fish."

"Oh, now, I didn't say that."

"It's hardly a secret, is it?" said George. "Dr. McKenzie says he was drunk when he was found."

"I'm afraid," said Mrs. Parker, dropping her voice down

from F sharp to B flat, "that he has been drinking a great deal more than is good for him." She sounded to Alex like a regretful parent who hears, once again, that her child has played truant.

"So did Professor Larkin—drunk or sober—object to Alice Marmott in his class?" asked George, pencil hovering over the folder.

"He did come into my office last week," said Mrs. Parker, "and say that he wasn't supposed to be teaching babies and where had she come from? Oh, dear, Alice Marmott wasn't an appealing girl. I tried to give her some advice and suggested that she take classes with her own academic level—she was a junior—and add some extracurricular activities—choir, basketball, the Outdoor Club—to her schedule, but she wasn't interested. Such a shame because Bowmouth has so much to give."

"Were there complaints about Alice from anyone else?" said George.

"Professor Garvey made several comments to the effect that Alice was unnatural. Always overprepared. Although I take what Professor Garvey says, as Professor Bello would put it, *cum grano salis*. And—now I hesitate to tell you this. . . ."

"Don't," said George. "Never hesitate to tell me anything." He parted his lips in what Alex had come to recognize passed as George's smile. Because of his minimum facial mobility it was a hair-raising expression, thought Alex, and he should give it up, but Mrs. Parker, apparently on the sergeant's wavelength, responded.

"Alice came to me with a complaint about one of our faculty. We do get so many complaints these days. Since the sixties the students have just not been the same, but I hadn't thought of Alice Marmott as the protest type. We have proper forms for student-faculty evaluations."

"Which faculty member and what was it about?" asked George.

"I don't like to, but it is murder, isn't it, so I must cooperate. Miss Marmott claimed that Professor Horst hadn't handed back her last semester's term paper, English 305, Twentieth-Century Poetry. Alice apparently questioned the rest of that class and found he hadn't returned any of the term papers even when the students left him self-addressed stamped envelopes. He just told her—and the others—they weren't going to get them back."

"I suppose that happens all the time," said George.

"Yes, but usually the instructor has told the students in advance, but Alice said it wasn't that she hadn't had it back —she'd made a copy—but that she received a *B* grade. It seems she has never had a *B* in English. In fact, until the poetry course she had a 4.0 average—that's all *A*'s. She found the entire class, thirty-eight students, received either a *B* or a *C*."

"I suppose that's quite possible too," said George. "Your point, Mrs. Parker?"

"My point is, officer, that Miss Marmott was not going through proper channels and was actually bypassing the English Department and going directly to the Dean of the Faculty of Arts and Sciences to report Professor Horst. She was charging him—her words—for refusing to return papers and for giving grades without the evidence of these papers to support the grades. Of course, several other *A* students were upset too. Students are entitled to their papers and can inspect exam papers too, if necessary, but there is no call to make a court case out of it, ruin reputations, destroy confidence in our faculty. I told Alice that *B* was an honor grade and there were other ways of handling the problem. I told her I would take it up myself with Professor Horst, but she would have none of it. She was quite unreasonable. A very stubborn young person. Students like Alice upset the whole departmental machinery."

"How fortunate then that she was killed," said Alex, losing his temper. "The whole department can rest easy."

"Oh, doctor, I didn't mean that at all." Mrs. Parker opened her eyes very wide and brought her gloves to her mouth. "It's just that things have been so difficult, what with Professor Larkin in the hospital and so many of the faculty out of sorts."

"Sorry, George," said Alex, when Mrs. Parker had been ushered out of the office. "Don't you ever lose your cool? No, I suppose not."

"Sometimes abruptness can be useful," said George, "although it's not my style. In fact," he added, "I try to have no style. Style means that you are predictable, and to be predictable is asking for trouble. Now, about showing Sarah the brief-case. . . ."

"Come for dinner. Sarah will be more relaxed, so will I, and we can even talk about something other than mayhem and murder."

George considered frowning and then consented. "I don't like to mix business, but I know Mike Laaka will be in the area tonight and he can meet us there."

Alex telephoned Sarah the news that George Fitts had agreed to step out of his official setting and join them for dinner, so she had rushed home, cut up chicken pieces and carrots, assembled a salad, and now stood back and gave the kitchen-dining room space a critical once-over. The room, with its scarred oak table and ill-assorted chairs picked up here and there from respective families, garage sales, and the local Goodwill, reminded her of a setting for one of those movies about alienated families growing up in a de-pressed corner of Nebraska. No curtains yet, cracked gray linoleum on the floor, and, against the wall, white metal cabinets that had undoubtedly been the last word in 1935. The ceiling plaster was stained and the window paint was chipped, the whole unhappy evidence of use and abuse by decades of college tenants. Only a handsome new sofa in a dark red print drawn up by the wood stove spoke comfort. "No point in making a real effort," Sarah had told Alex, "not when we don't know whether we're going to stay in this house." To which Alex had replied that he certainly hoped not, what with the constant stream of cars at odd hours as the medical students came and went on day or night duty or worked off tensions by hurling footballs and Frisbies around the yard.

Now George, never one to pay attention to the inadequa-cies of a room unless a crime had been committed therein, advanced and laid a heavy file folder on the table.

"These are the papers from Alice Marmott's briefcase and from her dormitory room—only copies, of course. We have a problem about choosing the senior faculty member who will also examine the papers, because all faculty, staff, and students who knew her even slightly are suspects."

"Including me?" said Sarah, pulling at the cork on a bottle of white wine.

"Well," said George reluctantly, "I must assume that some of you are safe and Alex assures me that—"

"Come off it, George," said Alex. "Sarah did not murder Alice Marmott. And if you don't trust what amounts to the entire college community, why not wait with the papers?"

"The evidence is too valuable. We need some kind of opinion at once. We have to know if anything seems out of place, so until we find an English faculty member who can account for his movements from before the hockey game until Monday when the thaw began, we'll have to rely on Sarah."

"Vera Pruczak might be safe," said Sarah. "She was at the *Mikado* rehearsal before the hockey game, then I saw her at the game, and afterward I'd guess she was tied up with non-stop rehearsals and the performance."

George consulted a small notebook. "Miss Pruczak is not of immediate interest since she has never had Alice Marmott in class or used her in any of her productions."

"Miss Pruczak only teaches drama, so she might not know whether Alice's notes made sense," said Sarah. "And I only had her in three courses. Try the department chairman —if you can find him."

"We are running a check on Professor Bello tonight," said George. "He seems to have had no personal experience of Miss Marmott. In the meantime, we have to make do with Sarah."

"George, you're inhuman," said Alex. "Let's eat first and do the briefcase later."

The broiled chicken and carrot dish was pronounced a success. "I like to know what I'm eating," said George. "You never know what goes into those ethnic dishes. And the apple pie looks good."

"Boughten, not made," said Sarah, feeling that she must maintain in the sergeant's eyes her reputation for absolute trustworthiness.

Following the pie and coffee, Alice Marmott's papers

were placed in neat piles on the dining room table. The dormitory papers and notebooks all neatly tied and labeled came from the previous semester and nothing seemed out of place, merely a testament to the time and thought that Alice had given to her work. Sarah frowned over a copy of the paper that Professor Horst had refused to hand back. It was a detailed analysis of Eliot's "Waste Land," and if length and number of footnotes were a criterion, Alice deserved an *A* plus. However, nothing about the paper seemed to be out of the way. The papers taken from her briefcase and representing the winter term's studies made a smaller pile. Xerox copies of critical articles having to do with Shakespeare's tragedies, a survey of scatological verse, an essay on Juvenal as a model of satire, a chronological list of Swift's poems to Stella, a Milton bibliography and notes for a paper on *Paradise Lost*, and a printout from an article on Anglo-Saxon philology. Sarah passed quickly over notes from Alice's undergraduate courses in Roman history and sociology, and then, at the bottom, she unearthed a list of questions for Professor Constance Garvey's novel course, suggesting that Alice was about to attack next in that direction.

"I don't see anything peculiar," said Sarah. "Except that she doesn't seem to have as many class notes as I'd expect— or any outlines for all those papers she was asking to write. I suppose she was one of those people who could keep everything in her head. I think the thing to remember is that Alice was a super student who annoyed quite a few of her instructors."

"Tell me," said George.

Sarah reached for the coffeepot and filled cups all round. "In the Shakespeare, Eighteenth Century, and Anglo-Saxon classes the texts themselves were stressed—standard texts, variants, footnotes, sources, but *not* independent research of the relevant criticism. That was supposed to come later. I'd say Professor Lacey didn't feel up to coping with Alice, Professor Larkin didn't need any extra headaches caused by her reading ahead of the assignments, and Professor Fletcher was very firm about telling her not to distract the other students from their proper job of learning the language and the literature. And she certainly did distract, always bringing in material we hadn't covered. Of course, I don't know how she acted in her undergraduate classes."

"More of the same," said George. "According to Professor Garvey, Alice thought too well of herself and did an unassigned research paper which Garvey said she wouldn't read until the end of the term. Alice also audited Merlin-Smith's Seventeenth Century class. He says she was, quote, 'aggressive and had to be told to be quiet and listen and that auditors had no rights.' A pattern seems to be emerging."

"Alice, the thorn in the professorial side," said Alex.

"There are always thorns," said Sarah, "but they aren't usually strangled."

The back door banged open, a gust of damp wind swept the room, and Mike Laaka, his slicker shining with wet, strode into the room, "Well, if it isn't the old homicide team back on the beat. Sarah, you're looking—"

"Yes," said Sarah, looking up. "Say it. Tired and frostbitten."

"Overworked, maybe, but presentable. Same with you, Alex. George, as usual, fresh as a new microchip. Me, I'm shot. Last weekend about trashed me." Mike struggled out of his slicker, pulled up a chair, and reached for the pie. As an old grade school friend of Alex's who had shared a good many tense moments with all three during the past summer, he considered himself at home. Mike had broad cheekbones and hair fair to almost whiteness, and in his heavy hand-knitted sweater he brought a breath of the north country into the kitchen. "Like my Christmas sweater? My grandmother did it and she's ninety-two. So what's up? George, I hope you're putting Bowmouth College in its place. Something I've been dying to do my whole life. Bunch of snots. Come into town, raise hell, drive into trees, toss hamburger wrappers and empty wine bottles around, and leave unpaid bills."

"Mike," said George, in the voice of a maiden aunt, "if we're going to work together, you can drop that attitude."

"It's a good honest healthy prejudice and I enjoy it. They briefed me at the State Police station. Female student strangled with a scarf. Frozen inside one of those sculptures, a Viking ship. God, couldn't you have picked some other time to find a body? Winter carnival weekend. Listen, there are probably twenty other frozen bodies lying around and you've just found one of them. Okay, what's new?"

While Alex and Sarah cleared away and stacked dishes, George went over the investigation with Mike, who, suddenly businesslike, produced, in his turn, a notebook. "I've got it," he said. "I'll cover the neighboring towns like a rug and hit the farms and little business places, and I'll help you follow up on the townspeople who were on campus. You're kinda lucky, in a way. What with the hockey game and that operetta, you've got two places where there were big bunches of folks all at once. You ought to be able to rule out those blocks of time for a lot of people."

"The rehearsals and performance should be easy," said Sarah. "The theater's way over behind the South Quad, so that most of the cast and the production team stayed put from the overture on. With Gilbert and Sullivan, most of the cast is needed for all three acts. The makeup people also did the costume changes, so they stayed backstage."

"The hockey game's another ball of wax," said Alex.

"You'd be surprised how people remember who was next to them," said Mike. "Especially in a tight little community like a college. The Colby supporters would know each other, and the Bowmouth crowd will know who had beer, who got punched, who threw up on the ice afterward."

"Like a big wedding reception," said Sarah. "You always seem to remember who wasn't there, who wasn't invited. The trouble is," she added, thinking of Professor Larkin, "the drunks who won't remember anything."

Mike reached for the cheese and hacked off a sizable wedge. "Not to worry. Everyone else remembers the drunks. We'll go over the whole crowd."

"And, Sarah," said George, "your impressions about the English faculty and students might be useful."

"But I'm new here this term."

"Keep your eyes open. Have you a friend who might know the department well? A reliable friend."

"He means have you a friend who didn't strangle Alice Marmott?" said Mike.

Sarah made a face. "I'm pretty sure about Mary Donelli.

She's very straight . . . only she's a bit soft on Professor Larkin."

"Might want to protect him?" said George.

Sarah puzzled for a moment. "Well, she might not be forthcoming about his faults."

"I'll make a note of it." said George, doing so. "Talk the faculty over with her, just informally, but leave out Larkin. I value your insights. Although your assistance last summer was not orthodox, it proved quite useful."

"It almost got her killed," put in Alex.

"I have no intention of asking Sarah to participate in this investigation. The professionals are quite able to handle the matter. But I do need some general information from Bowmouth insiders. We're starting from scratch with this girl." George picked up Alice's briefcase and reached for his hat. "Sarah, I'll leave her papers with you. If anything strikes you later, call me. Thanks for the dinner. Good night, Alex."

Mike Laaka lingered, apparently wanting to renew past memories, talk about boyhood days, horse racing—the hot chances of a three-year-old named Risk Dancer who just went a mile in a minute and forty seconds—and the events of last summer. Sarah left them to it and crawled into bed with a bundle of student essays. "The Death of Ivan Ilyich" had turned out to be a watershed, some students leaping ahead with new insights, others slipping deeper into the mire. These latter were now making new hash of "Bartleby the Scrivener." Somewhat later, her pencil fell from her hand. Just before she fell asleep, the papers from Alice Marmott's briefcase slid by in review, passing one by one before her inward eye rather like that other Alice's pack of cards. She had a dreamlike sense of something off-key, something missing.

EIGHT

I t began to snow early Friday morning, first a few tentative
flakes, then thicker clumps, whirling against the gray morning sky and building into little triangular drifts in the corners
of the college buildings. By the time the tower clock in the
Starbox Administration Building struck eight, the new snow
had hidden the dingy lumps of melted snow left from the
week-long thaw and put a clean face on the whole of the
Bowmouth campus.

It was if the snowfall marked a new phase in the progression of winter and put some distance between the people of
the college and the untimely death of one of its most promising students; as if there were now time to appraise their relationship with Alice Marmott and, if there had not been such,
to cause one to grow posthumously.

Those students in the North Quad dormitory who had
known Alice by name or by sight began to wonder if they had
not known her better than they had supposed, had shared,
perhaps, an intimate or an exclusive moment with her. One
recalled stopping by the open door of her single room and
listening for a moment to the sounds of piano music from her
radio. She had stuck her head in the door and said, "That
piano sounds nice," and Alice had said, "Well, it's really two
pianos—Brahms wrote it for four hands," which remark had
not seemed encouraging, and the student had gone on down

the hall. Another young woman remembered borrowing shampoo from Alice in the dorm shower and thought she had seemed reluctant to lend it. A young man in her undergraduate history section thought she reminded him of his aunt, Sister Mary Victory, not a favorite relative.

Official Bowmouth College also had its moments of remembrance. The assistant librarian recalled how easily Alice Marmott had made her way from the various file card catalogs to the stacks and the special collections; she had even asked to use the microfilm index to unpublished dissertations. The registrar struck Alice's name from the list of junior class students and shook her blue-tinted head several times over Alice's 3.9 average, and the chancellor signed a letter expressing his distress and "that of the whole college community over the tragedy." The editor of the *Bowmouth Review* set aside a line box on the front page for Alice, and the Women's Crisis Committee called an emergency meeting. Over at the English Department Mrs. Parker pulled Alice's folder from the file set aside for English honor students and put it for the moment in one marked "inactive."

Sarah Deane, bent almost double into the now hard-driving snow, wished she had thought of her ski face mask. By the time she made it into the English Office she could no longer feel her feet. Seeing Mrs. Parker emerge into the hall, Sarah asked whether classes might not be canceled for the rest of the day.

Mrs. Parker's expression told Sarah that she had suggested the unthinkable. "Heavens, no! Bowmouth never closes. Not in—well, simply years. Once I think in summer session, VJ Day after World War Two, and before that on Armistice Day in 1918, and I believe for Appomattox, or was it Lincoln's funeral? Missing classes because of the weather is not considered a proper excuse. And the Bowmouth faculty —so loyal. They make every effort." Sarah, who knew a warning when she heard one, nodded.

"If the weather is really heavy," went on Mrs. Parker, "arrangements are made. Students not living on campus can sleep in the gym, and the Faculty Club has guest rooms. For the regular faculty, of course."

"Of course," said Sarah.

"Off limits to adjuncts and fellows," said Mrs. Parker brightly. "Those people can use the dormitory lounges—a chance to get to know some of the undergraduates better."

Sarah swallowed a grimace and took her way to the Fellows' Room to collect Mary Donelli for lunch. Together they battled their way through the storm to the cafeteria where the churning mass of students with pinched faces and red noses resembled the survivors of an unsuccessful polar expedition.

Wedged into a corner table, Sarah explained to Mary the interest the police had in the English Department faculty members.

Mary was enthusiastic. "Call it revenge or call it wanting to help nail the rat who did it, but I'll start thinking. Of course, hardly any of the senior faculty are what you'd call psychologically normal adults, and that bunch in the West Quad, the adjuncts and the poets-in-residence and all the junior faculty have plenty of weirdos mixed in. But that's college teaching for you. Even me and thee in the fullness of time. We'll start developing crotchets and quavers."

"But what do you think we can do besides collect general impressions?" demanded Sarah, wanting to move away from speculations on her and Mary's future eccentricities. "I'm up to my eyebrows in work, and I'm an absolute stranger here."

"Well, you could audit some classes and so could I, because I've got more time now that I've passed my orals—I'm just sitting in on Amos's class and Lacey's. Anyway, no one will question us because grad students can always sit in on undergrad classes. Except I don't want to spy on Amos."

"I told George Fitts that, but it's not spying. The police just want general ideas about the faculty, the ones who knew or had Alice in class. No big deal."

"I can ask Drago if he's noticed anything. He says finding Alice was one of the worst experiences of his life."

"Like my trip to the morgue. But going back to Amos Larkin, how many people on campus wear navy scarves with a thin magenta stripe?"

"None that I know of. That scarf is an old school thing, his Cambridge college, whichever one it was. But you don't mean—?"

"They say it's possible."

"Oh, hell. Hell." Mary paused, frowning, and then shook her head vigorously. "He couldn't have. He was absolutely polluted all Friday, completely out of it, and then almost frozen to death and put in the hospital."

"People who drink aren't predictable. They can kill and still let themselves freeze to death."

"You said Amos was half dressed when you found him. So maybe he scattered his scarf around along with the rest of his things and the wrong person found it and used it."

The police are suspecting everyone, not just Professor Larkin. I'll bet George Fitts has a folder with my name on it, and yours, and even Alex's. He doesn't believe in innocence."

"A Calvin come to judgment?"

"Of that ilk. Okay, so we'll keep an eye out for odd faculty sensibilities—when there's a free minute. Lord, nothing's getting any easier. Anglo-Saxon, for instance. I can see why Fletcher doesn't want us wandering off the beaten path. And then Shakespeare. *Lear* and *Timon of Athens* by next Friday."

"So be thankful for Lacey. He just jounces along. No sweat and no Alice to make him look like a turkey. He can devote his time to bosom measurement. I expect him to start coming to class in cross garters and a tricolored codpiece."

Sarah looked at her watch. "Come on, it's time for the eighteenth century, although with the storm I'll bet there won't be many loyalists. My morning classes were only at half strength even if Mrs. Parker said no one at Bowmouth ever skipped classes."

Mary pulled on her jacket and jammed a red knitted hat over her head. "You're wrong about the class; it'll be a full house. Amos's first day back."

She was right. The eighteenth-century graduate seminar was up to full strength. "Just a bunch of vultures," said Mary, as she and Sarah pushed their way into the classroom. "Morbid curiosity. I'm here because of a legitimate interest in my field. And out of friendship. Amos needs a support group."

"When you have a minute," said Sarah, "you'll have to clue me, why Amos Larkin?"

"It's probably basic biochemistry, but later on I'll tell you about something funny that happened to me on the way to the parking lot."

"You and Professor Larkin hooked bumpers."

"Later, I said. It's a long story. Anyway, when Amos is mostly sober and on a roll talking about Swift and Pope and Co. in that voice of his—well, he absolutely makes my head explode."

"Shut up, here he comes, and God, doesn't he look awful!"

Amos Larkin stamped into the room, little clots of snow from his boots leaving a trail behind him. His sheepskin coat was pulled high around his neck and his tweed hat wore a topping of fresh snow. No scarf. Sarah noted this; judging from Mary's expression and the low murmurs in the class, everyone had. Sarah supposed that every detail of Alice's strangulation, especially the long scarf wrapped around her neck, had been reported, not only by Drago but by the entire hospital and medical school network.

The graduate students watched in silence as Professor Larkin pulled off his outer clothes and with perceptibly shaking hands unpacked his briefcase. Sarah, regarding him without sympathy, thought him thinner, paler of face, and redder of eye. Altogether he reminded her of a much worn suit of clothes just returned from the cleaners—pressed and cleaned, but flattened and diminished.

The professor's voice, however, a sort of Yankee variation of the Richard Burton pipes, was intact. "I have your essays on *A Tale of a Tub*. Those of you who have received an unsatisfactory grade—and I remind you that *C* is unsatisfactory for a graduate student—will now apply themselves to greater effect, which means"—here Amos Larkin fixed the front row with an angry red eye—"doing the assigned reading instead of free-lancing through the entire eighteenth century. I am missing papers from Amanda Tibbs, and since you, Miss Tibbs"—here Amos Larkin glowered at Sarah—"have so mysteriously appeared in this graduate seminar without my permission, the least I can expect from you is an essay. Have you perhaps an explanation?"

It was time to put a stop to this nonsense. Sarah cleared her throat. "My name is Sarah Deane. I'm a graduate student, a teaching fellow, and I've handed in an essay on *Tale of a Tub*."

A pause followed this announcement, and then Professor Larkin said, "Please see me after class, whoever you are."

Vera Pruczak was right when she called him a beast, thought Sarah as she opened her notebook. But it was a diminished beast that Sarah met alone after class. Professor Larkin no longer seemed interested in who Sarah might be. In fact, he looked so ill she thought for a moment that he might collapse then and there. However, after muttering something about a clerical mixup, he waved her away, and Sarah's last view of him was sitting slumped at his desk, his head in his hands.

She made it home through the snow. Just. Twice she had to back up her old VW and take a running header at the drifts building across the road. Then, with briefcase and a wrapped package of fish under her arm, her head lowered into the wind, she struggled toward the house. Alex stood by the door, a dark figure with a leaping dog. "Patsy's gone native," he said. "Thinks he's back on the steppes."

"That's *Russian* wolfhound," said Sarah. "Patsy's entirely Irish."

"Well, he's reverted to something. he loves it out here." Patsy, in answer, hurled himself at Sarah, knocked her into a snowbank, and rushed back to Alex and then spun around, taking little snapping bites at the whirling snow.

"Barbara Woodhouse hasn't had much effect," lamented Sarah, picking herself up. "But I suppose I haven't done what she says. I spend more time saying '*What* a clever boy' than I do saying 'no' and 'down.' "

"His birthday present shall be a choke collar and a proper run," said Alex.

"Let's go in," said Sarah, lifting the fish and her briefcase out of the snow. "I've about had it with winter."

They sat hunched on the red sofa by the wood stove soaking up heat. Then Alex put down his mug of whiskey. "I have news. The autopsy. Alice was strangled, no doubt about it, and by the scarf found around her neck. No other signs of violence."

"She wasn't raped? Nothing like that?"

"No. She was probably taken by surprise and it was over

quickly. The police are sure that she was then carried into the Viking boat by way of the ladder. Not only a bit of material from her coat but appropriate scratched areas on her stockings and skirt."

"And the scarf?"

"No doubt there. Professor Amos Larkin, Emmanuel College, Cambridge. Navy with cerise stripes. Took his BA and MA degrees there and later did some lecturing in the south of England."

"Was anyone else at Bowmouth at that college?"

"Possibly. The police are checking. But it narrows things."

"It should be easy to find out. People usually don't hide the fact that they've studied at Cambridge. It brightens up a curriculum vitae no end. The whole business screams Amos Larkin, doesn't it?"

"That scarf was apparently a hallmark of his. The police have had him on the mat twice, and he says he can't remember where he had it last or, for that matter, when he shed his coat, his shoes, or his jacket. Drunks and hypothermia victims are disoriented and often start doing odd things like taking off clothes in zero weather. Well, as his self-appointed doctor, I hope he stays off the sauce long enough to give George a few more details about last Friday. George and the assistant DA are itching to charge him. They probably have almost enough evidence."

"I can't see that all this is going to help him stay sober. Ready-made reasons for drinking yourself blind. Suspected of killing a student and not sure whether you did it or not. I didn't think I was going to feel sorry for him because he can be so abominable." Sarah walked over to the sink and opened the fish package. An opaque blue eye seemed to look at her reproachfully. "I wish they'd behead these first," she said. "And be-tail them. I don't like to know I'm eating an animal."

"So go vegetarian," said Alex.

"I should, but I like fish—and meat—and chicken. Your compleat hypocrite. Do you think he'd do something desperate? Suicide?"

"I've asked if he wanted to see a psychiatrist, but he was rather rude—in fact positively bloody about it."

"Don't say bloody," said Sarah, pushing the fish heads into a garbage bag.

NINE

Saturday the snow slacked off, and by Monday the dishrag-gray sky had faded into an ambiguous mix of cloud and pale blue, while here and there small squares of sun found their way into the frozen campus.

"Why didn't I choose the University of Florida?" complained Mary Donelli, meeting Sarah at the row of mailboxes in the small room off the English Office. Mary held up a folder showing a pelican regarding a bikini-clad lovely.

"Who's sending you those?" asked Sarah, whose mail never seemed to hold such exotica.

"It's a symposium for eighteenth-century addicts, and look at these. The social season's begun." Mary held up two undersized envelopes, one yellow, the other cream. "The senior faculty crank up once a term and have the fellows and adjuncts and other strays over for a feed and a drink. It gets them off the hook of being civil the rest of the time. Anyway, I see that Professor Fletcher and Lady Fletcher are having an 'informal supper' on Wednesday, which doesn't give us much time to refuse, and Vera Pruczak is on deck Friday with, you guessed it, an 'informal supper.' "

"Should I go? Alex can't on Wednesday, I know."

"You wanted to study the faculty, didn't you? Vera's wingding was sort of fun last year. Everyone got smashed and sang dirty songs and played sardines. Her house is a real winner because she's never thrown away anything—I mean, it's absolutely haunted."

"And Patrick Fletcher?"

"Austere. Polished mahogany, antique prints of antique things, books in full calf bindings. Hoity-toity intellectual interior, but fetching. The missus collects—pots, baskets, birds, insects, butterflies, weavings—all in gorgeous glass cases."

"Like Vera Pruczak?"

"No. Vera accumulates; Mrs. Fletcher—she does something in the anthropology department—collects with a capital C. Museum ambience. Anyway, I'll walk over there with you. It's just off campus near the library right next to the chancellor's house. Prestige setting."

Museum is right, thought Sarah, as she and Mary walked into the Fletchers' large Georgian house on Wednesday at the prescribed hour of six o'clock. All the marble-floored front hall needed was velvet ropes.

"You can tell we're second-rate stuff," said Mary, as they climbed the circular stairs to leave their coats in the designated bedroom. "Six o'clock for dinner yet. Real nobs eat at eight-thirty."

"But the invitation did say supper," said Sarah. "And Lord, look at all this." She stared around the bedroom, in which long hanging pieces of batik alternated with mounted carved wooden figures.

"This is nothing, just backwash. You should see the rest."

Sarah walked over to a full-length pier glass and smoothed her short dark hair, which in winter had a regrettable habit of standing up in little spikes. She wore her new black dress with a small white ruffed collar. "You look just like Hamlet's sister," Alex had said as he left for his evening medical conference. "It's a good dress for a faculty function," Sarah had answered. "The no-nonsense statement with melancholy overtones."

"That's a good outfit," said Mary, as they came down stairs. "I wish I weren't so stunted." She indicated her cranberry sack. "I always end up looking like an overdressed footstool. Oh, hello, Professor Fletcher." Mary arranged her face in a minor smile. "And Mrs. Fletcher, too."

Mrs. Fletcher, tall as her husband, with a high arched nose and a formal mouth, her splendid fall of blond hair held back by a tortoiseshell clip, extended a beautiful white hand in welcome. Hardly the hand of an archaeologist, thought Sarah. A heavy gold chain around the neck and waist of her rust-colored dress suggested the prosperous chatelaine—someone at home with valuable tapestries and chalices. "I was just telling Sarah what great collections you both have," said Mary. "That bedroom is very impressive."

"Sumatra and Indonesia," said Mrs. Fletcher in a low, husky voice. "Patrick and I spent a sabbatical in that part of the world. Please help yourselves to something to drink. We have wine and homemade mead—Patrick thought mead would be just the thing for this party—but if you're feeling sensible, there's also gin and whiskey."

Mary moved off toward a table centered by a large triangle of pale cheese, and Sarah walked about two connecting sitting rooms, inspecting the various exhibits, nodding every now and then to a familiar face in the clumps of fellows and adjuncts that stood around the rooms holding glasses. The first room was decorated with the spoils of a stay in India: brass gongs, a bronze god with multiple arms—Vishnu, or was it Shiva?—and a nasty-looking figure with an extended tongue, Kali perhaps, all set on heavily carved dark tables. The other room proved to be animal land, with prints, sculpture, a large aquarium, and, on the wall, lighted glass cases of assorted insects and butterflies. The butterflies were stupendous, Sarah thought, velvet blues, iridescent emeralds, reticulated yellows.

From the second sitting room, Sarah wedged her way through a knot of people standing at the entrance to what was obviously the sacred center of the house, the library—one of those libraries with a ladder on a track. She stationed herself next to Drago Collins and listened. Professor Fletcher appeared to be giving an impromptu show-and-tell. "The two iron helmets with the bronze plates are really copies of seventh-century ones, as is the gold collar. The original collar is in Stockholm. They're nicely made, I think, and they don't disgrace the genuine objects—this sword hilt, for instance, and the bronze plate, both from northeast England."

Sarah listened with one ear, her eye wandering to framed hand-colored maps decorated with the figures of ancient British kings: Hengist of Kent, Ælla the South Saxon, Cherdik the West Saxon, Ida of Northumberland, Offa, Ethelbert, Edwin, Ethelwulf, in blues and reds and gold, clutching enormous unsheathed swords. Below the maps on a table stood a photograph of a much younger Patrick Fletcher in a circle of flanneled men at the edge of some ancient ruin. A large silver-framed double picture showed the professor and his wife peering into a fjord on one side and, on the other, sitting in a pirogue wearing topees.

The "informal supper" turned out to be a hearty crab dish and a ring of rice and vegetables. Professor and Mrs. Fletcher passed dishes, explained their treasures, and referred pointedly to each other as Patrick and Ingrid, as if this one night all were permitted to be free with first names. No one dared.

"Someone—maybe it was Drago—called him Patrick in class after the annual dinner," said Mary, "and Fletcher withered him. You don't kick status around with these birds."

"You read too much satire," said Sarah. "I've certainly spent worse evenings, though I do feel like a young person from the provinces. Very untraveled."

The evening wound down with a demonstration of early music on alto recorder and crum horn. "We should probably curtsy," said Mary, as she and Sarah climbed the stairs for their coats. "Such affability and condescension, as Mr. Collins might say."

Sarah reached home to find Alex draped over their sofa with the telephone balanced on his chest. He was making the kind of noncommittal noises that a doctor makes when a patient is demanding an immediate diagnosis and prompt action. "No, no, of course not. . . . I see. Mmmmm. . . . Yes and no. . . . I'm sure you do. . . . Yes, I see that. . . . Well, we'll just have to wait it out. . . . Yes, tomorrow."

"Someone with the flu?" she asked as he hung up.

Alex leaned back against the cushions and stretched. "No," he said with a sigh. "Someone with a dead stepdaughter. Alice Marmott's family, such as it is. One stepmother."

"Wicked stepmother?"

"A rather irritated stepmother. George Fitts felt that she wasn't devastated with grief—more annoyed. Full of complaints about being stranded in Boston in the snowstorm and ending up on the coast of Maine in that rinky-dink airport in Rockland—her words. Seems they do things better in Ohio. She wanted to talk to me—you know, the attending physician."

Sarah collapsed on the sofa next to Alex and began pulling at her fleece-lined boots. "That must have been a miserable conversation."

"It's the kind I usually hate worse than hell—telling families about a death—but Mrs. Marmott seemed more worked up about the fact that Alice had transferred from Ohio State to Bowmouth. Told me she knew no good would come of the girl's going east."

"Oh, dear. Poor Alice."

"Well, poor Alice with a big fat scholarship prevailed. I'll be seeing the second Mrs. Marmott tomorrow, a session I could do without. Now tell me about the home life of Professor Patrick Fletcher. Did it seem like the setting for a murderer?"

"No," said Sarah, arranging her head comfortably on Alex's shoulder. "More like the Smithsonian."

Alex found that the second Mrs. Marmott had plenty to say. After giving lip service to the idea that, in her words, "the evildoer must be brought to justice," she enlarged on her main theme, the burden of which was that it was a serious mistake for anyone—especially the young—to put a toe over the Ohio state line.

Mrs. Marmott was a large woman in a speckled wool ensemble. She had a pouting mouth and slightly protuberant eyes and spoke in a sort of singsong whine. George Fitts had been easing her into a series of memories of the early Alice Marmott, who, it appeared, had been about eight years old when the present Mrs. Marmott had been taken to wife by Alice's father.

"She was always in corners," said Mrs. Marmott, sinking back in disapproval into the one comfortable chair—a Danish modern number George had removed from the student waiting room. The sergeant maintained that if people being questioned were physically comfortable, they wouldn't realize that being eight inches lower than their interrogator put them at a psychological disadvantage. From this interview Mike Laaka had been banned as one who might confirm in Mrs. Marmott's mind all the looseness of the decadent East. George Fitts, smooth of head and face, severe of mouth, hands folded, inclining toward his victim in an attitude of interest, inspired confidence. Now he tapped his pencil gently on his desk and asked what Mrs. Marmott meant, "always in corners." Was Alice often punished this way?

"Oh, no, she was always dutiful. In a corner with a book. An early reader she was." And Alex, listening, thought that she spoke as if Alice had contracted an infectious disease for which there was a perfectly good vaccine. "Not books I thought suitable for a child her age, not nice wholesome stories. The dear Lord knows I tried with Alice, being as it isn't easy to be the mother of someone else's child, especially when the mother was RC—though her father was Methodist and so am I. I suppose it left a mark on the child. But she stopped going to mass when she was fourteen. A stubborn piece, Alice, turning against everything Warren had to offer."

"How so, Mrs. Marmott?" said Alex, who saw from a slight movement of George's head that he was to be part of the conversation.

"Against her family and those good community influences: Sunday school, the Girl Scouts, the Y. Alice said they were boring. Now I ask you, sergeant, and you, doctor, Girl Scouts boring with all those opportunities for the outdoors and trips to Cleveland?"

"How about school?" asked George. "Friends, clubs, activities?"

"Oh, Alice wasn't one for any of that. We pushed and poked at her until we lost heart. High school meant nothing to her except for her lessons. Oh, she joined the German and

Latin clubs. Imagine what that did for her socially. Of course, she was straight *A*'s except for a *C* in gym, but she'd do things like tell the social studies teacher that Ohio history was trivial. The nerve. I tell you it wasn't easy having Alice in the house, and my own boys so well rounded."

"Friends?" prompted George.

"No friends, no chums. Always in the corners like I said. The corners of life." Mrs. Marmott, pleased at her figure of speech, smiled complacently.

"Quite a turn of phrase you have, Mrs. Marmott." George spoke in an unnaturally warm tone, and Alex forced himself to nod agreement. Alice, it was all too clear, was a stranger in a respectable middle-class, middle-American, middle-Methodist household.

"Perhaps she had boyfriends," said George. "Ones you didn't approve of."

"Boyfriends, my foot," said Mrs. Marmott, suddenly sprightly. "Why, she had no fun at high school at all. Nothing. No proms or going steady, the way we used to. Or slumber parties with the girls. And no one from around Warren thinks about going all the way to Maine to a place like Bowmouth College. Maybe Carnegie Tech or Rensselaer or Alfred, just to be different, but most of our young people are perfectly happy right in Ohio. Alice got a nice scholarship from Ohio State and offers from Western Reserve and Kenyon and Oberlin. And majoring in English literature when the future is in business, and computers are the wave of the future. My very words. The wave of the future." Here George and Alex nodded with solemn faces as if convinced of this remarkable truth.

"Then why did she want to go to Bowmouth?" said Alex. "Even if she wanted to leave Ohio, why Maine and Bowmouth?"

"Of course Bowmouth almost paid her way with that scholarship, which shows they must have been hard up for students. And then she got herself hypnotized with all those books she read. Dragons, Vikings, and swords and King Arthur and Shakespeare, and the man who wrote *Robinson Crusoe*," said Mrs. Marmott, wheeling easily over ten centuries of literary history. "Alice went through just masses of college catalogs and found out what professors were in what fields, and then with that special scholarship—more than Ohio State gave her—what could we do? And then she started talking graduate school, which was the last straw on my back."

"What was?" said George, whose pencil was making increasingly small circles on his pad.

"Graduate school. As if Alice thought she was special when I had the boys coming along."

George held up his hand and Alex could almost see the meshed cogs in his brain whirling, discarding this, selecting that, patience was all. "Alice was insisting on a graduate program as well as the BA?"

"I said she could insist until she was blue in the face but four years was it, and if she found some way to go through graduate school in those same four years—well, she was welcome to it. Though"—here Mrs. Marmott sagged visibly; Alice had obviously been the stronger force—"I suppose in the end if she'd gone and paid for it herself, I'd have let her have one extra year, and then she'd have to get a job."

"It sounds as if Alice was trying to do it all in one big gulp," said Alex. "No wonder she didn't have time for anything extra."

"You have Alice's letters with you, Mrs. Marmott?" said George. "We'll need to make copies."

Mrs. Marmott reached inside her large plastic handbag. "Not that writing home was Alice's strong point. You'd think with her own father passed on she'd perk up and make an effort. But it was always just one page on Sunday. 'I'm fine and working hard.' Aggravating."

"Health problems, Mrs. Marmott?" put in Alex. "Drinking, taking pills?"

"If you mean alcohol or drugs, no. Alice didn't hold with anything like that. Not because it was against scripture, mind you. Not for a good sound Christian reason. It was because they affected your mind, might hurt her study. Totally selfish, she was," said Mrs. Marmott, in a fine last burst of spleen. Then, collecting herself, she shook her head. "Not that I'm not grieved the way things have turned out."

George helped the second Mrs. Marmott to her feet and said that a car would take her back to her motel.

"So," said Alex, as George returned to his desk. "No boyfriends, no girlfriends, no drugs, no alcohol."

"And no gambling, no speeding, no loving stepmother," added George testily.

"If Mrs. Marmott couldn't stand her," said Alex, "then perhaps someone else couldn't. Grinds don't always make easy neighbors. I know a student who knifed another for not sharing his notes. I doubt if Alice shared hers."

"We're working that angle," said George. "Mike's been going to some of the usual student hangouts listening to the chat."

"I'll say," said Mike, coming in without knocking. "But it won't wash. I can't do the student act. I told them I was a graduate forestry student, transfer from U. Maine, but I sat down right next to a real one."

"Don't pull the modest act," said Alex. "I'll bet you picked up something."

"Nothing much. No one seemed to know the girl at all. I hit several student traps and made almost zero. Found two girls from her floor, and all I heard was that Alice played classical stuff when she studied, took an early A.M. shower, wore weird clothes, and told one girl that half the English faculty were incompetent or frauds or something, but that she couldn't leave because of her scholarship. I found some of the students who were signing the petition about Horst not returning papers, and they said Alice was very insistent about it, talking about students' rights, but none of them really knew her."

"Yet someone knew her well enough to kill her," said Alex.

"Like a redheaded drunk with a long scarf?"

"I'm sure Amos Larkin is at the top of George's list," said Alex. "But how about the rest of the faculty? What do they say about the department's losing a top student?"

George opened a new folder. "The chairman, Professor Bello, didn't know her personally but said he was sorry to lose an honors candidate. The others said things like 'gifted, advanced, interesting, disruptive.' Patrick Fletcher called her an exceptional student but academically unruly—whatever that means."

"It means," said Alex, "that Alice was too much of a good thing."

"I think you should go for the boyfriend and the drug angle," said Mike. "Show me campus trouble and I'll show you a boyfriend or a drug mess. Don't give me all that shit about Alice only loved to study. That doesn't happen today."

"I think it does," said Alex, "but not often. But you have a point. There might be sex under the rug somewhere." He stood up and began pulling on his duffle coat. "Back to medicine. I've got patients and a clinic this afternoon."

"I think," said George, "that you are both using sex and drugs for an excuse not to think."

"What do you mean by *that*?" said Alex, coming to a halt.

"It's the easy way out these days, isn't it? But sometimes it isn't sex and drugs. Sometimes it's simple vanity and greed. Or lost temper. Or," he added, snapping his folder closed, "alcoholism."

That Thursday night, Sarah tossed her briefcase in a corner and herself on the sofa and said, "I've had it. Too much to read, too many papers to correct, too many papers to write, *and* worrying about Alice Marmott. Who did it and why."

Alex leaned back in his chair, lowered the sports section from his nose, and said, "That's up to George and company. You're not to do anything but serve up a few warm impressions. When you can."

Sarah leaned back against the cushions and closed her eyes. "My impressions are pretty cold, but I am beginning to think dark thoughts about Mrs. Parker. She drips too much honey, and she knows absolutely everything about everything. Maybe she and her friend the registrar hoisted Alice up into the Viking ship. A woman's assault team to strangle and carry."

"That's a real jump in the dark."

"Alice was trying to turn the department upside down with her campaign against Professor Horst. Mrs. Parker wouldn't like that. It's *her* department. Or maybe she and the registrar were a duo and Alice found out."

"If you're suggesting a lesbian relationship, that's almost

fashionable now. Besides, the registrar, Miss Prism, is like the chancellor. Sanctified, above reproach."

"You can't mean Miss Prism?"

"Of course I can. What's the matter?"

"Did she have a handbag?"

"You're off your hinges, my love."

"I don't doubt it. And before I forget, tomorrow's Olivia Macbeth-Pruczak's party and you're invited. Again. You can't weasel out of all these things or I'll have to find someone else. Miss Prism, maybe, if she's free."

"All right. You may tell me about Miss Prism."

"Twenty-eight years ago Miss Prism left Upper Grosvenor Street with a perambulator that contained a baby of the male sex and never returned. She mixed up her manuscript with the baby. It happens all the time with novelists. First things first."

"I think an icicle fell on your head."

"And you'd better brush up on your reading."

"So it's Friday," said Mary, as she and Sarah met in the Fellows' Room for their cups of late morning coffee.

"My freshman students are getting real mileage out of poor Alice Marmott," said Sarah. "One of them came to me saying she wants to start a short story called 'Frozen Bodies.' "

"It's that time of year," said Mary. "That time of year when you in me behold a real sense of the yuckiness of things."

"I know," said Sarah. "I keep yawning and thinking what's the point of spending my vital juices on Alfred's *Preface to the Pastoral Care* and the *Blickling Homilies*. Who cares when everything seems to be going to pot?"

"Or to coke," said Mary. "Or just plain booze."

"Shall we pick you up for Vera Pruczak's party? I made Alex promise to come. He sees too many medical types. He needs to loosen up and read Oscar Wilde or someone like that."

"Vera's house is the place to loosen. Wait till you see Castle Pruczak. Zounds."

* * *

"What's all this about a castle?" said Alex, as they turned into the bottom of a long driveway. "It looks like a perfectly ordinary house."

Which it did. A long white frame building, a porch running down one side with a collection of snow-bound rocking chairs tilted crazily along its length. The dark red door still sported the grizzled remains of a Christmas wreath, but aside from this decorative note, the house was the sort of farmhouse seen scattered all over the hills and valleys of New England.

But Sarah, stepping through the front door with Mary, heard Alex behind them say, softly, "Good Christ." It was, she thought, a suitable response.

Inside was riot, swarm, fandango, cacophony. Compared to the vistas now opening up, Professor Fletcher's interior had all the austerity of a Shaker keeping room. Sarah, moving cautiously forward, had the sensation that all the sets of all the stage productions of the world had mated with all the junkyards and pawnshops and given monstrous birth. She could see, because the walls of the hall opened into a huge rectangle, that the interior of the farmhouse had been gutted and reinvented. Only a large and ordinary fireplace, now manteled in green velvet and tassels, suggested that once upon a time a farmer and his family had reckoned their accounts, churned milk, brought in new lambs to the fire; had perhaps been born, christened, wedded, and died in this house.

"Watch it," said Alex, as Sarah, in the lead, almost fell over a five-foot varnished crocodile.

"Darlings!" cried Vera, sweeping up in a purple tartan caftan. "So glad. Look out for Tick-Tock."

"Tick-Tock?" said Sarah, recovering and setting the animal back on its claws.

"My first time on the stage. Ever. They gave me Tick-Tock when the run was over. After all, he was a lead part. They ran him on a little track."

"You played a scene with a crocodile?" said Alex, to whom nothing by now in the dramatic world was surprising.

"No, darling. *Peter Pan.* I was one of the fairies and understudied Wendy. Got to play her twice. You remember the crocodile swallowed an alarm clock and when it ran down he was able to snap up Captain Hook. Now come along in and mix. I've made the most marvelous punch. Everything in it. You, darling, what *is* your name? Dr. McKenzie—Alex? Will you help me lift the bowl to the table, and remember I do want you for one of my productions. No point in wasting that sardonic sexy look and those black eyebrows on your patients." And Vera, leaving Alex with his black eyebrows up, floated off in the direction of two suits of armor guarding— judging from the odor of garlic—what must have been the kitchen. Sarah could make out the shape of a stove, over which was fastened an impressive sculpture piece made up of whitened bones.

"Didn't I tell you?" said Mary. "Catch those posters, will you."

Sarah swiveled around, trying to focus on the old theatrical posters that covered the walls from ceiling to floor, overlapping here and there, some hanging in tatters. They were hard to take in, as their owner had overhung them with pictures and objects of every known material and shape and massed groves of tropical plants in front.

"Those are new, those stuffed bats on the ceiling," said Mary. "At least I hope they're stuffed."

"And," said Sarah, feeling a little sick, "shrunken heads." She pointed at two very small dark heads with long black hair hanging past their ears.

"I hope they're papier-mâché," said Mary, "but I won't ask."

"Don't," said Alex, inspecting them. "And those are very authentic-looking blowpipes."

Vera floated by. "USO trip, darlings. Korean war. We stopped on the way at this island."

Sarah edged along away from the heads and came up to ceiling-high shelves. Memorabilia in spades. A pair of lace mitts, a little rack of glass animals with a broken unicorn among them, two fans, one elaborate, all lace and ribbons with *Margaret* worked across it, the other a palm leaf.

"A palm leaf?" said Sarah, puzzled.

"*Rain* and *Lady Windermere*," said Mary, indicating two

framed theater programs. Sarah, fascinated, ignored the increasing sounds of jollity coming from the punch bowl and moved around the room. A poster from *Death of a Salesman*—"best wishes to little Vera" from Lee J. Cobb—a program from *Arsenic and Old Lace,* under which on a tiny platform stood a small bottle of elderberry wine.

"How on earth did you have time to write all those novels?" said Sarah, as Vera materialized again by her side and fingered lovingly a fez hung next to a poster for *The Skin of Our Teeth.*

"Never made it big, dear," said Vera. "Not on Broadway, anyway. The ingenue, the understudy, the woman scorned. I started writing while I sat around backstage, and then when I had some money I started collecting these lovely old bits. That's Caligula's tunic, and the ring Claudius drops in the goblet, and the hatbox with the head in it from *Night Must Fall,* and the medicine Regina wouldn't fetch from *The Little Foxes.* And now come along, I've organized a treasure hunt with drama clues for a perfectly marvelous prize. You can eat and look at the same time."

The organization of the treasure hunt reminded Sarah strongly of the Queen's croquet, and after working her way from a clue having to do with *Amadeus* and Ivory Soap to one about Shirley Temple in *Captain January* she bumped into Alex peering into an open door.

"Oasis," he announced. "This is where it's at." He indicated a large, square, almost empty room well-lighted by a fluorescent tube running the length of the room over an equally long desk. On the walls in businesslike array hung clipboards, charts, and timetables. Sarah walked around the room in wonder. "All that stuff out there and then this. Look, here, Alex." Sarah picked up a piece of paper. "It's part of a new one. A list of possible titles: Lady Morgan at Midnight, The Fall of the House of Morgan, A Bosom Bared."

"Are we supposed to be in here?"

"She didn't say not to," said Sarah. "I've never been in an author's den. Look, there are all her books." She pointed to a shelf of the distinctive red, yellow, and black dust covers that marked an Olivia Macbeth novel. "And here's the end of a chapter: 'Lady Rosalind turned on the shrinking childlike figure of Lady Morgan. "You vicious puling baby. You think you can turn the duke against me with your soft little ways." Lady Rosalind's velvet bosom heaved, her face contorted. "Now drink this, and it's a far kinder death than you deserve." ' "

"Strong stuff," said Alex, reading over her shoulder. "Lady Morgan is in a bad way."

Sarah turned to a clipboard. "She's done her research. Foxglove, digitalis, henbane, nicotine, prussic acid, arsenic—and adder venom with a question mark."

"I think I've seen all the henbane I can take for one night," said Alex. "Let's gather Mary, if she wants to be gathered, and blow home."

Mary proved agreeable. "You've saved me from winning the treasure hunt. I think the prize is a tame python."

"But have you seen her workroom?" said Sarah, as they reached the car. "All business. I've just read a nice purple passage about Lady Rosalind about to poison the young Lady Morgan."

"I'll bet she's using Mrs. Parker," said Mary. "I've seen Vera giving her the once-over lately, and I don't think there's any love lost there. Professor Lacey made it into the last novel—a gambler with six capes on his greatcoat who seduced and abandoned every heroine in sight—and Constance Garvey came out two years ago as a nurse suspected of eating babies."

"The hospital has never seemed so peaceful," said Alex. "Just trauma, disease, and hemorrhage."

"You don't suppose Vera Pruczak tests out her plots," said Sarah. "Like strangling very bright English students."

"No," said Mary thoughtfully. "She's more likely to do in the faculty—except she can skewer them in books."

"But those trappings," said Sarah. "Bats, heads, varnished crocodiles—necrophilia rampant."

"Just froufrou," said Mary, as the car rounded the corner and pulled up by a well-lit apartment building. "Good night all. I'm going to climb to my lonely garret, and if I'm lucky some craven village youth will climb into my bower with his crum horn."

TEN

That night the weather turned into what the locals called downright ugly. Sleet followed the snow, then came a warming, a spate of rain, then a freeze, so that by morning the roads were glazed and rutted, and large branches, heavy in their sheaths of ice, broke and fell across the roads. Sarah, coming home from a hazardous trip to the supermarket, accelerated to make the uphill turn onto Sawmill Road and her thirteen-year-old VW bug coughed and died. An hour later at home, after the car had been diagnosed as probably terminal and towed away, Alex arrived back from the hospital lamenting over an ice collision and a smashed fender. "It's days like this that make a practice in Mississippi tempting."

"Or the Bahamas," said Sarah. "Well, at least a weekend of rotten weather will let me catch up with some work. And stay away from the English Department. Everyone's in a temper, even Mrs. Parker. She's been cruising up and down the halls like an attack force. Arlene and Linda are in hiding, and most of the faculty are behind barricades." Sarah walked over to the stove, examined its innards, and reached for a log. "The more I think about Alice Marmott, the more I think she was strangled in a fit of spleen."

"Sounds like the hospital. Staff and patients. A lot of spleen going around."

"Remember the old idea of humors: phlegm, blood,

choler, and black bile? The weather has everyone out of balance."

"George did mention temper as a possible cause, but that sounds too simple. But I do think the faculty connection is the way to go, because Alice Marmott was—to the exclusion of anything else—a top student. Academic all the way. A mad whirl of library, lectures, seminars. She was a perfectionist and wasn't going to let anything get in the way of that perfection."

"Are you saying it's Alice's fault that she was strangled?"

"No. I'm saying that Alice was an undeviating force and that she may have met another force moving in the opposite direction."

"That would fit Professor Horst. He's built like a bulldozer. He wouldn't have had much trouble with Alice and certainly could have carried her up into that Viking boat."

"How about the rest of them? Alice was tiny, not over a hundred and five pounds, I'd say."

"Yes, she hardly came up to my shoulder, even shorter than Mary Donelli. Anybody could move her around." Sarah looked out at the handful of icicles that hung in front of the window and sighed. "Oh, for just twenty-four hours of sun!"

But the weekend wound up in an increasing foulness of weather, with a cold malignant wind that blew into every corner of that part of Maine, and by Monday morning Sarah was in a fit mood to think the entire English faculty capable of murder. However, arriving on campus she was forced to revise her opinion that anyone could move Alice Marmott. She caught sight of Vera Pruczak struggling across the North Quad against the wind, her capes billowing, her hands clutching the air trying to balance, and decided that Vera would have to be ruled out as a lone murderer. Vera was hardly five feet tall herself and, without her lendings, a shadow of a thing. The idea of her shouldering and carrying a dead body up a ladder seemed ridiculous.

But all the other notables of the English department appeared reasonably agile and strong—even the alcoholic Amos Larkin. Professor Constance Garvey was built like a Valkyrie, and Mrs. Parker—as Sarah had noted before—had, despite the softening effect of those pastel cashmere twin sets and soft wool skirts—a notable chassis.

As for faculty achievement records, Sarah decided to begin a program of private research. Professor Lacey, for instance. A quick check in the library proved that he was, as she might have suspected, short on production. Two published books, and only three not very recent efforts showing up in the indices of the periodical literature. One, a full seven years ago, turned out to be a brief exegesis of four Shakespeare sonnets; another, three years back, had been done with a Carmine Wong, B.A., and proved to be an analysis of erring Shakespearean ladies. Professor Lacey seemed to have had a sexual frolic with the whole thing, cross-courting from Gertrude to Cleopatra to Cressida, and the like. It was all done with a dazzling display of analytical psychology, indicating that either the professor or Carmine Wong had spent some time on the couch.

Sarah cornered Mary and Drago for a conference. In flight from the college cafeteria, they sat squeezed into a narrow booth at the local burger joint. "Greasy spoons are sometimes needed for balance," said Mary, dipping a limp French fry into a pool of catsup.

"To answer your question," said Drago, "Lacey is no psychologist. That's Carmine Wong. She transferred from the West Coast somewhere. I went out with her a couple of times: psychoanalytic freak. Had a fellowship here and audited one of Lacey's classes. She was really built, in a sort of subcompact way, and they began turning up as a couple in nooks and crannies around the campus."

"I thought Lacey was married," said Sarah. "Plus kids. I saw him at the hockey game. Is his house way off campus? Otherwise his wife must be awfully close to the scene of action. Or is it what they call an open marriage?"

"The Lacey house is miles away, but Mrs. Lacey is a real watchdog," said Mary. "She turns up at all the college events with husband on the leash, but I'm sure he plays around when he gets the chance. I suppose Carmine must have done the sweating over the psychology and Lacey allowed her to put her name on the paper, maybe took her into a utility closet with him as a fringe benefit."

"Anything else of interest?" asked Sarah.

"Constance-the-dragon Garvey is more impossible every day, but that's just her normal progression toward driving her students to the brink. She's a champion nitpicker. Gives pop quizzes even to grad students. Wants students to memorize names of the minor characters, incidental place names. Has some kind of theory about minutiae as a guide to the author's real theme. Alice tried to argue about it, but Garvey mowed her down. As for Horst, he's turning into a sort of zombie. I think he's battery-powered and his cells are weak. And I've heard some of the students are going ahead with Alice's protest action as a sort of memorial to her. Rosy Parker's trying to keep the lid on and hold the line." Mary squashed a piece of hamburger bun into the catsup and pushed her plate away. "How about the hot fudge? We might as well go all the way."

Sarah nodded absently. "But Professor Bello? He's absolutely invisible. Isn't he supposed to run things, take classes, come out of his cage sometime? Professor Horst's affair should be bothering him."

"Not that I've noticed," said Mary. "As for coming out, he does do some tutorial work with honor undergrads, and I hear he's taken over Merlin-Smith's Milton section for a while because Merlin-Smith has tonsillitis or smallpox or something. You can catch Bello at four today."

"No one has a line on Bello," said Drago, beginning on a second cheeseburger. "He may be an impostor, for all we know. But he does publish. An article every year. Parker types them, and copies are served up from time to time. I'd say the whole high command except Bello is getting twitchy. They may all start to drink like Larkin, what with gendarmes all over the place. I'm nervous myself."

"And I'm beginning to avoid people wearing scarves," said Mary. "What's the matter, Sarah, don't you want your whipped cream?"

"I thought you didn't want to look like a footstool," said Sarah, scooping off the top of her sundae.

It was hard, Sarah decided, sitting in the back of Professor Bello's class, to know whether a professor you'd never seen in action was any more nervous than usual. Howard

Bello was one of those gray individuals whose voice and contours and clothes all fogged at the edges. Rumpled jacket, rumpled roundish face, gray and thinning hair, gray spotted tie. He seemed to know the subject well enough—today it was *Samson Agonistes*— but the class before him slumped in apathy. Remembering that his special field was not Milton but Emerson, Sarah wondered if the Sage of Concord roused him to give out more of a spark. As it was, she was not able to imagine that he could have mustered the spirit to strangle a student, much less dispose of the body so imaginatively. Energetic, Professor Bello was not. He was all passion spent with a vengeance.

Transferring to Professor Horst's five o'clock undergraduate poetry class across the hall, Sarah decided that *bulldozer* was right. Massive, body slowly rotating from the blackboard to his open notebook, he reminded Sarah of one of those earth-moving machines that slowly but inexorably create ditches, sewers, and highways where all was once verdant and flowering. What Professor Horst was doing was forcing the raw material of poetry through a series of calculations and transmutations and coming up with a kind of grammatical algebra.

Today, he was butchering—Sarah chose the word advisedly—John Donne's "Go and Catch a Falling Star." He quartered it, sliced it, pounded it; he separated bone from lean, integument from connective tissue, cooked it up, and reintroduced it as an almost unrecognizable cafeteria display of nouns proper and improper, adjectives, gerunds, infinitives, verbs active and passive, moods imperative, indicative, and subjunctive. These he jostled in columns, divided, square-rooted, took averages and medians, found standard deviations, and shook the lot into a line of equations that would have astonished the Dean of St. Paul's.

It also seemed to astonish the students, who from time to time brought up mandrake roots and faithful women and were shot down. Sarah decided that the professor was a bully and wondered that Alice had been so firm about going for him. It certainly added up to a motive for Horst, but as Sarah had learned from her past dealings with Sergeant Fitts, motives were not high on his scale of useful information. She looked up as Professor Horst at the blackboard began a dismemberment of "A Valediction, Forbidding Mourning." A murderer if there ever was one. Typecast.

Sarah met Alex late that afternoon in the waiting room of the hospital and told him that her car was being junked. "The garage said they'd give me three hundred dollars and I'd better take it, so I did. I'll have to ride with you until I can come up with something else."

"We'd better get going, then. Another storm is coming."

"I haven't gotten over the last one. Well, I've been looking over some of the English faculty, and my vote goes for Professor Horst. He's got his own pet poetry theory, and he's pushing it down the students' throats. They're just undergraduates and they think they should understand a poem before it's mangled. You've heard about all the fuss English departments are making about deconstruction?"

"No, I haven't. I just try to understand what I'm reading."

"No one reads for simple meaning any more; every text has a lot of meanings that can't be reconciled, that don't make conventional sense."

"You're not making conventional sense. Get back to Horst."

"Well, he's gone the deconstructionists one better. He doesn't just take the text apart, he turns it into numbers and then grinds it up. And he never listens to his students. He's a sort of robot and a real brute. And Alice had it in for him. You should see what he did to John Donne. Talk about the anatomy lesson."

Alex pulled his coat closer around his neck and shook his head. "That won't fly. The police won't care if Horst murders poems."

They walked to the parking lot and climbed in, and Alex started the car and drove it slithering and fishtailing toward the main road.

"Professors often don't," he said.

"Don't what?"

"Listen to students. It's a notable failing of theirs. I can think of dozens of teachers who don't listen and who ride roughshod over their subject, but they aren't murderers. How about Professor Larkin and that Wagnerian woman. Do they listen? Are they brutal?"

"Larkin doesn't encourage dialogue, maybe because he's usually fighting a hangover. Constance Garvey—I've sat in on one class—is straight out of P.S. 50 circa 1920: 'Stand up, Miss Blank, and recite without error the names of all the characters from *Middlemarch* and how they advance the subplot.' Patrick Fletcher is courteous but firm. Keeps your nose in the text. Meticulous about assignments. Chairman Bello is a cipher, but a gray one, and Professor Lacey listens if a student's measurements are interesting enough. He's a lazy womanizer."

"Do you think he might have womanized Alice Marmott?"

"She was into books, not sex. As previously noted."

"Still, he may have been into Alice."

"Honestly, Alex. She despised Lacey. Called him on facts."

"Honestly, yourself. It happens all the time. Eager student wants best of both worlds, dresses like a nun but yearns for carnal experience. Lacey obliges. Naive student falls hard but is guilt-ridden. Can't face straitlaced Ohio scene. Wants marriage, puts heat on Lacey. She's more than he bargained for, can't warn her off, home life, maybe job in jeopardy. Lacey stalks Alice, finds scarf near or on conveniently drunk Amos Larkin, and strangles Alice. Two things at one blow. Get rid of Alice, who's shown signs of 'taking action'—he'd know about the Horst action pending—and, second, leave circumstantial evidence to implicate Larkin, who's in no shape to know what's going on, perhaps even undresses Amos to make sure he doesn't ever wake up. Murderers don't usually leave Class A evidence such as an easily identified scarf unless there's a reason."

"Unless the murderer owns the scarf and is drunk. I must say, Alex, you used to be a sensible medicine man. You'd better take yourself over to Olivia Macbeth and help her with her next novel. Alice was no undercover nymphomaniac."

"She may have wanted to be one. Wanted to be ogled if not laid."

"That, Dr. McKenzie, is a completely male conclusion.

You've been talking to Mike Laaka. Women students have better things to do than hang around wanting to be leched by tomcats like Lacey."

"Have you read Freud on sublimation and repression?"

"Another impossible male. Alice had Ph.D. envy, not penis envy. Lord, look at the snow"—this as Alex made the turn for Sawmill Road—"it's really coming down, at least six inches since noon. You'll have to gun the car up our driveway."

This Alex did, coming to rest against the square side of the Sheriff's Department's all-purpose four-wheel-drive Bronco.

Mike Laaka leaned out, barely recognizable in a fur-bearing cap with earlaps. "I'm making a house call, just like doctors don't anymore, and I've brought us some fried clams. Open up the damned house. It's cold enough to freeze the balls off a moose."

"What a picturesque expression," said Alex. "Are you running for sheriff?"

"The tourists like it. Think they've bumped into a real Maine character."

"They have," said Sarah. "Come in and I'll brew something hot."

They sat around the kitchen table, fried clams, French fries, and cole slaw dispatched and coffee cups at the ready.

"Okay," said Mike. "Time for work. Here's what we have and here's what we want. First, approximate time of death."

"During the hockey game?" asked Alex. "Or after?"

"During, we think. Seeing that Alice was alive just before the game and wasn't seen by anyone after. Of course, the murderer, having put her on ice, so to speak, didn't make it easy. The Viking ship was below freezing and what with the hosing adding other ice layers and then the two-day thaw— well, none of that helps the pathology timetable. But even with some guessing about body tissue and stomach contents, it's a pretty fair judgment."

"I'm glad we've finished dinner," said Sarah.

"I waited, didn't I?" said Mike. "Anyway, we're putting the hockey-game time from seven-thirty to, say, nine-thirty.

That's allowing for three periods, intermissions with ice cleaning. After that the North Quad was swarming."

Sarah seemed to hear again the yells, the stamping of feet on the floor of bleachers, the banging of the puck, the slamming of players against the boards. "It was absolutely wild. The place was packed, and everyone was shouting and waving."

"The game of the year," put in Alex.

"George figures that most people will remember who they saw but will be fuzzy about the timetable—who was where and when. Best we can do, probably. Anyway, the North Quad—in fact, the whole campus—was pretty empty during the game, with not too many people leaving the rink to go outside for air. After all, it wasn't over ten above, so if they stepped out they'd step right back again."

"How about the *Mikado* people?" said Sarah.

"George has a list of the hockey game absentees. Vera Pruczak turned up in the middle of the game, but the stage-crew people stayed at the theater working on lights. There was a cleaning team doing the East Quad offices and the library, some grad students in the chem labs, ditto the physics labs, and, natch, the hospital personnel coming on duty, going off, or responding to a beeper. Then we've the report of the security people who worked the parking lot and the South and East Quads. Nothing there. We're trying to track down anyone who came near the North Quad just before or during the game."

"I suppose there were a lot of waifs and strays where they shouldn't be," said Sarah.

"Or even studying," said Alex. "Alice probably wasn't the only hardworking student around. And music. I heard a piano from somewhere. Music students don't always go ape over hockey."

Sarah frowned at the darkened kitchen window, trying to remember. "Well, as you know, the English office was open. I went there to pick up my libretto. Mrs. Parker was there and said she'd be late for the game, a student she had to see, and that Professor Garvey was expected. Professor Fletcher was in his office—I could just make him out through the stained-glass panel he has over his door. And Professor Larkin was in the Faculty Common Room."

"Resting up for his big scene, maybe," said Mike. "We're getting quite a dossier on Professor Lushwell—that's what some of the students call him. What was he wearing?"

"I didn't really look him over because I was in a hurry. He had his coat on, then and at the game—buttoned up wrong. I don't know about the scarf, and I suppose I would have noticed if he wasn't wearing shoes."

"He had boots," said Mike. "We've got him verified with high-laced field boots until the end of the second period, and then with boots off when he was found. Some say that at the hockey game he was wearing a scarf, some say not. I've heard he was reciting up a storm there, regular sideshow."

"Aren't you a little rough on him?" said Alex, remembering that Amos Larkin was now his patient.

"His doctor is being protective? Well, I'm not that tolerant of drunks. Ones that don't try and get help. Especially teachers. Parents are paying hard cash to have their kids taught by Lushwell."

Sarah swept the dinner leftovers into an unappetizing jumble and scraped the whole into the garbage bin. "No, Patsy," she said, as the big dog nosed into the container. "But Mike," she said over her shoulder, "do drunks or hypothermia victims always throw their clothes around? It was so cold out there. I have another thought."

"Shoot," said Mike.

Sarah reached for Mike's empty coffee cup and filled it. "Alex had an idea that I laughed at, but now it sounds better. What if someone was trying to murder Professor Larkin too? Implicate him with the scarf, undress him, and freeze him to death."

"Don't either of you go trying to complicate things," said Mike. "I'm worrying about Alice-who's-dead, not Amos-Larkin-who's-alive."

"He almost wasn't," persisted Sarah.

"It was close," said Alex. "The idea isn't that far out."

"Listen, Larkin was almost dead through his own damn fault. And don't tell me to go to Al-Anon and learn to understand. I have, but I see too many OUI manslaughters to squeeze out a tear for the drunks. So you two bleeding hearts try and think of who else you saw that night while I drink your coffee."

"You're all bark," said Sarah. "Have some fruitcake. It's left from Christmas so it's a little tough, just like you."

"Ought to go with fried clams," said Mike, unperturbed. "Now get out your pencil and start writing up those people you saw at the hockey game."

Sarah bent over her paper and tried to return to the hockey rink. She saw Professor Horst sitting there smoking his pipe, and Vera Pruczak in her knitted helmet and high boots, and Ivan Lacey under domestic restraint, Mrs. Parker and Miss Prism coming in late, and Mrs. Fletcher and her husband, yes, down by the ice late in the third period. No Professor Garvey at all, and no Amos Larkin after the end of the second period. The trouble was that much of the time Sarah had had her nose buried in *The Mikado*. And besides, the rink was such a madhouse that it seemed to her that anyone could have taken a chance to sneak out to strangle and hoist a body and come back to cheer for the home team. Finally, Sarah came up with a list that included at least half the senior English faculty. "Of course I don't know the department irregulars," she said. "They're housed over in West Quad."

"We've pretty much cleared that bunch," said Mike. "None had Alice in class, and the majority gave the hockey game a bye, and the others are accounted for."

"I have the same problem as Sarah," said Alex. "I'm new here. But for what it's worth . . ." He indicated his list, showing columns of times, places—many with question marks—and names, mostly the attending physicians of the Mary Starbox Memorial Hospital, together with a smattering of interns, residents, nurses, technicians, and medical students.

"Fine," said Mike. "How about conspicuous arrivals and departures?" But Alex could only add a urologist and a pediatrician who left together and two residents, their scrub suits visible under their parkas, vanishing just before the final score, causing considerable annoyance in the ranks of fans.

"It may turn out to be a random assault with no particular victim in mind," said Mike.

Sarah frowned. "Alice wasn't raped, they said."

"Maybe too cold. No, I'm not being funny. He might have started, but the ice and temperature were too much. But since Alice could have identified him, he killed her."

"I suppose it might have been like that," Sarah agreed.

"Anyway, security's been doubled, and the women are being warned not to walk alone."

"Alice was certainly a loner," said Sarah.

Mike floated cream across his cup of coffee. "Dessert," he explained. "Now, Sarah, did you see a ladder when you met Alice by the Viking boat?"

"No, but I didn't look around for it."

"Okay, that ties in with student reports that it was stashed behind the bushes. That ladder was mighty awkward. Twelve-foot and heavy."

Sarah turned and stared out the window, where the back-door light illuminated a blustery circle of the winter night. "Tomorrow's going to be impossible. The snow is going sideways, not down." She turned back to Mike. "I've been thinking about the ladder and Alice. I'd say not Vera Pruczak. She's so tiny. Smaller than Alice herself. Legs like a spider."

"Brown Recluse," said Alex, "or Black Widow."

"You don't have to be a lady wrestler to strangle anyone," said Mike. "Surprise and technique. It's just a knack."

"A knack for strangling?" said Sarah. "You *are* horrible."

"Vera might have strangled and someone else did the ladder bit."

Sarah remembered her picture of Mrs. Parker and the registrar working in concert and nodded. "But still, two people out there in public, strangling and hoisting a body—"

Mike drained his coffee, hauled himself out of his chair, and reached for his fur cap. "So keep your ears open, you and your friend Mary, for any close friendships in the department, working or sleeping arrangements. Something Alice might have had a line on—or interrupted." He bent toward the window. "You're right about the snow. Looks like Sarah will have a holiday."

Sarah sighed. "Bowmouth never closes. Regardless. Mrs. Parker told me very firmly. Loyal students, loyal faculty."

"Always thought these fancy-dancy college people had

no sense," said Mike, struggling into his heavy jacket. "Tradition, money, button-down shirts, and water on the brain. Anyway, I'll know where to find you. And you, Alex. Hospitals never close either."

ELEVEN

O ne look from the bedroom window the next morning told Sarah that this particular piece of the state of Maine had simply disappeared in the night. Trees, telephone poles, houses, barns had all become one blurred undulating white.

Alex appeared at the door fully dressed, with a small canvas bag in one hand. "I'll stay at the hospital tonight. I'm on call. Maybe you'd better pack a toothbrush too. If we get through this stuff we may never make it back. I've arranged for Patsy to be fed and loved by Nick Smith next door. He's off duty for two days."

"Poor Patsy," said Sarah, reaching down and pulling him from the center of the bed where, as soon as Alex had slipped out, the dog had jumped, returning albeit briefly to his rightful place.

"Patsy'll have a ball. Nick has a new female husky and Patsy's in love. Don't worry, she's spayed, but Patsy isn't sure."

"Then he's frustrated," said Sarah, pulling woolen stockings from a drawer. "We should breed him. I'd hate to have him die out—his line, I mean."

"And I'd hate to find nine of Patsy's puppies trying to climb into bed. One Irish wolfhound at a time, thanks. Look, get yourself together because the snow is really coming down again. Call me around five at the hospital and we'll take a weather reading."

But by five o'clock there was no question of anyone leaving the campus. All day Sarah had fought her way from class to class, face and neck stung by a wild wind and whirling snow. By one o'clock the cars in the parking lots had become undefinable shapes, while beyond by the main campus road a huge yellow snowplow like an expiring dinosaur had collapsed into a snowdrift, its mechanical head raised as if in distress.

Sarah, a wanderer in an arctic waste, groped her way to the English Department. She could no longer see her feet or feel her cheeks and hands, and all thoughts of Alice Marmott's murderer had given way to the simple need to be warm. In the halls of the department bundled figures gestured, pointed to the windows, stamped their feet, and spoke in high excited voices. "You'd think none of them had ever seen snow before," said Mary. "A lot of excited sheep."

"It's storm mentality," said Sarah, touching her cheeks experimentally. "You know, us against the elements. Remember all those people in Buffalo caught in that big storm? They're still having anniversary parties."

"My idea of hell," said Mary succinctly, "would be to have to go to a party every year with some of these turkeys. All the top brass is going to have a bed tonight." She indicated the row of lighted faculty offices. It was true. Most of the senior faculty had arrived with small overnight bags, and some had already left for the Faculty Club. Others, in the happy knowledge that a hot meal and a nearby bed were waiting, loitered in their offices or joined a colleague for a drink from whatever bottle could be produced from desk drawers.

"Of course," said Vera Pruczak, meeting Sarah and Mary in the hall, "rooms for women faculty are something else." Vera was dressed in a green Gore-Tex one-piece suit with extra pockets—a sort of space-age variation on Winston Churchill's one-piece number. She wore a fur kepi and was ringed by mufflers.

"The men, poor lambs, may possibly have to double up," said Vera crossly, "but the women *always* have to double or even triple up. Our rooms are on the Faculty Club third floor with one WC down the hall. Former maid's rooms from the good old days. Iron beds, curtained cupboards, and an extension cord to one outlet. And just try for a hot bath. The men siphon off all the hot water with their everlasting showers. And my poor darling cats, all alone tonight, although I did leave out the Friskies and plenty of water, but when I think of the cat box—"

"At least you have a bed," said Mary. "As far as Bowmouth is concerned, the fellows and the adjuncts can use the floor."

"But you're young," cried Miss Pruczak, becoming Olivia Macbeth before their eyes. "Why, when I was young we'd sleep anywhere. Just drop in our tracks. Strikes for Equity, all-night rehearsals, peace vigils, waiting in line at the booking office. In any weather."

Holding her bat-wing sleeves high, she lifted her chin bravely and became the gallant twenty-two-year-old ingenue facing a cruel snow-covered world.

"Oh, but my dears, that was years ago." Miss Pruczak lowered her arms, her shoulders dipped, and her face turned forlorn. "Now I'm too old for that sort of fun. Too, too old." And immediately she became a friendless crone and brought a hand up to her now visibly withered cheek, then reached over and touched Sarah's with unimaginable pathos, gave a faint cackle, and was gone down the hall, her booted feet shuffling, her hand in the shape of a claw, clutching her woven book bag to her waist.

"Marvelous," said Mary, as she disappeared.

"Too bad to waste it on us," said Sarah, in considerable awe.

"Not wasted, she knows we're a discriminating audience, but it still doesn't make me want to sleep on the floor."

"Or in the North Quad dorms and lounges. They'll all be packed with stranded students and everyone will be whooping it up all night."

"I have it," said Mary. "Right here. The Fellows' Room. We'll swipe some cushions from the waiting room."

But the Fellows' Room had already been turned into sleeping quarters. Drago Collins and four other male teaching fellows had made it into something like a scout encampment complete with sleeping bags, rucksacks, and a small alcohol stove on which a dark fluid bubbled in a beaker.

"Hot rum punch," said Drago. "We're ready to spend the winter. *Ein feste Burg,* but you're welcome to wedge yourselves in."

"Thanks, but no thanks," said Mary. "Sleep tight."

"That's the idea," said Drago, taking a long glass rod and whirling it expertly in the beaker.

"How about the student waiting room, then?" asked Sarah.

"Right," said Mary, moving across the hall. "Let's nab it before someone else gets the idea."

But someone had. Stretched full length along the Naugahyde sofa lay Amos Larkin, one arm dangling to the floor and bubbling snores rising from his parted lips. A pint of Jim Beam stood guard with his briefcase on a small table.

Sarah backed up. "Ugh. We can't stay here."

Mary, arms akimbo, stood silent for a moment and surveyed the sleeping professor. Then she shook her head. "My long-range plans may include spending the night with Amos, but not now. We'll have to move him."

"Where to?" said Sarah, moving to the door. "We can't just pull him out into the hall where everyone will see him." Why Sarah did not want this to happen she could not have explained, but somehow she shrank from being the final agent in what seemed to be Professor Larkin's almost certain expulsion from Bowmouth College.

Mary considered. "The department's still crawling with people and there's bound to be someone in the Common Room. The light's on. We'll just have to take him to his own office later. He can sleep on the floor like the rest of us, only he's got a skinful to help. Look, you do a recon trip to see if his office is locked, and I'll stand guard here to make sure we keep dibs on the room. Take off your coat and look as if you belong. Otherwise, Parker will send you on your way. She acts as if the department is her own private box stall—the cow," added Mary.

" 'What oft was said and ne'er so well expressed,' " said Sarah, hanging her dripping coat over a chair.

"That should net you a *C* in Eighteenth Century," said Mary. "Get going."

Sarah, walking with a businesslike step, briefcase in hand, marched down the hall and directly into Mrs. Parker. The secretary, decided Sarah, thinking of Mary's metaphor, did look a little like a well-groomed bovine trotting out of her stall to check the passing traffic.

"Why, Miss Deane. Still here. You should be making your evening's arrangements. If you don't find a place in the North Quad dorm, they're keeping the women's gym open to all comers. And remember, we've had incidents, so don't walk alone."

Sarah turned the subject. "But you, Mrs. Parker. I hope *you* have a place to spend the night."

"Oh, I'm completely set. I have a room in the Faculty Club. Professor Bello arranged it even if I'm not quite faculty. One of the VIP guest rooms because, of course, we won't have visitors in this storm." Then, as if suddenly aware that Sarah was edging toward the sacred row of offices, "Where are you going, Miss Deane? There are no appointments now. Most of our faculty are packing up for the night or are in conference."

"I'm going to the ladies' room," said Sarah firmly, and strode off to the end of the hall and turned right. Thank heavens the building designers had seen fit to locate the women's lavatory in the same corridor as Amos Larkin's office. Next door, in fact. She banged into the room, flushed a toilet and ran water, and then slipped out and reached for Professor Larkin's doorknob. Locked, damn it. The key was probably in his pocket and they would have to frisk him.

Sarah turned to go and then in the next office, from what was a partly open door, heard Professor Lacey's voice—unmistakable, that high cultivated whinny—saying loudly, "No, Rosalind. That's too much. Absolutely not." A pause, a low murmur, while Sarah, one foot arrested in the act of leaving, hung onto the doorknob. Then, "You know I'd do anything" —Ivan Lacey was now wheedling—"in fact I *have* done anything . . . but I can't do this. Don't you see, can't you see, that it's absolutely impossible? What does Fletcher say? Have you talked to Horst and the others? And Howard? Are they all for it?" Then Professor Lacey's voice sank, there was a scraping of chairs, and Sarah, moving like the wind, made it down the corridor and back to the waiting room before Mrs. Parker could catch her.

"Parker's on the prowl," she panted. "She wants to make sure we all have a nice safe place to spend the night. Obviously not in the department. How is Drago getting away with it?"

"Oh, he's probably buttered her up or she doesn't know. Now we'll just turn off the lights, close the door, and wait. When the place is cleared out, we'll grab Drago to help carry Amos."

Sarah pointed to the snoring professor. "You mean we sit here in the dark with that?"

"He's harmless. Look, we've got to eat. If you have some change I'll sneak down to the coffee and sandwich machine in the basement. We can't have Parker finding you again."

Mary switched off the light and Sarah felt her way to a chair as far from Amos Larkin as possible. She wondered what she would do if the professor woke up in the dark and began blundering around in a drunken rage. But all was peace, and after an interval Mary appeared with an armful of plastic-wrapped food and two cans of Moxie. "The new improved Moxie," she said. "It's all that was left."

"Improved," said Sarah, who had been trying to like Moxie for some twenty-odd Maine summers, "means that it's marginally easier to swallow than the old improved Moxie."

"And Sleeping Beauty?"

"Still sleeping, as you see."

"Okay. Things are pretty quiet now in the main hall. There's a light in the English office, so one of the clerks must be working late. Nosy Parker's office is dark, and only a few other lights are still on. I've asked Drago to come along in a while and help with the transfer. Now let's lie low for an hour."

"I forgot," said Sarah. "Larkin's office is locked."

"Oh, shit. Well, we'll get Drago to help search him. See if we can shake the keys out of his pockets."

The keys did shake out with gratifying promptness, and with Drago supporting the shoulders and the head, and Mary and Sarah each with a leg, the professor—coat, briefcase, and bottle centered on his midsection—was carried down the now darkened hall and into his office. Only occasional rumblings from Amos Larkin's interior indicated to the transporters that they were carrying a live body.

"I feel like an absolute ghoul," said Sarah, dropping the professor's leg and unlocking the office. "All we need is a grave."

"I'll switch on the desk light and make a space on the floor. He's a 'demd, damp, moist, unpleasant body,' as Señor Mantalini would say." Mary pushed a typewriter table away and closed the door. "That's that. I'll fold his coat for a blanket."

"Aren't we being maternal?" said Drago, letting the professor slide to the floor with a thump.

"Maternal or something else," said Sarah.

"Right now," said Mary, "my thoughts do not that way tend." She turned to go and, as she did, her arm swept a stack of papers from the edge of the desk, scattering them like a pack of cards.

"I'll leave you ladies to do the housekeeping," said Drago, putting Amos Larkin's bourbon on his desk. "We've got a poker game going."

"What a mess," said Mary, kneeling next to Amos Larkin's armpit and reaching for a folder.

"Look at this," said Sarah, recovering a manuscript. "It's a paper by Alice Marmott: 'Manuscripts and Early Editions of Swift's *Cadenus and Vanessa* Compared.' And there's a note clipped on. 'Dear Professor Larkin. I know this is not part of our assignment, but I thought you might give me your criticism because I would be interested in submitting the paper to a periodical for publication.' "

"That Alice was certainly something," said Mary. "I suppose the police made a copy of it and will use it against Amos. Are there any comments from him?"

"It doesn't look as if he's even read it," said Sarah, turning over the pages. "At least no notes and queries."

"I suppose he just dumped it on the slush pile with everything else." Mary held up a folder announcing a Samuel Johnson symposium, an envelope marked URGENT—FOR YOUR IMMEDIATE CONSIDERATION, and a sheaf of departmental memos having to do with meetings long gone by. "My thesis chapters are probably buried in here, the rat," said Mary.

"We'd better leave before he comes to and finds us reading his mail."

"It's time someone read his mail. He obviously hasn't. Besides, I think he's out for a while."

To which remark Amos Larkin opened both eyes and said clearly, "Not out." He then closed them, turned slightly on his side, and began to snore softly.

Sarah had reached the door when Mary grabbed her leg. "No, wait. He's gone again. Look at this. It looks like Mrs. Parker is planning a move. It's her whole CV."

"She wants another job?"

"Looks like it. All her vital statistics in glowing colors. Honor student at Appleton High, B.S. in business administration from Midcoast Community College, then a job in a bank with strong recommendations, and then Bowmouth College —'rising to position of executive trust.' What's executive trust?"

"The English Department, I guess. As Howard Bello's sitter-in."

"It's quite a blurb. From this sheet you'd want to give her tenure or make her chancellor of the whole place."

"Put it back and turn out the light," said Sarah. "You're making me nervous."

Together they tiptoed back down the now darkened hall. Only two faculty offices still showed a late-staying occupant, and the light still came from under the English Office door.

"Linda or Arlene probably trapped there, grinding out someone's amended reading list," said Mary.

"Hush," said Sarah.

"Pooh," said Mary. "We're orphans of the storm. Let's open supper and enjoy ourselves."

But a dinner made entirely of coin-machine products is a discouraging experience. "Tastes like shoes and wet toilet paper with whiskey fumes," said Sarah. "I'm going to bed. You take the sofa because I'm too tall. I'll use the cushions from these chairs." Sarah pulled four cushions from four so-called easy chairs, arranged them in a row, and then said, "I forgot my teeth." She reached for her briefcase, produced a toothbrush and a tube of Crest, and slipped into the hall. Returning, she reported all offices dark except for the English Office and the Fellows' Room. "And it's still howling outside, so I don't think anyone's going to turn up. We're safe for tonight."

Mary in turn assembled her toilet kit, left, and returned. "I almost went in to the English Office to tell them to go home, and then it occurred to me that Arlene and Linda are hanging out there for this night just like us. I'll bet Parker doesn't know."

"And to think she's in a position of executive trust," murmured Sarah sleepily from the floor. "Good night." And she pulled her quilted coat up around her shoulders and closed her eyes.

Mary, after considerable wriggling, settled into one position, her parka on, the hood over her head. "It's getting damn cold in here," she complained.

"I suppose the heat is turned down at night."

"Yes, but this room is supposed to have its own electric baseboard heat. They put it in some of the offices a while back. Maybe the storms knocked the wires down. And good night to you."

And as from a far country rose the muted voices from the Fellows' Room: My eyes are dim, I cannot see, I do not have my specs with me.

For Sarah it was like one of those nights she remembered from traveling, shifting uneasily between wakefulness and sleep with real and imagined people. Once she thought that Amos Larkin was in the room demanding his whiskey, but it was only Mary turning on her sofa, muttering to herself.

She woke suddenly, perhaps an hour later, to the sound of the Fellows' Room door opening and someone shuffling down the hall. The men's room, she thought, pulling her coat more tightly around her. The waiting room had turned into an ice chest. Keeping her eyes closed she floated off to a family trip on Amtrak, lighted stations, sudden metallic clangs, pattering feet in the corridor, toilets flushing in the next compartment, and then she was on an ice floe that was breaking away from the mainland while Alex and Patsy looked on from the shore. Patsy barked and Alex called not to forget her blanket. "It's cold in Nebraska." "But I'm not going to Nebraska," she called back, "and I've forgotten my blanket." "Wear your wool socks then," shouted Alex, and he and Patsy walked away, and Sarah could see that they were going toward a warm and pleasant meadow, dotted with wildflowers. "Wait, I'm coming," she called, but they kept moving away, and now she saw that the gap of water between the ice floe and the land had widened and she was slipping, slipping away. . . . Slipping in fact off her narrow bed of cushions and onto the cold linoleum floor of the waiting room. "Damn," she said.

"Are you freezing?" said Mary from the sofa. "I am."

"Yes. I was dreaming that I was caught on an ice floe."

"Look, I'll go out and rummage in the lost-and-found—it's a shelf in the English Office. I know there are a couple of sweaters there. Otherwise we're going to get hypothermia."

"Double hypothermia," said Sarah, shivering.

"I hope the door's unlocked. I suppose Drago and his buddies are all warm in their sleeping bags. Why didn't we think ahead?"

"Just go in your socks," said Sarah, half remembering her dream.

"Who's to hear? The place is a morgue and about twice as cold." But she kicked off her shoes, stood up, smoothed her coat, and slid out into the hall.

Sarah saw that it was just getting light. The blackness of the windows was giving way to a glum gray, and there were great blobs of snow on the glass as if some monster hand had hurled cotton against it. But if Mary hurried up with the sweaters, there was still a chance for a couple of hours' sleep before the place came alive. Sarah had just pulled her knitted hat over her ears and curled down again on her cushions when she heard fast footsteps and then someone falling heavily against the door. She jumped up and found Mary struggling to her feet.

"My socks, I slipped on the floor, I was running," she gasped.

"You shouldn't have been running," said Sarah sensibly. "You'll wake up the whole place."

"Oh, God . . . Sarah. It's awful. Don't go in there. Holy Jesus and Mary, it's so awful."

"Don't go in where? Mary, what's the matter? Get in here, I'll turn on the light." Sarah pushed the wall switch, reached for Mary's arm, and almost dragged her into the room and pushed her into the nearest chair.

"I turned on the light and she was there. I touched her hand. She's absolutely cold. I've never felt skin like that . . . and she was blue. Not breathing. There was no point in CPR or anything. And she was so damn cold. Oh, God, Sarah." Mary hugged herself, shaking.

Sarah could never remember afterward how time both sped ahead shrieking and stood completely still. How she stood there with Mary and debated about resuscitation and telephones and waking Drago and the others and at the same time raced down the hall. All she knew was that she was there at the English Office door saying over and over to Mary, "But who is it, who is it?" And Mary, panting, finally answering, "Mrs. Parker. It's Mrs. Parker and she looks so awful."

She did. Sarah leaned, nauseated, trembling, against the wall. Mrs. Parker, as if caught in an unsuccessful gymnastic act, sprawled face down on the floor. Her fur-trimmed coat was rumpled around her waist and her skirt was reefed up to her knees, with one high-heeled booted foot caught under the ankle of the other. Her left arm had hooked itself around an open dictionary as if she had seized it for support as she tumbled; her other ended in a tight fist shoved under her chin. Her face, as much as Sarah could see—or wanted to see—was a slate blue, as if a bruise had suddenly overgrown itself and spread. The keyboard of the office computer rested, end up, across Mrs. Parker's fur collar, and the wheeled desk chair, which must have spun away as she fell, now faced the wastebasket.

The room was cold, as cold as the waiting room, and there seemed to be a faint odor like marzipan turned rancid hanging in the frigid air. For a moment, Sarah stood turned to stone, only the heavings of her stomach reminding her that she herself was alive and protesting. In the hall, Mary was being thoroughly and effectively sick.

Then everything was a jumble. Another argument with

Mary about resuscitation—rejected—a search for a telephone in an open office. "Why isn't there one here in the English Office?" Sarah asked Mary. But every office was locked. "Even Professor Larkin's," she said in surprise.

"But we didn't lock him in," said Mary. "We'll have to get Drago and the others. There's a pay phone in the basement."

"And we'd better close the English Office door and not let anyone in," added Sarah, as suddenly the awful image of George Fitts rose before her.

But the telephone in the basement was out of order, so Drago, roused, hair on end, eyes squinting, was told to try and make it to the hospital. "A doctor," said Mary. "Any doctor."

"No," said Sarah. "Dr. McKenzie, he's a medical examiner and he's at the hospital. And call the State Police," she called after him. "Ask for Sergeant Fitts."

"Christ, Sarah," said Mary, staring at her. "What do you want with the police?" Mary had spent several minutes to good purpose in the washroom and by dint of much splashing now had a reasonably healthy color back.

"It seems like the thing to do. A precaution."

"Are you trying to say someone did something to her? It's just a heart attack, isn't it? Or a stroke?"

"Her color," said Sarah. "And that funny smell."

"I didn't smell anything," said Mary.

"You didn't stay in there long enough. But maybe I'm jumping to something."

"I'll say you are. I was there when Uncle Arturo died. A heart attack. He fell right over, and he was a terrible color."

"I suppose she must have been working late," said Sarah, gladly taking heart attack instead of homicide as a diagnosis. "And, oh, Lord, she must have been in there all the time we were arguing about who was using the room. If we'd only knocked, tried the door."

"I honestly thought it was Arlene or Linda spending the night, not Mrs. Parker. She has her own office with everything in it—the telephone switchboard, the works—except, of course, the computer and the copy machine. I've never seen her *work* anywhere except in her own office. She just went in and out of the English Office with papers for the clerks to copy or stuff to load in the computer. Jesus, I can't get her out of my head, how she looked. Do you think she had high blood pressure or a leaky heart or something and didn't tell anyone? No, don't answer, I don't want to talk about it. Let's talk about something else, anything else, like—well, why did you come to Bowmouth?"

"Oh," said Sarah, forcing herself, "you know, a Ph.D. and all that. Alex wanted to practice here in Maine and a fellowship opened up at Bowmouth and we'd decided to try living together. It was a sort of compromise."

"He seems like a good guy to compromise with."

"Yes," said Sarah, without really listening—and then, with agitation, "Oh, but I wish he'd get here. It isn't that far."

"Take a good look out the window," said Mary. They were back, huddling, in the waiting room. "Anyone coming across the quad would have to tunnel."

But then they were there: Drago, face red with cold; Alex, snow clinging as far as his chest, his hood pulled over his head.

"I've called Professor Bello," said Drago. "At the Faculty Club. He's coming right over."

"Now show me," said Alex, without any preliminaries.

Mary was almost incoherent. "I hope we didn't let her die by mistake—I mean we thought it was too late for CPR because she was almost rigid and cold."

"Take me to the room, won't you," said Alex quietly, and Sarah remembered that one of the things she liked—no, loved —about Alex, that comforted her, was that he never shouted or blustered but went ahead with what had to be done, never anticipating, never blaming.

Alex disappeared into the English Office and closed the door. Mary and Sarah retreated to the waiting room.

"I wish they'd do something about the heat," said Mary, slapping her sides.

"Exercise or they'll be finding us on the floor. I know some aerobic stuff."

"I hate exercise in any form," said Mary. "Okay, one, two, three."

Thus it was that Alex found Sarah and Mary almost perspiring, leaping, turning, and counting. Sarah slid to a stop. "Survival," she gasped.

"Good idea," said Alex. "The electric baseboard heat is off in the English Office, Mrs. Parker's office, and the waiting room. The custodian showed up and found that someone had pulled the switch in the basement. They'll start up the heat as soon as George and his team have checked for prints."

"Prints?" said Sarah stupidly. She had by now convinced herself of the heart attack.

"You mean it wasn't a sudden something?" asked Mary.

"It was sudden, all right," said Alex, "but I'm certainly glad no one tried mouth-to-mouth. It's a guess, and you're not to talk, but I'd say it was poison. The odor, her appearance, and a Thermos—on the floor behind the desk. Same smell. Anyway, you two stay here and keep moving. I'll send for some blankets. It's going to be a long morning."

The morning did indeed stretch out beyond measuring. There was the arrival of George Fitts, apparently by dogsled, since Sarah could see no sign that any snow-removal efforts were under way. But there he was with the homicide team with their cameras and cases of chemicals and instruments and a pathologist who bounced with unseemly enthusiasm, rubbing his hands and exclaiming about the snow.

It seemed to Sarah that the arrival of the State Police brought not only blasts of freezing air from open doors, it forced a confrontation of the real and harsh world with the arcane, at times almost precious, world of the English Department. In halls and offices where heated debates over sabbaticals, classroom assignments, the virtues of deconstruction, the new Marxist fiction critic, the proper teaching of semiotics, the faculty salary scale, which translation of Dante to use, the quality of the instant coffee, who should never be given tenure, who was responsible for the washroom toilet paper— where all these had held sway, now heavy boots, plastic bottles, sample jars, measuring tape, fingerprint powder, and the body bag took over. Somehow the English Department seemed like a paper kingdom, easily crumpled, easily overthrown.

At one point Drago and one other fellow were permitted to fight their way to the cafeteria for breakfast under police escort. This welcome meal helped clear Sarah's head so that it became obvious, as she and Mary first huddled in blankets and then jumped and ran around the waiting room, that she, Mary, Drago and his poker game, and the whole English Department community were implicated in Mrs. Parker's death.

Alex appeared briefly in the waiting room some time after nine o'clock, saying that he had hospital rounds but would be back and that the telephone service and the heat were about to be restored.

"George has things in hand."

"Which means?" said Sarah.

"That you and Mary are to stay put. The lab crew wants to finish with the offices and washrooms. You're to use the lavatories in the basement—a policewoman will go down with you. You're both to try and remember everything about last night. I think the English Department will be sealed off, for today at least. The police are picking up all the arrivals— faculty, students, and staff—that turn up this morning and sticking them in the big seminar room downstairs for an interrogation. Of course, you overnighters are of great interest."

Mary looked at Sarah in consternation. "Oh, my Lord. Amos."

"Oh?" said Alex.

"It's Professor Larkin," said Sarah, deciding that Mary didn't want to be the informer. "He'd been drinking, and we dragged him from the waiting room into his own office last night. We didn't lock him in, just left the key on his desk, but this morning when we were trying to find a telephone, his door was locked."

"You mean he's gone?"

"Or he's in there now." said Mary. "He might have come to and locked himself in."

"I'll check right now." Alex stepped quickly out of the room; five, ten minutes passed, and then Alex stuck his head in the door. "No Amos Larkin. But it looks like someone left by the fire escape at the end of the hall. The window's open."

For a while, Sarah and Mary, the heat restored, settled to going through their briefcases, correcting papers, checking texts for graduate seminars. Then Sarah looked up.

"Mrs. Parker. How did people feel about her? I hardly knew her."

Mary seemed glad to talk. "Of course, she ran the whole

place and that doesn't make for universal popularity. The fellows and adjuncts and underlings didn't take to her much. Neither did I. She seemed always to be in the way of my knowing or working with the faculty on my courses and program."

"She certainly protected Professor Bello," said Sarah.

Mary nodded. "Protected them all. It was impossible to slip down the hall to see if someone was in his office without being nabbed by Parker and told that Professor So-and-so was much too busy to see you. She was always smiling up a storm, but she wouldn't budge an inch. Everything went through her office switchboard, and half the time she wouldn't put you through. I don't know if all the faculty wanted it this way or not. She must have annoyed some of them, taking everything into her own hands that way. I've heard Amos Larkin sharpen his knife over her head, but he does that to everyone, and then she saved his hash a couple of times."

"Maybe she was the real thing," said Sarah. "You know, a dedicated secretary—or administrator. Like Alice Marmott was a student. Two of a kind."

But the mention of Alice acted like a cloud. Two dead people in two short cold weeks. "Sorry," said Sarah. "Forget I said that. The two have zip in common."

"Right," said Mary. "But I've thought of something to make you smile. Picture what's going down in the seminar room. The students, the fellows and adjuncts, the clerks, and God knows who else all milling around with the senior faculty, and they not able to hide out in their offices or under their desks. Students accosting teachers, teachers having to listen to students."

"And the English classes canceled," said Sarah. "Do you know, Mrs. Parker told me that that hadn't happened since VJ Day because everyone was too loyal, and now—"

"Stop it," said Mary. "Pick up your Anglo-Saxon grammar and decline for me the following verbs: galan, grafan, hladan, and sacan."

TWELVE

Halfway through the first strange morning without the directing hand of Rosalind Parker, Sarah and Mary were joined by trimly uniformed Deputy Sheriff Susan Cohen, who informed them that they were not to communicate with each other further until they had been questioned by Sergeant Fitts. Sarah, who remembered Susan from the past summer, said, "Hi, there," but the deputy smiled in the sort of way which established that persons of the law did not chitchat with witnesses. So Sarah and Mary worked away on the contents of their briefcases and each tried not to notice the arrival through the snow and up the stairs of two men with a stretcher, the stamping of feet down the hall, and the slower, more cautious steps of the burdened men on their return. Finally, after a sandwich-and-coffee lunch had arrived in a cardboard box, Mary and then Sarah were summoned into George Fitts's presence.

He had taken over the Common Room—a move Sarah was sure would not sit well with the faculty. There he sat at a library table amid the last evening's litter. The cleaning team had been barred so that periodicals, coffee cups, filled ashtrays, and sections of yesterday's newspapers were scattered about, and the green leather chairs still bore the imprint of yesterday's faculty bottoms.

As usual, George, though in the room, was not of it. He

remained the detached person whose extreme tidiness of trousers, necktie, and shirt suggested that he had not just slogged through drifts of snow but had deftly dropped from some other world. Sarah had at times played with the idea that George was an agent from some more sanitary planet sent to solve the problems of an unruly species. She remembered that he had once told her he was a fisherman. It seemed appropriate. She could see him standing motionless on some far-off planet's riverbank and then, with a slash of his arm, whisking a silver-scaled fish from deep waters.

Now, as Sarah watched him move his notebooks, his sharpened pencils, his recording equipment to one side of the table to make room for a fresh pad of paper, she would not have been surprised to see steel antennae grow from the sides of his bald head. And when he asked Susan Cohen to leave them alone, she thought his voice had taken on a foglike quality so that his words slipped into the air with a minimum of resonance. He took off his rimless spectacles, huffed on them, wiped them with a folded handkerchief, and then walked to the window and pushed back the interior wooden shutters that shaded the room. A bleak blue-white light fell on the furniture, making it look even dustier and harder-used than before.

George indicated a low chair. "Please sit down, Sarah. Begin with your arrival in this building yesterday afternoon and go on until Alex's arrival. You know me by now"— George gave her his vestigial smile—"everything. And let me judge what's important."

Sarah, folding her hands in her lap obediently, took a breath and began. Minute by remembered minute she took George through the evening. Oddly enough, he did not linger unpleasantly over the discovery of Mrs. Parker's body, for which she was grateful. Instead at the end he turned her around and leapfrogged her from incident to incident and bore in.

"Professor Larkin. Are you sure he was drunk?"

"Yes," said Sarah. "He was right in the waiting room sleeping on the sofa, snoring. I smelled the whiskey. He had a bottle with his briefcase."

"Could he have pretended to be drunk . . . or asleep?"

"Well," said Sarah doubtfully, "it's possible."

"Then you have no real proof that he was drunk, not just putting it on?"

"We didn't do a blood test, if that's what you mean," said Sarah with irritation. "Mary and I just assumed—I mean he was always getting drunk. He's an alcoholic."

"But that may not stand up in court. Would you swear that because he was sleeping, snoring, smelling of whiskey, and had a bottle of liquor nearby that he was drunk? Did he do, say anything to show he was incapacitated?"

"He didn't wake up when we dragged him to his office— only once later and then passed out again."

"If you wanted to convince someone you were drunk, what would you do?"

"I guess I'd slosh some whiskey in my mouth, maybe drink a little bit, sprinkle it around my clothes, and leave a bottle next to me while I pretended to be passed out. Do something crazy."

"Like be found in the waiting room so you'd have witnesses that you were drunk? Like allow yourself to be dragged to your office?"

"All right," said Sarah reluctantly, "but everyone knows he drinks."

"Exactly so. I'm just making a point," said George. "Professor Larkin was probably inebriated. It's a fair presumption."

Sarah remembered the locked office. "But where is he? We thought he'd stay put until the morning."

"That's why Professor Larkin is so interesting. He couldn't have been so completely out as you both thought. He was able to lock his office door. I've had a call from one of the sheriff's men that he turned up just now for breakfast at the student cafeteria. He'd left his tie and shirt in his office but took his outside coat and one glove. We've found disturbed snow on the fire escape exit, also the other glove. He must have climbed down the hard way. He seems to have spent the rest of the night in the cloakroom of the cafeteria, on a pile of coats, but he claims, naturally, that he can't remember any of this."

Sarah exclaimed, but George moved on to other matters:

footsteps, sounds of falling objects, bodies, doors closing, telephones ringing.

"I'm not much help," said Sarah. "Footsteps once from the Fellows' Room, but most of the time I had my coat pulled way over my ears and my hat on. And the wind was howling."

George made a note, pulled out a file marked *Drago Collins*, and turned a page. "A men's-room trip is claimed. Now what's this about Professor Lacey and Mrs. Parker having an argument when you were testing Professor Larkin's door?"

"Oh, it didn't make sense. About something being impossible and he asked Mrs. Parker—he called her Rosalind— what Fletcher, Horst, and Bello said about it. It sounded like a departmental squabble."

"Did Mrs. Parker help set departmental policy?"

"To some extent, perhaps. She was a privileged person. Sort of royalty. Last night she told me she was being allowed to spend the night at the Faculty Club in one of the VIP rooms."

"Pretty special treatment," said George, making little pothooks and lines on his paper. A secret code from another planet? Sarah wondered. George saw her watching. "My own shorthand," he said. "Now, did she say anything to suggest she was planning to spend the night here? No? Well, did Mrs. Parker use the equipment in the English Office, the word processor, the printer, the copy machine? After all, she was tangled up in the computer when you found her."

"Mary told me that Mrs. Parker resented the computer. She liked to type department material and keep department records herself."

"Interesting," said George. "Most women like Mrs. Parker in a clerical position would have felt they had to learn the computer."

Sarah corrected him. "Executive. She never considered herself clerical."

"Did she always bring a Thermos to work? Did other members of the faculty? How about the clerks, Arlene and Linda?"

"I don't know about Mrs. Parker, but the two clerks bring their lunch sometimes because the English Office isn't supposed to be left alone. I've seen others from time to time with lunch and a Thermos. You'd better ask them. Some people get tea, coffee, or cocoa from the hot water that's kept going in the mail room—that's the little annex off the English Office. The faculty can also have theirs here in the Common Room." Sarah indicated a somewhat tarnished urn on a tray with an array of cups that sat on a side table. "I suppose someone keeps it supplied. Arlene or Linda, maybe. Then there's a hot plate with water in the Fellows' Room for us and any others, like the adjuncts."

"Adjuncts?"

"Sort of semi-faculty without official status, temporary lecturers filling in gaps. Real nonentities as far as the department is concerned, more so even than the teaching fellows. But none of those were around last night."

"For which I'm grateful," said George. He turned to a knock. "Yes, Deputy, come on in. That's all, Sarah. Your Thermos will be impounded, as will the others, of course, and I'll be seeing you later this afternoon, around five." And then, looking up, "Come in, Alex."

Alex, face crimson with cold, dark hair snow-crusted, stood, stamping his feet at the entrance; as he moved toward Sarah, George indicated the door. "Later this afternoon, then."

Finding herself excused, Sarah made her way back to the waiting room. Here she found, on the edge of their chairs, the two English Office clerks, Linda and Arlene, plus a magenta-faced Constance Garvey, all being guarded by the efficient Deputy Cohen. Collecting her coat, she heard Professor Garvey threaten the deputy in a furious whisper for the unlawful search of her briefcase and office while the two clerks poked each other and smiled. Sarah nodded to them and made her way downstairs to the door to the North Quad, where she paused to read a sheet announcing the cancellation of all English classes and asking all personnel and students with connections in the department to report to the State Police Office in the Faculty Common Room. Well, classes wouldn't be canceled forever, Sarah thought, and she had papers to correct and library research to do—useful distractions, all of them.

She opened the door and shrank back for a moment as

the cold sheet of air slammed against her face. Then, butting her head into the wind, she pushed her way through a narrow slot of snow to the library. Here she fell into the well-worn routine of marking student papers, finishing *Antony and Cleopatra* for Ivan Lacey's seminar, and beginning Swift's *Battle of the Books*.

It wasn't until the library reading-room clock chimed three-thirty that she came up for air and began to wonder what more she could possibly say to George Fitts. Blast it, here she was up to her ears in another murder mess. And Alex too. But Alex—he seemed to thrive on these terrible puzzles, or at least was drawn in by the medical questions. She, Sarah, had stumbled into those past accidents and now look, just when they both were trying to settle down and see if they liked living together in what was billed as the peace of rural New England . . . and yet there was Alice Marmott. The death of Alice demanded attention. From all of them. And the death of Rosalind Parker. "Damn," she said suddenly aloud, slamming volume one of the *Works of Jonathan Swift* down on the library table.

"Please, I'm trying to study," said a young woman opposite Sarah. "Go have your fit somewhere else."

Sarah nodded an apology, packed her books, and made her way through the frozen passages to the cafeteria to see if real food and multiple cups of tea would restore equanimity. Here she found Drago Collins in the center of a huddle of graduate students. From his gestures she knew he was re-enacting last evening's events just as he had been warned not to. She slipped around his audience and caught up with Mary at the end of the cafeteria line.

"Amos Larkin has now absolutely disappeared," said Mary, as they settled at a table. "How he got out in one piece I'll never know."

"George Fitts will," said Sarah. "He'll know when he left, how he left, and where he is now. Speaking of which, where does Professor Larkin go to? Around here?"

"He lives in that old gray clapboard farmhouse on the hill just beyond the soccer field. There's a field of cows and a ski trail that goes by. I looked up his address once, just in case."

"In case of what? Honestly, Mary, what *is* it about Amos

Larkin? So okay, if he straightens out he might be interesting, but now he's nothing but trouble. You're not in the Salvation Army, are you? Do you feel you have some sort of mission?"

"It's more complicated. Not just the eighteenth-century connection. I said I'd tell you about our parking lot adventure."

"Now's the time," said Sarah. "But the way you're going, you're going to end up as an abused person."

"When I first had him as an undergraduate, he wasn't this bad, only an occasional hangover. A weekend souse, so people said. Well, that's when I got interested in the eighteenth century—Pope, Johnson, Swift, and all those—because Amos was so damn sharp in class. Then one day, a late Saturday afternoon beginning my second year in graduate school, I was coming over to the department on my bicycle and I cut through the department parking lot to the sidewalk. I suppose I wasn't looking, because *wham!* there he was."

"What do you mean 'wham'?"

"Literally. His car just went right through the parking space, over the curb, and onto the sidewalk into a railing. And me. Knocked my bike right out from under me."

"What happened to you, for God's sake?"

"I was lucky. I went off and landed in a pile of leaves. Had my wind knocked out and felt like I'd been shaken by a rat."

"No, you'd been hit by one."

"Listen, will you? I took inventory and I was okay and my bike was almost in one piece. He'd just spun it around, caught it with his fender, and bent my wheel."

"Romantic as hell. Did he carry you tenderly to the emergency room?"

"Not exactly. It was a sort of hit-and-run without the run. By the time I'd stood up and looked myself over, he'd passed out in his car. He'd been drinking and lost control."

"You're damn lucky not to be dead or mangled."

"I know, but then after I saw I was in one piece, I decided to go my way. I mean I was mad as hell, but I didn't see any point in charging him with attempted manslaughter or anything like that."

"It might have been beneficial if you had. And maybe saved someone else."

"Yes, but I didn't want to start yelling police and have him arrested, because even if I was mad I did admire him. Anyway, that's all there is to the affair, and I'm not really looking at him as a lost sheep, so if it's not Swift and Pope, it's probably chemistry or because I like men who have voices like Richard Burton."

"Try and find someone with a voice like Placido Domingo and you'll live longer."

"Well, I don't want some pure-living doctoral candidate, voice or no voice. It's better like this. I can think about Amos, but since nothing can come of it, it doesn't use up much of my time, and I can get on with my work. Let's say he's a sort of hobby."

"He's a lot more hazardous. He's a menace, and twice lately he's been very close to a murder. That should put the fear of something into you. I'll bet it gives George Fitts something to chew on."

It did that. George lifted Amos Larkin's folder from the stack and slapped it on his desk. "I'm giving Professor Larkin the morning to recover from his drunk, and then if the D.A. doesn't decide to hold him, I'm going to put him through a session that should keep him sober for a week."

"Or send him back to the bottle," said Alex. "Who's on deck now?"

George ran his finger down a list. "The two clerks, plus Horst, Garvey, and Fletcher and, if I can fit them in, Professors Bello and Merlin-Smith. Sarah's coming back at five with Mary Donelli."

"What about Mrs. Parker's house, her neighbors?"

"That's for tonight. There's a team over there now. We'll clean it out as fast as possible. Mrs. Parker has a cousin who wants to hold a service in the house before the burial—when we've finished with the autopsy."

"What have you found in the offices? A supply of poison, a loaded Thermos?"

"We've made a Thermos collection and found other drinking material. Quite a collection of hard liquor," said George with disapproval. "Amos Larkin isn't the only one taking a nip. Two candy addicts—giant Hershey bars hidden in Kleenex boxes—plus assorted pills and powders, all of which the lab will tackle. One thing: It does indeed look as if Mrs. Parker was considering another job. We found her résumé in at least five offices and fifteen copies in her files."

"Why on earth hand her résumé around the English Department if she was looking for another place? You usually don't advertise if you're planning to leave."

"Perhaps she was asking for a raise or was under notice and was trying to be retained. I've made a note to ask the chairman."

"Sarah tells me she was a very positive character—in a commanding-officer kind of way. Acted like she owned the department. Not like someone about to be booted out."

"It will all come out in good time," said George. "In the meantime I've asked Mike Laaka to stop by and sit in because he says he knows one of the clerks and he seems to be able to make people relax. Something I don't attempt. They're both out there waiting, Arlene Burr and Linda Lacroix."

Linda came first. Thin, tight purple sweater, short purple skirt, high boots, a mane of blond hair, a sharp little chin, and eye makeup that would have done Nefertiti proud.

"That snow," she said, shrugging off her coat, a synthetic orange fur. "I was stuck in the women's gym. Wild. All those students I can do without in the daytime, let alone spend the night with." She sat down and then said, as if mindful that she had an official duty to be devastated, "Oh, God. Poor Mrs. Parker. Was it sudden? Like I mean she was okay last night. On the warpath as usual. Poor Mrs. Parker," Linda repeated, without conviction.

George put Linda through her paces, and what emerged between the lines was a version of Mrs. Parker that approximated one of the more heavy-handed Caesars. Alex, sitting off to the side of George's desk, made sympathetic noises.

"Yeah, really," said Linda. "She made sure we did everything perfect or back it'd come. And back. Which was a real pain because everyone makes mistakes, and I never thought Professor Bello cared too much because he's sort of casual, not always with it, if you know what I mean. Not that I had anything against Mrs. Parker, but she made the English Office into a sort of boot camp."

"Did she spend much time in there with you?" asked George.

"Not spend. She bombed in and out, checking up. Arlene got it more in the butt—I mean in the tail—because she hasn't been there as long as I have and didn't know the routine that well."

"Can you run through a typical day with you both and Mrs. Parker?" asked George.

But George and Alex learned that no day was typical. Usually the two clerks sorted the mail, printed up copies of book lists, class lists, English major lists, exams, departmental memos, plus copies of periodical articles requested by the faculty.

"But everything went through her hands first," said Linda. "She didn't trust us an inch, and I've been here five years and am getting my B.S. in June in business night school. Telephone calls—we didn't even have the switchboard. Mrs. Parker saw the mail before we sorted it, and brought us stuff she didn't want to bother with herself. Of course, she was a whiz typist and she typed faculty manuscripts—you know that publish-or-perish stuff they're supposed to turn out. At least she used to." Here Linda stopped and gazed at her burgundy finger nails with some satisfaction.

"Used to?" said Alex on cue.

"Yeah. She was first lady typist to almost all the faculty until the word processor and printer showed up. Well, I'm pretty good at technical stuff, and I've had two courses, so I got the hang of it pretty easy and helped teach Arlene. Pretty soon the faculty and the fellows were slipping us work to do, and Herself didn't like it one bit." Linda smiled, crossed her booted legs, wiggled her pelvis, and thrust her pointed chin and two pointed breasts at George.

George sat unblinking. "Mrs. Parker was envious of your computer know-how," he said.

"She said she hated the computer, that the personal element was lost, so maybe she was jealous of us. She hated the faculty coming in, leaving their manuscripts, making jokes, using our coffee machine. We'd stay late sometimes to get something out for one of them, and that would piss her off.

Because she was the one who did that sort of thing—staying late and being noble."

"Then she often did stay late like last night."

"Yes, but I don't know why last night. Fussing with her files or doing some special typing. She never told us what she was up to. Maybe being that her husband was dead, she didn't have much to go home to. She always talked a blue streak about team effort, but if we were a team I didn't notice it. Like we were serfs and she was Queen Guinevere and the rest of the faculty mucky-mucks were Sir Gawain and knights of the Round Table." George made a note, and Alex reflected that Arthurian matter had somehow filtered into the English Office.

"And you took care of the hot water for the hot drinks in the department?" said George. "Tell me exactly how that worked."

"We keep the big coffee machine going in our office and a pot of hot water for tea or cocoa. Everyone's supposed to leave money, but not everyone does. We supply the Faculty Common Room, but the fellows come in and get the stuff for their own room from us. And, like I said, some of the faculty stop around and have a cup while we do some copying for them—just to waste some time, I guess. Sometimes they fill up a Thermos when they've got appointments through lunchtime. I know Professor Larkin has a Thermos because he dropped it once and the glass inside smashed and whiskey smelled up the whole hall."

"And Mrs. Parker had her own Thermos?"

"Yes, with her name stuck on with tape and the college seal on it. They sell them in the bookstore—expensive, a real rip-off. Parker would get her hot water in our office and take her Thermos back to her office. She'd wash it out in the ladies' room and keep it on her desk along with a supply of cocoa."

"Did you all get your cocoa from one big community container?" asked Alex, thinking it was time to zero in on what must be topic A.

Linda looked shocked. "No way. That isn't sanitary. They used to have a big jar and one spoon, but after I got here I put a stop to that. It's a wonder they didn't all have trench mouth. I bought these little packets for cocoa and coffee, and tea bags too. And then when some people like Mrs. Parker wanted diet cocoa, I added no-cal packs, and now some people are asking for decaf tea and decaf coffee packs. It's turning into a real drag."

Real drag is right, thought Alex, as he considered the difficulties of poisoning anyone through their chosen drink. "Did Mrs. Parker take any regular medicine that you know of?"

"How do you mean? Did she do drugs, or just take aspirin?"

"Any of that."

"Well, not that I know of. I've seen Bufferin on her desk, and once I saw some diet candy in her open drawer when she called me in. I asked her if she was trying for a bikini in the summer, just a dumb joke, but you didn't joke with that lady. She bit my head off like I was spying on her."

"Tensions?" asked Alex, seizing on what might be the theme in Linda's answers.

"Oh, sure, tensions. Get this done, copy that, Professor Fletcher wants it by three, Professor Garvey doesn't like the class lists being late, the bookstore wants the order. Push, push. Old crab."

Here Linda paused, realizing she had again spoken harshly of the dead, but she was mercifully spared further indiscretions by the arrival of Mike Laaka, who blew into the room like a gust of north wind, tossed his fur hat on a chair, draped his jacket over another, and grinned at Linda.

"Hey, there, it's Linda Lovely. They got you on the hot seat, Linda?" He turned to Alex and George. "Linda worked for the Sheriff's Department for a while. Didn't know you had a job in a classy place like this."

"Classy is as classy does," said Linda, visibly cheering. "After a couple of murders, this place isn't so classy as it thinks it is."

George sighed. "I'll fill you in on Linda's statement so far. Later." Mike, although introducing a note of familiarity, might also distract a witness whom George was bringing into the proper stage of intimidation.

Mike grinned at Alex, put his feet on a low table covered with periodicals, and turned to Linda. "So who killed Mrs.

Parker, Linda? Any ideas about her? Was she Lady Bountiful or Mrs. Bitch?"

"You may answer the deputy's question, Miss Lacroix," said George.

"Hello, Mike, or do I have to call you deputy or something? Long time no see. Well, Mrs. Parker was a bitch or a lady bountiful depending on who you were. Arlene and I didn't come in for much of the bountiful business, but she dripped all over some of the faculty. The men, anyway. Brought in homemade cookies, flowers from her garden, that sort of stuff."

"Any special favorites?" said Mike.

"Oh, she spread the shit around pretty evenly." Linda, far from being intimidated, settled back in her chair and appeared to be enjoying herself. Mike Laaka with his handsome broad face, his very blue eyes, could, Alex thought, be counted on to warm up the women. Especially the likes of Linda, so carefully dressed to accentuate her finer points. Mike was looking at two of them right now with a kindly eye.

"Professor Bello probably got more attention than the others," Linda went on. "Him being the chairman and all that. He's not much on looks because he's sort of moth-eaten, but he's the boss."

"From whom all blessings flow," said Alex.

"Perks, salary schedule, office assignments, committees, you know. Of course, she had her hate list. Like Garvey and Vera Pruczak. You ask me, she was jealous of Vera, who didn't give her the time of day and called everyone 'darling.' And she pretended to cooperate with Garvey, but that was more . . ."

"Shit?" said Mike.

George gave Mike a look and nodded to Linda. "Thank you, Miss Lacroix. Leave your address and your work schedule with Deputy Cohen in the waiting room. Mike," he said, after Linda, wiggling her neat little fanny, had sauntered out of the room, "don't encourage her."

"Come off it, you've learned something. No love between Garvey, Pruczak, and Parker. Now I've got a prelim on the search of Parker's house." Mike produced his notebook. "The team's still in there, but for what it's worth, Parker was a member of the Book-of-the-Month, the Methodist Church, and the DAR. She's got mail from the Republican Party, catalogs from all over, gets *Time, House and Garden, People, Consumer's Digest,* the *Bowmouth Alumni Magazine,* and *PMLA.*"

"What's *PMLA*?" said George.

"Glad you asked. Publication of the Modern Language Association of America."

Alex leaned over and twitched a blue and white periodical from under Mike's ankle. "You've got your feet on one. Sarah gets it. Learned articles on English studies. Mrs. Parker probably felt she had to keep up—especially if she was typing manuscripts the faculty submitted to it."

"Nothing much more in the house except she has a room set aside as a home office and her bookcase is full of books by the English faculty, all signed. *To Rosalind with many thanks,* et cetera, et cetera. The house is small to medium, with a garden and a garage out back. The neighbors say she's never done anything to make them sit up and take notice except maybe complain about a dog chasing her cat. The cat's boarding next door now."

"So," said George, "if you can keep it low key, Mike, we'll have the other clerk in. Arlene Burr. That Linda was quite helpful."

"And very sharp," said Alex. "I doubt if she's missed many tricks."

"I agree," said George. "I think she'll open up more in time."

"She needs appreciative attention, which is what I'm good at," said Mike. "People like to have humans around."

Arlene Burr turned out to be Linda's opposite. While Linda was on the edge of being scrawny, Arlene was simply comfortable. Where Linda's eyes were shrewd and watchful, Arlene's were open and untroubled. Arlene had dark hair pulled back with two hair clips, was round-faced and full-lipped. Zipped into her padded coat she reminded Alex of an ambulatory quilt. This taken off she sat revealed, plump in all dimensions.

George took her through the same questions as he had Linda, and except for an occasional giggle or a look of real distress, her answers were much in the same vein. Mrs. Parker ruled with a strong hand and pounced in and out of the English Office.

"Linda got all hot about it because she thought she could run the department as well as Mrs. Parker. It didn't bother me because this is just a job, but Linda's ambitious. When she gets her degree she wants to move up."

"In the English Department?" asked Alex.

"Well, somewhere, but with Queen Bee Parker around, she didn't stand a chance. There was really too much work for Parker to handle it all, but she tried. To her we were second-class citizens. We were to call the faculty 'Professor' and be respectful. No first names. I mean, *really*. Of course, people like Vera Pruczak said call me 'Vera' and some others too. But like I said, she never got to me the way she did Linda." Arlene paused, giggled, turned sober, and said, "But I suppose I'm sorry she's dead because we might get someone worse, and besides it must mean that what with Alice Marmott being killed too, we've got a maniac loose in the department."

George brought Arlene to a halt by handing her a sheet of paper. "Did you type the original of that for her?"

Arlene bent over Mrs. Parker's résumé, read it carefully, and then shook her head. "No, I didn't, and Linda didn't either. At least not on our typewriters. We have Smith-Coronas and this looks like Mrs. Parker's IBM. And the copy isn't made on our copy machine, the paper's too heavy. But I've seen it before. Just a look. Professor Bello came into our office when Mrs. Parker was in on one of her raids, and he put it right on the table next to me. He said he knew how valuable she was without seeing it written up, and then she snatched it and said it was just for his file, and then they both went out into the hall, and I think he said something like 'Rosalind, you know how impossible it is.' "

"Did you ever see her depressed, unhappy, or ill?" said Alex.

"Oh, sure, she had her moods. We knew some days we had to keep our heads down. Linda said she was probably going through the change, but I think it was mostly when something in the department came unstuck—which it did a lot. I mean the computer class cards got messed up sometimes, or one of the faculty wouldn't turn up for an appointment. But she never stayed home. I mean even if she had flu and was spreading bugs all over the place, she'd come in because she was afraid the whole place would fall on the floor without her, or one of us would get into her office and fool around with her files."

"Anything unhinged her lately?" asked Mike.

Arlene bit a nail thoughtfully and then nodded. "Alice Marmott's campaign against Professor Horst. The fur sure flew on that one. We heard them going at it in the hall once when our door was open. Parker telling Alice that Professor Horst was conscientious and had a reason for what he did, and no, she couldn't have an appointment, and yes, if Alice had her petition with the class signatures on it, why, she'd be glad to take care of it."

"And Alice didn't buy it," said Alex.

"Alice had a soft voice so I couldn't hear her exactly, but it was something about the whole class going to the dean. Anyway, that whole day Mrs. Parker stomped around blowing steam, and I'll bet when Alice turned up dead Mrs. Parker wasn't all that sorry."

"Did you ever see them together after that day?" asked George, and Alex suddenly began to see the impossible connection might just be possible.

"The night of the hockey game," said Arlene promptly. "Mrs. Parker saw Alice in her office and then took her into the Common Room. I was just leaving, but I heard her tell Alice that they'd be more private in there."

Alex gave George time to note this bombshell by returning to Mrs. Parker's fatal drink. "Do you put cocoa packets in the Common Room?"

"We take in the fresh water for the coffee and take out the dirty cups like we were some sort of maid, and the cleaning people vacuum at night and tidy up. We check the tea bag supply and put out a bowl of cocoa packets like we have in our office. The cocoa disappears fast. I think Professor Garvey sneaks the no-cal ones and takes them home."

"She does?" said George, alert.

"She dropped her handbag once in our office and everything spilled out, including five of those packets. She's a cheapskate. Voted against a raise for the clerical staff last year."

"Okay, Arlene," said Mike, who often grew impatient with George's careful interrogations. "Who didn't like Mrs. Parker? Whose toes did she stomp on?" And Alex had a view of a high-heeled Mrs. Parker doing a flamenco on numerous exposed bare feet.

"That was funny too," said Arlene, to whom much of what Mrs. Parker did seemed that way. "A lot of toes. Like she always seemed to have the last word. There'd be a big dust-up about some department proposal and everyone would run around having conferences in each other's offices, and then Mrs. Parker would get into the act and visit around, and then there'd be a faculty meeting—she always sat in on those—and everything would be settled her way, only Professor Bello's name would be on the memo. You'd have thought she was chairman."

"Give us an example of Mrs. Parker getting her way," said George.

"The electric heat one year ago," said Arlene. "Thank God she did, but it was one big rumble. The waiting room used to be a seminar room and the clerks used to be squashed into the mail room and Mrs. Parker used our office. Then she began working on the idea of having her own special place— the office across the hall. Only Garvey was in there. Well, the Dean gave approval to have the seminar room turned into a waiting room because students hanging around for appointments just sat on the hall floor or leaned against doors getting in everyone's way. When the okay came through, they put in electric baseboard heating because the waiting room was always too cold. No proper radiators there. When the workman were here, Mrs. Parker got busy and didn't stop until Garvey got moved next to Vera Pruczak—they cut one office into two —and Parker got Garvey's old office complete with electric heating. We got heat in the English Office too."

"Then the baseboard heating was for those three rooms only," said Alex. "The English Office, Mrs. Parker's new office, and the waiting room. But how could a secretary move a tenured faculty member just like that? It's impossible."

"Mrs. Parker always ran around saying nothing's impossible. And for her I guess it wasn't. She was all smiles for weeks. I used to call her Miss Piggy, all sweetness and an iron hoof. If you're looking for an enemy, I'd say Garvey would like to have killed her. She hates being in that little office."

Arlene, dismissed, stood up to leave, but Alex held up his hand. "One more thing. Linda called Mrs. Parker 'Herself' and you called her the Queen Bee and Miss Piggy. Did she have any other names . . . ones you gave her or anyone else?"

Arlene grinned. "Linda had a whole bunch. Herself, Her Majesty, the Queen of Sheba, Guinevere. Let's see—I heard Professor Horst say "damn bitch" once, but I'm not absolutely sure he meant Mrs. Parker. Professor Larkin would come into our office and say, 'Where's Nosy Parker?' and one of the fellows, Mary Donelli, who's always making cracks, called her Lady Cashmere because of those expensive sweaters she wears. Professor Fletcher called her Mission Control. That's about it, except Garvey said 'Mrs. Parker' like she wanted to curdle your blood—oh, and Vera Pruczak never called Mrs. Parker 'darling.'"

Arlene buttoned up her padded coat and departed, and Mike grinned at Alex. "Like I've always said, just another blackboard jungle. Chew, snap, tear, swallow. These ivy-covered walls don't fool me. And how about those cocoa packets? Why, Garvey probably took them home and slipped in the poison—cyanide, wasn't it, George?"

George stood up, walked to the window, and scowled at the snow-filled scene below—a phenomenon beyond his jurisdiction and management. He returned to his table and made several notes. "Yes, cyanide. All lab results so far, the clinical symptoms, point to it. Autopsy this afternoon. But don't go jumping the gun on Professor Garvey. Not many of them liked Mrs. Parker."

"But you know," said Mike, "most good secretaries attract enemies like some kind of magnet."

Alex grinned. "Mike, are you about to be reasonable?"

"Listen, secretaries have to deflect bullets for their bosses and they have to run an office. If the secretary is a pussycat, then all those inflated egos would bump into each other."

Alex stood up and in his turn inspected the view from the window. He saw a man and woman walking slowly past a snowbank, their arms around each other, and he thought of Sarah and the quiet good life in a sleepy New England winter.

"Executive types don't make friends," Mike was saying.

Alex sighed and came back to his chair. "Even the most executive secretaries aren't usually murdered."

George pressed a portable intercom button, newly installed. "I have Vera Pruczak on deck, then Professor Merlin-Smith. Alex, I'd like you to stay, but they'll be starting the autopsy in a few minutes. Take your choice."

Alex, weighing the attractions of a live and voluble Vera Pruczak and a most silent Mrs. Parker, chose the dead over the quick. He stood up. "I'll check up on some hospital patients at the same time and come back."

George nodded and turned to Mike. "I'll start with Miss Pruczak, if you'll check with the college heating engineers and find out why the electric heat failed here last night. It didn't in any other building. I can see the telephone being disconnected by the murderer, but I'm not sure why the heating. Then come back here."

The departure of the two men was interrupted by the arriving Vera Pruczak, who cried out, "Alex McKenzie, it's you, darling. Now can't you just spare one minute and read for me? I think you *will* do for Albany, because you're not right for Edgar, and Gloucester is probably beyond you. Hello there, Sergeant Fitts. Isn't this all too Sherlockian, and it's Deputy Laaka, isn't it? You got me for speeding last summer down by Chickawaukie Pond. I tried to talk you out of it, but you were absolutely steadfast. A credit to your uniform."

"I'm plainclothes," said Mike, "and you were doing eighty."

"Nothing ventured, nothing gained," said Vera. "You're not going, both of you? Because I always do better with an audience. All right, Sergeant Fitts. Shoot. Where was I on the night of the murder? Answer, naked as a jay and shivering in a cold bath in that damn women's dormitory in the garret of the Faculty Club, that's where."

Alex left feeling like the butler whose exit has been topped by the leading lady. He made his way through the narrow corridors of snow past the parking lot, noticing that although no car was yet visible, a plow was blowing a funnel of snow into the air over by the rim of the lot so there was a good chance that by tonight the stranded population would be free to leave. He hoped that some agency, civic or miraculous, had cleared Sawmill Road so that he and Sarah could retreat and for a little space of time pull up the drawbridge, sit by the stove, watch the snow come down against the window, and then make love.

But later, standing by the autopsy table listening to the pathologist expound to two watching residents on the merits of Mrs. Parker's organs and the efficiency of cyanide as a killer, Alex was once again reminded of the great insult of violent death. It hung over them all, and, like Sarah, he saw Alice and Rosalind Parker demanding attention, demanding sacrifice of time, intelligence, and effort. A scarf strangler, a Thermos bottle poisoner was loose at Bowmouth, right now going his or her way, perhaps meeting classes, counseling students, giving lectures, and perhaps even trying to decide about the next victim. Should it be the scarf again, or something new? The pillow, the ax, the hit-and-run? No, Alex told himself resignedly, this was not the time for the drawbridge.

Mike Laaka joined them for the final stages of the postmortem. He watched as the pathologist took his last tissue samples, finished with his slides, sluiced down the table, and then pulled a sheet back over what was left of Mrs. Parker.

"Some lady," said Mike. "There's going to be a power vacuum in that department. But you know none of the faculty I've run into strike me as exactly docile, as if they wanted someone to run them." Then, as he and Alex turned to leave, "So what showed on the post? Anything besides cyanide poisoning?"

Alex looked grim. "Matter of fact, yes. Double mastectomy about three years ago, they think. I don't know if she was in a remission or what. They'll be looking at the slides."

"My God, you mean Mrs. Parker had cancer?"

"Apparently. But the surgery wasn't done at this hospital. We're checking with the Maine hospitals and in Boston for a start. Also to see if she's been getting chemotherapy. No record here."

"Doesn't this put suicide in the picture?"

"Yes, but why would you do it by staying late at work in the middle of a snowstorm?"

"Say she'd just had a bad report, the cancer had spread. She'd want to die in harness. She lived and breathed the English Department. You know that might explain about those résumés turning up. Not for a new job, for her obituary. Making sure the facts are straight and properly complimentary. Let's hit the cafeteria for coffee before we have to listen to this Merlin-hyphen-Smith, who's been off on sick call. He's sort of interesting because he's been to Cambridge like Larkin. But man, this cancer business makes it a whole new ball game."

Over coffee, Alex persuaded Mike to put the suicide theory on hold and sum up George's progress.

"I went back in the middle of the Pruczak event. She is some kind of comedian. At first I thought she was going to audition George on the spot. Said he was a special type and there was a part in her *King Lear* production—Edmund, she said. I gather Edmund was a very questionable type."

"She didn't offer you a part?"

"Just looked at me and shook her head. Anyway, Pruczak said she left the English Department when Parker was still in her own office at her typewriter. This was about seven o'clock and only Fletcher, Garvey, and this guy Merlin-Smith were still rambling around. Arlene and Linda were in their coats getting ready to leave. She didn't see Larkin because, as we know, he was passed out in the waiting room. Pruczak said she decided to go on over to the Faculty Club to find a room without someone like Garvey in it. Nothing more of interest except she saw Sarah and Mary Donelli in the hall earlier and met Ivan Lacey coming up the stairs. Seems he'd forgotten something."

"A lot of them seemed to have forgotten something that night. Who else did George work over?"

"A whole mob of the grad students, lecturers, other oddballs. He went through them like a machine gun. The Fellows' Room gang were having a poker game and punch bowl sing-along and didn't hear anything all night—or if they did they don't remember. That Collins guy said he got up when it was still dark to take a leak in the men's room and saw the light on in the English Office but didn't think much about it—I'd say he doesn't think much about much—and didn't see any other lights. Nobody else claims they used the men's room, but two others said they used an empty beaker for a urinal."

"Fascinating," said Alex.

"So except for Collins helping Sarah and Mary lug Professor Lushwell into his own office, the poker party stayed put with the door closed. Look, that session with Merlin-Smith should be under way. Make that Merlin-Wimp. He heehaws and acts like he's a star of the department, but I'd say he's a real loser. Anyway, George wanted you to drop in."

It was obvious to Alex when he walked into the Common Room that George had been exercising some of the more iron aspects of his personality, and Professor Merlin-Smith was not heehawing. Alex took a seat at the far side of the room and, picking up the thread, gathered that this particular member of the English faculty had been on campus during the estimated times of Alice's death, had taken to his bed with flu thereafter, and had just resurfaced in time to be suspected of both murders. Tall, bony, slack of eye and jowl, his elongated face folded into a pattern of misery, Professor Merlin-Smith shifted about in his chair as if it had tacks on it.

"So," George was saying, "you weren't baptized Merlin-Smith, were you? I have some records here that say you were Eustace Earl Schmidt when you were in high school and when you entered Princeton."

"Merlin was my mother's name," said the unhappy professor. "I chose it as a compliment to her. Merlin doesn't go with Schmidt."

"I see," said George. He snapped his ballpoint pen up and down several times with a repeated *click-click.* "You took the double name after you'd come home from Cambridge."

"I may have then . . . yes."

"Were you at Cambridge at the same time as Professor Larkin?"

"I don't know if we overlapped. It's a large university. We were in different colleges. I was at Downing."

"And you learned that there was a little more prestige in a hyphenated name. Schmidt was dull compared with Merlin-Smith."

The professor pulled at his knitted tie. "I don't think you have the right to insult—to cross-examine in this manner."

It was a final effort. George stood up and leaned forward on his table. "I have the right, Professor Smith, to ask any question I consider necessary to help me understand why two persons associated with the English Department were murdered. If you changed your name, you may have changed something else. You may have altered records, you may be lying about your relations with Alice Marmott and Mrs. Parker. Do you know, Professor Smith"—this as the professor shrank back into his buttoned gray cardigan, becoming to Alex's eyes almost concave—"that Alice Marmott was strangled with a long scarf, the kind worn by British students at British schools and universities, and that we have that scarf? I imagine you own just such a scarf. Perhaps several, since you are no doubt proud of your association with Cambridge University and this Downing College. And now you may go, professor. We will call you again."

"My God, George," said Alex, after the professor had fumbled his way out of the room. "What are you doing to that man? Have you found cyanide in his desk?"

"No," said George, closing his notebook and lifting out a new folder. "But I've been in touch with Princeton. He started his undergraduate program there, but he didn't finish."

"You mean he's a fraud, bought his diploma?"

"Not necessarily. But he may have gotten his degree from a place less distinguished than Princeton. We're running down his records."

"But his scarf wasn't found around Alice's neck. Larkin's was."

"He may not have found that out. I want him to start thinking. And we've found this note in his office, clipped to a copy of one of Mrs. Parker's résumés. *Please realize that what you ask is highly improper. I think I've done enough and have always been cooperative. Please reconsider.* It's signed *E.M.S.* Now add this to Sarah's memory of Professor Lacey saying something was impossible, to Arlene's of Howard Bello saying the same, and to Drago Collins's recollection—this when I interviewed him—of Professor Horst slamming out of Mrs. Parker's office saying something like 'The hell I will. There's a limit.' And the same résumé was found in Horst's office. In fact, every one of the senior faculty got the résumé except Vera Pruczak and a Professor Joseph Greenberg, who checks out clear of both murders. He's just back from a symposium on the West Coast. Office next to Larkin's. So now, what about the autopsy? Anything besides cyanide?"

"I'm afraid so," said Alex. And he told George about the mastectomy, adding, "It makes suicide a possibility."

"Suicide in the department office, not in her own—or not at home? Well, it's possible, but for now I'll go on considering it a homicide. And the two homicides may be connected since we now know that Alice and Mrs. Parker met together in the English Department before the game—and not by accident, since they both mentioned an appointment. Well, as you know, I fish. It's a matter of waiting. The proper bait, the quiet line. The English Department is a very interesting pool."

Alex stood up. "A contaminated pool, I'd say—or maybe it's the old cigars in here. I'm going along to try and catch Sarah before she comes to see you. It's almost five."

Alex saw Sarah coming through the arch that led to the North Quad, head bent, collar up to her ears, briefcase clasped in her arms.

"Wait a minute," he said, steering Sarah over to a dormitory entrance.

"George said five and it's three minutes to. You know George."

"Time he developed some flex. Look, I have to work late. Meet me in the hospital dining room for dinner."

"Candlelight and hamburger flambé. Okay. Not much choice since you have the car. Mind if Mary comes?"

"Of course not. And don't let George get to you. I've just watched him unravel one of your faculty."

"Consider me warned," and Sarah took off down the path toward Malcolm Adam Hall.

Sarah arrived before Mary Donelli and was introduced to Professor Joseph Greenberg, a tall, lanky individual with bushy black hair, high cheekbones, and dark eyes framed by wire-rimmed glasses. He smiled an angular friendly smile, cut George Fitts short at the word "professor," and said, "I'm Joe

Greenberg and you're the new teaching fellow. Welcome to Bowmouth, though you're probably wondering why on earth you decided to get mixed up with this particular college." Another smile and he was gone, leaving Sarah to savor the agreeable notion that here was one well-disposed human attached to the department. Sitting down on the indicated chair, Sarah thought that all the scene needed was a maid arriving with a tray set with tea things and a decanter of sherry. The curtains were drawn, the ashtrays had been emptied, and the lamplight hid the elderly overused furniture. George sat at one of the Common Room writing tables, his bald head illuminated like a globe from an overhead wall sconce light.

"Mary Donelli is late," said George with disapproval.

"She probably has a class," said Sarah. "You can't just leave your students, even for the police."

"Yes, you can," said Mary, bursting in. "And I did, but then I ran into Joe Greenberg coming out. I hope he's innocent."

"Professor Greenberg was in San Francisco during the suspected time period," said George primly.

"Well, good for him," said Mary. "The department needs all the honest people it can hang onto."

George clicked his pen up and down, a sure sign that he felt time was wasting. "I've been discussing Bowmouth with Professor Greenberg. The problem of why Alice Marmott chose Bowmouth. Can you tell me why a student like Alice would choose a small New England college when she had very good scholarship offers in Ohio? Mike Laaka suggests Ivy League snob appeal."

"Almost Ivy League," said Mary. "Almost but not quite. I think it's Bowmouth's special program for exceptional students. It's quite well known. Hunks of money: complete scholarships with a chance to find work on the campus, the library, in the hospital, the cafeteria."

"Top people on the faculty?" said George.

"Well," said Mary, "they *have* managed to snag a few big names. In our department, there's Horst, who, even if you don't like him, has published a long poetry series, and Professor Fletcher has a whole shelf of Old English commentaries plus a monster study of *Beowulf,* and Amos Larkin has written studies on Swift and Pope. Even Lacey's done some things a while back, and Joe Greenberg has a raft of published articles, *PMLA, Studies in the Novel,* and so on. Of course, the department always has a few established poets drifting around."

"There's Vera Pruczak," said Sarah. "Though," she added thoughtfully, "I don't suppose she'd have been much of a drawing card for Alice because Alice didn't strike me as the type to be attracted by a writer of gothic romances. She seemed more like a pre-nineteenth-century type—even pre-sixteenth-century."

"I am reading one of Olivia Macbeth's novels," said George, looking as if he had been sucking lemons. "They are exaggerated and quite violent. Now," he said in one of his sudden switches of subject, "can you think of any reason for Mrs. Parker to be wanting to leave Bowmouth—or to have had her job terminated?"

"Lord, no," said Mary. "You mean that résumé, the one we saw in Professor Larkin's office? Mrs. Parker almost owned the English Department—or acted like it. And who would dare fire her?"

"President Truman fired MacArthur," said Sarah.

"It would have to be like that," said Mary. "Right from the chancellor, because Professor Bello doesn't act as if he had the stomach for it and the dean is wishy-washy. Of course, Garvey has probably been yearning to do it, but she hasn't the clout."

"What if the whole faculty got together and agreed to remove her?" suggested Sarah.

"The whole faculty couldn't agree on anything like that. They can't even agree about the freshman comp exams," said Mary.

George acknowledged this truth since his interviews with the English faculty had certainly demonstrated the force of Mary's statement. He then led the conversation back to the discovery of the body, went over the timetable once again, and then dismissed them with one more question. Had Mrs. Parker a voice, was she known to sing? Anywhere?

"I know zilch about Mrs. Parker's private life," said Mary, "but I've never heard her warbling in her office or in the halls."

"Sing?" said Sarah, puzzled. Then, thinking of Vera Pruczak and *The Mikado*, "You mean on stage, a performance?"

"Choir," said George. "My men have reported a choir robe among her things. Or something like it."

"Not that I've heard of, but I haven't been here long enough." Sarah said this again, trying to make it clear to George once and for all that she was a newcomer to the department and a poor source of information. Then, as a robed and coiffed Mrs. Parker rose before her, "She might have done as Katisha."

"Or Poor Little Buttercup," said Mary.

"The trouble is," said George, who rarely acknowledged trouble, "that I can rely on so few in the department for disinterested information, so your being new might be an advantage, Sarah. No one at the college seems to know about her singing, but Miss Prism has told me that she went regularly to church, so my men are going to check with the church choirmaster. Now I thank you both and good night."

"I suppose," said Mary, as they made their way down the stairs, "by 'disinterested' he doesn't mean me, because I expect someone has told him that I've been mooning after Amos. Which I really haven't. It's all an act . . . pure fiction."

"Of course."

"Who needs a catastrophe like Amos in her life?"

"No one," said Sarah. Then, thinking that Mary might want distraction, "Isn't that Professor Greenberg ahead?"

"Joe Greenberg. Looks just like Abraham Lincoln and gave the best novel course I've had yet. Sat in on my orals and asked decent questions. Let's catch up."

They all ended up in the hospital dining room—Mary Donelli, Sarah, and Joe Greenberg, the last explaining that he had an evening class and was stuck on campus for dinner. "I need a change from dinner at the Faculty Club. Young hopeful graduate students, for instance." He grinned his lopsided grin at the two women.

"Except," said Mary, looking around, "this place is totally depressing. I hope we can get through dinner without choking."

Sarah agreed. The hospital auxiliary had done its best with a frieze of leaves and geraniums and framed posters of New England scenes—a covered bridge, a lighthouse with surf—around the walls, but the fact remained that hospital dining rooms are for people who have medical things on their minds, not food and conviviality. By six-thirty the hospital staff is frayed, and relatives choosing such a place for their evening meal are mindful only of the family member in crisis or waiting for morning surgery on one of the floors.

The atmosphere had its effect. The three went through their vegetable soup in silence, and then a message came down that Alex would be late, held up by a new admission. Mary, always the first to bounce back from gloom, said, "Okay, let's be leisurely, then. We can solve the murder and get the English Department back on the track. Didn't George Fitts say to keep our eyes open?"

"Not just *our* eyes, he says it to everyone in the department, I suppose," said Sarah.

"Why not? What do the police know about the vortex we all work in? For instance, Joe, what's this about Mrs. Parker and her résumé? Do you think she was going to offer herself to Harvard or what?"

"I didn't get a résumé," said Joe Greenberg. "I gather Vera and I were the only ones not so honored—of the senior faculty—and the senior faculty are the ones who seem to interest the police."

"But why not you two?" asked Sarah. "Did the others like Mrs. Parker better, or were they closer?"

"Well, I wasn't Mrs. Parker's greatest fan. I objected to her sitting in on the faculty meetings, and she knew it. And I did my own typing, never used her for any of my articles. Not that she wasn't very efficient, but I like to work on my own things. Vera Pruczak always kept her at an armed distance. I think Rosalind Parker thought Vera wasn't 'real faculty' and Vera thought Rosalind wasn't a real human. But, you know, none of the rest struck me as being genuinely fond of the woman." He looked over at Sarah. "For instance, the Garvey-

Parker hate fest is something even the freshmen know about —in case you think I'm talking out of turn about department secrets—and Amos Larkin went around saying 'Nosy Parker' in a loud voice."

"But Professor Bello liked her," put in Mary. "She ran interference for him day in and day out."

"Well, Howard loathes administration and makes no bones about it. We take turns being the department chairman, and he was overdue. I think he was enormously grateful for the way she kept the students away from his door and all the nuisance paperwork she saved him. Anyway, I don't know why Vera and I were singled out. That résumé makes no sense to me unless Mrs. Parker had presentiments and was working up an obituary."

"Well," said Mary, "it wasn't wasted. I saw the write-up in the student newspaper. The résumé plus all sorts of glowing bits. Trusted and honored employee, interests of Bowmouth at heart."

The three sat quietly, each seeming to see Rosalind Parker as she had so recently appeared, brimming with life and authority. Mary remembered how Mrs. Parker's emergence from her office had galvanized the hall loiterers into action—or into hiding: students back to the waiting room, Arlene and Linda to their typewriters, faculty returning to their offices. Joe Greenberg remembered her in faculty meetings, held in the downstairs seminar room: Mrs. Parker, her smile, her lizard shoe tapping, her pencil poised above the spiral flip notebook, her deferential cough when something concerning her purview came up; Howard Bello deferring to her agenda, Jakob Horst scowling, Vera making wicked little sketches of the faculty in period costume, Pat Fletcher, urbane, unperturbed, bringing the subject back on course; Lacey impatient; Connie Garvey, arms folded, finger drumming, never looking Rosalind in the eye; Amos Larkin, slouched at the end of the table. Sarah remembered Mrs. Parker in her office, the auburn lacquered head tilted toward the clear-glass door window, watching every passage in the hall, issuing forth to capture those without appointments, those with whom she had traffic. Of course, thought Sarah, her window *would* be glass. None of those macramé or poster-covered windows for someone whose finger was in every department pie.

Then Joe Greenberg looked at his watch and pushed his chair back. "Time for English 307 and *The Sun Also Rises*. Let's try this again in cheerier surroundings."

"So," said Mary, when she and Sarah were alone, "what do you think? I heard from Drago that Mrs. Parker had had a mastectomy. That means cancer."

"Honestly," said Sarah. "Talk about loose lips. What is Drago, a hospital CIA man?"

"Hospital people jabber just as much as the rest of the world. Do you think Mrs. Parker did a suicide or had a death wish? Did Alice Marmott? Or did Mrs. P strangle Alice and kill herself with poisoned cocoa?"

"No way," said Sarah. "If ever two people were busy living, they were Mrs. Parker and Alice."

"Mrs. Parker certainly was the sort to go down fighting, hanging on until the last ditch. Maybe that's what the two had in common."

"Fighters who were busy living? Maybe. If it's important that they have something in common, if the two murders are tied together, that might be it."

Mary stirred her beef stew into a sluggish whirlpool. "So define your terms. 'Busy living' is pretty general."

"Busy with power, then. Alice, strength through study, up the scholar's ladder."

"But not knowledge for its own sake?" said Mary.

"Not since she went into such a fit over a *B* instead of an *A*."

"But she could be both, pure scholar and practical. She had to keep that scholarship. Knowledge for its own sake *and* good grades for practical reasons. Money, getting into the graduate program."

"And Mrs. Parker? Power? Strength through what? Influence, efficiency." Sarah looked at Mary's stew with disapproval. "You're not going to improve that stuff. You should have had the cheese noodle thing. It's hard to ruin cheese." Sarah looked around the room again. Two nurses, stethoscopes still around their necks, stood in the doorway and beckoned to another at the counter. An elderly woman, fumbling with a basket of knitting, a handbag, and a novel, seated herself heavily at nearby table, and a young woman in a long white coat moved quickly across the room to a middle-aged man and a teenage boy sitting by the wall under a darkened window. She bent over them, seeming to whisper a few words. The two rose quickly, napkins left on their chairs, and hurried out, their faces masks of controlled distress. Sarah gave a long sigh, seeing the deaths of Alice Marmott and Rosalind Parker take their places in a constant passing parade.

Mary, watching, shook her head. "I suppose hospital dining rooms and waiting rooms serve the same purpose as those ghastly medieval sculptures, you know the half-living, half-skeleton figures with bones scattered around you see in cathedral sculptures. *Timor mortis* and all that."

Sarah pulled herself together. "We'd better forget object lessons and concentrate. It's Alice and Mrs. Parker we're supposed to be thinking about, and for what it's worth, if you're looking for some common ground, I'd say that neither Alice nor Mrs. Parker would give an inch. To me they were tough women who acted as if they knew exactly what they wanted and damn the torpedoes. Look at Alice with her campaign to get her paper back from Horst, and wanting to do unassigned work, and Mrs. Parker running the English Department like the Pentagon, taking over from Howard Bello. Why, she was the de facto chairman. I think they were a match."

"Who was a match?" said Alex, joining them, sliding a filled tray in place.

"Alice for Mrs. Parker, Mrs. Parker for Alice. Stone wall meets stone wall," said Mary.

"If that's the connection, I don't buy it," said Alex. "How about our murderer? Another stone wall?"

Mary finished piling her dishes on her tray and then shook her head. "No, not another stone wall. Say the murderer is sort of a freewheeling agent who ran into one of the stone walls."

"Yes," said Sarah. "This agent meets Alice, who blocks him or threatens him somehow; he removes her and then meets Mrs. P, who does the same. Alice and Mrs. Parker as a team."

"Mrs. Parker would never team up with a student because

students were nonpeople to her, obstacles," said Mary. "They got in the way of her running the department. Like some librarians and books: The borrowing of books gets in the way of an efficient library. Good night, because I have a freshman quiz to type up."

Forty-five minutes later, Alex shot his car up Sawmill Road. Just before turning into the driveway, he pointed across the darkened snow-filled fields to the long shadow of a building. "George told me that's Amos Larkin's farmhouse. No lights on. Do you suppose he's just sitting there in the dark?"

"And drinking in the dark," said Sarah. "If it were anyone else we might stop in, but he'd probably throw a bottle at our heads. Although"—she sighed, feeling again an unexpected twinge of sympathy—"it's terrible to think of him there in the dark maybe wondering if he's killed someone."

"Not always alone. I heard he was married once, but something happened to his wife, I'm not sure what," said Alex, as the car came to a swiveling halt against a snowdrift at the top of the driveway, "Anyway, there's not much we can do for someone who doesn't want help, but for us a bottle isn't a bad idea. I'll do my hot-toddy special. To pick you up and put you down. You've had a time of it."

"You too," said Sarah.

Inside, she collapsed on the sofa and accepted a steaming mug of a dark fluid in which a piece of lemon floated. She took a careful sip and blinked. "My God, what is it?"

"Sort of a Dickensian punch," said Alex, coming over and sitting down. "The kind travelers could count on at the old coaching inns. Lean back and let's go into a time warp."

"One other gaudy night," said Sarah, putting her head against Alex's shoulder. "And I feel as old as Cleopatra's grandmother."

"Whom 'age cannot wither. . . .' "

"Don't be gallant. We're both too tired."

"Hold my hand, drink my drink, and kiss me." Alex leaned over and traced the outline of her eyes, drew his finger down her nose and lightly around her lips.

THIRTEEN

The next few days brought to the college the realization that something was indeed rotten in Denmark—that is to say, in the English Department—and with it came a certain satisfaction. English departments are always suspect, a nest for mad poets, confused socialists, misguided communists, and closet fascists, all straw brains viewed as arguing endlessly over the value of porno novels, fighting over new critical heresies, or nattering about the trivia of grammar, mode, and genre. The faculty and students of those schools and departments that supposedly dealt with the world of facts—engineering, mathematics, physics, the life and earth sciences—took particular relish in the murders and went about shrugging to each other: Well, what did you expect? Look at that Pruczak dame, some kind of witch; and Amos Larkin, drunk as a skunk at the hockey game; and Lacey, makes Don Giovanni look like a boy scout—you call them a faculty?

Sarah Deane, as a member of the tainted department, found herself caught in that well-known phenomenon, the midwinter slump. This was made more unendurable by repeated interviews with George Fitts, classes held in either overheated or underheated rooms with edgy and poorly prepared students, these events broken by slipping and sliding trips around the campus with a wind that cut like a razor through cloth and wool. Alex, too, found himself on a down slide. Two of his hospitalized patients ready for discharge on Tuesday developed untoward symptoms; the pipes froze at the house on Sawmill Road; Patsy in an act of boredom pulled out and shredded the leather laces from his boots, and on a stolen half-hour for a bird walk he missed a rare boreal owl by ten minutes.

"All this," said Sarah, "and somewhere a murderer is sneaking around swiping scarves and cyanide, ready to do in the next victim," to which Alex replied that the new Korean flu strain would probably catch them first, but for what it was worth, had she heard that Mrs. Parker, except for a small legacy to a niece and nephew, had left her estate, house and all, to Bowmouth College?

"Perhaps the chancellor poisoned her," said Sarah, in a weary voice. "Or the bursar. Colleges love getting property. But it really shows you, doesn't it?"

"Shows what?"

"Bowmouth was her whole life."

"Her death, too. I hear there's to be a chapel service and then a reception . . . or something like. At her house. George had to give permission since the police have been in charge there."

This news was confirmed Wednesday morning by Professor Bello. Along with the usual department flotsam in her mailbox, Sarah found a two-page communiqué. It announced "with profound regret" the death of a "most valued member of our department, who, throughout her long association with Bowmouth, never stinted in either her service or her concern for the college." The statement went on to describe the secretary's generosity in leaving her house to Bowmouth and to announce a reception for the entire English Department faculty that evening following the chapel service.

"Does that mean us?" asked Sarah of Arlene, who had turned up at the mail shelves.

"Yes, that's what the word 'entire' is supposed to mean," said Arlene. "Fellows, adjuncts, part-timers. According to Professor Bello, Mrs. P had this sort of memo about funerals and services and wanted something afterward at her house. Everyone is supposed to go, but not the husbands and wives and boyfriends and, natch, not Linda or me. Which I don't mind one little bit. After all, she never invited us to her annual spring wingding. She must have really forgotten that she started out just like us. If you want a ride, let me know; everyone's doubling up with cars because the roads are still packed with snow and there isn't much parking."

So it was that Sarah and Mary found themselves again with Joe Greenberg for the ride to Mrs. Parker's house at five o'clock that evening. Each had skipped the chapel service, Mary and Sarah because of late classes and student appointments, Joe Greenberg for what he described as a queasiness about the whole affair. "But tonight is a command performance. Howard caught me in the hall. The Faculty Club is catering and Melanie Prism is managing it. It sounds absolutely awful."

Mrs. Parker's house was in a fairly new residential enclave south of the campus, the houses all built, as far as Sarah could see from over the drifted snow, on a variation of the colonial New England ranch, a hybrid that had never seemed to bother the builders of the late twentieth century. Mrs. Parker's brown shingle model with white plastic shutters was marked by a dark line of cars, one with the roof lights of the State Police. The walks to both the front door and the side entrance had been neatly shoveled, and a uniformed man stood next to a kerosene heater in the open garage.

Sarah walked in from the street, feeling with each step more and more of an intruder. Despite the secretary's funeral directives, she could not feel that Mrs. Parker welcomed either death or these people—certainly not the latter without herself present in hostesslike posture at the front door.

The front hall was a commonplace area with a table, mirror, and two stiff chairs, and just beyond by what might be a downstairs lavatory stood a man in a brown suit, his impassive face and his planted feet identifying him as police. In an odd way, the man's presence in this very ordinary house acted like a miasma; he transformed it into a scene of the crime. The curtains—a patterned brocade—and the French copy furniture became repositories for hidden notes and fingerprints, the carpet a harborer of hairpins and bloodstains.

Directed to take their coats to the second floor, Mary and

Sarah climbed the stairs. The carpet was thick gray with such a heavy stair tread that it was like walking on a sponge. This flowed "wall to wall" and spread, apparently seamlessly, into three open bedrooms. The first two, obviously guest rooms, their beds covered with coats, were fitted with white-painted matching furniture, the kind advertised as "suits" in the Sunday papers.

The room with the fewest coats belonged, obviously, to the deceased, there having been a reluctance on the part of the visitors to use this chamber. Sarah and Mary entered hesitantly, and then, overcome by a mutual curiosity, looked around. An aerial photograph of the Bowmouth campus in a gold frame and a misty pastel of Bowmouth Pond hung on peach plaster walls. The bed was a large fourposter with an eyelet lace canopy.

"Lord," said Mary, "you'd think she was coming right back." She pointed to the bedside table with the *Bowmouth Alumni Review* for February, a box of tissues, and an alarm clock. "And look at her reading."

Sarah saw Mary move over to a painted bookshelf on the other side of the bed. A complete Shakespeare in soft leather and, next to this, a blue cloth volume, *The Fruit of That Forbidden Tree.*

"Pornography?" suggested Mary. And then, peering more closely, "No, it's one of Merlin-Smith's things; the subtitle is *Essays on Paradise Lost.*" She reached for it, opened the front, and read, " 'Best wishes for a Happy Christmas from Eustace.' "

"Put that back, Mary," said Sarah. "We've got to go down." But Mary had opened another book, Shakespeare's *Sonnets* in a plum cover, introduction by Ivan Lacey. " 'To Rosalind with affection, Ivan.' I'll bet anything it wasn't affection," said Mary. "Parker was one lady even Lacey wouldn't try to grope."

"What are the books, then, fallout from Mrs. P's typing jobs?" said Sarah. "Who is the real Parker, the classics or those?" She pointed to the lowest shelf, filled with Barbara Cartland and Norah Lofts. After all, she reflected as the two women started slowly downstairs, perhaps Rosalind Parker was a closet scholar, hiding her light under her typewriter by day and having immortal longings by night. Shakespeare with a chaser of Barbara Cartland.

At the foot of the stairs they met Professor Greenberg. "We'll stay as long as is decent," he said. "But it may be a while. Pat Fletcher says there's a rumor that the chancellor may turn up. In the meantime, I suppose, we can eat and drink."

Sarah walked into the living room and wove her way to a corner by the fireplace, leaving Mary to move on and say hello to some of the gathered crowd. Mary, who had been to Bowmouth as an undergraduate, probably knew most of the guests. Or were they guests? Visitors? Mourners? What was this, a cocktail party, a reception? Surely not a good old-fashioned wake. There seemed to be no sense of the celebratory: Good old Rosalind, here's to her, let's drink her up. A sober bunch, dark clothes, grays and navy blues, with here and there a frayed tweed jacket and a turtleneck or, on one Einstein figure, a black sweatshirt with a white collar, one of the poets-in-residence, perhaps.

In a dining alcove beyond, Sarah could hear the rattle of an ice bucket and the murmur of voices. She watched Ivan Lacey, navy-blue blazer and crimson and blue striped college tie, emerge holding a tall glass filled with what appeared to be mahogany varnish. Patrick Fletcher joined him and gestured at the walls, pointing out a series of framed watercolors, "Scenes of Old Bowmouth." Sarah, looking about, decided it was one of those living rooms for display only. The pristine, never-sat-on slipcovers in peach and powder blue, the velvet gray rug, the glass coffee table with a book of photographs, *New England Heritage Houses*, and *The Royal Wedding* with Prince Charles and Lady Diana beaming out from the glossy cover. Behind her the bookcase was filled with an array of china figures holding dogs, balloons, or sheep, its bottom rows filled with beautifully aligned books, their dust jackets perfect. And next to the bookcase, the fireplace mantel with two Wedgwood vases with white carnations and, below, an absolutely clean fireplace with three immaculate birch logs set on gleaming brass fire dogs that could never have known smoke or flame. For surely, Sarah reasoned, the police hadn't been bustling around cleaning and polishing and smoothing pillows. Or had Miss Prism done this—doing service for her friend—under the eye of the police? Or again, perhaps the suicide idea wasn't that far out. Sarah, up to now, had not held with the idea that Mrs. Parker, her cancer notwithstanding, would have deliberately poisoned herself. She had felt that Mrs. Parker must have left her house the morning of the storm with every expectation of returning to it. And because of the storm would, as they all had, hurried and left a few things in disarray. Sarah would have to ask. Had the police found dishes in the sink, a girdle perhaps drying in the bathroom, laundry in the hamper, a few unpaid bills? Rosalind Parker was obviously house proud, the sort who, if planning the end of her life, would have plumped sofa cushions, made her bed, tidied her underwear drawer, and so presented a tableau of absolute order. Perhaps, preparing for this posthumous reception, she had had extra cleaning help so that the police had found the house in its present state of spit and polish? Sarah was about to move off with the vague idea of telephoning Alex when Ivan Lacey and Patrick Fletcher walked over to the bookcase and began an examination.

"Your *Poems from the Anglo-Saxon*," said Lacey. "That new translation. And she's got one of mine here and one up next to her bed. I took a sneak look. But did she ever really read, you think?"

"She had to, she typed the manuscripts," said Fletcher, lifting out the first of a brown cloth-bound set. "Here's Howard in all his glory, *The American Renaissance, a Critical Survey*, 'To Rosalind with many, many thanks.'"

Professor Lacey turned toward the living room entrance and frowned. "God, how long do you think we have to hang around here? Isn't Prism going to say something or do something? I think that chapel service should have taken care of the matter. It was long enough."

"I'll find out." Patrick Fletcher strode away purposefully toward the front hall while Ivan Lacey drifted back to the drink table.

Putting aside the idea of telephoning, Sarah felt that it now became a matter of some interest for her to find out who had not sent or inscribed their work for Mrs. Parker. She sidled over to the bookcase and came up with *Patterns in Poetry*, by Jakob Horst, and the offering from Ivan Lacey, *The Center of His Sinful Earth: A Sonnet Reexamined*. Since no one seemed to be paying attention to anyone else, she opened different faculty-authored books as if this were a natural thing to do on such an occasion. All but the Olivia Macbeths came with a fulsome and personal inscription; Vera had written a cool *With best regards*. Conspicuously missing among the senior faculty were Amos Larkin, Joe Greenberg, and Constance Garvey.

"Can you hold out a little longer?" said Joe Greenberg, coming up behind her so quietly that Sarah jumped. "A guilty thing surprised? It's okay. The books were meant to be opened and admired."

"I don't see any of your books on show," said Sarah.

"I mostly write articles, and they don't display well. Besides, as I've said, she didn't do my typing."

"Nothing from Professor Garvey or Professor Larkin either."

"I'd say Mrs. Parker would rather have a green mamba in the house than a book by Constance Garvey. As for Amos, not much love lost there. But every fall when Vera's new novel came out, Rosalind would ask her for a presentation copy, coy as hell. Vera probably thought she'd better come through or Parker would schedule her Intro. Drama classes in the boiler room."

"One thing I overheard—I couldn't help it, he was shouting—Professor Lacey telling Mrs. Parker that what she wanted was impossible. And Alex told me George knows about other confrontations where Mrs. Parker was told that something was impossible."

"I can't imagine what was so 'impossible' unless she wanted to be made chairman—which as far as I can see, she almost was."

Here they were joined by Mary. "Gather round. There's going to be a Miss Prism statement. The Dean of Arts and Sciences is doing a sub for the chancellor. Another statement. And then we can go home."

The visitors now showed signs of increased animation—Sarah had settled on "visitors" as the most suitable noun; it suggested the detached, the temporary, and would do for friend or enemy. For surely, if he existed, the poisoner was present. To savor more completely the absence of the secretary. Or would he? Or she? Who hadn't come? Sarah, as the crowd moved in a stately herd to the end of the living room and spilled out into the front hall, tried to take note of absentees—ones she knew, anyway. No Constance Garvey. No Amos Larkin. No Vera Pruczak. Three standouts on any occasion. Howard Bello, yes, over by the bay window, partly hidden by a hanging spider plant; Professor Merlin-Smith, there by the velvet wing chair; and Professor Horst, over by the arch to the hallway.

A respectful hush followed the appearance of Miss Prism in blue crepe (she's matched her hair, thought Sarah), who proceeded to remind the group of the reason they were so sadly met. Here several glasses were hastily put down and cigarettes snubbed out. "Rosalind always looked forward to her spring party. It was an occasion when the colleagues with whom she worked could forget their daily concerns and join with her in celebrating the end of the winter semester, the coming of spring, the excitement of the next commencement. Because Bowmouth was never far from her heart and her beloved English Department. . . ."

Miss Prism went on in that vein for what Sarah felt was an intolerable ten minutes. She was succeeded by the dean, who, rather tentatively, began a rehash of his most recent encounters with the secretary, her unflagging zeal in the performance of her demanding job. What emerged when he had finished, Sarah decided, was a précis of a relationship in which the dean had rarely come out the winner.

Now certainly they could go. Sarah looked about and found Joe Greenberg in argument with the sweatshirted man, who was brandishing a a copy of the *Bowmouth Alumni Review*. Mary had disappeared entirely. Sarah worked her way out to the hall, already thronged with faculty in coats and boots, and then made her way past a kitchen passage where she could see someone clearing a tray of glasses. She walked through to what must have been the original "utility room." No Mary, but here, if anywhere, was the real Mrs. Parker. The rectangular room reproduced almost perfectly her English Department office. Tall file case, oak desk with an IBM typewriter, the Bowmouth calendar showing the South Quad Music Building, a sectional bookcase with row on row of *PMLA*s. On the desk, a *Thesaurus,* an array of Norton anthologies—drama, literature, poetry—a Bowmouth College *Who's Who, Bartlett's Quotations,* an Old English dictionary, a *Manual of Style,* and a slim volume, *Academic Protocol.*

"Good God," said Mary, turning up, the sound of a flushing toilet behind her. "It's home away from home. She's cloned her office. But, Jesus, why bring it all back with you every night?"

"Because Bowmouth *was* home, I suppose," said Sarah. "And her office once belonged to Professor Garvey, so it was a sort of plum, one of the spoils of war. Why not copy it here, the better to gloat."

"You're supposed to be thinking kind memorial thoughts," said Mary. "Let's get our coats, and then I'll detach Joe Greenberg. He's locked in with that kook Eli Frango, the one who does those imitation epics with internal rhyme schemes—absolute junk."

Back in Mrs. Parker's bedroom, its carpet now scuffed from many alien shoes, Sarah took one more look around. "You don't suppose she was really interested in literature, and that's what she had in common with Alice Marmott, and the super secretary act was just a cover, or just one part of her personality?" She turned to Mary, but found her standing at a partly open sliding wardrobe door.

"Someone's been looking over Mrs. Parker's closet," Mary said. "Since we've been here. Even I wouldn't do that."

"You're doing it right now," Sarah reminded her.

"It's open, so why not? God, look at these. I remember all these outfits. Lady Cashmere with a vengeance. No polyesters for Mrs. P."

Sarah, telling herself firmly that such an inspection was the absolute bottom in taste and manners, found herself joining Mary at the doors of a closet that took up almost the entire wall. The police—or was it one of the "visitors"?—had obviously been searching. Dresses and suits were shoved into little clutches of blues, apricots, pinks, and primroses, silk, voile, knit, pale tweeds, challis, soft spun wools. But there next to a yellow number, like a crow among songbirds, in an opaque vinyl garment bag hung a long full-sleeved black garment. "For evening funerals," said Sarah, touching through the plastic sheath what seemed like a heavy black trim.

"Halloween," said Mary. "Or maybe one of those secret female societies where everyone wears evening dresses in broad daylight and carries candles."

"And call each other 'honored matron'? No," added Sarah, remembering. "George Fitts asked about Mrs. Parker singing in a choir. It must be a choir robe."

"Or her graduation gown," said Mary. "As she has made perfectly clear to all of us, she was a college graduate. Some people hang onto their gowns like trophies. Come on, let's move it."

They found Joe Greenberg in Mrs. Parker's office. He was in his overcoat perched against the arm of a black desk chair stamped with the Bowmouth seal in gold and thumbing through a stack of commencement programs.

"She's got a regular collection of these," he said. "They go way back, the forties, the fifties. She's even marked them up. I knew Rosalind was devoted to Bowmouth, but now I'd say she was obsessed."

"It makes sense," said Sarah. "Living alone, a widow. She was in love with the college."

"In love with it, but after her fashion," said Joe. "I'm ready to go, because if we stay any longer we'll be in for a scene with Melanie Prism."

"One thing," said Sarah, as they crunched through the snow to the car. "Did Mrs. Parker sing in a choir . . . or did she wear a long black dress to faculty parties?"

"I've seen her at a hundred dressy college receptions, always in light colors. It was a sort of joke. Lacey called her the pastel princess. If she sang in a choir it's news to me." He started the car and then returned to the subject of the home office. "Rosalind was more of a workaholic than I'd imagined. I'd always pictured her coming home, working in the garden, playing bridge, that sort of thing. Of course, I've never seen her out socially at anything apart from college affairs. But then I don't see much of anyone from the college on the outside. We get enough of each other at work. Except for Amos Larkin. My wife and I used to go camping with him when his wife was alive, but not lately, of course. He's avoiding everyone."

Alex was busy stoking the wood stove when Sarah got home. He looked up. "You look frozen. Was it ghastly?"

Sarah thought for a moment. "Unreal. Maybe I should have gone to the chapel service. Put myself into a proper frame of mind. This way it was like some weird cocktail party for people who don't have friendship in common, only their jobs, and the hostess doesn't show up. Because she's dead."

"Anything useful? For George?"

"First, did the police find Mrs. Parker's house in perfect shape—as if she expected to kill herself?"

"No," said Alex. "I remember George telling me that after they were finished, he asked one of the policewomen to put her things in order, do the laundry, make the bed for the reception. Miss Prism supervised."

Sarah nodded. "For me that shoots the suicide idea. Mrs. Parker wouldn't have left a mess."

"Anything else?"

"For what it's worth, Professors Garvey, Larkin, and Pruczak were absentees, Mrs. Parker has a possible choir robe in her closet, and she kept a collection of Bowmouth artifacts —pictures, desk chairs, and old commencement programs. Make of it what you will. I'm going to correct a few freshman papers and try a long hot bath."

"Wait. I've been thinking again, what we've been talking about. Getting a handle on peace and quiet. And security. So may I interest you in marriage?"

"What?"

"You know, licenses, double harness, rings, plight thee my troth, the knot intrinsicate."

"That's life, not marriage, and makes me think of asps."

"Proposing to an English teacher is always hazardous. You said a long time ago you'd mull it over. I'd hate to think of you without me—to sound the self-centered note."

"Or, like Mrs. Parker, in love with the college," said Sarah, remembering her own words. "Look, Alex. I love you, I love you. But. But we're in tumult and disorder. Murder, confusion, everything swirling around in a crazy academic vacuum. I like—no, I love living with you. At least I think I will when we start living. But there's the English Department gone loony, and you being the medical examiner on the spot, and all of us trying to keep our eyes open for Sergeant George, so let's talk about it when we've had at least five successive days of New England peace and quiet."

"I thought I'd put the bee in your bonnet. Again. An earwig in your ear. Food for thought."

"The earwig? How romantic. Stick to medicine."

"Get you to your hot bath. I'm going out to gather leeches."

FOURTEEN

Sarah decided Thursday morning that Alex had enough on his plate without her going into the amorphous plan she and Mary had for auditing faculty classes and making notes on their oddities or suspicious remarks. Nothing would probably come of it, and Alex had before him a disagreeable session. Later that morning George wanted him to sit in on the second interrogation round of those two unpleasing personalities from the English Department faculty, Professors Horst and Garvey. She left him in the parking lot muttering about hospitals, police, and frozen pipes and made her way to Malcolm Adam Hall, where she found Mary sitting alone in the Fellows' Room, huddled over a cup of coffee.

Sarah dumped her briefcase on the table and attacked the subject. "Maybe it's a big fat waste of time, our sitting in on other classes. No one's done anything weird or signed a confession. So let's either forget the idea or chivy them a bit. Brown-nose it, irritate them."

"How do you mean irritate them? Drop notebooks, come in late, throw fits, give up our fellowships?"

"Be more like Alice."

"You're mad." Mary put down her coffee and shook her head. "No one could be like Alice."

"I mean act like her. Ask in-depth questions, talk about

doing a research paper, look up some esoteric footnotes and expound."

"Listen, we've enough to do with our own classes without turning into fake brains. Alice was a genius. We're normal, common, garden-variety graduate students. Besides, look at Alice. Trying to turn into an Alice may turn us right into the morgue. Use some sense."

"That's the point. Common sense. We won't overdo it. Just see if we cause a ripple under someone's skin. Don't enrage, irritate."

"In our spare time, shall we imitate Mrs. Parker? Type manuscripts and offer our services to Arlene and Linda? Try for the cyanide as well as the scarf around the neck? What does Alex say about all this? Or Sergeant George Fitts?"

"I'm not going to worry Alex about some simple little plan, and George wouldn't understand how some of the faculty react when students get uppity. You're the one who said that only English Department people could understand what makes the place tick."

"I'll unsay it."

"We'll work out a schedule. Who to audit, who to badger. And who to leave alone. For Alice. That's what you said, too."

"I will learn to button my damn lip—and it's whom, not who."

Alex, after dropping Sarah, drove to the hospital, parked, made his hospital rounds, and then picked his way carefully on the walks, now stiff with packed snow, to the English Department and the now transformed Common Room. Newly installed tape recorders, telephone extensions, a personal computer, an intercom system, and large-scale maps hung over the bookcases and the watercolors of the Lake District, all of them combining to overmantel the room's scholarly carapace.

Alex pulled off his coat and nodded a good morning. "Okay, George, get your big fish equipment ready, because these are your heavyweights, aren't they? I mean literally."

George indicated a chair near his desk. "I want you visible. Less temptation for them to overbear. Yes, it's usually strong tackle with these. Proper rod, double hooks, forty-pound test line, copper leader, live bait. Muskie, bluefish. Have a club ready. But first, today, let them take the hook and run. Easy on the strong-arm."

Jakob Horst, when brought to rest in the leather chair, seemed to Alex more bull than fish. He had small eyes and a thick fleshy neck and moved one foot back and forth in a hooflike fashion. His was the sort of figure that, with his jacket stretched across the chest and his trousers tight over the thighs, looked as if his clothes had shrunk in the wash. But fish or bull, he was, Alex decided, one mean customer. The one who had butchered John Donne, who had taken his interest in mathematics and imposed it on the shifting sands of literature.

George took Professor Horst swiftly through his academic and domestic career and then made his first serious cast. He had refused to give Alice Marmott back her paper, hadn't he, and wasn't there even now a hearing pending with the dean?

The professor became truculent. Student grades and student papers and the way he ran his classes were his business, and he'd damn well thank the police to stick to theirs. George inclined his head almost in deference, as if granting a point. What was the professor's opinion of Mrs. Parker? Did she perhaps take too much on herself? Offered this bait, Professor Horst simply said with a grunt that he supposed she did her job well enough. No, he didn't resent her sitting in on faculty meetings; she'd find out anyway what was happening. That was as near as the professor came to criticizing the secretary. Had he ever had a major disagreement with Mrs. Parker? Nothing major—little things, sure—not worth mentioning.

"Everything concerning Mrs. Parker is worth mentioning," said George austerely, but still not bearing down.

"Oh," muttered Dr. Horst, "things like classroom assignments, exam schedules, textbook orders. Nothing important."

And George let him go.

"You'll see," he said to Alex, whose eyebrows were up. "Let him have some line. Some of those hooks will stick in his craw. Now we have Professor Garvey."

"You have her, not me," said Alex, shifting his base to

a more distant chair, where he settled back and studied the new arrival. Constance Garvey was designed by nature for battle. Forehead broad, chin outthrust, shoulders wide, chest —breast was too kindly a word—like an escarpment. A massive presence in gray flannel, she sat with booted feet square on the floor, a black fur cossack hat centered on the top of her pulled-back gray hair. She needs a balcony to review the troops, thought Alex. Or, taking George's image, a very sturdy aquarium. All in all, Professor Garvey's bulk and breadth reduced George to a translucent shade, and as for Alex, he felt a sudden urgent need to start himself on a program of super vitamins.

George, working with a fine line and a tough wrist, took Professor Garvey through her early history—this most notable for her captainship of a champion water polo team—and along to her present eminence as the senior tenured English faculty member. Here George snapped his line back, inflicting injury. The loss of her office to the likes of Mrs. Parker, the increasingly low student enrollment in her undergraduate course—George had all the figures—the canceling of a graduate seminar, the indignity of a tiny office next to a "popular novelist"—these were bitter fruit to Constance Garvey.

"I'd had that office for ten years, and to have a secretary —a clerical person . . ." Here Constance Garvey snorted. Alex had not thought it was possible for a human to snort properly, but this was the real thing. "I've never believed," she went on, "in that *nil nisi bonum* nonsense. Mrs. Parker didn't know her place. She even tried to advise me on what texts to order. And my classrooms. I told her time and again that I had a dust allergy and needed rooms with open space and windows, and last term she put my freshman class and a graduate seminar in the basement."

"Do you drink hot chocolate, Professor Garvey?" said George.

Constance Garvey, brought up short, sat up and blinked.

"You have a Thermos, I believe," prompted George. "Do you fill it at home or do you use the supplies in the department?"

Professor Garvey recovered. Yes, the Thermos the police had collected stayed usually in her office, used only for cocoa.

No, it could not be mistaken for another person's. Hers was blue, stainless steel, one of a kind. Yes, sometimes she took a cup of chocolate or coffee in the Common Room. Yes, she had from time to time used the cocoa packets from the English Office—"which I pay for, and that is more than some do —the two clerks, for instance."

"Friendly get-togethers with colleagues," suggested George. "Meetings in each other's offices."

"The English Department is not a restaurant, and I do not stop and waste time in get-togethers. I teach my classes, meet my students, and go home—and," said Constance Garvey, showing her dorsal fin, "if you're making notes on our drinking habits, I suggest you attend to Professor Larkin, who disgraces the entire college and drags the English Department down with him. I have seen Professor Bello and the dean about his removal."

Brought back to the period of Mrs. Parker's death, Professor Garvey said she had met her last student at about five, made a call to make sure she had a bed at the Faculty Club, and said good night to Mrs. Parker. "I make it a point to be civil, although as usual she was playing the martyr, pretending the place would fall apart if she didn't stay late. I had dinner by myself, went to my bedroom—on the third floor, disgraceful quarters—and locked myself in. I had no intention of sharing the room."

After more prodding, Constance Garvey revealed that, yes, she had once left her room sometime after nine. She had forgotten her freshman anthology in the seminar room downstairs in the English Department building. "The snow was a disgrace. No attempt to clear the walks. I had to fight my way."

"But you got through," said Alex, picturing Professor Garvey cleaving her way through the drifts.

"Of course. The book was where I left it. No, I met no other member of the department. I did not go upstairs. Yes, there was a light, several lights. The Fellows' Room and the English Office. Sheer carelessness. Yes, I went directly back to my bedroom."

"And relocked the door?"

"Of course."

"So no one can say that you actually spent the rest of the night there?"

Silence. Glaring. High dudgeon.

"Are you on a diet, Professor Garvey? Do you choose the low-cal packs of cocoa?" Alex had to admire George's change of pace.

"If you are suggesting that I use the diet brand, you are quite wrong. I don't believe in harmful substitutes for natural and wholesome foods. The rest of the faculty? I neither know nor care. I pay no attention to their personal eating habits."

"What was your opinion of Alice Marmott?" said George, doing another switchback.

"You asked that question following her death, so kindly consult your files for my answers." Professor Garvey began pulling on her black leather gloves. To George's further prodding, she said that as far as she knew, Alice Marmott and Mrs. Parker had no connection with each other. "Mrs. Parker may have found Alice Marmott's wish to take graduate studies improper; I certainly did. In fact, I thought Miss Marmott rather grotesque. She could be most irritating in class."

"Thank you, Professor Garvey. We will finish with the English faculty offices by tomorrow. Please leave your current teaching schedule with Deputy Cohen. We will want to see you again." And George turned his back.

Professor Garvey, for once the dismissed, not the dismisser, rose in surprise and before she could have the last word George closed the door behind her broad back.

"This cocoa business is more and more difficult," he said.

"They all drank it, didn't they?" said Alex.

"And the packets that fell out of Professor Garvey's handbag—the ones that Arlene saw—were no-cal. The paper cover is blue. No mistake."

"What if Garvey's on a diet and won't admit to being overweight? Or are you thinking that Garvey went home, filled the no-cal packets with cyanide, and put them in Parker's office? Wouldn't that be terribly difficult? Packets like that are glued closed or heat-sealed."

"Difficult but not impossible if you worked carefully with a razor blade. As the manufacturers say, these packages are 'tamper-resistant,' not tamper-proof. And if Mrs. Parker was working late at night and ripping open a familiar-looking cocoa packet to put in her Thermos, would she examine the seal? I doubt it."

Alex rose to leave. "And what sort of fish is Professor Garvey?"

"Which would you choose?"

"No question. A shark. Hammerhead, I think."

The next few days fell for Alex and Sarah into a sort of rhythm. He, from hospital, to clinics, to the medical school, to see the Chief Medical Examiner in Augusta, and to go over the interviews with George. Nothing seemed to be moving ahead because George seemed much occupied with running time and place checks and trying to find out if there were hidden ties that bound Alice Marmott to Rosalind Parker.

Sarah, like a sort of well-wrapped robot, went from class to class, to her own seminars, and to whatever undergraduate lectures she could find time to audit. Although it went against the grain, she tried to become a more conspicuous presence. In Old English, Shakespeare, and poetics, she found that she could usually come up with something that brought the class to a halt and caused an exasperated instructor to explain some arcane reference, some question about a conflicting text.

She interrupted Professor Horst in the middle of a ruthless dissection of Wordsworth's "Lines" on Tintern Abbey to ask whether the poet's heavy use of adjectives gave the nouns more numerical weight than he had assigned them in view of the lack of strong verbs. Sarah had concocted that one at breakfast, and it was good for at least ten minutes of class confusion and singled her out, if not as a lesser Alice Marmott, certainly as a new class nuisance. She broke into Ivan Lacey's explication of Act IV of *The Winter's Tale* to ask whether Shakespeare used fewer or more plant images in the late plays. Professor Lacey backed and filled and tangled himself into a number of references to unweeded gardens, while Mary, joining in the hunt, asked if he could diagram for the class the exact process of grafting plants so that Shakespeare's lines about marrying scions to the "wildest stock" would make the metaphor clear. In Professor Fletcher's class Sarah asked if she could do a paper on the great vowel shift and was told in no uncertain terms to stick to the course as it had been devised, that as a beginner she wouldn't know a vowel shift when she met one—a remark only too true.

"Hell," said Mary, meeting Sarah in the Fellows' Room late Thursday morning. "This is pointless. Lacey always goes to pieces over any questions that don't have to do with sex, and you can't deflect Horst with anything short of a road grader. We're driving everyone crackers and not finding out a thing about Alice or Mrs. Parker. Fletcher puts us in our place, and as for Amos—well, I can't go after him. He's on my doctoral committee, for God's sake. Let's desist."

"Good morning, ladies. Miss Donelli, Miss Deane." It was George Fitts, who had slid into the room like a visiting shadow. "Have I surprised you?"

Sarah made a strangled noise, and Mary examined the contents of her open briefcase. "We're talking over the murder," Sarah said, pulling herself together. "It's what everyone does. Topic A."

"Sit down, Miss Donelli," said George, pulling up a chair. "I've heard from several sources and from you yourself—though perhaps you weren't aware that you were telling me—that when Professor Larkin's name comes up, you react, are defensive. That perhaps you don't see the man objectively."

Mary went crimson. She sat down at the table and for a moment turned the pages of a textbook. Then finally she said, "I'm not serious about him. It's sort of a game. He doesn't know I exist, so there's nothing personal. I've never even had a cup of coffee with him. I just make jokes, you know, for kicks."

"I see," said George. "Then you won't be disturbed when I tell you that we may be about to arrest him for the murders of Alice Marmott and Rosalind Parker."

"What!" Mary and Sarah said it together, but then Mary turned away. "Oh, Christ."

George waited a moment while Mary, shoulders moving, struggled with herself. She turned back, her face crumpled with distress.

"You do care," he said impassively.

"Of course I care. He's one of the few really decent

teachers they've got in this place. The others—well, okay, most of them know what they're saying, but he's good. Like Joe Greenberg. Both of them, brilliant sometimes. Even better than Fletcher."

"Professor Larkin has been brilliant lately?"

"No. Oh, hell, you know he's been on a drunk. Off and on but more on lately. I don't know what's eating him. I mean, shouldn't he have some reason for drinking? He didn't drink all that much when I first came here. Just sometimes on weekends, at faculty parties I heard, but now—" Mary didn't finish.

"But you're going to arrest him?" said Sarah. "Did you mean that, or were you just upsetting Mary?" George sometimes appalled her.

"I meant it. But not immediately, not today. The District Attorney is going over the evidence. Professor Larkin was on the site on both occasions, and his scarf was used to kill Alice. He left his office in the middle of the night Mrs. Parker died, used the fire escape, and dropped a glove. Obviously not so drunk that he didn't make it to the cafeteria."

"It sounds awful when you list it that way," said Mary, subdued.

"I have a piece of advice," said George. "I see you heading for trouble, Miss Donelli. Except for your regular classes with him, stay clear of Professor Larkin. Perhaps you didn't know, but he was married."

"Oh," said Mary in a small voice.

"His wife died six years ago. You would have been an undergraduate then. Not a mysterious death, a brain tumor. You students probably didn't know. He was left with a small boy who was taken away from him last year because of the alcohol problem. Lives with his grandparents."

Mary looked a fraction brighter. "That's plenty of reason to drink. Your wife dying and leaving a child."

"I don't think finding yourself a single parent is a reason to go on drinking, putting your child and your job in jeopardy. He's unstable, and he may have turned to murder. Stay away from the man."

"Yes, sergeant," said Mary quietly. Too quietly, thought Sarah.

"As for you, Sarah, be cautious with Larkin too. If you

must talk with him make sure someone's around. Remember, the police are trying to protect all you people, and we know how difficult it is not to be careless, not to be sentimental."

"Thanks ever so," said Mary. "The State Police may have a human side, but I've missed it."

"Just remember what I've said is for your own good." George rose, reached for his hat, and departed.

"What a creep," said Mary, glowering at the closed door. "He's made me feel that I've been obscenely chasing Amos Larkin. Well, I'm about to give up this business of trying to aggravate the faculty."

"I wish you'd give up on Amos Larkin. Honestly, Mary, find someone who won't go after you in a drunken tantrum."

"Then you believe he did it?"

"Not yet, but you heard George."

"Screw George. He's some kind of an iceman. Look, Sarah, we're both going to go insane with all this. The sun's out, the temp's up. Let's take a jog around the campus, get some air into our lungs. I haven't a class until four-thirty. We can do our running and then drive into Camden for lunch."

"I wanted to audit Garvey's undergrad novel class at two."

"And screw that too. You can catch her act tomorrow. It's always the same."

"Okay," said Sarah suddenly. "I've had it with this place. Talk about academentia. Let's go."

The campus walks were shoveled clear. The sky was a thin blue, and the sun had turned the snow into a light-shifting dazzle.

"Take it easy," said Sarah. "I'm out of condition."

"So am I. Work it up slowly."

They ran around the North Quad, down through the arch to East Quad, banked around the Art Building, back across by the Life Sciences Library, jogged past the Biology Building, and around the corner of the Administration Building.

"Down to the pond," shouted Mary.

"It hurts," called back Sarah. The air burned a path down her throat, singed her lungs, her nose ran, her thumbs froze, her feet disappeared—it was as if she were running on stumps. But she pounded after Mary, and then they both stood, backs to Bowmouth Pond, breaths smoking, looking up at the college. Every building stood window deep in drifted snow, every roof frosted with little caps, the guardian trees clotted with white.

"Land of enchantment," said Mary. "To quote Sergeant Fitts, I could become sentimental."

"It's this view that always gets to me," said Sarah. "You can imagine noble purpose, high moral commitment, pure learning."

"And pure loathing. And homicide."

"Don't be so cynical. Today it's magic casements. I think I'm getting a second wind. Come on, we'll go around the South Quad, up to the med school, and back to the English Department parking lot." And Sarah set off, a steady pace, one-two, one-two, now and then slipping on the packed snow, once tumbling into a drift with Mary falling behind her. Sarah felt the months, the years lifting off. She was back in high school in January running around the soccer field; she was in fifth grade, playing fox and geese; she was in kindergarten lying on her back, making angels and looking up into a cold winter sky.

"I'll race you," she called back to Mary. "To the parking lot." And she took off, dodging students, faculty with briefcases, the heat from her running now sending a warm buzzing through her hands and feet, and trickles of perspiration down the sides of her woolen hat. Mary ran behind her and then suddenly accelerated, passed her, laughing, cut around a huge drift of snow by the edge of the parking lot, and hurtled directly into a figure coming in the opposite direction. It was like a scene in a comedy short. Up went Mary, off went her hat, up went the man, off went his cap, his briefcase shooting away at an angle and disappearing into a snowbank. Everything was all legs, arms, Mary on her back in the drift gasping, the man face down in the snow, apparently trying to swim his way to the surface. Sarah collapsed helplessly on the path, laughing so hard she began to choke.

Mary sat up roaring. "Shit, I've got a whole blasted bushel down my neck. Do something, Sarah. Give him a hand."

Sarah reached for an arm and pulled, and the man, getting some purchase with his feet, emerged, sat up, his hair matted with snow, his eyes wild. It was Amos Larkin.

"Oh, Christ," said Sarah. She dropped the professor's arm as if it were electrified, so that he dropped back into the apparently bottomless drift.

But Mary, looking on with horror, just sat there, and Sarah had to reach again and help the professor to a more stable sitting position.

"What the bloody hell," said Amos Larkin. "Don't you look where you're going?"

"Oh," groaned Mary. "We've done it again. I don't believe it. I'm sorry."

"What the hell have you done again? You've done quite enough now." Professor Larkin rolled out of the drift and began scooping chunks of snow from the back of his neck.

Mary sat there in the snow. "I'm sorry, that's all. I don't believe it because it's the same place. Almost. But I guess we're even. I knocked you down and you knocked me." And then with more attention, "You've got snow all down your neck."

"I'm aware of that." Amos Larkin stood up, pulled off his sheepskin coat, and began shaking it. Sarah, torn between assisting at least one of the victims or taking off and leaving them to sort it out, now found that the heat of her body was melting a patch of snow and it was soaking into her corduroy trousers. She jumped up. "Your briefcase," she said to Professor Larkin. "I think it's in there." She reached down, found a handle, and set the case on the walk.

"I know you, don't I?" demanded Professor Larkin of Mary, who was still sprawled in the snow, looking like an avalanche victim.

"Yes," said Mary. "I'm—well, I'm a candidate . . ."

"For what? Manslaughter?"

"English. Eighteenth century. And," said Mary, her voice gaining firmness, "you're just as up for manslaughter as I am. I said we're even."

"And I say what the hell are you talking about?"

"Oh, you know. The bicycle. Two years ago. Right over there at the end of the parking lot. When you drove into me or I rode into your car. Knocked my wind out and wrecked my bike wheel."

"I don't know what you're talking about."

"I never told anyone because I thought you'd be embarrassed, and I was in your class and had just started graduate school. It was in the fall. I thought we'd better forget it." Mary lost her temper. "You'd been drinking, if you want to know, and after all, I was okay except for my bike wheel needing about forty dollars' worth of repair. So knocking you down now isn't as bad as you think because you're just a little bit wet and I might have been killed."

Amos Larkin stopped brushing his coat. "Say all that again."

"I can't possibly. It's ancient history. But"—Mary, calmer now, cresting along with her temper—"if you would return those four chapters of my dissertation, I'd know whether I can go on from that point of view. You see, I'm saying that Swift wasn't so much of a satirist per se as a sort of frustrated reformer who—"

"Hang Swift," said Professor Larkin. His coat dangled from one arm. He seemed to have forgotten that the temperature was barely in the twenties. "What's this about a bicycle? You weren't hurt?"

"I said I wasn't. My breath was knocked out so I just lay there gulping and my bike wheel was bent. The gears had to be remounted."

"But you didn't get up and tell me you were okay."

"You were in your car. You'd driven past the parking space right over the curb—it left a big scratch on your fender. Anyway, when I got up and found I was in one piece and picked up my bike, you—well, you were asleep."

"You mean passed out."

"Yes, I guess that's what I mean."

"Then say it."

"Okay, okay." Mary was almost shouting. "Passed out. Drunk. Gone. Out of it. Stinko. Blotto. Zonked. Is that what you want?"

"Yes," said Professor Larkin quietly.

Sarah thought it was time to intervene. Things had gone

quite far enough. "Come on, Mary, let's get lunch. We're sorry, Professor Larkin." God, she thought, of all the people to knock into a snowbank.

"No, wait," said Amos Larkin. "Let's get this straight. Absolutely straight. I knocked you off your bike with my car. Fall, did you say?"

"The second week of November. A Saturday late in the afternoon, almost five."

"That would be right. Almost exactly right." He paused. "Did you say lunch?"

"No, I did," said Sarah firmly. "Miss Donelli and I are going for lunch. Together."

"It's Mary," said Mary. "Lunch is a good idea."

"So come on then," said Sarah. "Goodbye, Professor Larkin. Don't forget your briefcase."

"Where were you thinking of?" said Professor Larkin.

"Camden," said Mary.

"Have you got a car? I gave mine up."

"An accident," put in Sarah, not without malice.

"I was, to quote, 'driving to endanger, operating under the influence.' Is that what you want to know?"

"I just thought——" Sarah stopped. She was losing her grip.

"My car, then," said Mary.

"Don't you have a class, Professor Larkin?" asked Sarah, without much hope.

"I have just finished a class, but thank you for reminding me," said Amos. "It must have been obvious for some time that my brain is too pickled to remember these details."

It wasn't exactly humility, thought Sarah. In fact he was beginning to sound like his old dangerous sarcastic self. Well, she certainly couldn't leave Mary alone with the man.

They drove in silence to Camden, along snow-drifted Route 17, past Chickawaukie Pond, looking like a glazed white platter set in front of the surrounding snow-covered hills. Mary drove—it was an old unheated green Jeep—Amos Larkin sat in the passenger seat, and Sarah, who had climbed into the back to keep an eye on him, sat on a pile of old blankets and bounced along uncomfortably, feeling like someone's unwelcome relative.

Settled at the Harborside Restaurant, Sarah tried not to watch Professor Larkin attempting with shaking hands to bring a cup of coffee to his mouth.

"Now," he said, "once more, in detail, tell me how, when, and exactly where I knocked you off your bicycle."

"You can't be serious," said Mary. "Not again."

"I am perfectly serious and for once perfectly sober."

"Okay." Mary put down her fish sandwich and began the now-familiar description.

Sarah, across the table, examined the professor. Unhealthy was an inadequate term. His nose, cheeks, forehead were reddened, although she charitably conceded that being knocked face down in a snowdrift may have aggravated his complexion. His eyes looked blurred as if the red rims and blood vessels and the blue of the iris had, like watercolors, run together. His sandy eyebrows, heavy as they were, could not overbalance the smoky shadows that rimmed the eyes, and his hair, a darker reddish mix, seemed to have been cut by a blind man with nail scissors. As for the chin, it was nicked and patched, with here and there a missed bit of stubble. All in all, a poor specimen; in fact, a fit subject for a Swiftian satire. He hardly looked as if he had the nerve to plan one murder, let alone two. Suddenly, Sarah was overcome with longing for Alex, whose eyes, though sometimes dark and forbidding, were clear, whose dark hair, though not a model of tidiness, was at least not a red rat's nest. But at the same time, Sarah thought illogically, if Alex were here she might even be able to muster a modicum of sympathy for the professor.

"You're sure it was a Saturday in November," Professor Larkin was saying. He frowned at his ham sandwich and pushed it aside. "Because I'd hate to think that I've knocked two students off their bicycles."

"It was the day before Armistice, or Veteran's Day—or whatever they call it. The tenth, anyway. I remember because the bike shop was closed on Monday for the holiday. And it was warm or I wouldn't have been racing around on my bike."

"And when you came to my car for an appropriate apology and money for a new bicycle wheel, you found me out of it. So, fearing for your future in eighteenth-century literature, you tiptoed away and never mentioned the incident to anyone."

"No, I didn't. Not then or later. You're on my doctoral committee."

"I am?"

"Yes, and you were supposed to sit in on my orals, but you didn't make it. Anyway, the whole thing seemed awkward."

"How right you are. Never embarrass a drunk."

Sarah glared at him. "Sarcasm doesn't go with lunch."

Amos Larkin looked up at Sarah as if noticing a third party for the first time. "The sarcasm is self-directed. The only thing I want to direct to this person . . ."

"Mary Donelli," said Mary.

". . . to Miss Donelli, are my apologies, forty dollars for her bicycle wheel, and my heartfelt thanks."

"Thanks?" said Mary.

"If as you say you never told anyone about the accident —not even Mrs. Parker."

"Why would I tell Mrs. Parker?"

"Why indeed? If you never told Mrs. Parker, and if I didn't knock two female students down on Saturday, November tenth, in the late afternoon—which, I suppose, is just possible—then Mrs. Rosalind Parker has been enjoying herself enormously."

Sarah, despite her intention of remaining a bulwark of disapproval and nonparticipation, said, "What do you mean? Did Mrs. Parker see the accident?"

"She missed very little, in or out of the department. Even on Saturday afternoon. Mrs. Parker's office window, her desk, overlooks that end of the parking lot, so she must have seen the whole affair. The next morning she called me on the phone and described the accident exactly as you have, except that she didn't tell me your name, which she must have known, you being a graduate student in English and she having had a memory for faces. She told me that I had driven into and injured—critically—a female student on a bicycle. She said that she—helpful woman that she is—had made it down to the parking lot just after the ambulance had gone away, found me passed out, moved my car with me in it away from the scene of the crime before the police could get there, called my brother—he's a member of my rescue squad—who drove me home. None of which did I remember, perhaps because it didn't happen quite that way. But I'd gotten used to memory lapses and I swallowed it whole. After all, there was the dent in my fender. The next day she told me that the student was still in critical condition and had been flown to a Boston hospital and added that she would probably be permanently crippled. When I asked for the student's name, she wouldn't tell me, said she wanted to teach me a lesson, pointing out that if it hadn't been for her moving my car, getting me away, I would be up for attempted manslaughter. I made several attempts to find out from local hospitals about accident victims and also called the Boston hospitals. It turned out that there was a rash of accidents that day in both places—none of them unaccounted for. That didn't make sense, but I didn't pursue it or turn myself in. Coward, lily-livered, or cirrhosis-livered, call it what you will."

"And until now," said Mary, "you've thought you'd maimed a Bowmouth student."

"Correct. And for over two years Mrs. Parker has made private little references to it. Progress reports on my victim, who, she implied, was somewhere in New England wearing braces and creeping around on crutches and let that be a lesson to me. Of course, she always had some little favor to ask: would I support her request to sit in on faculty meetings, get her a card to the Faculty Club, arrange an invitation to some VIP college reception? Lately, I've gotten pretty sick of it all, have even thought of telling her to go ahead and have me arrested, tell the world she's solved the mysterious Bowmouth hit-and-run, the one nobody knows about. Of course, this past year I haven't been in any shape to help her with her little projects, and I think that she was working on getting rid of me as someone who not only wasn't useful to her any more but was an embarrassment to the department. But you see why I'm saying thanks. You're not on crutches or wearing braces, so at least that's one nightmare I'm rid of. There are others."

It was, Sarah thought, a horrible story, with both secretary and professor seen in a thoroughly unlovely light. Mary, she was sorry to see, was smiling across the table, which, considering that Amos Larkin had just told them why he had a most powerful reason to murder Rosalind Parker, was unfortunate. Sarah would have to keep her eye on Mary and never let her be alone with a man about whom she obviously hadn't a grain of sense. In this spirit, she looked at her watch and said it was time to go.

"But I haven't finished my sandwich," said Mary. "Nor has Amos—I mean Professor Larkin."

"I think being knocked down and having the goodness not to sue gives you every right to call me 'Amos' or any other name you can come up with. I'm sure the students have plenty."

Sarah, remembering "Professor Lushwell," turned her head.

"Professor Lushwell, for instance," said Amos, reclaiming his sandwich and peering into its interior.

"Would you like to order a drink?" said Sarah, thinking that this might be the quickest way to bring Mary to her senses; Mary who, becomingly flushed, was still smiling across at a possible strangler.

"You mean, Professor Lushwell with his shaking hands needs a fix?" said Amos. He removed a piece of ham from the sandwich, let it fall to the plate, and took a large bite of rye bread.

"I didn't say that," said Sarah, furious to find herself on the defensive with this derelict.

"But you thought it. Yes, I'd give half my life for six ounces of alcohol. I see that you are here with your friend to make sure that the sinister dissolute professor doesn't frighten this trusting young woman—or, worse, take his remaining Emmanuel College muffler and tie it around her neck. Isn't that the problem, Miss—forgive me. What is *your* name?"

"It's not Amanda Tibbs, ' said Sarah angrily.

"Who? Should it be Amanda Tibbs? She's an undergraduate, isn't she? Have I done her wrong too? Alcohol does leave these blank spots. In fact, this whole past term is full of holes. So if you are, or are not, Amanda Tibbs—well, I don't remember. I'm behind on reading my papers, meeting students, opening my mail, my socks probably don't match, my stomach's yelling at me, and if Mrs. Parker were here—God forbid—she'd probably call my brother. Since she isn't, I guess I'll order a glass of milk. Some people swear by it. So your name is?"

"Sarah Deane."

"Fellow of the college?"

"Teaching fellow. From Boston University." Sarah presented these facts with austerity and scowled at Mary for good measure.

"And you are suffering from being a fellow, almost as bad as being an adjunct lecturer. Life always below the salt."

"I'm perfectly happy at Bowmouth," said Sarah, thinking that she sounded more and more like Mrs. Pardiggle while Amos Larkin was coming out as a wit or, more like it, a life-long adherent of satiric literature.

Amos Larkin accepted a glass of milk from the waitress, gripped it with two hands, and drank it down in three gulps. "One thing I've learned, get poisonous liquids down in a hurry."

"Like cocoa laced with cyanide," said Sarah. It came out of her mouth without the least intention, as if some inner fiend was preempting her speech for its own dark purposes.

"Sarah!" exclaimed Mary. "What are you saying that for? What are you trying to do?"

Professor Larkin put down his empty glass of milk and looked Sarah full in the face. "Since I've never knocked you off your bicycle, it must be something else. You must think, you must be convinced, that I murdered Mrs. Parker—and that other one, Alice whatever her name was."

"Alice Marmott," said Sarah in a low voice. Something like a sense of shame was taking over. What was she doing attacking this man in public? Of course, he was one of the chief suspects, but that was the business of George Fitts. Who was she to start acting like the FBI and the WCTU rolled into one? Surely she could support Mary, keep an eye on her, without turning into some sort of female barracuda. And more to the point, wasn't there more to be gained from an investigative point of view by a show of compassion, by sympathetic questions? God's gift to a secret police she wasn't. She lifted her head. "I didn't mean . . ." she began.

"Yes, you did. Either you're worried that you two women might be cooped up with a murderer or you hate drunks—or both. Are you in any of my classes?"

"English 603—Pope, Swift, and Johnson. I like the syllabus very much," she added, in what she hoped was a conciliatory tone.

"Don't try and make it up. Your suspicions are appropriate and so is your former tone of voice. It's a tone I use myself. I was around when both murders were discovered, and I had one hell of a reason to want Mrs. Parker dead. But, for what it's worth, I had no reason to want to lose Alice. Alice wrote a paper on Swift's poetry—unassigned, needless to say—that I can even remember. Alice was the kind of student, if you'll forgive me for saying . . ."

"Say it," said Mary. "We're not Alice Marmotts—even though Sarah thinks we should try."

"Neither of us can touch Alice," said Sarah firmly, thinking, Lord, Mary's so addled she's going to give us away.

"Well, it's probably good for the profession that an Alice Marmott—what an awful name—comes along only once or twice in a lifetime. The scholar born. The one who cuts through the tripe, the rodomontade, the cant, and gets to the heart of things. Her paper could have been published as is. I didn't make a mark on it. Oh, in class she was a pain in the ass because she had to know everything, get everything right, but every teacher wants every ten years or so to read a paper from a student like Alice. So even though that hockey game is a big blank—yes, Sergeant Fitts, when he was flourishing my scarf in my face, made it clear that Alice was strangled during the Colby-Bowmouth game—I don't think that even blind drunk I would have killed a student like Alice. Or any student for that matter. When I drink, I'm told I grow very sorry for myself, nasty, and sarcastic—too much Swift, you'll say. I become obnoxious, run off at the mouth, and pass out. As I did in North Quad, where someone as a good joke removed my shoes and my coat the better to freeze me."

"How do you know you didn't just lose them wandering

around out there?" said Sarah. "I've heard hypothermia victims often pull their clothes off."

"It's a guess. I think someone helped me. My boots are high ones with long laces. I doubt if I was in any condition to undo them."

Mary's eyes widened. "Do you think you might have been set up? A convenience for the murderer?"

"It's possible. It might have been handy to have a soused English professor frozen near the corpse of Alice—the corpse with his scarf around her neck. Even if I lived through the night, it was a good bet that I wouldn't remember any of the details of the evening—which I don't. I've been told I made a fair spectacle of myself at the game. It would have all fitted. Drunk kills student, drunk passes out, drunk freezes, drunk dies. Case solved."

He seemed to Sarah to be calling himself a drunk more than was necessary. Was it sort of a cathartic *mea culpa* or self-pity, a bid for sympathy? Or—more sinister—had Amos Larkin, even drunk or partly feigning drunkenness, strangled Alice because—because why? Well, because Alice had written a publishable paper on Jonathan Swift and Amos Larkin hadn't written anything in a dog's age. Had lately been too fried to have put together anything worth publishing. Two birds with one stone. Get rid of an annoying student who, as she was doing with Professor Horst, might bring suit for improper professorial behavior and at the same time pick up an essay that might help rescue an endangered reputation. Sarah roused herself to hear Mary explaining to Amos Larkin why he had not murdered Mrs. Parker.

"I know you woke up later and went somewhere," she said, "but earlier I'm sure you were too far gone to put the cyanide in the cocoa or in her Thermos, because even when we carried you to your office you didn't come to. Mrs. Parker always guarded her Thermos like a baby, and she would have known you'd been drinking that night. She wouldn't have let you near her office."

It was plain to Sarah that as a fellow investigator—at least as far as Professor Larkin was concerned—Mary was a total loss. By the time they got back to the college, Mary would have provided enough support and comfort that the professor would have emerged as the hero of the piece. Again she looked at her watch, reached for the check, and rolled up her napkin. But Professor Larkin held up his hand.

"Wait a minute. What do you mean, you two carried me?"

"Well," said Mary, now at ease enough to giggle, "Sarah and I had the legs, but Drago Collins took the heavy part, your head and shoulders."

"Collins, stocky, black hair and glasses? How helpful. And you made this little procession down the hall?"

"No one saw us. We needed the waiting room to sleep in." Mary did not add that the presence of a snoring and bourbon-reeking professor would have added to the night's discomforts.

"I've heard," said Amos Larkin thoughtfully, "that drunks have to hit some sort of rock bottom before they take their condition seriously. I've landed on several hard bottoms, but this may be it. Associate Professor Lushwell, a motley to the view, being lugged drooling and snoring down the hall by three graduate students."

"You didn't drool," said Mary. "I wouldn't dwell on it."

"I damn well am going to dwell on it. And as Miss Deane has twice noted, it's time to be going. My stomach has survived the milk, though it was touch and go for a while. I may try it again, especially if I have to convince Sergeant Fitts—and Miss Deane here—that I'm not a double murderer."

After Mary had left Professor Larkin at the foot of the hill that led to his house, she turned to Sarah. "He *is* sharp."

"Too sharp. And clever," said Sarah. "I think we've been treated to an excess of cleverness. Contrite alcoholic doing fast footwork around motives and opportunities. He's a fox even if he is a drunk. Don't let yourself be taken in."

"With you around," said Mary with asperity, "there's not much chance."

"I'm not always around. Just don't take any moonlight walks or trips down a darkened corridor. Use the buddy system. George Fitts told us to. Look, it's almost four o'clock. I've just time to catch Merlin-Smith's undergraduate lecture on Milton."

"I had him on Milton. Weary-dreary, but he covered the

ground. He loves Milton, thinks they're soulmates, and disapproves of Donne because of the sexual metaphors. And he snuffles. Amos at a party once called him Professor Merlin-Pecksniff to his face."

"The trouble with Amos Larkin is that drunk or sober he makes you laugh, and I think that's dangerous. Think fox. Mr. Todhunter. The gentleman with the long whiskers and red tail."

"And I'm Jemima Puddle-Duck who goes pit-pat-paddle-pat right into his jaws."

"Remember you heard it here first," said Sarah. "Want to come to the house this evening? Dinner and telly. Or paper correcting."

"And I could be safe from sneaking up to Amos's house with a carton of milk and a hot-water bottle? Thanks, but no thanks. I think I'll go out on my own and hit the hot spots."

"You're impossible," said Sarah cheerfully. It was hard to act like a housemother with someone as buoyant as Mary. But, Sarah told herself as she clambered out of the Jeep, she's vulnerable, a sitting Jemima duck.

Professor Merlin-Smith, now fixed in Sarah's mind as Merlin-Pecksniff, did indeed snuffle. And fidget. He went over the metrics of *Paradise Lost* and wrote little squiggle notations on the board to indicate stress and rhyme scheme, told his students in a reedy voice to look for echoes of the *Areopagitica*, spoke at length about Heavenly Visions and Voices Divine, and then began a rehash of the catastrophic events of Book IX.

The students were quiet for the most part. Four o'clock classes were notorious for student lassitude, and Eustace Merlin-Smith did nothing to rouse them out of their torpor. Ruffling through the pages of the text, he called upon a student to begin reading.

Sarah, sitting at the back of the room, listened with half an ear, remembering Dr. Johnson's words that "*Paradise Lost* is one of the books which the reader admires and lays down, and forgets to take up again. None ever wished it longer than it is." Even Professor Merlin-Smith seemed to be suffering from the reading, although the student's monotone rendition may have contributed to this. Sarah's judgment was that Merlin-Smith seemed insecure, snuffled, had poor color, and acted threatened if anyone raised a hand. Then she looked out the window at the snow-topped roofs of the college and began to think of other things. Rosalind Parker, for instance. Her choir robe. Did she really sing in the choir? Sarah tried to picture the secretary, imposing in her robe, a score in open hands, lifting her voice in a cantata. Did choir members still wear black robes? Most of the choirs Sarah had seen lately were clad in trendier colors, light blues, greens, even gold. Burgundy and navy for the more conservative denominations. Perhaps Mrs. Parker was a lay preacher or some sort of deacon.

"I see," said Professor Merlin-Smith "that we've been joined today by one of our teaching fellows. Miss Deane, isn't it?"

Sarah jumped as if she had been stung by a hornet.

"You students who seem to read with so little sense of the meaning and rhythm of the lines might benefit from hearing from a new voice." Professor Merlin-Smith twisted in Sarah's direction. "Miss Deane, could we persuade you to read Milton's lines as I'm sure they were meant to be read? Will someone pass the text to Miss Deane?"

It was absolutely malicious. A young man with a ginger beard and a sardonic grin passed over a book.

Sarah began to say no and then thought better of it. Wing it. Surely after all these years in academic life she could get through a little Milton without disgrace. She plunged in, a little awkwardly at first, but as the lines unrolled, forcing their beat and movement on her reading, she took heart and wound up in good form with Eve about to do in Adam and womankind in one fell bite.

There was a pause and a slight rustle in the class, but whether from boredom or from appreciation Sarah could not tell.

"Thank you, Miss Deane. Very nice indeed. Now perhaps you'll join in our little discussion and tell us what you think Milton is accomplishing here—poetically as well as thematically—remembering the carrying force of the first eight books."

Oh, no, you don't, thought Sarah, smiling at the professor with clenched teeth. "Professor Merlin-Smith, it isn't quite fair for me to say anything when your class is right in the middle of Milton's central development. What do they think—you, for instance?" Sarah whirled around and handed the text back to the student with the ginger beard.

"I think," said the student, grinning, "that the snake has all the lines."

The resulting chatter from this remark and the sound of the period bell allowed Sarah to escape, her teeth still bared in what she hoped was a professional grimace. Merlin-Smith was a worm of the first water. Alex had told her he had elaborated on his name and possibly fudged his undergraduate record, so he was probably one of those who would do something devious to save his skin. A specialist in little acts of meanness and calculation. But the big time, murder? She doubted it. But now, no more classes, thank God. Time to meet Alex, go home, take Patsy for an evening walk.

Following a very good omelette with peppers and mushrooms and cheese, Sarah poured coffee out for Alex, tea for herself, settled herself before the stove, and said in a casual voice, "We bumped into Amos Larkin this morning."

Alex sat down next to her, balanced a cup on one knee, and put an arm around Sarah's shoulder. "And what came of bumping into suspect number one?"

"Lunch came. With Mary and me. Not my idea. George had just finished warning us about him. Anyway, here's something to think about. Mrs. Parker was blackmailing Amos Larkin about an accident that had never really happened—well, never happened the way she said."

"Explain yourself."

So Sarah told about Mary and the bicycle and how for well over two years Mrs. Parker had used Amos Larkin's "crime" to gather in a host of favors.

"And that's a damn good reason for Amos Larkin to poison Mrs. Parker," said Alex. "Have you called George?"

"I haven't had time. But doesn't it show Mrs. Parker in a new light? If she could bring Professor Larkin to heel, what else has she been up to?"

At that question a heavy rapping sounded at the kitchen door. Alex put down his coffee, sighed heavily, and stood up.

It was Mike Laaka, with fur cap, fur gloves, and a quart of coffee ice cream.

"Come in, Mike," said Alex resignedly. "What's with the ice cream? Do you think we need cooling off?"

"It's a theory of mine. Fight fire with fire. Cold with cold. But the visit's semiofficial. I've got informations and questions."

"Let Sarah lead off first," said Alex. "She has the day's bombshell, and it's not going to do Amos Larkin any good." He dug into the ice-cream carton. "Ben and Jerry's, nothing but the best."

Sarah pulled up a chair for Mike beside the stove and filled him in on the day's excitements, ending with, "And you see Mary's off balance as far as Professor Larkin goes, and Mrs. Parker may have had a sideline in blackmail. If with Amos Larkin, why not the others? It would account for her power base. Mike, have you found out anything about the other faculty that Mrs. Parker might have tied into?"

"George has dug up a few irregularities, though Larkin is leading the field because of the scarf and now this bicycle business. George will have to go through the hospital records to make sure he really didn't slam into someone before he hit Mary. But we've got more on this Merlin-Smith/Schmidt guy. Not a Princeton graduate. George found out that he changed his records. Began at Princeton and finished, after a year off, at Penn State. Then, he doesn't have a Cambridge University degree, though he seems to have given the whole English Department that idea. Just a junior year abroad at Downing College, which I gather isn't one of the prestige places. Parker might have used the info as a bargaining chip."

"Lord, lord, how this world is given to lying," said Sarah. She accepted a bowl of ice cream from Alex and took a tentative taste.

"Any more dirty linen?" asked Alex, coming back to the sofa with his ice cream.

"Constance Garvey hated Parker's guts, but that's no secret, and she's interesting because she's been palming low-cal cocoa. No one can stand the woman. I heard that Larkin once called her the 'new Gorgon'—whatever that means."

"It's not a friendly remark," said Sarah.

"I'll file it away," said Mike. "Now, Howard Bello, the chairman, is clean so far and in a tailspin over losing Parker, and I've sat in on a grilling of Ivan Lacey, who let us know that he's loyal and true to his dear wife and children, who he kept dragging into the conversation, and he's tired of fighting off female students. They apparently line up to get into his classes."

"Perhaps they do," said Sarah. "He doesn't work them, and they all read the passionate parts of the plays together. Mary Donelli calls him the Black Stallion, but that may be maligning the horse."

"Well, we called on Mrs. Black Stallion, and she backed up his version of things, but she was some defensive. Maybe Lacey has left his hoof marks on a few local fillies. But no proof so far."

Alex shook his head. "I think it would be pretty stupid for Lacey to fool around with Bowmouth students."

"I agree," said Mike. "And the college is entirely surrounded by very small, very gossipy towns. You can't buy a six-pack of beer without someone turning up at your house with the pretzels."

"How about Professor Patrick Fletcher?" asked Sarah. "He's a smooth one, and he was working late the night of Alice's murder."

"Yes, and he came late to the hockey game, but we've come up with nothing except complaints about his pipe tobacco and the view that some of the underlings think he's an arrogant bastard. Of course, he's published a raft of scholarly books, which may account for the superior air. Jakob Horst is more likely. George thinks there's something funny about not giving those papers back."

"Your turn, Alex," said Sarah. "Any medical lore to add?"

"Nothing except the fact that Mrs. Parker was done in by cyanide and there seem to be multiple ways of finding the stuff."

"Like?"

"All the labs. Biochem departments, undergrad and grad

labs. The Life Sciences buildings, the med school and its research branch. The hospital research extension."

"But not just lying around."

"Precautions are taken, but things are looser than you'd think. Lots of the labs have a sort of open-door policy, with people wandering in at all hours to check on experiments and results."

"You mean anyone can walk in and ask for a cup of cyanide?"

"Not quite, but most people here have access to lethal material. A lot of household products, pesticides, and plants have a cyanic base."

"How comforting," said Sarah. "And to think only Mrs. Parker got poisoned."

"It's one reason why police hate to deal with colleges," said Mike. "Everyone goes on about freedom of speech, and no one pays attention to these people playing around with poisons and atoms. We're trying to trace all the college connections. Drago Collins and one of the ER nurses are a duo; Linda, the clerk, has a cousin in the hospital ICU; and guess who has a brother in the med school who teaches anatomy?"

"I don't have to guess," said Alex. "I know him. Amos Larkin's brother, Francis."

"And has access to cyanide," Sarah guessed.

"Correct," said Mike. "I gather Amos drifts over to the med school from time to time. Passed out in the gross anatomy room one fine afternoon. Woke up to find he was the only living thing around. Sobered him up for a while, according to his brother, who says he's tired of playing nurse and lecturing Amos about his liver."

Sarah finished her ice cream, gathered up the dishes, and then with a sudden thought turned to Mike.

"Did you ever find out if Mrs. Parker sang in the choir? She's got a black robe in her wardrobe."

"I know. George asked me to chase that down, but I haven't got around to it. It's a low priority. Long black dresses are a dime a dozen. Maybe she's a practicing witch."

"That's been suggested. Or she belongs to a secret society, or it's her graduation gown. It just might be worth looking into. What's the name of her church?"

Mike pulled out a notebook. "Cedars of Lebanon Methodist Church."

"Try and call them," said Sarah. "It's not that late. Someone might be around."

It was surprisingly easy. It was choir practice night, and Mike found out that Mrs. Parker had from time to time been a substitute alto. The choir robes were dark red; the men wore white shirts with dark ties, the women white collars. No black robes except for the minister. Most of the church choirs in the area had switched to colors years ago.

"Mike, let's go," said Sarah suddenly. "Right now. Over to Mrs. Parker's house. Let's see the thing. You know, if she was squeezing Amos Larkin, there might be more to find out even if a black dress seems completely trivial. Couldn't we sneak in without getting George all stirred up?"

"George doesn't stir, he strikes. Think of a better reason."

Sarah considered, going slowly in her mind over Mrs. Parker's memorial cocktail party. The presentation books, the Bowmouth watercolors, the duplicate office, and then: "Those old commencement programs. Why has she kept those? Joe Greenberg said she'd made notes in them."

"George has checked them out. Not very interesting. Mrs. Parker underlined the names of honorary degree recipients—some women, a man or two, though she only knew one of them personally, a local woman," said Mike. And then as if falling into the spirit, "Okay, what the hell? I can talk my way past the deputies on watch there. Of course, George will cut off my head in the morning, and yours too."

Mrs. Parker's house now really stood out from its snow-buried neighbors. Not only the walks were shoveled; the roof, the chimney top, and the gutters had been cleaned and searched, the yews and arborvitae had been vacuumed, and the foundations probed.

A light burned in the front window, and a sheriff deputy's car, with the deputy in the driver's seat, stood in the driveway. Mike went over, spoke to some purpose, and returned. "All right. Go in and solve the case. But if you do, George will never forgive you. He doesn't want amateurs buzzing around finding hairs on the soap and blood spots, especially after his own men have sucked the place dry."

The trip to Mrs. Parker's bedroom proved immediately that the black dress was a proper academic robe. Black velvet front panels, sleeves circled in three black velvet bands.

"Pretty fancy outfit," said Mike.

"It's a doctoral robe," said Alex. "Bachelors and masters don't get the velvet."

"Well, that's that," said Mike. "Maybe she swiped it or is doing some mending for one of the faculty. She made cookies for them, so why not take home a gown or two?"

Sarah ran a finger down the front panel and thought wistfully of all the slogging work and time it took to merit such a costume. "You don't suppose she had a secret PhD or bought a degree? People do, you know. Or maybe it's for dressing up. Wishful thinking, fantasy."

"You mean she's like the sergeant who keeps silver bars in his bureau drawer?" said Alex.

Mike sat down on the edge of the now stripped bed. "George went over her background. She had a BS, and she'd audited a few courses at Bowmouth. No graduate credits. After all, she was a full-time—night and day—secretary. She didn't have any advanced degree, and George hasn't found any caps or tassels or hoods. If she's dressing up, the robe is it."

Sarah turned and headed for the stairs. "Maybe you're right, Mike. She was mending someone's gown—Howard Bello's, maybe. She did everything else for him. Anyway, since we're here, can we see those commencement programs and those honorary-degree names? Who was the woman that Mrs. Parker knew?"

"Some name like Wilma or Thelma Wiggins. She's a sculptor and was in Parker's class in high school. Made good in NYC and got an honorary degree, in 'seventy-nine, I think it was."

Down in Mrs. Parker's office, Alex ran through several programs and frowned over the underlined names. "Some of these are fairly recent. She's marked one or two honorary degree recipients in almost every program. In 1982 Bowmouth gave a degree to Robert Penn Warren, to Agnes DeMille, and a man called Dunstan Royall—'benefactor, community leader.' She's underlined him. Two years back an Evelyn Giles of the American Red Cross got a degree and three underlines, as does a Dorothy Yardington for 'community leadership in education.' "

Sarah quickly ruffled through several more programs. "Two more underlined, an amateur geologist and an artist, both women."

"Women she admired," suggested Alex.

"Women," said Mike, "she did not admire. Judging from reports. She played to the men. Everyone in the department makes it a point to tell us that she was never buddy-buddy with the female faculty or staff, never had lunch or went out for a drink with them. Except Miss Prism. And Linda told us that she said several times that it was a shame that Bowmouth went coed."

"Not a member of the sisterhood," said Sarah. "Let's try this on. Rosalind Parker has made Bowmouth the end and be-all of her whole life, she gradually builds a heap of faculty perks—the club, department meetings, her own office—but she's not faculty."

"So in her bedroom she plays like she is," said Mike.

"What she does," said Sarah, "is go over all the names of people who were given honorary degrees, especially the women, to see if somehow she would qualify. Which she wouldn't. Dead end. Back to square one."

"Right," agreed Alex. "It would be impossible. Unless you're a public personage, a benefactor, have done some noteworthy deed, are an artist or writer or government bigwig, it's out of the question. Absolutely impossible."

Sarah struck her hands together. "That's what he said. Professor Lacey. The night that Mrs. Parker died. He said that it was out of the question, absolutely impossible. Listen, you don't suppose Mrs. Parker actually asked for an honorary degree?"

"Then she'd really lost her grip on reality," said Alex. "She should have known the academic world better than that. They don't sprinkle degrees around like salt."

"But she had almost the whole senior English faculty eating out of her hand," insisted Sarah. "Maybe she thought she'd win out and bought the gown to be ready. She'd been at the college over thirty years. She must have thought she was a local treasure and should be rewarded. That she deserved a degree." Sarah sat down in the Bowmouth chair and drew her coat around her shoulders. The house, since the police had taken full possession, was now kept at a spartan fifty degrees. "If she had the same sort of hold over other faculty members as she had over Amos Larkin, she might have made them propose her. People like Professor Fletcher and Bello—even Horst—have quite a lot of influence, I suppose."

Mike shook his head. "Now just hold it. One PhD robe and a soused professor being squeezed don't make a case. There is no sign that Parker had found out about any of the irregularities that George has dug up. No notes, no letters, no files. If she knew about Merlin-Smith and Princeton or any girlie episodes of Lacey's, she kept it in her head. And if Mrs. Parker had been going around the English Department bleating about an honorary degree, some of the faculty would have mentioned it to us. They would have known she was a mile out of line. I think you're making too big a deal out of that black gown. Think of all the things that turn up in closets. Circus costumes, whips, spurs, ticklers, stuffed cobras, pickled gall bladders. Why, Mrs. Parker didn't even have a reversed cross or a bucket of blood on the stove. Forget it, Sarah."

"Oh, dear, and I thought I was on to something."

"Let it simmer for a while," said Alex.

"Anything else catch your fancy?" asked Mike. "Since you're here, you might as well take a look."

Sarah with Alex beside her made another round of Mrs. Parker's home office—the framed pictures of Bowmouth, the pile of periodicals, the cupboard of office supplies. On the bottom shelf stood a regiment of dictionaries and style handbooks. The usual. Sarah reached for Skeat's *Etymological Dictionary* and in doing so tumbled a small green paperback behind it. *A Handbook for the Computer Novice—Word Processing Made Simple.*

Sarah held it up. "Mrs. Parker didn't use a computer, did she?"

Mike walked over. "No. It was a real sore point, seeing how Linda and Arlene were starting to get a lot of business from the faculty that Mrs. P used to handle."

Alex thumbed through the handbook. "Looks like Mrs. Parker was on speaking terms with word processing. See, she's checked some sections, made notes."

"I'll bet she'd been practicing," said Sarah. "On the quiet. You know, if you can't beat them, join them. That would explain her dying in the English Office with the computer keyboard knocked over. I couldn't understand *why* she was in there with her cocoa."

"George found the book and has already speculated that she was trying to learn elementary computer operation," said Mike. "Or was trying to run some department disks. A checkup on the two clerks."

"The learning idea makes a lot of sense," said Alex. "Mrs. Parker knew that even the most complex electronic typewriter couldn't compete with a word processor."

"Yes," said Sarah with growing excitement. "She must have felt she'd lose control of the department if she couldn't get a handle on the competition. She probably was going to emerge fully armed someday and send those clerks back to copying and filing papers. How can you find out if she was actually using the machine when she died?"

Mike shook his head. "When she fell across the table and onto the floor she pulled the cord out of the socket and just about ruined the keyboard. George is still working to get decent prints from under the spilled cocoa. Anything on the screen would have been lost when the power was cut."

"Unless she'd saved it," said Alex. "On a disk."

"Sorry," said Mike, "but no disks. George checked particularly. No disks in the machine. George is going over the disks on file in the office, but so far they're just routine English Office stuff that Parker had printed copies of. But you know it'd make a good TV show. Secretary practicing on computer drinks poison cocoa, and then as she expires taps out a secret message about the murderer, but as she's about to transfer his name from the screen to the disk, death grabs her by the throat and she falls over, knocking out the power and the message, and the murderer is in the clear."

"Stick to horse racing," said Alex.

"Don't I wish? All the Kentucky Derby preps are being run, and I can't even get away for an hour to watch them on the tube. Okay, let's pack it up here. You've both made enough trouble, for me and for yourselves, and I don't think we've moved one inch ahead. In fact, George will probably think you've set us back three weeks."

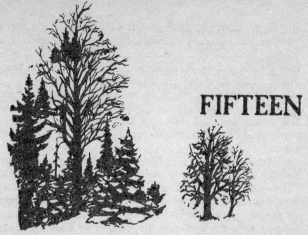

FIFTEEN

The next day—Friday—Sarah, bracing herself, sat in on two of Constance Garvey's morning classes, after explaining that her own field was the novel. The professor, thus flattered, gave her a *humph* and proceeded to demonstrate her often repeated theory: "If you can't see the trees, you can't see the forest." This interesting reversal of an old favorite could be followed in Professor Garvey's fanatic pursuit of the tiny detail, the tedious, and the peripheral in several well-known nineteenth-century novels. It was literature as Trivial Pursuit. What was Jane Eyre wearing when she first met Mr. Rochester? What was the name of his dog? What sort of cheese did Mr. Murdstone name when testing David Copperfield on his arithmetic? What book did Becky Sharp toss out of the carriage window? What instrument did the Warden play? What was Mr. Woodhouse's favorite dish? How did these facts relate to the action, the statement, the controlling metaphor, of the whole? And so on and on.

Sarah, relieved of any need to remember what Professor Garvey was talking about, came to the easy conclusion that with those heavy-ringed hands—the professor favored knuckle-bending garnet and gold numbers—she could have tossed an elephant, let alone handled Alice Marmott. As for Mrs. Parker—well, cyanide was hardly punishment enough for the ousting of an associate professor from her office. Opportunity, yes. Motive, certainly. Supply of low-cal cocoa packets, absolutely. Cyanide? That just needed a little research and friends in the right places. Sarah could just hear her say in her deep voice, "I have rats to get rid of."

She turned her attention back to the class to find Professor Garvey threatening the class with an hour quiz. "I take off ten points for each error of fact and judgment," she was reminding them. "And last term I gave eleven *F*'s in the final exam."

As an antidote to Constance Garvey, Sarah decided on a sudden impulse to sit in on Joe Greenberg's undergraduate "Development of the English Novel" class. The fifty minutes so spent served as a needed reminder of why she had wanted to major in literature. Today it was *Clarissa*. Students, arranged in a circle, were encouraged to develop ideas, no matter how feeble, and were led through the intricacies of Clarissa's seduction with a sure and delicate hand. In fact, students who might have originally groaned over the epistle form of the novel were now galloping enthusiastically from letter to letter, the females of the class crying rape and the males pointing out that Clarissa was asking for it. All in all, a lively class in which students seemed to care about what they were saying. Sarah mentioned this as she and the professor walked down the hall after class.

"I like to keep things moving, even if they get off the track sometimes. It's hard to make a book like that seem urgent. The eighteenth century is like the Middle Ages to them." He opened his office door. "Come in a minute and tell me how goes it with the teaching fellow."

"Distracted by murder. Alice and Mrs. Parker keep circling around in my head and jamming the jobs I should be doing. I do have one question, a crazy one. Did Mrs. Parker have any expectations of getting an honorary degree?"

"From Bowmouth? God, no. At least not that I knew of. That would have been idiotic, which she wasn't. She was a very good secretary and got plenty of recognition, some would say too much. The college gave her a staff award a few years back, but an honorary doctorate? No way."

"So no pressure on you about it . . . or anything else?"

"I think she knew I wouldn't give in to any ideas like that."

"Then how about a sort of in-house blackmail? I found out yesterday that Professor Larkin was being worked over." And Sarah told him about Mary's bicycle accident. "He wouldn't have found out about this fake crippled student if Mary hadn't blurted it out yesterday when she knocked him down."

"Oh, God, poor Amos. That's fiendish. He's having enough trouble with the bottle and his son being taken away without Mrs. Parker's moving in. I suppose in your book, Sarah, that means motive."

"I'm not keeping a book, but I know George Fitts is. Anyway, I've been thinking that if she was squeezing Amos Larkin she may have been doing it to someone else."

"I've never heard of anything like that. I doubt if she'd try anything with Vera or Howard or Pat Fletcher. And how would you like to try and squeeze Connie Garvey or Jakob Horst?"

Sarah said she wouldn't and left to make her way to the mail room. There, overhearing Arlene and Linda recapping in detail a day with Mrs. Parker, she thought to herself, That's the way to go. No one knows more about the inner workings of a department than those who take care of all the nitty-gritty, tedious, and unlovely details. The two clerks see the faculty in their natural state, not trying to impress students or each other, and perhaps the two of them have not really loosened up with George and Mike. Anyway, she reflected, Mike had given the impression that the police investigation was stalled on dead center with only Amos Larkin as a genuine suspect. And, much as she deplored the professor as a person, Sarah was not entirely convinced that a man who was staggering drunk on the two murder occasions had enough wit and coordination to manage the killings. She walked into the clerks' office and greeted the two women, all the while wondering how she would be justified in poking into the ways and means of the English Department as well as discussing the peculiarities of Mrs. Parker.

Linda was stuffing memos into brown manila envelopes and Arlene was stacking a new shipment of desk copy novels for Professor Garvey's course. It gave Sarah an idea.

"Look, Linda, Arlene, I'm thinking about writing a sort of mystery story—a novel about a college. But I'm keeping it a secret until I've done the research."

"You mean you're using us," said Arlene, whirling around in her chair. "And the murders and what goes on here?"

"Not exactly. Just getting general ideas, sketching in the characters," said Sarah cautiously. It sounded believable; everyone in the English Department wrote *something,* and Vera Pruczak would have broken in the two clerks to the idea of a fiction writer on the prowl. "I'm sure," she added, "that Vera Pruczak gets some of her ideas from all of you."

It was a lucky shot. "Why, Vera was in the other day," exclaimed Arlene. "She says I'm to be the model for Miss Belinda in her new novel. Miss Belinda's in love with this lord, but he knows that her brother has gambled away her whole estate."

"And I was the model for the housekeeper's daughter in the last one," said Linda. "I went mad and tried to push Sir Joshua into the big bake oven. But, honestly, I'm not that turned on about her stuff. I mean, life is real, and now that I'm the acting secretary I haven't the time."

"It turns me on," said Arlene. "Instant glamour. So what are you going to do? Have a college like this with a fiend loose?"

"Not quite like this," said Sarah, wondering what sort of book to propose.

"Go supernatural," said Arlene. "That's big now. Vera doesn't have ghosts; her characters just *think* they see them."

"That's a good idea," said Sarah gratefully. "Visiting space people, open graves, and children walking. Interstellar vampires. Anyway, I thought you could help me with some of the characters. Like Mrs. Parker. Things the police wouldn't be interested in—you know, personality quirks. I'll change the names."

"I want to be recognized," said Arlene. "But make me thin."

"Slim, dark-haired Princess Arlene from the Planet Zip. How's that?"

"Sounds good. Okay, this is fun." Arlene stood up and hung a sign—LUNCH HOUR—on the outside of the door. "That keeps most of them out except for types like Garvey, and she's got one o'clock seminar. And now that the switchboard's been moved in here, we can take the calls. Linda hopes to get Parker's office, but Garvey wants it back. Never a dull minute."

"Of course," said Linda, examining her nails—today an apple-green polish—"we may get an empty office without trying. When that Sergeant Fitts makes an arrest, if it's one of the senior faculty here, we'll have an extra office."

Sarah paused, digesting the formula: murderer caught equals office space available. "For a start," she said, "tell me about Mrs. Parker. The little things. For instance, do you suppose she wanted to be real faculty? Get an honorary degree? Something like that."

This produced a torrent of opinion and information about the secretary, the upshot being that yes, she acted like faculty, talked like faculty, ordered people around like faculty, and she probably would have killed (as Linda put it) to get one of those Doctor of Humane Letters the college dished out at commencement. "Doctor of Typed Letters." Arlene chuckled.

"Could she have made the faculty propose her?"

"She made them do everything else," said Linda. "So why not?"

Arlene agreed. "And it wouldn't hurt the college to give some of the staff those fancy hoods. Maybe not Mrs. Parker, but how about Klaus, the night watchman, or Mrs. Flanders in the bookstore? They've been here for ages and have given their life's blood. All they get when they retire is a watch or a silver dish."

It wasn't the worst idea Sarah'd ever heard. Better, she thought, than decorating some oil baron or warmongering congressman. Further questioning revealed that Mrs. Parker didn't talk about her health, was rarely sick, but had gone to Boston last year for a checkup and tests. "She seemed okay, though," said Arlene. "She could always work us right under the floor."

As to the secretary's interest in word processing, "We think she was interested but she wouldn't let on," said Linda. "After all, we were getting a lot of the manuscript traffic, and she was missing out on those little acknowledgment notes. You know, 'My sincere thanks to my devoted typist'—that sort of crap. But you can't fit that into a mystery novel."

"I can write about how the invention of the nuclear typewriter threatened the college secretary who had just mastered the word processor," said Sarah. "It's the same idea."

Here the little switchboard blinked, Linda said, "English Department," and Arlene beckoned Sarah off into the annex where the mail shelves and the lost-and-found lived. "Look, don't tell anyone, but we think Parker had something on Horst. Maybe it won't fit in your novel, but someone should know. I think she was worried about what Alice Marmott was going to do to him. Parker liked knowing something about everything, but she wouldn't have wanted some student to be in on it. Alice's case was getting off the ground and Parker wanted to stop it. I'll bet Parker found out that Horst was doing something he shouldn't have or that he'd lost those students' papers. I heard her say once that he'd better be careful."

"In my novel," said Sarah, "I've got a blackmail scheme. There'll be a weird space woman character, Mrs. Proudie"—thank you, Anthony Trollope, she said to herself—"who infiltrates the college and is blackmailing everyone in sight."

"I always said Mrs. Parker would make a great sheriff, so why not a great blackmailer? Of course, she did have something to hold over Professor Larkin's head, seeing as she was always bailing him out of trouble. And she might have caught Lacey. I bumped into him once wrestling with one of the students in the Fellows' Room, and he was unzipped. I never told anyone, but he should watch out. You should see the Doberman pinscher he's married to."

"And Professor Fletcher. He'd do as a gentleman were-wolf."

"He sure thinks he's high and mighty. I don't think

Parker would have anything on him. Mr. Old English Leather sucking on that pipe and saying to us, 'My dear girl, have you a minute?' Mrs. Parker was plenty respectful to him."

"Come back in here," called Linda. "What are you saying?"

"Just that Fletcher is the big gun of the department. Olivia Macbeth may be the Hollywood star, but he's the prestige man. All those articles and books. He's always getting requests to speak or do a colloquium somewhere. Listen, I've got to eat lunch." Arlene sat down at her desk and pulled out a carton of strawberry yogurt.

"Are you set as the new secretary then?" said Sarah to Linda.

"I hope. God, the work that woman got through. I've been polishing up Howard Bello just like Parker did, because he doesn't know anything about running the place, but I may have to start working late to sew up the job."

"As long as you don't turn into Mrs. P," said Arlene. "Sarah here tells me the Parker character in her mystery will be blackmailing one of the other characters."

"It's all a secret, remember," said Sarah. "I'm just collecting primary material." That sounds legitimate, she thought. Then cocking her head to the door, "What's that noise?" She could hear heavy footsteps, shufflings, and bangings.

"Thank God," said Linda. "The State Police. They're moving out of the Common Room and setting up a field office in a trailer next to the hockey rink. Now we'll get the waiting room back, the faculty back to the Common Room, and the students off the floor. And I forgot; we're to report to the police this afternoon there. Me and Arlene now, Mary Donelli at four, and you at four-thirty. All the faculty again tomorrow. They must be getting ready to grab someone."

"Or," said Arlene, "they haven't a clue and are going to put the heat on us. Truth serum or nerve gas. All the latest technology."

"Sarah, that's where you are." Mary Donelli stuck her head in the door. "Hurry up. It's a makeup seminar at one on the eighteenth century, for when Amos was out—in the hospital."

"Out is a good word for it," said Linda.

"He was sick," said Mary angrily.

Oh, brother, thought Sarah, she is absolutely gone. Before Mary could expose herself further, Sarah pushed her out into the hall.

"Wait up," called Arlene. "Sarah, if you want more local color for that novel, go on the ski club trip next Monday."

"What's she talking about?" said Mary, as they hurried down stairs. "What novel?"

"I was just trying to find out more about nothing. What ski club trip?"

"The English Department ski club. See also the English Department bowling team and ball club. The chairman before Howard Bello was big on community spirit. But except for the skiers, it's more or less fallen apart. The skiers get a break on the bus and the lift tickets. There's usually a dinner afterward."

"The faculty go?" Sarah started for the stairs.

"Sure, some of them. Joe Greenberg and his wife. Horst and wife, and Lacey without wife so he can pinch ski pant bottoms, and Fletcher and the missus. They're both experts. Vera to the party afterward."

"So maybe we should go. Does . . . ?"

"Amos? No way. Drunk or sober, he's not the clubby type."

They reached the first floor seminar and made their way to seats. Professor Larkin was bent over the desk at the head of the room unpacking his briefcase. Then, holding a stack of papers, he looked over the house. Not by the twitch of an eyebrow nor the curl of a lip did he acknowledge the presence of his companions of the snowbank. Sarah was glad that he appeared sober and showed signs of being capable of conducting the seminar to its two-hour limit.

"I have here, for better or for worse," said Professor Larkin, "a collection of your recent papers on Swift. Pick them up after class, and I'll schedule some of you for conference. Three interesting contributions, which I will read." He reached in a pocket and produced a pair of dark-rimmed glasses fastened together at the nose with a piece of tape.

The first paper dealt with Swift's conflicting views of the

nature of man, and Sarah found herself wishing she'd hit on that particular angle. She noted that Amos Larkin's hands still shook the paper he read, but from her distance he looked a fraction healthier. Next he picked up a paper, "Swift's Satire —The Poetry of the Anti-Sublime." Sarah saw Mary's shoulders rise and her color change. I wonder if he's reading it as a sort of apology, she thought. But no, the paper stood on its own, and Sarah, as if seeing her friend for the first time, heard the paragraphs roll forth, each illustrated by appropriate lines of poetry. Mary was succinct and pertinent, and each point was made in turn so that the whole stood at the end like a well-built house.

"That," said Professor Larkin, "is a chapter from a graduate student's dissertation and is the sort of thing I'd like to have from all of you."

The third paper read, Sarah found to her horror, was hers, a trifling effort she hadn't been able to finish properly.

"This writer doesn't go far enough," said Amos Larkin. "She has conviction, but not the courage of it. It peters out. But since it's a good beginning, I hope she'll finish it someday. Not for me. For her own pleasure."

Pleasure. A word that hadn't occurred to Sarah lately in connection with her classes. Not for instruction, for discipline, but for pleasure. Well, well. For a moment she forgot her fury at the man in front of the class. Only for a moment and then remembered. Amos Larkin, the fox. What could be more disarming? Because even a hung-over sot would have noticed that Mary was forgiving and Sarah was antagonistic. What better way to put Mary firmly in his camp and to put a damper on Sarah than to read their papers? Except Mary's chapter was good; it deserved praise. And—well, what he'd said about hers was right too. She'd had an idea and hadn't taken it far enough to test its validity. She frowned and drew an angry series of fox faces on her paper and then realized that the professor had begun an introductory lecture on Samuel Johnson. Jonathan Swift was past history. She tried to pay attention, only too aware that Mary was still sitting next to her in a daze of happiness.

An hour later, with an assignment on the great lexicographer long enough to keep students tied up for a year, Sarah gathered her books and with Mary collected their papers. She had a $B+$.

Mary said what Sarah was thinking. "This isn't because of the snowbank incident, is it?"

"Miss Donelli, you've written four good chapters. If you'd written poor ones I would have told you so. Now go along and do four more. And you." He looked at Sarah. "Have you a question?"

"No, Professor Larkin," said Sarah meekly. She had come to the desk with a sharp retort on her lips and some intention in her role as a quasi Alice Marmott of asking whether she could extend her paper into a real research effort. Now, such a thing seemed cheap and self-serving. She retreated.

To make up for what she told herself was a complete lack of investigative backbone, she resolved to strike some sort of spark from Professors Patrick Fletcher and Jakob Horst.

Professor Fletcher was spreading himself. Finished with battles where ravens circled as warriors hacked and hewed themselves to death, he moved on to Old English charms and riddles. For a little while Sarah forgot duty and listened with enjoyment as the professor read to them what he called a free translation of the "Storm" riddle.

> At times I roil the ocean   flinging down
> to stir the surges   and drive the flint-grey
> waves to the shore   foaming the waters
> battering the wall.   Darkly rears up
> the dune over the deep;   darkly behind it
> admixed with the sea   another surge roars . . .

Then, obviously in an indulgent mood, Professor Fletcher launched into the delights to come after the spring break when the students would be allowed to tackle the epic poem *Beowulf*.

Sarah raised her hand and asked whether she should begin to read background material such as the history of the Viking invasions in Britain. As expected, Professor Fletcher not only cut her short but roasted her slowly over the fire by asking her to read aloud an appropriate elegy called "The

Ruin." Sarah faltered, as she knew she would, and was told not to annoy the class again.

Professor Horst, whose classroom was in a drafty corner of the old biology building—a sure sign of Mrs. Parker's disfavor—had today chosen "Dover Beach" to dismember. He lectured from the blackboard, breaking chalk, breathing heavily, and soon the whole surface was covered with a maze of shredded lines, curves, triangles, and plus signs. Sarah, sitting front and center, tried to nod brightly every so often and shield her paper, on which she was drawing a picture of the classroom door.

After the bell rang, Sarah stood in line to talk to the professor. His coloring, she had thought during his blackboard performance, was on the hectic side and suggested that he might be coming down with a cold and fever. But now, on closer inspection, she decided it seemed likely that there was more than one heavy drinker in the department. She stepped up to his desk. "I'd like to try analyzing a poem, giving the grammar numerical weight as you do."

"You're one of the teaching fellows, aren't you?" said the professor. "Well, avoid contemporary work if you're just starting this sort of thing. Choose regular rhythms and rhyme schemes. I myself have trouble with some of the newer poets."

"And," said Sarah, "you'll read and criticize what I've done?"

"When I have time."

"And I may have my paper back?"

Jakob Horst threw his head up. "What do you mean by that?" he barked.

"I've heard that, as a matter of policy, you don't always."

"I sometimes don't hand back undergraduate papers because I have no intention of making time-consuming comments on every feebleminded paper that comes to me." He turned away and began slamming his pocket calculator and his graph paper into his briefcase.

Sarah said, "Thank you very much. I'll start with Tennyson," and left the room and headed for the English Office. Tennyson seemed a safe enough choice for something she had no intention of doing. The sun was making a small afternoon effort, and the walkways were heavy in melting slush. Four o'clock. Half an hour until her appointment with George in his new field office. And then, perhaps, an early dinner and the new Olivia Macbeth that Vera had left off for her yesterday. Gothic romance sounded unbelievably restful and undemanding. She made her way to the English Office, intending to pick up her mail, and found Linda and Arlene unpacking the restored computer.

"I'd like to know what Mrs. Parker thought she was doing, fooling around in our office," said Linda. "It wasn't enough that she was Queen Bee, she had to move in on our word processor."

"So look where it got her," said Arlene, who was gingerly pulling the keyboard out from two blocks of Styrofoam.

"We should have guessed," said Linda, "because there've been funny things for a couple of months, like my paper punch and the scissors turning up on Arlene's desk." She wrestled the printer out of its carton, looked up, and scowled. "Now that I'm secretary, I'm going to keep it under lock and key."

Arlene rested the keyboard on her lap. "Hey, Sarah, do us a favor and pick up your Thermos, it's still there in the mail room. The police returned them all ages ago. Everybody got a big laugh out of your Raggedy Ann model, asked who the kid was."

"We're trying to clear out the place," said Linda. "Your Thermos is just the top of the heap. Stuff going back for years, unclaimed student papers, freshman texts. And that Parker was something. Nothing thrown away. Look at these, two whole boxes of used lift-off cartridges with her supplies. Maybe she'd figured some way to use them again. She was always making us hand in the used printer cartridges before giving us a new one. Well, out they go because things are going to change around here, believe me."

Sarah, without reasoning why she did it, reached into the basket for the two orange boxes and pocketed them, saying something about her mystery research, a statement accepted by Arlene and Linda, both long inured to the eccentricities of department personnel. Call it "evidence," she told herself, although how Mrs. Parker's typing mistakes could contribute to the investigation was for the moment beyond her. She set out for her appointment with George Fitts, turning over this and that, and soon found herself through the North Quad arch and at the newly planted State Police field office, a dingy white trailer with wires spouting from its dome like a creature about to be electrocuted.

The trailer's interior resembled the gutted insides of a large fish, gray and cold, a suitable backdrop for angler George Fitts, who opened the door himself. Mike Laaka, on one flank of the long metal desk, teetered on his chair, a great hazard to himself and to a stack of file boxes. And there was Alex, arms folded, sitting on a chair on the other side of the desk, part of his face obscured by the hooded desk light. The visible side of his face gave her a short wink.

"A joint interview," said George, "sometimes useful. Especially since Mike and Alex and Sarah have been acting together by looking into academic costumes without my knowledge. Remember, please, all of you, that this case is far from being over, so do not act on your own. You will harm more than help. Now, Sarah, have you anything to tell me, anything you've seen or heard lately?"

"Very little," said Sarah. "Except for some typing gismos Linda's throwing out and some little things Arlene hinted at."

"I don't expect miracles. The little things will do nicely," said George.

"Well, first, Arlene in the English Office felt that Mrs. Parker knew something about Professor Horst," said Sarah. "So what if Alice had come up with something that Mrs. Parker absolutely had to keep quiet, like the truth about Jakob Horst and the student papers. Or the business of blackmailing Amos Larkin."

"You mean a chain reaction," said Alex. "Alice finds out something Parker knows and Parker kills Alice. So who kills Parker, Alice's ghost?"

"It's just a starter," said Sarah.

"Let's just say Alice knew something or was going to do something and someone felt she would be better off dead," said George. "For now, let's leave Alice and consider Mrs. Parker alone."

"Her cocoa habit, for instance." said Mike. "She had her

own labeled Thermos with the Bowmouth seal, so no one could have made a mistake, and she kept a supply of low-cal cocoa packets on her desk. No one else's Thermos had any traces of cyanide, although Garvey's had traces of the low-cal stuff. What do you think, George? Did someone insert the cyanide in the cocoa packs in the A.M. and Parker just didn't get around to drinking her cocoa until after dark, when she was all alone—which was damn convenient for the murderer?"

"It didn't work that way," said George. "Linda says she remembers taking some finished copy into Mrs. Parker's office just before five that afternoon, and the top was off her Thermos and was half full of cocoa—the Thermos top makes a cup. We think she washed it out and later that night refilled it from the hot water in the English Office and added one of the low-cal packs, probably from the supply on her desk. Now we've tested those—as well as all the others—and they're okay, so we're going with the idea that the cyanide was put directly into her Thermos. We doubt that the murderer would have planted just one poisoned cocoa packet, not if he wanted to be sure of killing her that night, and we're sure it was planned for that night."

"Because of the snowstorm?" put in Sarah.

"The snowstorm was helpful—so many people milling around. But we think that the electric heat was turned off deliberately sometime after seven or eight. All but three rooms—the student waiting room, the English Office, and Mrs. Parker's office—are served by the old furnace, and the heat stays at about sixty degrees all night. But in those three rooms the heat went off. Looks like the murderer wanted to make doubly sure about Mrs. Parker having her cocoa. After all, a hot drink might be a necessity for someone working late in a cold room. It was just above freezing when we first examined the body."

Sarah nodded, remembering her shivering attempts to go to sleep.

"It almost had to be a member of the department, someone familiar with the new heating system, who knew about Mrs. Parker's plan to work late," continued George. "Also someone with access to Mrs. Parker's office, who could slip in while she was out for a minute."

Sarah protested. "That doesn't eliminate anyone. Mrs. Parker didn't make a secret about staying late, and the department was a regular party scene. Everyone going in and out of offices, having drinks, talking about the storm and where they were spending the night."

"Maybe only our friend Lushwell can be eliminated," said Mike. "Too polluted to handle the Thermos loading."

"If he wasn't playing possum," said George, "though I've confirmed from my own observation that his hands shake. Now, Alex, any new thoughts on the cyanide problem?"

"Well, as we've said, it's not that hard to get hold of. I've checked, and although the hospital and research labs do keep fairly strict tabs on lethal material, someone with an in or a friend could probably get their hands on it. I know you're interested in Amos Larkin's brother Francis, and he does go everywhere. But he's got a spotless reputation and runs a tight ship in the Anatomy Department. Another point. The cyanide may have been lifted ages ago and kept on hand just in case."

"You mean," said Sarah, "the murderer could just have kept it in his pocket waiting for Mrs. Parker's Thermos to be left unguarded. Or," she added thoughtfully, "he waited for a time when he knew Mrs. Parker would be alone working late, maybe even knew about the computer practice sessions. He —or she—could sneak in after everyone left and talk about how jolly it is to have cocoa to keep you warm."

"No one knows exactly what piece of work was keeping Mrs. Parker late. She even skipped dinner because she told Linda she had so much to do that she'd get a sandwich from the vending machine in the basement."

"I have it," said Sarah. "The murderer gives her a manuscript to type that night—needs it first thing in the morning —knowing that the only way she can finish it on time is to use the word processor. The murderer knows she's been practicing. And the length of the manuscript ensures that she stays quite late. If she used just the typewriter she would have refused, but now this will show that she can compete with the clerks. Question: Why does he want her to die in the English Office, not in her own office? Is it any easier to have her dead in the one place rather than the other? Anyway, the murderer lies low. Literally. In his office with the lights off. Slinks in after everyone has left to see how she's coming along."

"And," said Mike, joining in, "says, Lordy, how cold it's growing."

"Tiddely pom," said Sarah.

"What?" said George sharply.

"Nothing," said Sarah. "He says, 'How cold it's growing. Mrs. Parker, what a treasure you are. Mustn't let our fingers grow stiff. How about a nice hot drink of cocoa? None for me, thanks, I'm having coffee.' Of course, Mary and I were lying low too, staying out of sight, so we never bumped into whoever it was."

"It might have happened that way," said George.

"Of course," put in Alex, "the murderer has the problem of the original manuscript Mrs. Parker was copying from. He would have to go back to his office after making sure the poisoned cocoa was at her elbow, wait for the crash and the thud, and then go in and remove the manuscript. Then—and this is crucial—if Mrs. Parker's body hasn't knocked the computer on its ear, he could unplug it. The machine loses the whole business and, of course, the murderer takes the disks —because George says there were none in the machine."

"I think Sarah can answer the question about the choice of room," said George. "Most of the rooms and offices in the English Department have the same door, half glass, half wood, right? But you can't see in every door. Sarah, can you describe the doors?"

Sarah in her mind walked into the entrance hall. The waiting room had clear glass; the Fellows Room' had the big poster from the Camden Shakespeare Festival covering it; the Faculty Common Room was a door of solid wood with a brass plaque, and the English Office had its glass panel covered with that heavy piece of purple macramé studded with beads. The rest of the faculty offices were uniform in all having some covering to give privacy—posters, wooden plaques, or, in Professor Fletcher's case, a large piece of stained glass in blues and greens so that distorted figures could just be made out. The two lavatories had solid doors. The exception was Mrs. Parker's office. Like the waiting room, it had a clear glass panel.

"Of course," she said aloud. "She had clear glass so she could keep tabs on everyone. I thought that before."

"So choosing the English Office makes some sense," said Alex. "You wouldn't want to arrange for your victim's death in a fishbowl. You'd want to visit her on the QT during the evening to cheer her on, and you'd want to go in after the body fell and retrieve your manuscript—and get out the computer disks. Always assuming that this manuscript request is what kept her late that night. And speaking of being kept late, I'm hungry. Dinner break."

"All in good time," said George, who never seemed to need food. "I want to go back to Sarah for a minute. Any other details?"

Sarah, feeling rather foolish, reached in her pockets and produced the two cartons of used lift-off tapes. "Linda found them in Mrs. Parker's supply closet. She apparently kept everything, but these are used, and keeping them seems a little stupid."

"I make my office people keep the used spools and typing ribbon for inventory check," said George. "It keeps them from pocketing supplies. My men, when they searched Mrs. Parker's office, probably assumed they were new tapes. Almost all typewriters use some system of correction tapes like this that lift typed characters from the paper, leaving it clean and ready to be retyped." He carefully opened the box, which showed a series of double orange plastic spools connected by white tape, and shook one of the spools out of his hand and examined it. "Clean, the first part, so perhaps they *are* new. No"—unrolling another inch—"it's been used, all right." He examined three more pairs. "All used, though about eight inches in the beginning and at the end are blank. Now that's waste of material."

"May I see?" asked Sarah. "I mean, if you've checked for prints on her office supplies." George nodded, and she stretched out a foot of the sticky tape, frowned, and passed it over to Alex. "Take a look."

"More games," said Mike. "Cat's cradle."

"No," said Sarah. "Not just letters. Whole words. Back-wards words because the spool picks the letters up as it runs counter to the typing . . . like my own typewriter. There's 'Merlin-Smith,' then a dash, then 'No Princeton B.A.,' then a space, and then 'Penn State degree, altered transcript.'"

"There's more," said Alex, unwinding the tape. "'Down-ing College, no Camb. degree.'"

"Just what we already know," said George. "It looks as if Mrs. Parker had her own private file."

"Not bad," said Mike. "A cute little info center. But why in her office?"

"Why not?" said Alex. "No one went near her office supplies. How about the rest of these?"

The next spool unwound revealed in short phrases and abbreviations the times that Amos Larkin had been rescued by the watchful Mrs. Parker—date given in each instance. The bicycle incident was described as Mary had given it, but with a series of notations about the crippled student's progress through Boston hospitals, through therapy centers, and then with a question mark: "Make student die of injuries?"

"Why, that devil!" exclaimed Sarah. "She was really into it. What about the other spools?"

"Wait," said George. "We'll have to mount these on paper."

"Evidence," said Mike with great satisfaction. "That's what we've been wanting. Nice sticky evidence."

George produced a pad of graph paper and, with Sarah on the scissors and Mike and Alex holding the ends of a spool, managed to make a creditable display of Mrs. Parker's ex-tracurricular work. Constance Garvey was featured on the third tape. At first her dossier seemed heavily larded with question marks and fragmentary comments: "Failed 2 sub-jects as undergrad., insulted jr. student, steals cocoa." Then, in caps, a triumphant "AGE FALSIFIED—66 NEXT YEAR, CV STATES 63."

"Parker finally had her," said Mike. "Old dragon Garvey is past retirement age. How'd she get away with that one?"

"Age changing is very popular."

"It's disgusting," said Sarah.

"Which?" said Mike. "Faculty members lying and drinking or Mrs. Parker collecting the dirt?"

"Both. The whole thing."

"Here's Vera Pruczak's tape," said Alex. "She seems to have frustrated Mrs. P. Just a series of queries about men in her life, whether she drinks, does she neglect research, does she practice witchcraft—Mrs. Parker must have seen the Pruczak homestead and eyeballed those bats and stuffed heads. Anyway, I'd say Vera's clean."

"So is Joe Greenberg," said George, "and so is the chairman, Howard Bello. Just a long list of departmental duties Mrs. Parker's taken over for him. Not enough of a lever there."

"Ivan Lacey isn't," said Alex. "He's been caught, what's the phrase . . . *in flagrante delicto?*"

"With his pants down?" said Mike.

"Looks like it," said Alex. "Four separate instances of, quote: 'ADULTERY—2X w/'—that's two times with—'students, 1X w/teaching fellow, 1X w/admissions clerk.' Busy Professor Lacey."

"I suppose that all that looking down cleavage and patting fannies wasn't enough," said Sarah. "He had to have some action."

"And look at this," said Alex. "I've had these subterranean feelings about Jakob Horst. He's been making me think 'substance abuse' since I first saw him. Parker's got it all down. 'powder fr. desk, analyzed = COCAINE. DEMEROL in raincoat pocket. Summer detox. admiss., left before release.' She does like caps. Anyway, more cocaine found this year, marijuana in his file drawer—and, see this, a note that Horst admits burning student papers during a drug period."

"Horst is a druggie," said Mike. "My, my. Parker missed her calling as a gumshoe. How about smoothie Patrick Fletcher?"

"Another blank, perhaps," said George. "All it says is his name and, with a question mark, 'Unpubl. MS'—that's manuscript, I suppose—then MO, FINN, SHOO' And the last tape has only 'Unpubl. MS??' and no name."

"I suppose," said Mike, "it's too much to hope that the entire Bowmouth faculty are rotten apples."

"Not all rotten," said Alex. "But with some notable worms. Okay, George, I've got the hospital lab report for you. Mrs. Parker's last checkup showed evidence of cancer spread. Lymph node involvement and secondary tumors. She was sent the report some weeks ago. The hospital in Boston wanted her back immediately for a new course of chemotherapy, but she said she had to wait until commencement, that her job came first."

A somber silence met Alex's statement, and then Mike shrugged. "Looks like that handing around of her résumé did have something to do with her obituary."

"Or the honorary degree," said Sarah. "I know everyone thinks I'm absolutely crazy, but now you see Mrs. Parker knew that time was running out. She couldn't wait for a silver pin or a luncheon when she was sixty-five, and all those special perks can't mean much if you're on the way out. But an honorary degree at this year's commencement would be a recognition of what she must have felt were her unique services. She would want to look her very best, and if she were doing chemotherapy, she might not. She made a great effort over her appearance. I'd say that the résumés were meant to show what a good candidate she'd make, not an obituary. And don't forget she had a pressure system, all those sticky little tapes, to force at least four prominent faculty members to go along with the idea."

"All the faculty have denied the honorary degree idea," said Alex. "How about Miss Prism, the real friend and confidante?"

George frowned. "It looks to me as if Miss Prism must have been the information conduit. Some of these details— age and university background—could most easily have come from research by the registrar. But Miss Prism has been very close-mouthed. I think I'll try the faculty again. Merlin-Smith is the most pliable. Anyone who lies about his academic record and hyphenates his name may talk. I'll pull him in tonight."

"Of course, double names are commonplace now," said Sarah. "All my married friends are using them."

"So think about it, Sarah," said Alex, coming over to her side. "Just plain Deane is a bit dull. McKenzie-Deane has a nice ring. Deane-McKenzie fits into the college scene."

"It does sound impressive," said Sarah. "But right now dinner sounds more probable than marriage. Is Alex excused, George?"

"I'll need him a while longer," said George. "But I'll drop him off at your house."

"So take the car and go home and put your feet up," said Alex. "George and I don't want you wandering around the campus at night."

"That's right," said George. "After all, you are a member of the suspect department, and we haven't zeroed in on any sound reason for Alice Marmott to be killed. Mrs. Parker, yes. Plenty of opportunity and motive. But not Alice."

Mike got to his feet. "I'll walk Sarah to the parking lot and pick us up some food," and then, as the two left the building, "So, Sarah, what do you think now about the efficient Mrs. Parker?"

"Efficient is right. I still can't believe that Mrs. Parker had a blackmail system in operation right here at Bowmouth."

"That's because you belong to the college scene," said Mike. "It takes tough town types like me to believe in it—all those tweed hat types and metal-plated women or weirdos like that Olivia female. And how about this unpublished manuscript notation? I'll bet Parker was on to something about Fletcher or Pruczak, like a porno novel. I can't make anything out of the Shoo and Finn business, but you literary folk can kick it around. Maybe Fletcher's got a lady love stashed away in town, half Chinese, half Irish. Shoo-wong Finn?"

Sarah, dropped at Alex's Volvo, had to admit that Mike might be on to something. No doubt George and his gang would be scouring the libraries and special collections—and looking in and under beds—for unpublished manuscripts or unpublished oriental mistresses. But not tonight. Sarah pulled her key out of the ignition. It was only six o'clock and and still quite light. Strictures about roaming at night surely didn't hold so early in the evening. She climbed out of the car and walked quickly to the main walk that led to the North Quad. The air was unexpectedly soft—another thaw on the way, perhaps—and the lamps along the way reflected themselves in blobs of color in the sidewalk puddles.

Sarah reached the English Department without any particular plan in mind beyond the vague idea of asking Arlene or Linda—if one or both were still at work—to let her look over the library in the Faculty Common Room. But just after she had turned up the walk to Malcolm Adam Hall, she stopped in surprise. Lights showed from two-thirds of the office windows. Of course, now she remembered: the special faculty meeting called for five-thirty. Notice had been posted on the English Office bulletin board. Faculty meetings usually took place in the large seminar room on the ground floor, and yes, there they all were. Sarah could see dark heads and shoulders strung out from window to window. Keeping her head averted, her briefcase held to the side of her face, she passed the partly open door, seeing with a corner of her eye Constance Garvey's profile, shoulder, and impressive breastworks. She climbed the stairs and stood irresolute in the hall. Why, she asked to herself, am I acting like a sneak? I have a perfect right to visit my own department, to ask to see the Common Room library, to knock on office doors, to visit its faculty. And a perfect right to snoop? demanded her conscience. No, she answered herself, but murder changed the rules, didn't it? In fact, after murder there were no rules. And besides, wouldn't a troop of State Police going through bookcases and files scare any suspicious manuscript into disappearing?

The halls were empty, but the English Office door stood ajar. Arlene looked up. "They're all downstairs sharpening their claws. I've got some memos to get out. Want something?"

"The Common Room library. I need a couple of references."

"Are you supposed to—I mean, only the senior faculty . . . ?"

"Come on, Arlene. That's Mrs. Parker's game."

This approach was good enough for Arlene to escort Sarah into the room, turn on the light, and offer coffee. Sarah, refusing, knelt down at the room-length bookcase and began checking the faculty collection. Periodicals in cases, single volumes in dust jackets, essay collections in leather, paper-bound monographs and studies. A tour through the frontispieces showed nothing that could be considered an unpublished manuscript. What about the MO notation? Magnum opus, possibly. An unpublished manuscript that was someone's great work. Or separate works, the manuscript and the opus? Well, most of the faculty's so-called great works were undoubtedly in the library, where they belonged, as well as on their authors' own bookshelves. And nothing here had to do with Shoo or Finn, joined or apart. These, like so many other of Mrs. Parker's notations, were probably abbreviations, and the facts behind these shorthand notes—the unpublished manuscript, for instance—may well have been part of the reason that Alice Marmott, on the last night of her life, had visited the English Department and met Mrs. Parker. Well, if the Common Room was a washout, how about the offices—why stop now?

Sarah slipped out and back to the entrance hall and listened at the stairs. Still the reassuring mumble from the meeting. Some of the offices showed lights and might be unlocked, their owners' coats and hats waiting. Yes, down the hall, there was Howard Bello's door invitingly ajar. And what a mess. Textbooks, letters, monographs, periodicals, mimeographed sheets, book mailers tumbled over each other and covered his desk, his file cabinet, his two chairs. Overshoes, two hats, a scarf, gloves, several coffee mugs, and an umbrella mixed it up with an overflowing wastebasket and yesterday's newspapers. He certainly needed not only Mrs. Parker but a personal maid, though perhaps she had done this service too.

Sarah, depressed, worked through the surface flotsam and the jumbled file cabinet drawers, then moved on to the glass-fronted bookcase. Here she found the professor's three-volume work on Emerson and the series on Bronson Alcott and Thoreau but no unpublished bound or unbound manuscript. And nothing suggesting Finns or Shoos.

From the chairman's office, after another check on the faculty meeting, she moved to Jakob Horst's office, also lighted. Very tidy, each object lined up. On the desk a pipe rack, on the walls a dark landscape and a calendar from a shoe company. Nothing unbound, no manuscript lurking in file or bookcase. Just a vast number of treatises on mathematical subjects and an impressive collection of European poetry and the professor's published poetry studies.

Another trip to the head of the stairs, another reassuring mix of voices, now raised in argument, and then to Patrick Fletcher's office. Also unlocked. What carelessness. Or did none of them have anything to hide—at least not in their places of work?

Professor Fletcher's office, of those visited, won the prize for taste. An antique brass student lamp with a blue glass shade stood on a handsome walnut desk with carved details, and ceiling-high walnut bookcases spread across one wall. Rattan blinds replaced the usual metal venetian ones, and the two office chairs were of designer quality. A set of hand-colored costume prints on the wall, a photograph of a gold collar from the National Museum in Stockholm, and a Persian rug on the floor completed the interior. Professor Fletcher had, in fact, settled in for life. And why not? thought Sarah, running her finger over his books. Tenured, a full professor, one of the luminaries of the department, and the author of at least six magnum opuses—what was the plural, magna opera? She hadn't yet gotten a grip on her Latin. And an impressive platoon of translations from the Old Norse, Old Saxon, Old English, Old everything else. There they all were, including the jumbo study of *Beowulf*—a trade edition and one in scarlet leather—all beautifully bound by the Bowmouth University Press. Money, money. Obviously Patrick Fletcher had funds unconnected with salary and royalties. But no visible or hidden unpublished manuscripts, not in boxes, or folders, or cased, or concealed in a notebook. Nor yet in the unlocked desk drawers.

Sarah dodged out into the hall, raced to the head of the stairs. Still in the meeting. What on earth was keeping them so long? It was past seven. Alex might be waiting at home, might even be worrying about her. But, since she was here, she might as well cover the territory. Her search was shortened, however, by the fact that both Ivan Lacey and Vera Pruczak had locked their offices, as had Merlin-Smith. Constance Garvey's tiny vaultlike office showed only teaching anthologies and paperback novels. Only Professor Larkin left.

She walked softly, trying to keep the soles of her rubber boots from squeaking on the linoleum, and turned the knob to his office. Unlocked and lighted. Watching the stairway apprehensively—the meeting couldn't last forever—she backed into Amos Larkin's office. And directly into Amos Larkin. In fact, only by grabbing at the edge of a file cabinet could she keep her balance, since Professor Larkin was on his hands and knees a few feet in front of the door.

Oh, God, thought Sarah. He's off again. She whirled to go, thinking that one mercy about his being drunk was that he wouldn't remember her entrance, when her arm was caught by the professor, now on his feet.

"You have an appointment?" He sounded entirely sober.

Sarah said the first thing that came into her head, a terrible habit that cropped up only under extreme stress. "Why aren't you at the faculty meeting then?"

"What do you mean 'then'?"

"I mean . . ." Sarah floundered. What she had meant was that if he wasn't drunk, then why wasn't he where he should be—at the meeting? "Where everyone else is," she finished lamely.

"Leaving you free to visit offices, Miss Deane?"

Sarah took hold of herself. "No, I wanted to borrow a book. I saw your light on."

Professor Larkin seated himself at his desk and turned his chair to face her. "And you always back into rooms when you want to borrow a book?"

"About Johnson. *Rasselas—Illusion and Discovery.*" Thank heavens she remembered the title; it was on her reading list.

"The library has three copies," said Professor Larkin. He picked up a letter opener and for a second balanced it on his middle finger. Sarah saw that his hands were less shaky, and this did not reassure her.

"They're out," said Sarah, going from one lie to another. "So I thought yours might be available."

"Because you think it's a wise idea to read the works of your instructor. To see which way the wind lies. Isn't that so?"

Sarah drew back her shoulders. "Yes," she said boldly. "It's not a bad idea to find out what your teacher has written. Especially if he misses a lecture, you can fill in."

"You mean if he comes drunk to the lecture and doesn't make sense. Is that what you are saying? Because reading what the instructor wrote in a sober moment may be all the sense you're going to get out of the seminar. And aren't you wondering why I was on my hands and knees on the floor when you came in? Didn't you say to yourself, 'He's off again'?"

"No," said Sarah. Another lie. She decided that Amos Larkin could read minds, hers anyway.

"I was looking for my staple machine. I'd knocked it off my desk. My hands still act like jumping beans. Okay, Miss Deane, you may have my book—for a week. Some of the criticism is out of date. I wrote it over five years ago and there has been some good material published since. Anything else?"

It was the perfect opening. "Aren't you writing something new on Johnson—or any of the others, Pope, Swift?"

"Hardly," said Professor Larkin. "I've been otherwise engaged."

"Or have a manuscript put away somewhere," said Sarah. "Unpublished." Which, she thought, is certainly sticking my head in a noose—or in a scarf.

"Everyone in the department has manuscripts put away somewhere, but thank you for your interest. Now, if you'll excuse me—"

He was interrupted by a knock and a head thrust in the door. Mary Donelli. "Professor Larkin? You're not at the faculty meeting."

"As you can see. Since I am undoubtedly the subject of some of their deliberations, I thought it was politic to stay here and tend to my own business. Come in, Mary."

Mary, thought Sarah. Oh, brother. "Hi," she said aloud. "I'm borrowing a book."

"Are you?" said Mary, and, to the professor, "I had to come back for something and thought I'd take a chance that you were here."

"Well," said Sarah, "I guess I'll go along."

Neither Professor Larkin or Mary did anything to delay her. Sarah gave Mary an intense look, intended to convey a red alert on not being caught in a murderer's office after hours, and left. At the end of the hall she met the dispersed faculty members hurrying to their respective offices. Joe Greenberg stopped her.

"Working late?"

"Just checking a reference. The Common Room library. And borrowing a book from Professor Larkin."

"I'm on my way to see him. Motion to kick him out. Faculty divided, but lots of evidence, provocation, reputation of the department at stake. I'm glad he wasn't there. It was nasty."

"And?"

"Saved, but just. One more false step, and so forth."

"He's in his office," said Sarah.

"Then I think I'll tell him he's still got a job. Any other news?"

"George Fitts is looking for an unpublished manuscript, perhaps a big one. A major effort. Do you know who might have one tucked away?"

"I'd say we all have. You know, breathes there an English teacher with a pen so dead. . . . But most of us are rather shy about unpublished great works. They hide out in our underwear drawers or in the bottom of closets and then once in a while we take them out and burn them. Of course, there's Pat Fletcher. Everything he writes is a magnum opus, so I doubt if he has any hidden clinkers. Published his first effort the year he got his B.A. And Vera, I don't think she's ever held anything back."

Sarah nodded agreement, adding, "Then what do the initials MO mean to you?"

"Modus operandi, money order, and mail order."

"Not magnum opus?"

"That too. And Missouri and month."

"That doesn't make it any easier," said Sarah. "What about Shoo and Finn?"

"Mickey Finn, Huck Finn, Finlandia, and shoofly pie."

Sarah was silent and then said, with sudden inspiration, "You don't suppose Mrs. Parker was writing a novel—everything exposed?"

"Why not? There's plenty of material in the department. Or perhaps a real-life documentary. Now, may I walk you back to your car? Mine's in the parking lot."

"But Mary Donelli's back there, in Professor Larkin's office. She might need walking."

"I'll walk you both."

Which he did, but his presence precluded Sarah's finding out whether Mary had just had a routine thesis guidance meeting—although the word "routine" hardly fitted Amos Larkin—or whether there had been dangerous undercurrents.

When Sarah walked into the kitchen, she came face to face with Alex—Alex, black eyebrows, smoldering eyes, looking exactly like Heathcliff after a bad day in the heather. He exploded. Where had she been, what had she been thinking of ? Because he knew she'd stayed on campus, he'd gone out to the parking lot with George and there was his car still sitting there. Didn't she know, hadn't she heard about the two murders?

Sarah, as sometimes happened with her, met temper with great calm. She pulled off her boots, shrugged out of her coat, and said in a level voice, "I've been doing some extra work for the English Department—on an empty stomach."

"You're not supposed to be *near* the English Department at night, and I was so worried I've eaten half the chicken I brought you."

"I don't need a guard every minute, Alex, not at six o'clock, and anyway I was escorted back to the car. Kindness of Joe Greenberg. And I can't fight without my dinner."

"Sarah, my love, I don't want to fight, but I was worried as hell. I almost called out the troops. I kept thinking that if we were married—"

"What? That I wouldn't visit the English Department in the evening if we were married? That I'd be home with an apron around my middle making mushroom quiches? Speaking of food, let me at it." Sarah brushed her hair back out of her eyes and went to the stove. "Don't say anything until at least I've had a drumstick. Hello, Patsy. Next time he comes home in a temper, bite his head off." Sarah reached for a kettle, a plate, and the pan of chicken being kept warm in the oven and settled herself at the kitchen table. Some minutes later, she looked up at Alex, who stood against the refrigerator, arms folded over his chest, still looking like a character from the Yorkshire moors.

"We weren't going to talk about getting married until we had five normal days in a row."

"I want to marry you, I want you safe, and I love you. Three things that are not incompatible." Alex managed a slightly more agreeable expression. "And think how happy your Grandmother Douglas will be. She told me when we visited that she prays for us."

"I know," said Sarah. "But she likes to pray for people."

"A wedding would be a real tonic for her. She could forgive us for living in sin as a real act of Christian charity. And my parents and yours are all for it."

"Parents usually are." Sarah reached for an apple and began to peel it carefully, not letting the skin break. "Have you been talking it over with your mother and father?"

"No, but I know how they feel. They were afraid I was going to fall for some dreary medical type or some dingbat blonde."

"I do love you, but it's got to be on hold until George Fitts clears up the cases."

"Contrariwise," said Alex, "you and I are now going to brainstorm and move two giant steps ahead on these murders because we both know a lot more about the academic scene and neurotic academics than either George or Mike. Now be quiet and listen. I have news. First, I called my father. His field —as you know—is Old English. For what it's worth, he says that Patrick Fletcher is the real thing—his *Beowulf* study is a monument—and to kindly keep our hands off the man. Also, George's commendations to you. Mrs. Parker did indeed lean upon at least one other faculty member for an honorary degree. Merlin-Smith, who has a noodle instead of a spine, admitted it. It came right out after George set his hook and reached for the landing net. Her résumé was in aid of the degree. She wouldn't take no, kept insisting. He thinks she was after some of the others. Sarah Deane is right, I am amazed, and so is George. But the question is, Does asking for a degree equal murder? Or did Mrs. Parker threaten to go public?"

"I'd guess the latter."

"All right. That probably takes care of motives for Larkin, Merlin-Smith, Garvey, and Horst. For convenience, let's put Vera Pruczak, Fletcher, and Bello aside."

"But can we? I'm thinking of that unpublished manuscript with the MO notation." Sarah began to cut her apples into slices and to heap them onto a plate. "What does MO mean to you?"

"Medical officer and molybdenum," said Alex promptly. "And mineral oil."

"Well, that's true to type, but I think magnum opus works better in the English Department context. How about Shoo and Finn?"

"Shoeshine boy, shoofly, don't bother me, my master's gone away, Finland, Finntown Road—that's over by Friendship—and Finsen light, blue-violet light once used to treat lupus. Helpful?"

"Not helpful. How about *Finnegans Wake*? Stick to the liberal arts. That's what I did tonight, if you must know. I gave the Common Room library and some of the offices a quick going-over for bulky manuscripts and drew a blank. Lots of published and bound works, but no manuscripts. Of course, as Joe Greenberg suggested, everyone probably has one hidden at home under the bed. I got away with the search since everyone was down at a faculty meeting deciding whether to can Amos Larkin."

"Did they?"

"No, but it was close. He hadn't been drinking tonight— I caught him in his office—nor in class the other day."

"Which means he can turn it off if he has a mind to. Better tell Mary to watch it. Especially if she really has a crush on the man. And you too."

"It's not that easy for Mary. After all, he *is* on her doctoral committee." Sarah cut a lemon, produced a canister of sugar and a tin of cinnamon, and began sprinkling the apples. "How does Alice fit in? Try this. Alice, who is gung-ho for research, finds some manuscript or a reference to it. Say a very feelthy piece of writing. Something that should stay in a closet. Something by one of the English faculty."

She reached for two sticks of piecrust and began creating two dough footballs.

"What if Alice went first to Mrs. Parker that night and told all and then found that Mrs. Parker wouldn't go raging in and confront the wicked person because that wouldn't be Mrs. Parker's style. She had her little ways."

"I suppose Mrs. P would lie low, wait, and *then* put on the heat. Little requests, little favors."

Sarah slammed her rolling pin down on a football. "From what Amos Larkin said, never a direct quid pro quo. Until it came to this degree business. Then she may have gotten tough." .

"Then a real quid pro quo sequence. Secretary wants honorary degree, faculty refuses—or one faculty member refuses—secretary threatens, will spill the beans, secretary is poisoned."

"If it was this unpublished MO Shoo Finn thing, where do you think Alice came across it—if she did? Maybe not in anyone's office or house. How about in the library? She lived in the library." Sarah pushed a piece of piecrust into a pie pan, dumped in the apples, and draped the second crust over the top. "There are special collections and unpublished manuscripts and dissertations by the yard. The more I think about it, Alice was super bright and super dumb. A sort of idiot savant. If she had actually found something vile, something libelous, she might have tried a frontal attack. Here she had bucked the home front to transfer from Ohio State to study literature at Bowmouth, and look at one of its luminaries— one of the hallowed breed—making mud pies."

"Shitting in the temple."

"You could say. But it's crazy." Sarah turned her pie to the light and squinted at it critically. "If anyone had written a horrible book, the last thing they'd do is have it in the library."

"Under a pseudonym?"

"Well, that's possible. And if Alice found it, she might have suspected someone in the department."

"Then you've forgotten what Joe Greenberg just told you about English teachers. They've all got manuscripts. I don't think most authors—no matter how gross the novel—would hide it at home because if they died suddenly, the family might burn it. Families do things like that. But libraries hang on to manuscripts."

"You mean, better to hide it in the library under another name, and a little codicil in the will can release it to the waiting world: 'Please see my novel, *Gross Out,* in the unpublished manuscript division of Memorial Library under the name of Peregrine Pickle.'"

"You've got it. Under Special Collections, on microfilm, or God knows where. But accessible and retrievable."

"What day is tomorrow?" asked Sarah suddenly. "Saturday? I've lost all track."

"Poor overworked Sarah. Tomorrow is Saturday, to be followed by what is known as spring break. One week. Not much of a break for us. We'll have to put any idea of a holiday off. I think the manuscript thing is worth going after."

Sarah took her pie, opened the oven door, and slid it on the shelf and then, as an afterthought, turned on the heat. "Who needs a preheated oven? I just made it for therapy. We can give it to Patsy. All right, I'll go through those copies of Alice's research notes and papers again—George left them with us—and then hit the library. And heaven help me, I'll try and skim over the stuff the department big shots have written."

"That should take you until next summer."

"No, but at least a good chunk of next week. I can put off my own work and dig. I might even ask Mary for more help. And now, good night." Sarah rinsed her hands and wiped them dry. "I'll start in with Alice's stuff right away. I've got a pie to keep me warm."

"Comforted with apples—but not with yours truly."

"Not tonight, but I'll save you a piece . . . and a flagon."

Alex leaned over and kissed the back of her neck, a neck already bent over a folder of papers. "I may have to find me a concubine."

"Go ahead, and may she resemble Constance Garvey."

SIXTEEN

Alice's papers had proved better than a sleeping pill. After working her way through ten closely reasoned and heavily footnoted pages on Milton's years at Christ College, Sarah had given up and set her alarm clock for five.

Now, leaving Alex to sleep, she hurled herself into the shower and by five-thirty was at the kitchen table having breakfast while running through her copies of the Alice Marmott collection—class notes, research outlines, and finished essays. No magnum opus, no large unpublished manuscript, thank God, though I wouldn't put it past her, Sarah said to herself. But super-grind Alice had planned and executed research papers for all classes except Professor Garvey's novel course and Professor Fletcher's Old English seminar. The only Anglo-Saxon material among the papers was three sheets on the phonology of the language. And no notes taken for the paper she had handed in to Amos Larkin. Surely there should be material here connected with that effort. In a folder reserved for notes on Jakob Horst's class on poetics, Alice had written and underlined twice "unfinished business." But what vaguely troubled Sarah, what she had missed when she first gone through the papers, was that someone might have gone through Alice's briefcase—she remembered it had been found tucked under her body—and done some selective lifting.

Sarah repacked Alice's papers, piled her dishes in the sink, filled her Raggedy Ann Thermos with tea, wrapped a piece of chicken and a wedge of apple pie in a square of foil, and checked for pencils and her yellow pad. Finding Alex dressed and ready for hospital rounds, she climbed into the car, intending to head for the English Department on the chance of finding Mary and enlisting her help.

In the English Office she found Linda, looking thoroughly annoyed, crouched over the computer printer. "Trust a foul-up. The creeps at the repair company gave us a different thimble."

"A which?"

"For the word processor printer—a sort of gadget that looks like a thimble. Has the alphabet and numbers. But this one has a bunch of dots and stripes and funny accents. Look. I did a printout."

Sarah saw a line of umlauts, cedillas, an upside-down question mark, a series of accents and dots, and what looked like the Greek alphabet.

"And those little bubbles like in Norwegian names," said Linda.

"Diacritical marks for different languages," said Sarah. "I think you'll be needing them for faculty manuscripts. Most of them probably use references to foreign studies."

"Parker used to do all the special stuff. She had a couple of special printing balls for her typewriter. That's how she managed to hang on to some of the manuscript business. Horst made her get one with math symbols, and I know Larkin has used those Greek letters."

"Well, now you can get into the act," said Sarah.

"And look at that thing like an ax or a balloon on a stick."

Sarah looked over her shoulder. "That's a thorn. Part of the Old English alphabet. And that loop with a stem is an eth, and the combined ae is an ash."

"Yuck," said Linda. "But where the hell is our old thimble?" And then, in answer to Sarah's query, "No, Mary Donelli isn't around."

Sarah left Linda to the contemplation of the thorn, the eth, and the ash and made her way to the entrance, where she was pounced on by Vera Pruczak.

"Are you much too busy to understudy Goneril and help with the lights? We're so shorthanded."

"Sorry," said Sarah. "I'm really flat out." And then, not to miss an opportunity, "Miss Pruczak, have you any unpublished manuscripts around? A novel or a critical study?"

"Darling," exclaimed Vera, "how did you know? Well, doesn't everybody? Mine, it's too embarrassing. My editor turns purple when I bring it up."

"Oh," said Sarah, surprised. Somehow, the sexual adventures of Olivia Macbeth's glowering heroes and passionate heroines with swelling bosoms and dangerous villains were, when it came down to it, too foul to tell. Olivia always drew a veil over these escapades and her men and women bedded down by blowing out candles, closing the door, and meeting all dewy-eyed at breakfast. "You mean X-rated," said Sarah.

"Lord, no," said Vera. "I've never gone in for that stuff. I'm too old. How my characters fornicate is up to them. I just get them to bed or into the hay or into an inn. Inns are best. All those different bedchambers and footsteps in the passage and the ostler whistling from below. Let the reader do the work. My hands are clean." Vera spread her hands, heavily ringed, braceleted, and spattered with blue paint. "Figuratively speaking," she added. "I'm working on the set. No, my secret is a magnum opus. A study of Falstaff. You know, the wise buffoon, the venial anti-hero. Through the ages. I blush, but I keep nibbling at it. It's one of those things you keep under the rug."

"I suppose everyone in the department has a secret manuscript."

"Except Patrick Fletcher, I suppose. All those scholarly works. Too depressing for the rest of us. And Amos too, but not lately. I wouldn't think Merlin-Smith has the bottom for a great work, nor Garvey, who has. Now I must fly. We're blocking out the first act this morning, and it's a devil because our Lear is only five foot three so we have to elevate him somehow."

And she was off, leaving the odor of Magie Noire wafting behind.

Sarah followed, feeling that getting a coherent answer on

the subject of unpublished manuscripts was as likely as finding daffodils blooming in the North Quad. She walked slowly down the cleared path toward the library complex. The Nicholas Starbox Memorial Library loomed at the end of the path, one wing fronting on the Quad, the other thrusting out toward the Life Sciences buildings. Of course, Bowmouth had a surfeit of libraries—music, art, science, and the medical school, each no doubt with its quota of unpublished great works. But be sensible, Sarah told herself. Only the main library would hold a large literary manuscript, be it pornographic, libelous, seditious, or utterly banal.

Established at the long table in the main reference reading room, she felt closer to the live spirit of Alice Marmott than she ever had in the classroom. Somehow the always sure excitement of the stacks, of books unknown, of passages unread, brought with them an increase of sympathy for the single-minded Alice.

The time sped. By three o'clock, Sarah, with a tower of books in front of her, had skimmed through enough of the published works of the English faculty to have a feel for their subjects and styles. Nothing out of the way and no startling departures from the fields she knew to be their interest. Amos Larkin, crisp and acerbic; Howard Bello, afflicted with Emerson, wandering back and forth, no more consistent than his subject. Consistency may belong to little minds, Sarah thought, but it would be certainly easier on the reader. Constance Garvey had a slim volume on *Middlemarch,* a slimmer one on Mrs. Gaskell, and a dreary tract on freshman writing —all published by an obscure university press. Ivan Lacey galloped enthusiastically away with the thesis that Shakespeare's Dark Lady of the Sonnets was actually the fair man in drag and, in the face of evidence to the contrary, had written several essays, claiming that Juliet, Ophelia, Perdita, Marina, and Miranda had all lost their virginity somewhere in the first act. Vera Pruczak in her single work on Tennessee Williams showed herself concerned only with problems of directing. Patrick Fletcher, however, proved the major obstacle in Sarah's reading marathon. Too many books. Old English, Latin commentaries on the Anglo-Saxons, chapters on Celtic offshoots, essays on Middle English and Chaucer.

These plus his triumph, the study of *Beowulf*. But in none a cross-reference, an allusion, even the whisper of an unpublished manuscript or a yet-to-come masterwork.

At last, with an hour to closing, Sarah finished skimming the dissertation abstracts and made her way to the basement stacks and moved in on the first of the special collections, the unpublished dissertations held in the Starbox Library. She came up empty-handed. Here were only those dissertations finished at Bowmouth. Ivan Lacey was the one person of the English faculty who had received his doctorate there, and his dissertation was a study of variant *Measure for Measure* readings with many murky footnotes. Nothing in the work suggested reasons for murder and blackmail. Unless. Unless Alice had latched onto it and found it a fraud. A plagiarism. Oh, God. It would take a lifetime to work her way through the mountains of Shakespeare studies. But Lacey's work seemed to her a third-class effort. No great work had flowered from it, no great fame to the author. But since the idea of plagiarism persisted, Sarah carried the dissertation over to the Xerox machine and copied the index and the first and last chapters.

Returning Professor Lacey's work, Sarah passed a line of empty carrels. No, not empty, there was Mary, bent over an open text scribbling on a file card. And sitting next to her, perched on a pair of library steps, his red head inclined over her arm, the fox: Amos Larkin. Hell. What should she do? She couldn't spend the rest of the year warning Mary. But what better place to eliminate an undesirable, if Mary happened to fit the description? Dimly lighted stacks, cul-de-sacs, storage rooms with file boxes and cartons. And since it was the beginning of spring break, the place was almost deserted.

Sarah looked at her watch. Twenty more minutes before the library closed. She could case one more special collection on this floor and at the same time keep an ear out for untoward noises. First, let them know she was around. Professor Larkin could hardly kill Mary with a witness around the corner. And, good, there was Merlin-Smith on his knees by a row of leather-bound folios, and—it was almost a reunion—Patrick Fletcher sauntering with a man Sarah recognized as the library director. Even if one of the three had murder in mind, there were two others to call. Sarah slowed her steps, turned toward Mary, stopped, and said, "Hi" in a bright voice. Mary looked up and said, "What are you doing here on a Saturday afternoon?" Sarah smiled, Amos Larkin lifted both eyebrows and nodded, and Sarah moved across the hall to examine other special collections.

Turning her head from time to time to watch Mary, Sarah made a lightning sweep of the long shelves. The Homer Gridley Library of Maine Cemeteries, the Women-at-Sea Collection, Commencement Addresses of Bowmouth Chancellors, The Lighthouse Keepers' Collected Diaries, the Midcoast Audubon Folios, the Hutter College Collection. What was that? Sarah, seeing the director now detached from Professor Fletcher, went over and asked.

"When Hutter College went bankrupt we bid for some of their library. Business records from one of the big paper companies, early annals of the Waldo Patent, a Sarah Orne Jewett collection, private press material, special monographs, plus a Hutter faculty collection. We haven't cataloged it all yet, so the books can't be checked out."

One glance at the stacks—shelf after shelf—told Sarah that it would take an entire day just to skim the surface of the Hutter College Collection. She was reaching for the nearest volume when she heard a sudden rustle and a thud from the nearby row of carrels. She raced over to find Mary kneeling on the floor over an open notebook, and Professor Larkin reaching down his hand.

"Stop," she yelled. "Hold it. You're not alone."

"Are you crazy?" Mary reared up.

"Inspector Clouseau?" said Professor Larkin.

"I dropped my notebook, do you mind?" said Mary.

"I heard something. I thought you'd fallen."

"Or was being strangled," said Mary. "Honestly."

"Miss Deane is an invaluable friend," said Amos Larkin. "Always on the spot."

"Are you leaving, Mary?" said Sarah in what she hoped was a controlled and austere voice.

"We have to," said Mary. "The place is closing up."

Amos Larkin leaned over and picked up Mary's notebook. "If you follow up those six references you might come up with something useful. Now, shall I walk ahead of you both or behind?" Sarah smiled distantly and in single file the three moved to the stone stairs, climbed to the first floor, and went out into the late afternoon air.

"Dinner with us tonight, Mary?" said Sarah in as cordial a voice as she could muster.

"Of course, dinner," said Mary. "Have you forgotten? Another faculty do. Professor and Mrs. Horst at home. You got the invitation because I was in by the mailboxes when you did."

"Oh, Lord, I completely forgot."

"Civilization returns to the English Department. Are you going?" Mary turned to Professor Larkin, who was buttoning his sheepskin coat and squinting into the darkening sky.

"No," he said shortly. "But I wish you both joy of it." And he strode off down the walk.

"What a crank," said Sarah.

"More bark than bite. And if you're trying not to drink, wouldn't a depressing faculty party drive you to it?"

"I think Alex has a conference tonight. Shall we go together? I'm trying out what they call a 'new-used' car, only forty thousand miles, and I can pick you up."

"Around six-thirty, then," said Mary. She sighed. "Another lost evening."

"I've another faculty invite tonight," Sarah told Alex when she got home. "They're jacking up the hospitality machine again, putting on a brave front pretending the department's back to normal. And tomorrow I'm going to take another whack at the library, but I'll have to keep an eye on Mary. She's getting altogether too chummy with Larkin. Hell, I wish one suspect would drop out or evaporate."

"For what it's worth, and against the dictates of medical ethics, I'll tell you that Merlin-Smith turned up in my office. Tests show a nice duodenal ulcer eating away. Says he's under stress and is thinking of accepting a job in some small midwestern college."

"Stress from being thought a liar and a murderer, or stress from having become a murderer?"

"Hard to say, but he's also got a very noticeable bilateral

· 241 ·

muscle weakness, so he might not have been able to carry that ladder or hoist Alice into the ice boat, nor yet the nerve to do the cyanide."

"You asked him about Alice and Mrs. Parker as you were tapping his knees?"

"I talked about stress in general. In my best fatherly manner. But I think as a murderer he's a long shot."

"You haven't a fatherly manner," said Sarah. "You probably frightened his ulcer into getting worse."

The House of Horst, as Mary Donelli called it, was over-pictured, overcarpeted, and overstuffed. It was one hundred percent Victorian with its innards intact—inglenooks, stained glass windows, tiled and carved fireplaces, whatnots, beaded curtains, fringed lamps, too much royal blue and crimson.

Drago Collins greeted the two women in the front hall. "Heavy, heavy hangs over thy head. Old Horst has bought out the nineteenth century."

Sarah nodded. Not camp, funky, or an interesting restoration, just solid and indigestible. Like the Horsts. Mrs. Horst, her cylindrical figure in puce knit with a cameo pinned at her throat, welcomed them in a throaty middle-European accent. At her side stood Jakob Horst, massive in his wide-welt corduroy jacket, thick tweed pants, pipe in mouth. His face—Sarah remembered Mrs. Parker's tape—had always been something of a Gouda cheese with lidded eyes so it was hard to tell whether he was still taking drugs. Users taking uppers and downers were pretty cagey, and since in class he always growled, it was hard to tell his natural state from a doped one.

Sarah, with Mary, joined the stream of guests moving toward a long table with a cut-glass punch bowl flanked by pots of ferns. She looked toward an archway and saw that an assortment of graduate students and fellows were milling about with members of the English faculty. All except Vera Pruczak and Amos Larkin. Sarah was almost sorry. The piss and vinegar missing.

The evening wore on. The food was acceptable but, like the furniture, heavy. A trip to the Horst upper regions and a quick look—Sarah by now having lost all shame—through bureau drawers, bookcases, and under beds, yielded no package looking like a manuscript. In the bathroom and medicine cabinet, Sarah found no sign of tourniquets, syringes, spoons, needles, or small alcohol lamps. Nor yet bottles labeled heroin, cocaine, cyanide, or "Drink Me." Downstairs again she joined a group watching Mrs. Horst show her mounted dried flowers, which was followed by a tour through a small greenhouse. Sarah found her mind turning to foxglove, poppies, nightshade, and hellebore. And cyanide? From peach pits, she remembered. Did the Horsts have peach trees?

A few interested questions as the guests gathered to admire an enormous ornamental castor bean plant revealed that Mrs. Horst was an enthusiastic amateur botanist and that growing herbs and flowers for drying and mounting was the passion of her life. Certainly it wasn't her husband. Sarah, following around, decided she was quite possibly frightened of him—or frightened of something he might have done. Mrs. Horst had shadowed eyes, her mouth twitched, and she kept rubbing her fingers down the side of her dress.

"How did the party go?" said Alex Sunday morning. "Did you have cyanide mousse?"

Sarah rolled over in bed and pulled her arm free from Patsy, who was trying to restore himself to bed status. "No, but we could have. Digitalis pie, belladonna coupe, hemlock quiche. She's a botany lover, collects flowers. Maybe peach pits."

"A nice hobby."

"So are they all nice hobbies. Vera and her shrunken heads, the Fletchers with their anthropology exhibits. Amos Larkin probably has something pickled in a jar. Have you found anything?"

"Lacey is a camera buff, has a darkroom and appropriate chemicals including some with a cyanic base. And George went over the computer disks, the English Department files, the Common Room library, and the faculty offices again. No manuscript, no great opus, foreign or domestic, no strange notations. So the library's your best bet. Have you found anything about Finns and Shoos?"

"I've checked some encyclopedias. The closest thing to Shoo is *The Shoemaker's Holiday;* that's a late Elizabethan play,

Ivan Lacey's period. For Finn, there's *fin de siècle,* which could mean anything; *Phineas Finn*—that's Trollope, which is Garvey's and Joe Greenberg's field; then a batch of Gaelic references—Fingal, Finn, Fioon—probably Professor Fletcher's turf; and then Joyce and *Finnegans Wake,* which I've found out is a special interest of Joe Greenberg."

"Finn to me is finnan haddie, which reminds me I haven't had breakfast. I'll go on digging into the cyanide possibilities and then look for you around noon. Maybe I can help in the library."

"Go to the ground floor, special collections. You won't have to worry about the place being crowded, it's Sunday before the holiday. I'll call Mary for extra help."

Mary answered in a hoarse croak. "It's Sunday. Go away."

"I need you," urged Sarah. "A research project."

"God, you *are* turning into Alice Marmott."

"Bring your lunch. It's an all-day project."

"I said I'd meet Amos in the library before nine. Dissertation help. I'm seeing him in public because of your fidgets about him strangling me. He's asked why I can't see him in his office like any normal student."

"Cut him short and be where someone can see you. We may be on to something. We're looking for connections." And Sarah described the problems of the unpublished manuscript, MO and Shoo and Finn. "We may have to go through all of Joyce. And then we've got poison plants and shrunken heads and peach pits."

"Study hath made you mad."

"If we can only tie things together."

"Like the man said, 'Only connect.' "

"I'll meet you about nine-thirty."

"Shut up."

Okay, connections, Sarah repeated to herself as she slapped together a bologna sandwich and filled her Thermos with tea. Arriving at the main library entrance, she was stopped at the stairs that led down to the lower-floor stacks by a student library assistant.

"Big doings down there," he said.

"What do you mean?"

"Moving day. The new rare-book vault is finished. You know, fireproof, air-controlled, moisture-tight, bug-proof. They're doing it today while the place is cleared out. All that junk: folios, manuscripts, first editions." It was obvious that this assistant was not in his job for the love of old books.

"But we can go down, can't we?" said Sarah, dismayed.

"Oh, yeah. By the side entrance. For research and necessary reference work. Show your ID. They'll let you through and check your things."

Murder, thought Sarah, appropriately enough. She retraced her steps down the long flight to the ground level, walked around to the side door, and went through a hall that led past a series of library offices. At the entrance to the stacks she was stopped, examined, and given a permission card by an elderly Miss Murdstone type.

"You must check your things in the supply room. And no more bringing lunch and fluids into the library. We've had incidents. Last month someone spilled a can of Pepsi on Emily Dickinson. You can eat in the old coal bin. We've just set up tables."

Sarah was directed to the supply room, a wire-cage space with rows of shelves accommodating a scattering of paper bags, Thermos bottles, shopping bags, rucksacks, and the like. A library aide relieved her of everything but her pencils and file cards and put her Thermos and sandwich on the shelf slot marked number twelve. "Now they've put the rare books down here we're being extra careful. All the literature collections are being moved today. Some of the English faculty are assisting." The aide indicated a passing parade of men in coveralls carrying cartons and being shepherded by the curator of rare books and the library director. Behind came Professor Garvey, Fletcher, Horst, and Merlin-Smith.

"So many of our works are not replaceable—not on our budget," said Miss Murdstone, joining Sarah. "Our signed Mark Twains, the *Kelmscott Chaucer*, those letters—Cotton Mather, Samuel Sewell, Robert Frost, Robert Lowell. So good of the English faculty to lend us a hand."

Outside of the supply-room cage, Sarah joined Mary Donelli, also relieved of her briefcase and lunch supplies.

"God, Sarah, what timing. Quiet as a tomb, you said. Why, we've got the entire library staff and the English Department underfoot and you're trying to research a homicide under their noses."

"Keep your voice down. I think they're all going to be too busy putting Cotton Mather to bed to bother with us. Look at them, it's like taking babies to their cradles." And indeed there was a nursery aspect to the lines of librarians, aides, and faculty cradling folios, vellum-covered quartos, cased manuscripts, and several wrapped bundles tied with ribbons.

"Okay, give me my assignment."

"Come over to the table where we can talk," said Sarah. "The Hutter College Collection is a great big mixed bag, so it's worth going through. It goes along one wall, yards of it, all the way to the new Rare Book Room."

"And I'm hungry already. As soon as they took my lunch away, I knew I'd be hungry."

"We'll eat early. Has Professor Larkin turned up?"

"Yes, he's over by my carrel. He's checking some of Swift's letters for me so I can go ahead with my next chapter."

"You didn't tell him what you're doing with me."

"Not in so many words. Just that you're doing some oddball research project and I'm helping."

"Oh, great," said Sarah. "Anyway, here's what we're doing." And she described for Mary the subjects of interest, with particular attention to be paid to any reference to *Finnegans Wake* and *The Shoemaker's Holiday*.

They parted, Sarah moving away to the opposite end of the stacks. But the bustling and rustling proved distracting. Not only were the rare books being relocated but the School of Forestry arrived to claim cartons of bulletins that were scheduled for transfer to its buildings and a music student began noisily hunting for a book of bound scores. Once Sarah was surprised to find Professor Fletcher and Professor Garvey at her elbow. "Look here," said Constance Garvey. "I didn't know they'd bought so much of the Hutter library."

"I just heard the other day. They've been sitting on it, but I imagine most of it is negligible," said Professor Fletcher, running a finger over a line of cloth-bound Bret Harte novels. "Pretty much run-of-the-mill." He nodded to Sarah and then added to Professor Garvey. "Nineteenth-century American novels and Maine maritime material."

"I hear the Rare Book Room is finished," said Sarah, thinking to drive the two back to their proper task.

"Hardly negligible," said Constance Garvey, ignoring Sarah and moving along a shelf. "Some privately printed Hawthorne and Poe, a great deal of Emerson, and studies by their own faculty. All very nicely bound. Oh, Amos"—this with a noticeable chilling of tone—"we're discussing the Hutter College Collection. The library seems to have kept it quiet."

"I went through some of it yesterday," said Amos Larkin. He was wearing his coat and had a folder tucked under one arm.

"Hello, Larkin," said Patrick Fletcher. He reached up to a top shelf and pulled down a volume. "One of your own efforts. *The Cutting Edge: The Satire of Jonathan Swift.*"

"So I see," said Amos Larkin. "Taken all in all, it seems to be standard stuff."

Again Constance Garvey protested. "Not standard. See here, medieval and Old English material. And a whole row of Dreiser criticism. Of course, it's all out of order."

"Really." Professor Fletcher did not sound interested. "Hutter College can scarcely have afforded a first-rate library. I agree with Amos. All quite run-of-the-mill."

"Gentlemen. Professor Garvey. There you are." The library director joined them, rubbing his hands and looking, with his triangular face, glossy black hair, and striped waistcoat, like a magnified beetle—in fact, like the Woggle-Bug in Sarah's Oz books. This personage—at his peril, thought Sarah—took Constance Garvey by the elbow. "I need *all* your advice on the display cases in the Rare Book Room Annex, which will be open to the public on request. Professor Lacey wants the Shakespeare in the center cases. Oh, Professor Larkin, I didn't know. How very nice. I mean, this is a joint effort, all of us, but I thought—"

"You thought I'd spill whiskey on your incunabula. Don't worry. I have no opinion about display cases."

"Now, Amos, you know you're welcome," said Patrick Fletcher, "only we thought all this wrangling about shelving and display would bore you to death. Vera begged off, and so did Howard and Joe Greenberg."

"Of course, there's nothing terribly exciting about the Hutter Collection," said the Woggle-Bug. "But the price was right, and we thought some unfamiliar reference material might turn up. Imagine, Hutter had all the unpublished and published works—including dissertations—of their own faculty bound in this olive leather and stamped with the college seal. Quite attractive, really, but my gracious, no wonder they went under. We also found two interesting Festschrifts written and bound for Professor Witherspoon. He lived to be ninety-six, you know, and stayed on at Hutter until he was made emeritus while everyone thought he'd died in harness at Yale simply years ago. Of course, these shelves won't be available for a while, though it is attracting some attention. I saw this young lady"—Sarah, to her horror, found a finger pointing at her head—"burrowing in the collection yesterday. I told her that none of the books could leave the room." He bestowed a cautionary smile on Sarah, who found herself moving into the shadows.

"Time's wasting," said Patrick Fletcher. "Let's finish with the display cases so we can all go home. As it is, I've got to call my wife and say I'll be late for lunch."

Professor Larkin lingered, fingering an anthology of early Scottish poetry. "Who was Professor Witherspoon?" asked Sarah, and then regretted it. No point in giving the man any leads.

"One of your old-fashioned sorts. Taught everything from soup to nuts: Old English, Chaucer, Shakespeare, the eighteenth-century poets—a real generalist. First at Yale, and then in his eighties he propped up Hutter College. Died quite some time ago. Didn't publish much, but I've heard he was a good teacher."

"Thank you," said Sarah primly. "I just wondered."

Amos Larkin studied her for a moment. "I don't think you just wonder," he said. Then he turned abruptly and took himself off. His eyes today seemed to Sarah not only clear but unnaturally penetrating.

For some time Sarah busied herself with the Hutter Collection. Checking on Mary, who was lingering over an illustrated copy of Pope's *Dunciad*, she allotted to each of them three shelves on each end of the stack, with emphasis on those books bound in olive leather with a gold seal. Unfortunately, since nothing was in its proper place, these were scattered through the shelves. But by noon she had made three trips to the table with bound volumes on everything from *Pilgrim's Progress* to *Acid Rain in Northern New England* and was just carrying off the latest pile when she heard a throat-rattling by her side.

"I'm sorry," said Miss Murdstone. "We've had a discussion—actually a request. Since the Hutter material has not been *thoroughly* examined and might be valuable, it's been suggested that we put the entire collection off limits for the time being."

"What?" said Sarah. "Who requested?"

"It was a group decision. The English faculty is always alert. So if you'll give me those books at once, we'll start loading them on the cart. I'm sure they'll be available in a week or so."

Sarah surrendered her books and stepped quickly around the stack to Mary's side. "Grab some books—those olive ones. Quick. Someone's closing the Hutter library. Here, I'll take three. They won't miss them for a while. They'll be busy clearing the shelves. Come on, duck back into the carrel row."

"It's time for food," said Mary. "We'll take the books with us, put a coat over them."

"Excellent advice." Alex stood behind them, his white coat hanging six inches below his duffle coat. "I thought you said the library would be uninhabited."

"The English faculty's swarming like bees," said Mary. "It's the rare books."

"We've all got to do some fast reading," said Sarah.

"After lunch," said Mary.

"Have you found anything, Alex?" asked Sarah.

"You mean my poison research? Nothing besides the fact that shrunken heads don't call for cyanide. Anyway, the lab says that the cyanide was straight—potassium cyanide crystals —not a derivative like furniture polish. The trouble was that it was all mixed in with powdered milk, cocoa, and Nutra-

Sweet. I've got my sandwich in my pocket. They don't frisk the medical types. It's this threatening white coat. I'll meet you in that new eating place."

"That's funny," said Sarah, as she and Mary reached into the shelves for their lunch bags. "My Thermos is missing. You know, Raggedy Ann. Slot number twelve."

"That'll learn you to have a cute Thermos."

"Damn. I've had it since seventh grade. It's sort of good luck."

"A nostalgia freak probably swiped it. Here, I'll give you half of mine. Diet lemonade."

"What I need," said Sarah, "is my tea." She moved along the shelves toward a far corner. "Oh, okay. Here it is, behind a bag. Someone's been moving things around." She lifted the red and blue Thermos, and they walked along to the new lunch area. This was a dismal underground cavern, a shaft of daylight filtering in from a grill-covered window high up on the wall and a single electric light hanging from a ceiling beam. Several scarred superannuated library tables and chairs were set in rows around the room. Sarah noted with relief only a few diners, the rest of the notables undoubtedly preferring to go back to their own houses, or over to the popular Faculty Club Sunday brunch.

"Ten minutes only," said Sarah. "Gobble it down." She unwrapped her sandwich, unscrewed the red cup top of the Thermos, and poured out the dark liquid. "Damn," she said. "I've forgotten the milk. I always put milk in my tea." She lifted the cup and sniffed. "This isn't tea, it's bouillon. Smell."

She passed the cup to Alex, who brought it to his nose and then carefully poured the fluid back into the Thermos and refastened the top. "I'm not paranoid, but I think you can just share my can of root beer."

"Oh, Lord, you don't suppose," began Mary. "Mrs. Parker's Thermos."

"No," said Alex. "It smelled like good old beef broth. Nothing more. A Thermos mix-up. There must be another Raggedy Ann fan in the library. But stay on the safe side."

"Cyanide smells like almonds, doesn't it?" said Sarah.

"Bitter almonds. Unmistakable, usually. But I'll have this analyzed."

Sarah felt a shiver begin at the top of her back and go all the way down to the soles of her feet. She changed the subject. "Did you get through any of the nature or pottery books?"

"I did some elimination work and—"

Sarah never learned what Alex had eliminated. There was a sudden rustle, a chair pushed back, a strangled cry, a thrashing, and suddenly, with great velocity, a Thermos flew across the room and crashed into the radiator behind Sarah. It rolled to the floor with a tinkle of broken glass and came to rest at her feet. Raggedy Ann's shoe-button eyes stared at the ceiling.

Sarah stared dumbly at the Thermos, Mary stood up speechless, and Alex hurled himself across the room, knocking two chairs apart and sending one student to the floor. Bending over a crumpled figure, he grabbed the arm of a hovering man and yelled over his shoulder to Sarah, "Call the ER to set up for cyanide poisoning!" Then, together, the two men, one carrying the torso and head, the other the legs, ran for the entrance and disappeared.

Sarah dashed to the telephone, gave the message, and, returning, stood with Mary, looking at the wreckage with unbelieving eyes. "That poor woman. God, it's as if we did it to her ourselves. Mostly me, though. Fooling around in class asking questions, goading some rat into trying again. Oh, hell. That Raggedy Ann Thermos. Everyone in the department knows it—Linda said they laughed at it."

Mary said the inevitable. "Your Thermos was poisoned. You said you wanted us to be like Alice Marmott, and you're the one who succeeded. What should we do now, go to the hospital? Does anyone live after drinking cyanide?"

"I don't know. But Alex wanted the Emergency Room ready for cyanide poisoning, so they're probably working on her. We'd better stay put for now. The police will be coming."

"I think I'm going to be the one following you around, and you can stop protecting me from Amos Larkin."

"Unless—" said Sarah. "After all, he was in the library."

Mary sighed and then nodded solemnly. "Yes. He was."

"God," Sarah said again, then turned to find that the librarian, Miss Murdstone, had joined them, evidently seeking relief in talk.

"Oh, poor Harriet. What do you suppose? A sort of a fit? She opened her Thermos—we've always made jokes about it, a child's Thermos, Raggedy Ann, she's had it since grade school. An epileptic, do you think? She's never complained of being ill, but then you know some people hide everything. Or an allergic reaction. That's what I think. Of course, it wasn't her Thermos—or it wasn't what she'd put in it. Consommé. That's what she always had and this was brown with milk, like tea or coffee. She spat it right out and then went almost crazy, spitting and grabbing someone's Coke and rinsing her mouth. A bitter smell, not like coffee or tea. Oh, goodness me, what have you got! Imagine!"

And the librarian reached across Mary to the table and fastened on three olive-bound books from the Hutter College Collection that had been uncovered in the excitement. "However did you? I thought I'd made it clear. There were six missing. Someone noticed. The bound faculty works." She reached over to Sarah's part of the table. "Here are the other three right under your jacket, and we've looked everywhere. One of the faculty spotted that they were missing at once—they're all numbered. Professor Fletcher, or was it Professor Garvey or Professor Lacey? Professor Garvey said it was light-fingered students, but I said it was just as likely to be faculty. They take anything and hide it in their offices. Poor, poor Harriet. She looked absolutely deathly, but what a blessing there was a doctor."

"You can't remember who spotted the books missing?" said Sarah.

"No. I was too distressed at their loss to pay attention, but I do know that I'm upset to find them here in the lunchroom. When they've been properly cataloged you may, of course, have access."

"But please tell the police not to let anyone out with those books, not even faculty," said Sarah, as Miss Murdstone, clutching the six books, made off toward the door.

Two uniformed State Police arrived to stop her exit, but Sarah found it impossible to interest them in the matter. They asked Miss Murdstone to show them the books and then escorted her in the direction of the Rare Book Annex, where the remaining members of the English faculty were penned.

Then, as the star witness, she returned empty-handed to the lunch area for questioning. She, Sarah, Mary, and five others were summoned to a luncheon table and told their tales, and the state trooper in charge told Sarah that the matter of particular books could wait. Nothing was going anywhere. The police were at all entrances. They had their orders from Sergeant Fitts: Sequester witnesses, take names, addresses, collect the Thermos parts, search the lunchroom, the storage-room cage, and the entire ground floor of the library.

"Did you even notice the titles or the authors?" asked Mary, when they could retreat to an empty table.

"No." Sarah groaned. "Just that one is a collection of Elizabethan essays, one a long Old English thing, and one a full-length Milton study."

"That's more than I did. One was on Auden, one on Joyce, but I didn't notice the third."

"Well, remember that *Finnegans Wake* has references to Jonathan Swift. It may mean nothing."

"And it may mean a hell of a lot. Anyway, it's easy to see someone didn't want one or more of those books to be on the loose."

"What if Alice Marmott got into the Hutter books—and that's the connection we've been looking for? Wait a minute, I'll ask."

Sarah walked over to a huddled group of library aides and hit pay dirt.

"They all remember her," Sarah told Mary. "Of course, being murdered does keep her in mind. They said Alice spent a lot of time down here, always asking questions. Used all the library facilities like a pro. She was even offered a job as a student aide, which she was considering. And listen to this, she *was* hired as an extra when the Hutton Collection arrived —just a few days before she was killed. She helped log it in, do the temporary cataloging, and shelve it."

"Santa Maria . . . or something like that."

"They're letting us go in a minute, the aides said so. Let's find George Fitts. I'll bet Alice was using some very special Hutter College stuff for those unauthorized research papers of hers."

But George Fitts was afield. "Probably with the lab team,

that poison incident," said the State Police corporal in charge of the trailer office. "You're Miss Deane, aren't you?"

"Is she still alive?" asked Sarah fearfully. "Harriet somebody. I don't know her name."

"We haven't had word to make it a homicide," said the corporal. "But we've a message from Sergeant Fitts that you and Miss Donelli aren't to be alone, and we're to give you protection on the campus."

"Thank you," said Sarah without enthusiasm.

"I hope you're satisfied," said Mary, as they turned toward the hospital."

"If it weren't for poor Harriet, I'd say yes. Those olive-bound books must be the reason my Thermos was poisoned. Not so much because we were classroom gadflies, but because I was identified as someone who'd been—what was the word? —'burrowing' in the Hutter Collection. But which one of the six books ties in to Alice's research?"

"We know a little about the subject of five of them. Auden equals poetry and that equals Horst; another was Old English, that's Patrick Fletcher."

"And the Elizabethan study, which is Lacey; and Milton is Merlin-Smith; and *Finnegans Wake*, with the Swift bits, equals Larkin."

"Okay," said Mary. "That certainly equals Larkin."

"And we probably won't know anything more until we get our hands on those books, and I'll bet they'll just evaporate—even if the doors are being guarded. Any faculty member worth his salt can bull his way past the police with a book under his arm. Can you just hear Fletcher or Garvey: 'My good man, stand back, I have a class to teach.' And all that nebulous stuff about Finns and Shoos and big manuscripts isn't going to convince anyone to put a freeze on a mere book."

"And," continued Sarah, as they pushed open the door to the hospital entrance, "since we can't get our hands on those six books, let's think about who has cyanide ready for all occasions. After all, poisoning Mrs. Parker took planning. The storm, knowing she was working late, the cold office, the cocoa habit. But whoever put it in the Raggedy Ann Thermos knew only about half an hour before he did it that I'd been into the Hutter books."

"The point being that someone had to have cyanide in his or her pocket right there in the library."

"Or be able to find it close by and scoot out during the rare-book affair."

"I don't suppose it could have been kept safely in the English Department office because the police keep coming back to search," said Sarah. "And there's something else bothering me about the English Office. Something Linda said."

"What bothers me is that you should hire a taster to try your food, but I don't want the job."

The woman at the hospital desk turned the wheel of new admission cards and came up with "critical." "No visitors," she added unnecessarily.

Followed by Mary, Sarah took the stairs to the fifth floor of physician offices and, slipping by the receptionist, walked directly into Alex's office. Fortunately, no patient in a state of undress was laid out on the examining table. Instead, Alex sat slumped in his office chair in a rumpled condition, a sheet of lab readouts in front of him.

"She's alive," he said. "Touch and go. But we got into action fast."

"And it was cyanide," said Sarah. "Definitely?"

"I thought everyone died with it," said Mary. "Mrs. Parker, Jonestown, Eva Braun and the Goebbels."

"Oh, it's lethal, all right. As little as three hundred milligrams of potassium cyanide can do it. But there's a specific and effective antidote. It's complicated, but what you're trying to do is break up certain killer combinations and restore enzyme function and cell respiration. Administer one hundred percent oxygen, sodium nitrite and follow it up with sodium thiosulfate, and so forth. It's just damn lucky she swallowed the stuff within in reach of an emergency room. Anyway, if she gets through the first four hours, recovery is likely."

"And she'll be okay?" said Sarah.

"You can't promise that. Cerebral symptoms may hang around."

"Christ," said Mary.

"But we got her fast, we've got a good toxicology team here, and the ER people were on their toes. George's lab team is working on it. We've also fixed it to keep tabs on you two, because looking through the Hutter library has, I'm afraid, marked you out as dangerous. I'll be around when I can. Otherwise, please stay together, and no walks or solos in dark corners."

"Tomorrow's the English Department Ski Club thing," said Mary. "I'm all paid up, lift tickets and all. Sarah said she might come."

"Stay home and read a good book," said Alex.

"We could go and stay glued together," said Sarah. "Keep on the bunny slopes in full sight of hundreds. But for now, we're missing six books—olive binding—that might be the key to the whole thing. We think Alice found out something and Mrs. Parker found out from Alice. The library people have them now in the Rare Book Annex."

"I'll see what I can do." Alex initiated a series of telephone calls back and forth to switchboards, to the State Police, to the library. "Okay," he said, pushing the phone away. "It's the best I can do. They will take inventory now of the Hutter College olive-bound faculty collection, and none of those books will leave the library. Not with faculty members, not with librarians, not with the chancellor himself. Also, the director pointed out that inside the spine of each book the library had already put a metallic disk that sets off a squeal when it goes past the library security desks. Standard theft protection. And everyone leaving the library from now on will be frisked. Mike Laaka will come to escort you to the library for a look at the books."

A head and the top of a blue scrub suit leaned into the doorway. "She's doing pretty good now. We're maintaining blood pressure. Washed out her stomach again to be on the safe side. Want to come and see?"

Alex stood up. "Keep your fingers crossed."

Mike Laaka marched them back from the hospital and down to the side entrance to the ground floor library. Perhaps because of the rather oppressive appearance of the rows of stacks, Mike was unnaturally silent. "Libraries like this get under my skin," he admitted. "All those moldy old books and moldy old females whispering 'hush.'"

"You never know," said Mary, spirits reviving. "They may be young, sexy, and homicidal."

A few minutes later, in the presence of a disapproving director and a purple-faced Miss Murdstone, the olive leather-bound volumes were brought from the shelves and put along a long polished table.

Sarah and Mary, feeling like criminals viewing the evidence against them, lifted and opened book after book. Then Sarah shook her head. "They're not here. Not one of the six we had."

"Of course they're here," said Miss Murdstone. "I brought them here myself. I put them directly on that shelf, the middle one, with the others. I left a note for Dr. Threadgill"—she indicated the Woggle-Bug—"to check them, and I asked an aide to see that they were placed in the proper order."

"But they're not here," repeated Sarah.

"Impossible," said Dr. Threadgill.

But it was quite possible. It was quickly established that the Annex door through to the Rare Book Room was open and that the latter chamber was peopled by librarians, aides, and those of the English faculty who had returned from, or had not yet departed for, lunch.

"Professor Fletcher and Professor Horst—" began Dr. Threadgill.

"Wait up," said Mike, taking out his notebook.

"And Professor Larkin—" said Dr. Threadgill.

"No," interrupted Miss Murdstone. "Professor Larkin was outside at one of the reading tables, but Professor Lacey had just returned."

"Of course, no one was allowed to leave after the incident—the emergency with Harriet," said an aide, "but the English Department people were allowed to keep their briefcases."

"We try to trust our faculty," said Dr. Threadgill.

"I am always very, very careful," said Miss Murdstone, her face twisted with fury.

Sarah, seeing that library fur was about to fly, spoke up. "I heard that no books were being let out of the library, and that they have metal seals that trip sound devices even if the books are in a briefcase. So the books must still be somewhere in the building."

"Quite so," said Dr. Threadgill. "We will search."

"The police will search," said Mike.

"You wouldn't know what to look for," said Miss Murdstone, now much agitated and looking about the room as if the missing books had deliberately concealed themselves.

"Just describe the books," said Mike. "We'll make out. Most of us know our colors and can read and write."

It was a remark, Sarah knew, that boiled up inside the sheriff's deputy as a result of weeks of working on the campus, where the often thinly veiled condescension of the academics must have rubbed against him like the scraping of a blister. She imagined that someone like the militant Constance Garvey or the heavy-fisted Jakob Horst must often have brought Mike and his fellows to a state just short of assault and battery.

Mike now turned his back on the librarians and told Sarah and Mary to go along. "It's our ball now, ladies. Take a breather, stick together. Corporal Meservy will keep an eye on you both."

That night after dinner, Mary called Sarah. "The Ski Club trip tomorrow, is it on?"

"Homicidal faculty with ski poles?" said Sarah.

"We can't do much more here, not until they find those books or until the police get the lab reports from your Thermos. So let's take a break. I'll bet you're hot stuff on skis."

"I haven't been downhill skiing since last year. My knees will probably dissolve."

SEVENTEEN

T hus on Monday morning, against inclination and better judgment, Sarah found herself, skis and poles over her shoulder, trudging behind Mary in the direction of the North Quad parking lot. The two buses chartered for this annual event were filling up—faculty and children, fellows and adjuncts, students staying on campus over the spring break, and even Arlene in powder blue and Linda in orange and yellow skin-tight ski pants.

Sarah loaded her equipment in the bus's luggage compartment and then, seeing the two English Office clerks, suddenly remembered. "I'll be right back," she called, and galloped down a path and behind the rink before Mary could call her back.

She found George Fitts in the trailer, unfolding a map of the campus. "Yes?" he said.

"The computer thing—that thimble. The one on the English Department printer. When you found it after Mrs. Parker died, did it have special characters on it—accents, letters for foreign languages?"

George moved his chart to one side and opened a notebook. "The English Office inventory at the time of Mrs. Parker's death shows a printing thimble, Special Multilingual 604." He ran his finger down a list. "Foreign alphabet letters and diacritical marks. Something you'd expect in a college office."

"But that's what's bothering me," said Sarah. "Mrs. Parker did all the foreign language stuff on her IBM typewriter with special printing balls, and Linda and Arlene just used the standard printer thimble. Linda thought the computer company didn't send back their own standard thimble —that they'd substituted a new one. But you're saying the repair people sent back the one they found on it."

"Correct."

"Then it must have been installed by Mrs. Parker—" Sarah stopped, puzzled. Mike Laaka came in and slammed the door so hard the whole trailer shivered.

"Wait, Mike. Go on, Sarah," said George, picking up a pencil.

"Mrs. Parker was the last one to use the word processor and maybe the printer," said Sarah. "I mean, she died next to it, with her cocoa spilled all over everything."

"Yes. We've finally recovered prints from under the film of cocoa."

"Then she must have been doing something that called for a special thimble. Or she was practicing foreign-language typing."

"I'd say so."

"Listen," broke in Mike. "This won't wait while you two play hunt the thimble. The cyanide report is in; they did a rush job. Potassium cyanide in crystal form. Not entirely dissolved. This because the tea-and-milk mix had probably cooled enough to slow up solubility, but also the lab people think the cyanide must have been put into the Thermos close to the time it was drunk."

"That's that, then," said George. "Now to run it down."

"Alex is working on that too," said Sarah. "To see if it's used in flower drying, or stuffing bats and crocodiles, or pot making."

Mary burst in, flinging the door open with even more violence than had Mike. "Sarah, come on, the buses are leaving!"

They departed with George's admonitions in their ears. "Ski together, have lunch together, go home together."

"All this girlie togetherness," complained Mary, "is getting me nowhere in finding a man."

"I thought you'd found one," said Sarah incautiously, and then, "I'm sorry."

"You'd better be and so am I," said Mary, as they climbed aboard the last bus and flung themselves on the last empty seat. And then, looking about, "I'm sure that little side trip to the police trailer has now confirmed your status as a sort of in-house spy."

"They're all too busy with themselves. Look around and see who's here."

They took inventory. Professor and Mrs. Horst, both in navy gabardine of forty years ago, sat together and looked stolidly out the window. Ivan Lacey sat with a graduate student who wore a one-piece racing suit that fitted her like a second skin. Lacey himself wore an Irish sweater, paisley scarf, and dark reflective glasses, and his long well-muscled legs were nicely displayed in tight red pants.

"The Black Stallion is looking trig," said Mary. "No Mrs. Stallion to cramp his act."

"At least Professor Fletcher isn't trying to look like a travel poster," said Sarah. The two Fletchers, presumably representing one of the few happy marriages in the English Department, sat, heads together in conversation. She in one-piece navy, her long fair hair pulled tightly back in a yellow scarf, he in a dark green parka and black pants, represented sense and restraint. Patrick Fletcher's pipe was held in his teeth; the light from the window emphasized the planes of his face. Sarah poked Mary. "If you don't fancy Lacey, how about Lord Patrick Fletcher?"

"Don't distract me. I'm trying to face up to Amos as a possible murderer. It's taking all my vital juices, so don't suggest substitutes."

They rode amid the chattering babble, excitement from the crisp air, the sun stretching over on the long white fields and the mountain foothills, and the knowledge that the whole week was vacation.

In the parking lot an energetic young woman whom Sarah recognized as an instructor in the European novel, handed out trail maps and indicated the children's and the beginners' slopes. "Make it back by five if you plan to take the bus to the Camden Inn for dinner. Those who plan to take the Campus Trail back to the college and join us in your own cars —well, remember Happy Hour doesn't last forever."

"What's the Campus Trail?" asked Sarah, as she and Mary began poling over to the beginning of the chair lift.

"Just finished last year," said Mary. "A long run down the other side of the mountain. It splits—over to Sawmill Road or down to the campus by Old Farm Road."

Sarah nodded and added to herself, Right down Old Farm Road and right past Amos Larkin's house. "But we're taking the bus back, aren't we?" she said aloud.

"If you say so," said Mary. "It's the easy way to get to the dinner."

The trails had been given sea and weather names and, to warm up, the first runs were taken on the novice slopes, Blue Skies and Zephyr. It became clear immediately that Mary Donelli, like many short compact persons, could zip down the hill, feet together, swinging and dipping, and that Sarah, taller, thinner, out of practice, was going to spend a large portion of the day pulling herself out of the snow and refastening her release bindings.

"It'll come back to you," said Mary cheerfully, stopping by a tangled Sarah at the foot of the lift. "We'll go over to the intermediate trails—Spindrift is nice—because what you need is more speed to build up your rhythm. Then we can hit the expert trails in the afternoon. I like Tornado. The moguls are great."

Alex sat in the reading room of the Life Sciences Library. He was surrounded by books on cyanide and cyanic derivatives, botanical handbooks, pamphlets on herbal remedies and taxidermy, nature field guides, books on silver and brass polish. To the left of his shoulder were heaped references on arrowhead poisons, shrunken heads; pot making among the Zuni, the Hopi, the Navajo; utensil making in Indonesia, Micronesia, and points north, east, and south; as well as compendiums on photographic chemicals and plant and crop insecticides. To his right lay Sarah's list of faculty-owned objects and a list of their interests and hobbies as she had judged from hearsay and from her visits to the houses of Professors Fletcher, Pruczak, and Horst.

Potassium cyanide. The possibilities were without end. He was beginning to think that cyanide was utterly commonplace, a substance any house-proud person might want at hand at all times, to clean, to polish, to develop, to eradicate —to kill. After all, the murderer, as Sarah had said, could not have known until almost the time of the latest poison event that Sarah had been zeroing in on the Hutter College books, so he must have had the cyanide available in some immediately useful form. Mrs. Parker's cyanide had not been a derivative; perhaps this would be the same. Materials like silver polish would either have to have its ingredients extracted or require a heavier dose than the straight cyanide. How about the Bowmouth chemistry and medical school labs then? But was there enough time for the murderer to race to a lab— hoping to find it open and empty—and grab the stuff? Or did he keep it at all times in his pocket, in his bureau drawer, in a capsule, in a bottle ready to drink, ready to drop into a Thermos? Allow, say, fifteen minutes, maybe twenty, to leave the Rare Book group, find the cyanide, get to the Thermos, and return. Alex let out a long exasperated breath, reached for another field guide, and ruffled through the pages, then back to the introduction. Here he was arrested suddenly by the word "killing." The word was imbedded in detailed directions and explicit warnings. He grabbed Sarah's list again, shouted, "Holy hell," jumped to his feet, and raced to the library desk and demanded a telephone from the alarmed librarian.

Lunch at the ski hut was only a short reprieve. Sarah felt that her knees and calves might need several years in a hot tub to recover their full use.

"You're warming up," said Mary. "The first few hours are the toughest. I think you're ready for Tornado."

"I like Spindrift just fine," said Sarah. "Look, Mary, go ahead if you can find someone safe to ski with. Drago Collins and his girl will let you stick with them. I heard him say he was going to hit Tornado in the afternoon. I'll find a safe partner and ski where I belong. Maybe back to Zephyr with the kiddies."

"No way," said Mary. "Safe is with me. Me with you. I'll tutor you on two more runs, and then we'll try the expert trails. You have to ski a little scared to get the feel."

Sarah sighed and reached for her goggles. "It's starting to snow. The visibility will be terrible."

"Follow me. I'll take it easy. You're still fighting the fall line. Just lean away, get up your speed, and then you won't have to do that little stemming I catch you doing."

"If I end up in traction, you'll have to take my classes."

Sarah did seem to find a second wind, and Spindrift now seemed a bit tame. She noticed that Patrick Fletcher and his wife—Ingrid, wasn't it?—were gliding up and down in front of her. And then with one accord, as if they had discussed it, the four of them started off at the top of the trail toward the complex of expert trails. At the top of Squall they found Ivan Lacey and his graduate student, he leaning over her and doing something intimate with the back of her knees.

Professor Lacey smiled at them. "Spindrift is a little boring," he said. "I'm just showing Phyllis, here, that it's all a matter of knee control."

"Quite," said Professor Fletcher. "At least there isn't a crowd on the expert trails."

Sarah, plunging down Squall after Mary, could see why. Squall had sudden drops, narrow spots just when one most wanted to check, and few opportunities for sideslipping. "This is the pits," she said to Mary as she picked herself out of a bush on the side of a trail. She stood up and resentfully watched Professor Horst and his wife appear in tandem, counting one-two-lift, two-three-lift, as they skiied down the slope in a style that went out with Lake Placid rope tows.

"Let's switch to Tornado," said Mary. "It's not much steeper than Squall and it's got more room. They widened it when they built the new Campus Trail off of it."

"The one with a cutoff to Sawmill Road and the campus," said Sarah, thinking of a hot bath with unspeakable longing. The sky had darkened and the snow was now blowing down in large blinding flakes.

"Well, we might consider taking it. It's a fun trail for the end of the day—just like a highway. You put your feet together and zip."

They moved into the chair lift line and, as often happened, a man ahead of Mary called "single" and Mary hopped onto the chair with him, while Sarah, doubled up with another stranger, swung behind her and began to consider murder on a ski lift. Mary's "single" had turned out to be Ivan Lacey cut loose, either by accident or design, from his graduate student. Sarah found herself with Mrs. Horst. With one ear she listened to Mrs. Horst in her heavy foreign accent—Hungarian, perhaps—discuss her children and the expense of putting all four of them into ski boots, skis, poles, the newest in release bindings.

Ahead the chairs swung in the steadily rising wind; the snow, blowing across the slopes, swirled into Sarah's face. Just above, she saw that Professor Lacey had bent his head toward Mary as if engaged in deep conversation; one of his mittened hands hung over the back of the chair and rested against Mary's neck. Sarah shuddered, not from the cold but from the ghastly vision of Mary being eased from her chair— Ivan Lacey lifting the chair bar and giving Mary a skillful heave-ho. The chair lift to the three expert trails, Squall, Force 10, and Tornado, rose much more directly and steeply than did the other lifts. Rose over the tops of the pointed spruce trees, over bare crags and hanging ledges, and at one point over a frozen waterfall that dropped away for sixty feet or more. It would be explained as a terrible accident, Mary had tried to catch a falling ski pole—a common enough occurrence on ski lifts. And who was to say no? Not Sarah, because the driven snow was now blinding her, even with goggles, so that the chair ahead was only a dim shape. Then abruptly the whole lift came to a swinging stop over a particularly nasty succession of tumbled rocks.

"The veather iss gettink heavy now," announced Mrs. Horst, pulling her parka hood over her head and setting their chair in motion.

"Look out," said Sarah angrily. "The seats are slippery." Maybe Mrs. Horst is the one, she thought, taking a tighter grip on the chair's supporting pole.

"Slippery," repeated Mrs. Horst. "Yes, fery slippery and so very cold iss gettink."

They could only sit swaying, the heavy boots and skis dragging down their feet, and then the welcome whine and the lift began to move again. Had someone fallen off? Sarah peered into the space below but saw no sprawled shape.

With great relief she saw the two figures ahead slide off the chair and slip off to the right. Mary's red parka with the two horizontal navy stripes was easy enough to follow. Sarah gripped her poles with her right hand, her companion flipped up the iron bar, and then, as Sarah was about to shove off, Mrs. Horst fell forward directly in front of her, a scramble of skis and poles. Sarah fell across her, a ski binding released, and the chair lift jerked to a stop.

"Damn," said Sarah, for Mary had disappeared. She pulled at Mrs. Horst, rescued her poles, and refastened her own binding. "Damn," she said again.

For a moment, Sarah considered staying near Mrs. Horst, who really seemed harmless, but then, wiping her goggles, she saw far ahead, in a sudden abatement of the snow, a red parka figure moving in the direction of the Tornado Trail. She flung herself in motion, saw the figure join another, and shoot over the headwall of Tornado. Throwing herself into a prolonged sideslip, she swooped up to the two, only to find two teenage boys. What now? No choice. She put her skis together and, abandoning safety, took three turns on the fall line, hit a sheet of ice, and windmilled into the air.

Collecting herself from this misadventure, she cleaned her goggles again, peered, and, yes, there was another red parka on the right shape and size person. It stood at the top of a wide deviating trail, apparently waiting. Obviously Mary, standing at the top of the Campus Trail. Pushing herself off, Sarah schussed down a hundred feet and took a wide sloping turn, her feet bobbling over the ruts and lumps, and then saw the red parka, reassured no doubt by Sarah's reappearance, take off down the Campus Trail. Had they agreed to take the trail or were they going by bus? Never mind, Mary was ahead. Had she possibly, in the face of everything, decided to pay a visit to Amos Larkin's farmhouse? Would she dare be so incredibly stupid?

Sarah poled herself furiously along the flat entrance stretch, past a troop of home-going skiers, muffled, goggled, and ski-masked. With their lowered heads and slogging pace, they looked like a crew of slaves returning from work on a distant sunless icebound planet. She forced her rubbery leg muscles, aching ankles, and increasingly numb feet into motion, but now, aggravatingly, the red parka pushed off and began a long glide down, around, and out of sight.

As far as Sarah could tell through the circling snow and wind, the trail was wide and well-groomed. In fact, had she been in any mood for pleasure, she would have found it a happy forgiving trip, sliding easily around each dip, hearing the occasional hiss and scrape of a skier going by. And now, at last, the trail opened and gave out on a broad sweep across a field and past Amos Larkin's back door. And there was Mary at the foot of the hill looking down on the farmhouse, its chimney smoking in an inviting manner, no doubt considering whether she dared stop with her watchdog just behind her. With a tremendous effort, Sarah poled herself over the edge of the trail, took the fall line straight, and came up with a swoop to Mary. Only it wasn't Mary. It was a short blond girl just taking off her hood and goggles and wiping her nose and chin clear of the gathered frost. She looked up at Sarah. "That snow is tough. I couldn't see a blessed thing. But God, isn't that trail heaven? Almost home." And she stamped her skis free of the clinging snow and was off.

And where was Mary? Sarah searched the road ahead and the field behind. More goggles, parkas, hoods, masks. But no one in red with navy blue stripes. Mary: was she at this very moment being tucked into a crevasse, or was Sarah just being a tired nervous wreck?

Well, no help for it. Ski on down and across to her own house—the Sawmill Road cutoff ran off to her right. It would be quicker than finding a telephone on a closed-up campus. Once home she'd call Alex, call George. Say it was an emergency and to start looking. As for the English Department dinner, as long as Mary was found in one piece, to hell with it. Sarah joined the trickle of skiers heading along the slight ridge to Sawmill Road, seeing every now and then someone split off for one of the houses that dotted the meadow between Amos Larkin's farmhouse and her own road. Finally, only Sarah and one tall trudging ski-masked figure, both walking awkwardly in their cumbersome inflexible boots, made their way toward the house on Sawmill Road. One of the medical students, she decided.

It was not until she reached over with her ski pole to release her bindings that she realized the other skier was not going ahead to the other half of the house. He had joined her. She reared up to face a gray woolen ski mask and yellow-lensed goggles. A navy blue arm reached for her shoulder.

Sarah, without thinking, began to edge toward the back door. The dark figure in the face mask nodded. "Sensible of you. We don't want a discussion in public. Now do as I say. Take off your skis." The voice was a husky whisper. Not familiar, and yet Sarah knew she had heard it before.

She bent over and released her ski bindings. Leaning down to loosen her runaway straps, she could think of fifty strategies. Run, jump, scream, pierce her visitor with a ski pole? But ski poles didn't pierce, they punctured. A five-inch puncture. Just enough to enrage an attacker. In fact, there were no strategies. The visitor was tall—in fact, in the failing light, seemed to loom hugely over her.

Move slowly, Sarah told herself; the only chance is in the house, and I hope he's not asleep at the switch. She pushed her skis into the snow and carefully hung her poles over the tips. Her companion collected Sarah's skis and poles and together with his own slid them under the steps leading to the back door. "Why be conspicuous?" said the husky voice. Then, in a conversational tone, "Go in ahead of me. I have a gun."

Sarah, awkward in her heavy boots, pulled herself up on the railing, reached in her zippered parka pocket for her back-door key, and opened it. Then, followed by the visitor, who closed the door behind them, she stepped inside and into the kitchen and gave a soft whistle.

For a moment the figure behind her paused, adjusting to the sound and to the room, and in that moment Sarah opened her mouth and screamed. And screamed. From every body cavity, she forced out air and screamed. And then, seeming to fill the kitchen, a huge gray wolflike shape jumped for the throat.

Alex made two calls. One to the house on Sawmill Road —with no answer—and a second to the State Police trailer, described to the corporal in charge certain details taken from the introduction of one of the nature field guides, and demanded the immediate services of George Fitts and Mike Laaka. Then he flung himself into his car and drove up to the Bowmouth Ski Basin at a dangerous speed, spinning on the ice and skidding around turns.

The parking lot at the foot of the basin was filled with churning cars and returning skiers, while at one end the two yellow buses were loading for the English Ski Club dinner. Alex found Mary Donelli flanked by Drago Collins at the entrance of the ski lodge. Mary shook her head as he ran up to her.

"I've had the loudspeaker call her, and I've checked the other side of the mountain where we were skiing. The ski patrol people are sweeping the trails now. She might have skied the Campus Trail all the way down—the parking lot or home. We talked about taking it but hadn't decided, so maybe I missed her there. Mrs. Horst says she had a spill when she got off the chair lift."

"Have any of the faculty disappeared?"

"At least half. I guess some left early by the Campus Trail."

"Stay here," said Alex, "and help keep the search going. I've left a message for George Fitts to get up here fast and Mike to check our house and the campus. I'll do the same." And he strode off back to his car.

Alex's timing, Sarah thought later, would have done Steven Spielberg proud. The dog sprang, the ski-masked figure swayed back, the kitchen door opened, Sarah screamed again, Alex lunged forward yelling, "Down Patsy," Alex and the visitor rolled on the linoleum floor, a kitchen stool spun around, and Mike Laaka filled the doorway.

"Only abrasions, I think," said Alex, pulling the ski mask

clear of the head and carefully lifting the long fair hair away from the neck. "No blood vessels broken and the skin's hardly marked. I don't think Patsy's a killer at heart, but he certainly knows how to take the starch out of someone."

"But the breathing," said Sarah, standing white-faced by the sink.

"Got the wind knocked out when she went down. That's the wheezing."

"I don't believe it," said Sarah slowly. She walked over and stared down at the face, the mouth open, gulping for air. One of the woman's hands, still with its mitten on, reached for her chest.

"Look out," cried Sarah, backing up. "She said she had a gun."

Alex ran expert hands down the woman's side, reaching into her pockets. "No gun," he said. "I'll get my stethoscope and take a listen, but she may have only cracked a rib. Sarah, will you call the ambulance?" He snapped his fingers. "Good dog, Patsy. You watch." This as Patsy stepped over to examine his handiwork. "Of course," said Sarah afterward, "Patsy hasn't a clue to what 'watch' means."

"It doesn't matter," Alex then said. "He knew what to do when it counted."

Now Sarah came back from the telephone and said again, "I don't believe it. I never thought of you."

Mrs. Patrick Fletcher had stopped gasping. She looked up at Sarah. "You should have, because Patrick told me about you. A destroyer. Like that awful Marmott girl, who went on and on, questions, questions. May I do a special research paper, I just love Old English, digging around where she had no right. And you, never leaving well enough alone. Destroy, tramp on something fine and destroy it. Meddle, meddle, meddle. Oh, I know you."

"But you—you didn't . . ." Sarah hesitated. Something was fearfully out of joint.

"What does it matter what I did or didn't?" The woman's voice was louder, more confident.

Alex returned, knelt before the woman, and, as he fixed his stethoscope around his neck, said, "Where is he?"

"I don't know." The woman turned her head away.

"Yes, you do. Sarah, did they ski together?"

"I saw them start over to the expert trails, but later on when it began to snow I couldn't tell anyone apart. That's how I lost Mary. Everyone was in goggles and masks."

"George is off at the ski basin," said Mike, "and he's sent a man ahead to the Camden Inn where the faculty's supposed to have supper."

"Try the library," said Sarah. "That's what this whole thing is about. Isn't it, Mrs. Fletcher?"

"I don't know anything about the library." The woman began struggling to a sitting position.

"Stay put, you," said Mike, and Sarah thought she could hear him add "bitch."

The woman subsided and fixed her eyes on the ceiling. Alex made his examination and then sat by the woman until the ambulance stretcher team arrived. "Call the State Police to keep an eye on her," Alex said. "I can't see anything but a bruised throat, but tell the ER people I want a complete check."

"Okay, let's get a move on," said Mike, as Mrs. Fletcher was rolled out of sight. "We'll start with the library. Sarah, you stay here and don't answer the door."

"You must be joking. Do you think I'm going to sit here wondering if Professor Fletcher is on his way down the chimney? I'm going to the library with you. I'm sure the missing books are hidden there and I can help. We can get the whole library staff going."

"Okay," said Alex. "But you're the number-one target."

"So I'll stay under heavy guard." Sarah reflected that a day's skiing had rendered her almost useless, a thing of wobbling joints and macaroni muscles. She leaned over and began unclamping her ski boots. Whatever happened, she wanted her feet back in normal shoes.

"I'll raise George on the car radio," said Mike, "and tell the library people we're coming."

Dr. Threadgill and the faithful Miss Murdstone—whose name to Sarah's satisfaction turned out to be Miss Pierre—met them at the ground-floor entrance. The library director clasped his hands. "There is, I fear, the possibility of an intruder. Someone going up toward the rotunda in heavy boots.

We are closing all the doors and have called the police. And we have not located the missing books."

"Find those and you might find Professor Fletcher," said Alex. "Come on, Mike, let's start with the main reading room."

Sarah sat for reasons of safety in the assistant librarian's office, a small chamber that adjoined the undergraduate reserve shelves and the reading room. Her companion was Miss Pierre, whom Sarah found still in a tizzy brought on by anxiety for the library and the thrill of actually being "on the scene." Miss Pierre was acting like someone just introduced to strong drink and finding a taste for it.

"I'm sure it couldn't be one of the library staff. I mean, to actually steal books and then hide them. Or to poison poor Harriet." (Sarah could tell that she considered the two crimes on a par.) "The Bowmouth faculty don't actually *steal,* and our aides and volunteers are screened, only the most reliable. Poor Harriet, the finest recommendations, and to think. But they say she's getting better, only her head's not quite right yet. I can tell you we've been run off our feet in Reference without her."

Sarah, looking out an outside window grill, saw the revolving lights of the arriving State Police car. She held her breath.

"And," said Miss Pierre, "our custodians. Thoroughly checked. Of course, the library is turning into a prison house what with students trying to get away with our reserve shelf books. They throw them out the window so as not to trip the detection alarm. And then this man in ski boots, clumping right into the stacks. I was working late on returns. But I didn't see who it was, and then you came and I had to stay in here." Miss Pierre sounded almost resentful.

Sarah heard the scuffling of many feet on a marble floor, rapid sounds of running down the hall, the echoing of voices from the main reading room.

Miss Pierre shuddered and pulled at her fingers.

"At least we don't have to watch," Sarah said sympathetically. "It might get nasty."

"Don't be silly, we've got a window," said Miss Pierre,

now proving herself completely corrupted. "We had one put in so we could watch the desk. Poor Harriet, I owe it to her to see everything. We can look right into the main reading room and up to the galleries."

So from behind the window they watched. The main reading room was lit, but the stacks flanking both sides were in shadow. Sheriff's men in brown uniforms guarded the foot of the two wide circular stairways to the upper galleries and shelves while gray-uniformed state troopers slowly and silently circled around the rows of long library tables and the two semicircles of card index cabinets and dodged in and out of the rows of stacks, rather like awkward dancers making stage right and stage left entrances. It was, Sarah thought, an enormous choreographed game of hide-and-seek set to the tempo of a pavane.

Then a bustle and scraping at the main desk and George Fitts stood forth, a loudspeaker unit pressed close to his mouth.

"Professor Fletcher. Please save us trouble. Come down now." His always hollow voice echoed around the galleries, and "Come down now" repeated itself in spectral tones. "If you have a weapon, drop it," called George. "The library is surrounded. Come down. We will hold our fire."

"I should hope so," said Miss Pierre. "Think of the bindings."

"We have your wife in custody, Professor Fletcher," said George. "She is in the hospital asking to see you."

A scrabbling noise sounded from the second-story gallery, and several volumes came flying out, pages fluttering, and like wounded birds crashed to the marble mosaic floor.

"Oh my, oh my, oh my," said Miss Pierre. "Those are the bound quartos, the Popham Colony History collection."

"Professor Fletcher, you're wasting time," called George. "Come down—resisting arrest will be added to the charges against you."

For an answer, the clatter of ski boots and two more books came down, looseleaf folios, scattering prints and text over the library tables.

"The Audubon Folio," moaned Miss Pierre. "The American Poets series—the large paper edition."

Miss Pierre was a treasure, decided Sarah. Perfect recall for any book, even if airborne.

And then Alex stepped out into the reading room and pointed. "There he is, George."

And Sarah, lifting her head, saw him. Professor Fletcher. Still in his dark green parka, his black ski pants. He stood quite still, backed up against one of the portraits of the past chancellors of the college, and then took several steps forward and leaned out into the space of the rotunda, hands wide apart and fastened on the polished brass rail as if he meant to vault gracefully into space.

For several minutes he gazed down at the scene below, apparently taking note of the absolute hush, the menace of the uniformed men standing suddenly still below him.

Sarah watched, rigid. Was he going to say something? Something memorable, an apt quotation? Or just curse them all and jump. Splat.

"I'm covering my eyes," said Miss Pierre. "Oh, dear, oh, dear."

Sarah did the same. A long pause, a collective *ahhh*, a splintering crash. A gap of silence, then a rushing of feet, out, down.

"He went out the window," shrieked Miss Pierre. "I looked. I couldn't help it."

Sarah opened the door and walked slowly over to the main desk. Alex joined her. "It's all right," he said.

"What? But he jumped," said Sarah. She found that she was shuddering as if caught in a windstorm.

"If my sense of direction is right," said Alex, "Professor Fletcher has jumped directly into that monster pile of snow that's been building under the main window of the rotunda. I'd say he's in danger only of snow down his neck and being treated roughly by George's men."

Which proved to be the case. And Sarah, going to a window, was rewarded by the sight of three State Police troopers headed by George Fitts hauling Professor Patrick Fletcher toward a waiting squad car.

"Thank God," she said.

"I suppose he knew about the snow pile," said Alex. "Thought he still had a chance to get away. Now where are those damn books we're supposed to be looking for, the answer to this whole blessed tangle?"

"We'll start searching again immediately," said Dr. Threadgill. "This is a job for professionals."

"The police are professionals," said Mike Laaka. "We'll do the heating systems, the lavatories, the offices. Yes"—seeing a scowl on the face of Dr. Threadgill—"the offices. This case isn't entirely wrapped up. Sergeant Fitts is busy with the main event, but we'll work on the tag ends. You may have a slippery-fingered librarian in here."

"I resent that," said Dr. Threadgill.

"Go right ahead and resent," said Mike. Sarah could see that he was enjoying himself. He walked over to one of the sheriff's deputies and pointed to the stairs.

"Olive leather with gold stamping," said Sarah.

"This young lady may help since she is familiar with the binding," said Dr. Threadgill graciously.

"So be it," said Alex. "Look, Sarah, I'll run over to the hospital and check on Fletcher's wife, and then I'll come back and pick you up."

For the next hour the complete library staff, summoned from home and from dinner, searched like so many vigorous ants. On top, behind, and underneath carpets, stacks, cabinets, shelves, carrels. They opened display cases, peered under folios, behind hanging portraits, moved book trolleys, searched the paper dispenser of the copy machine and the crannies of the microfilm library. The deputies crawled high and low among the heating pipes and radiators, ran hands along ledges, dumped wastebaskets, and opened toilet tanks and bowls.

Sarah, moving from one center of activity to another, floated into the main reference room—Amsterdam, Amulets, Anderson, Andersonville, Ankora, Anna Purna, Anthrax, Antiques, Archaeology, Arthropods, Astrology, Astronomy, Beethoven, Bellamy, Bellevue, *Beowulf* (here Sarah paused and searched earnestly), Bishop, Borax, Botany, Brahms, Buddy System, Burton-on-Water. But nothing, nothing bound in olive leather with gold stamping.

She moved over to the far side of the rotunda, instinctively avoiding the spot where Patrick Fletcher might have chosen to fling himself, and walked into the Founder's Room. This proved an austere chamber done in crimson and mahogany where portraits were being lifted down by two deputies. She retreated and walked down the hall to the the Eliza Starbox Memorial Children's Room. The light was on and the children's librarian was hurrying out with an aide. "Everything's just as it should be," she was telling the aide.

Sarah slipped in and sat down at one of the low round tables. The whole day was beginning to weigh on her like a coat of lead. She reached for the pile of nursery books from the center of the table. *Everybody's Mother Goose, The Tale of Squirrel Nutkin, Goodnight Moon, The Cat in the Hat.* A few of Sarah's favorites mixed in with new and strange titles. I'm getting old, she thought. I don't know even half these books. Did anyone even read the books she grew up on—her mother's, her grandmother's books? *The Secret Garden, The Snow Queen,* the Nesbitt books, *Peterkin Papers, The Princess and the Goblin.* And her mother's and grandmother's favorite set, the good old Book House. Six volumes, from nursery rhymes to little biographies of noted people and excerpts from the likes of the *Mill on the Floss* and *David Copperfield.* Six volumes in olive leather. Olive. With gold stamping. By Olive Beaupré Miller. Sarah jumped to her feet. If you wanted to hide books, why put them behind a radiator or in the toilet? Why not match them up and put them in a part of the library no one would search? Sarah jumped up. Of course the Book House set was an oldie. Did modern children's libraries even carry it?

But Bowmouth was old and prided itself on the fact. She rushed over to the low shelves and began running through the matched sets, Child Craft, World Book, the Scribner Classics. There it was: My Book House, six volumes and, standing next to them, six almost matching olive-bound strangers. Sarah pulled them out and began opening books and on the third found it: Volume 47 of the Hutter College Collection. Professor Witherspoon. *Beowulf, the Finnsburg Fragment, and Sutton Hoo.* "A reappraisal of the Old English texts in the light of the artifacts found in an Anglo-Saxon burial ship." Finn and Shoo had come to light.

When the library excitement had died down, when Miss Pierre had been soothed and entrusted with the return of the five books of the Hutter College library that did not figure in the devious doings of Professor Patrick Fletcher, and when Dr. Threadgill had fulminated on the abuse of library material, Sarah was permitted to sit down with both Professor Fletcher's own study of *Beowulf* and Professor Witherspoon's work and make a comparison.

Alex pulled up a chair on one side, Mike sat on the other.

"You mean," said Alex, "Shoo isn't a sneeze or shoofly pie?"

"And Finn had nothing to do with *Finnegans Wake*," said Sarah, opening Patrick Fletcher's book and finding a tender inscription to "My dear wife, Ingrid, without whose constant support this book would never have been possible." Sarah shook her head. "What he means is that without Professor Witherspoon this book wouldn't have been possible."

"So the unpublished manuscript—of Mrs. Parker's note—meant Witherspoon's," said Alex, "because I suppose having it privately printed and bound by Hutter College isn't exactly like having it published."

"And," said Sarah, "the MO, the magnum opus, was Fletcher's. The trouble was that none of us in the Old English class had gotten as far as *Beowulf*—except, I suppose, poor Alice. None of us had done any background reading—Fletcher certainly didn't encourage it—though he didn't know until a little while ago that Hutter College had printed up its faculty works—and that Witherspoon was at Hutter. Witherspoon had been at Yale for years and Fletcher did his graduate work there. The introduction to Witherspoon's book says something about it being taken from a seminar series he presented at Yale. Anyway, the two books are twins—not quite identical but very, very close. Paragraph after paragraph."

Alex reached for the books and turned several pages. "And Alice Marmott helped log in the Hutter books. She must have confronted Fletcher with the awful news—or Mrs. Parker. Or both. Maybe she didn't tell him the source of her information, because if she had then Fletcher would have made that book—or the whole Hutter College pile—go up in smoke."

"Do you think," said Sarah, "Mrs. Parker knew what this was all about?"

"She might not have known a Finnsburg Fragment or about Sutton Hoo, but she sure as hell would have known plagiarism. Now she had her knife at Fletcher's throat and could really go after that degree."

Sarah thought for a moment and then made a regretful noise. "I blew it. Alice almost told me the night of the hockey game. She said she'd been doing research on archaeological finds—said that pre-Viking relics had been found at Sutton Hoo. It went right out of my head. Sutton Hoo's in Suffolk. A whole ship cenotaph was found there."

Mike Laaka held up his hand. "I know I'll be sorry if I ask, but please, tell me about *Beowulf*—in twenty words or less."

Sarah laughed. "I haven't read it yet, except in translation. It's a long poem in Old English, an old Germanic language, probably early eighth century. The manuscript lives in the British Museum and it's about battles, warrior heroes, swords, faithful henchmen, two monsters and a dragon."

"Dragon like Constance Garvey?"

"Right, but in the end Beowulf, the hero, meets up with this fearful dragon who has a gold hoard and Beowulf dies. *The Finnsburg Fragment*—"

"That's the Finn clue?"

"Yes, and it's another slice of the same. And Sutton Hoo —Mrs. Parker's abbreviation said SHOO, not S. HOO—is a place in England that an actual burial ship was found. Anglo-Saxons buried swords and helmets and eating and drinking vessels in the ships so the dead warrior could sail to the next world. Though the Sutton-Hoo ship didn't have a body. Christianity was creeping in."

"Then it was kind of appropriate," said Mike, "that this professor of Old English and a *Beowulf* expert buried this hotshot Old English student in an ice ship. Some of the sculptures were a lot easier to get at, more out of the way, and didn't need ladders."

Alex and Sarah stared at Mike.

"You mean," said Mike, "you didn't think of that yourselves? Shows what too much schooling does. Absolutely paralyzes the brain. So long. I'll pick up Mary at the ski slope and tell her that Lushwell's in the clear."

EIGHTEEN

One hour and a hot bath and a gallon of tea later, Sarah made her way to the kitchen and found Patsy asleep in a corner and, on the counter, an impressive array of cartons and serving dishes. Alex was at the stove with a tea towel around his waist. "I bought one of everything," he said. "From the Philippine take-out. Mike's bringing Mary over for dinner. She wants to know what's been going on. I'd forgotten that she doesn't know about Mrs. Parker's expanded blackmail game. Mike says all he's told her are that the Fletchers are in custody and that Amos Larkin is off George's list."

At which point Mike banged on the door and Mary appeared. "I've got to go," Mike said. "George wants me for a wrap-up, so it's goodbye. It's vacation for the overworked deputy. I'm off to the races—the Woodward, the Blue Grass, the Derby Trial. Life as it was meant to be lived."

"Not the Derby?" said Alex.

"Back on duty Derby Day. Can't have everything." And he closed the door behind him.

Mary, still in ski pants and sweater, accepted a glass of Alex's latest drink discovery, described as a Canadian special called "One-Two-Three," a tincture of whiskey, maple syrup, and lemon. Mary took an appreciative sip and walked over to inspect the kitchen tables. "This Philippine food's probably a lot better than the English Department dinner, except I paid eight dollars for that one."

"You mean the Ski Club dinner's actually taking place?" said Sarah. "After all that's happened?"

Mary took a healthy gulp of her whiskey. "An object in motion tends to stay in motion. What are two murders more or less? Keeps the conversation going. I'll bet they all still suspect each other, and with good reason. Bunch of crooks."

"Not all," said Sarah. "Here and there an honest face."

Mary selected an egg roll and settled down at the table. "Fill me in, for God's sake. All I know is that Amos Larkin didn't kill anyone and that Professor Fletcher did and somehow his wife got into the act, and what was in that book we were all looking for? And Alice Marmott. How does she figure in?"

"Do you want to start with the cyanide and work back?" said Sarah, joining her at the table.

"Cyanide by all means," said Mary, sipping her drink. "And say it all slowly, because it's been hard work on the ski slopes trying to find where you'd been kidnapped from."

"Which I wasn't. Skied into my own trap. Come on, Alex. Sit down. The cyanide thing is your baby."

Alex cleared a place at the table and put down a jar of mustard and a bowl of duck sauce. Then, joining them at the table, he shook his head. "If we'd had just the two murders we might still be on square one, but the poisoning of Sarah's Thermos speeded things. Potassium cyanide crystals not completely dissolved meant that the murderer—and we can call him Patrick Fletcher now—had to be able to get his hands on the stuff in a hurry. He may have been watching Sarah because of her asking to do research in Old English—the Alice Marmott act she's now told me about—but Fletcher couldn't have anticipated her going through the Hutter collection; he didn't even know himself about their library being at Bowmouth, or that Witherspoon had ended his career at Hutter."

"Did Fletcher have cyanide in his pocket?" asked Sarah.

"I wouldn't have thought so," said Alex. "Not to do a Rare Book Room job."

"But how could he have slipped away to get it?"

"His house!" said Mary excitedly. "His house. The Fletchers live just off campus. Don't you see, he could run over, grab the stuff, and make it back without trouble."

"Yes," said Alex, "it would have been just possible. Assuming that he kept it at home." He rose and brought over a heaped dish in which tiny shrimp and pea pods poked out of a nest of thin noodles. "To manage the poisoning of Sarah's Thermos—the one he thought was hers because no one would believe there were *two* Raggedy Anns in the library —there wasn't time for the murderer to dash over to any of the college labs. So Mary's right. Fletcher was the only one of the English faculty who lived next to the campus. But even if he can do a four-minute mile it would be a risky run. His absence for ten, even fifteen minutes would be noticed."

Sarah reached for a plate. "So what are you saying? That he did have it in his pocket or had it stashed in the library."

"Who was his handy helpful assistant?"

"What! Oh, Lord, of course! How could I miss it. He said he had to call his wife about being late for lunch. What Fletcher must have done was to call her and tell her to get over to the library fast with the family supply of cyanide. But where did he get it? Pure potassium cyanide?" She turned to Mary. "I kept telling Alex to look up what kind of poison went into taxidermy and shrunken heads—you know Vera Pruczak and her crocodile Tick-Tock and those other awful things, and Mrs. Horst and her herbs and dried flowers. And with Horst being into drugs, who knows what supplies *he* had. And there were the Fletchers with all those old pots and jars, and Lacey had his own darkroom, and Amos Larkin with a brother in the med school. I don't know about Constance Garvey."

"Garvey probably exudes cyanide," said Mary, "from every pore."

"Anyway, I told Alex to start working with the anthropology and nature books, the botany texts, and photographic guides. And he did."

"When we were trying to figure out Mrs. Parker's death, the source of the cyanide was a real puzzler. It was too available. In fact, I'd decided that cyanide was about as available at Bowmouth as instant coffee."

"That's good to know," said Mary. She reached for a second egg roll. "Tonight's not the time to work on my diet."

"It finally came together," said Alex. "I jumped when I saw the word 'killing' in the butterfly field guide. Cyanide in a crystal form is used for killing bottles by butterfly collectors, and I knew from Sarah's description of her visit—"

"Yes!" shouted Mary, upsetting her glass. "The Fletchers. La Casa Fletcher. Those endless cases of butterflies. And they're so proud of their collections—Professor and Mrs. Perfecto and their little culture tours. Shit, that's my whole drink." She unfolded her napkin and began sopping up the spreading liquid.

"You see," said Alex, passing over a paper towel, "I had a butterfly-collecting phase when I was twelve or so. But I couldn't bring myself to kill them with tweezers, and I wasn't allowed to fool with cyanide. The idea is for the butterflies not to go into a spasm and fold their wings."

"You're not doing much for my appetite," said Mary. "But I could use another of that whiskey potion—One-Two-Three. What you're saying is that all Professor Fletcher had to do was help himself to the family killing supplies to poison Mrs. Parker and yesterday telephone to his wife for a dose for Sarah's Thermos. All *she* had to do was dash over to the library while Fletcher slipped outside for a minute, palmed the stuff, and dumped it into Raggedy Ann. Easy as pie. Do you think Mrs. Fletcher helped him do in Alice too?"

"I think he probably took care of Alice by himself," said Alex. "George's questioning of the hockey game fans showed Mrs. Fletcher was a full-time spectator, while Fletcher wasn't. But she claimed that her husband was just around the corner, never left the rink, and so forth. She was his cover. And the police had so many other suspects coming and going that night that Fletcher was lost in the shuffle of candidates."

"I hate to be simpleminded," said Mary, accepting her refilled glass, "but *why*? Why kill Alice and Mrs. Parker and try to poison Sarah's Thermos? Patrick Fletcher had everything—he was what they call a distinguished man of letters. Full professor and Mr. Old English at Bowmouth with a devoted wife and that museum of a house. And he was always bombing around the country speaking and doing symposiums. What I mean, why blow it all by getting into murder?"

"I defer to Sarah," said Alex. "Do you want to tell Mary why?"

Sarah looked at the table. "Okay, if Alex will go on being the food dispenser and poison consultant. I'd like that Luglug and some Chicken Adobo, and Mary's plate is empty. Okay. It's like this. Don't start with Alice, start with Mrs. Parker."

"Our mother superior of reverent memory," said Mary. She leaned back in her chair and held her glass just under her nose.

"Mrs. Parker made it her business to mind other people's business," said Sarah. "As we know. When I first got here I couldn't believe she had such a grip on the place. Professor Bello was invisible—by choice, I guess—but a lot of them seem to have handed over everything but the actual teaching and writing to her."

Mary nodded wisely. "And so she got too grabby for her own good. Was that it? Professor Fletcher didn't want her to have any more perks than she'd already taken? After all, she was the *secretary.*"

"You mean the honorary degree business?" put in Alex. Mary exclaimed, and Sarah filled her in on Mrs. Parker's academic gown.

"Well, no wonder he killed her," said Mary. "Fletcher wouldn't be able to stand seeing Parker in a doctoral robe."

"No one in the department could. They all told her it was impossible, but that wasn't why she was killed." Sarah took a tentative taste of the Chicken Adobo and then pointed at Alex. "Tell Mary why Mrs. Parker wanted an honorary degree right now, at this spring's commencement."

"Cancer," said Alex. "She was at the end of the line. What good were all these special perks if you were dying? Mrs. Parker wanted some lasting mark of recognition. It wasn't reasonable, but she'd stopped being reasonable, and then she had her special power base."

So as they worked their way through the cartons of hot and spicy food, Alex explained Mrs. Parker's extracurricular activities, and then the three settled down by the wood stove on the red sofa.

"George is sure now that Miss Prism was Parker's information pipeline," said Alex, handing around the brandy. "It'll be tough to prove, but he doubts whether Parker could have gotten her hands on some of that data without help in high places. As registrar, Miss Prism could search out transcripts and chase down old records. And George found out that Melanie Prism and Rosalind Parker were childhood buddies, went through grade school, high school, and the first two years of college together. And Prism was instrumental in getting Parker her job with the English Department."

Sarah lifted her face out of her brandy glass. "As I suggested once, perfect friendship."

"No more than that, I think," said Alex. "But a strong enough tie for Mrs. Parker's purposes. She seems to have been the dominant character of the two and probably told Prism she was acting in the best interests of the college. But Parker had the blackmailer's chief fault—she always wanted more."

"Like Oliver," said Mary.

"Yes," said Alex, "but they often end up like Mrs. Parker. And among the faculty who seemed to be in the clear was Patrick Fletcher. Just some strange notations about FINN, MO, and SHOO—which we took as one word—and an unpublished manuscript on his tape which Sarah will explain sometime. Anyway, Mrs. Parker started to be very insistent about the honorary degree and to sprinkle résumés around with not very encouraging results, when who should appear . . ."

"But that poor dumb brilliant Alice Marmott," said Mary sighing.

"No one could have predicted Alice," said Sarah. "The super-scholar who could even work Mrs. Parker under the desk."

"Go on, put me out of my misery."

"Alice, because she spent all her free time burrowing in the library, caught Fletcher out. He was very nasty when Alice asked to do a critical paper in Old English. None of the faculty encouraged it, but Fletcher almost threw Alice out of class because of it. Half his life he must have been waiting for something to happen, for the shoe to drop. Anyway, after I found out that Alice had helped log in the Hutter Collection, it seemed likely that she'd dug up something unsavory. I'll bet that Alice went to Mrs. Parker and said, 'Look what terrible thing I've found out about Professor Fletcher's *Beowulf* study' —his magnum opus—and Mrs. Parker added the information to her blackmail bag."

"And now," said Alex, "she had a hold over the big gun in the department. She must have thought that someone like Fletcher might have enough weight to get that honorary degree for her."

"I don't know if it's the whiskey, but you're muddling my already muddled head," complained Mary. "You mean Alice and Parker both knew the same something against Fletcher?"

"They must have. But Alice first. Alice was in the English Office the night of the hockey game with Mrs. Parker— confirmed by Arlene. Alice must have told Mrs. Parker that Professor Fletcher was not the paragon everyone thought. Alice, who was direct to the point of foolishness, who would never back down, probably went to call Fletcher on it and was stopped by Parker, who stopped everyone."

Mary sat up. "Parker would say, 'Miss Marmott, I am always ready to help. Please tell me your troubles because you can't see Professor Fletcher. He's much too busy'—which is what she always said."

"So Alice, all indignant, told Mrs. Parker why she had to see him."

"Told her why what?" shouted Mary. "You've lost me."

"I've been telling you. Professor Witherspoon and Professor Fletcher wrote the same thing. But Witherspoon did it first."

"You mean the great god Fletcher stole someone else's stuff? Stole, copied, lifted? Come on, Sarah."

"What do you think we were poking through all those dissertations and Hutter Library books for?"

"I didn't think. For some weird fact, some exotica. The proof that the murderer had used an Old English cyanide recipe, maybe, or that Alice had found proof that Garvey had shat on a manuscript."

"No, it's simpler than that. Plagiarism, as it's called in the trade. Anyway, Alice, who never gave up, undoubtedly hung around, and when Fletcher left the English Office building on his way to the hockey game, she confronted him. End of Alice. It was almost easy. North Quad deserted, Amos Larkin passed out, his scarf available. Strangle Alice, undress Amos—hoping he'd freeze to death—go through Alice's briefcase and take out any suggestive Old English material and, for good measure, take out notes from Amos Larkin's class, the better to pin the death on him."

Mary was silent for a minute and then shook her head slowly from side to side. "Poor Alice, poor Amos. Oh, my God."

Sarah leaned back against the cushions of the sofa and looked into the open stove door, seeing the fire throwing up leaping shadows on the walls and darkened windows. Anyone walking in would see only the sleeping dog and three friends enjoying a late evening drink and civil conversation. One of those scenes that people outside of the academic community imagine to be the daily rule. Easy, friendly, even erudite debate, reasonable differences expressed in reasonable ways. Lives lived as an example to the young. "Hah!" she said aloud.

"Hah what?" said Mary, startled.

"I know," said Alex, suddenly clairvoyant. "It isn't fitting, is it? All this talk about adequate doses of cyanide and murdering professors and dog-eat-dog faculty and criminal secretaries."

"I've never had any cozy idea that Bowmouth was in the least civilized," said Mary. "It may have its bright lights but there's still a nest of vipers down in the cellar."

"I suppose," said Sarah thoughtfully, "that if Hutter College hadn't gone bankrupt binding all their faculty's writing in that expensive olive leather, Professor Fletcher would have ended his days here in all honor, probably having an Old English chair named after him. Professor Witherspoon's book had been originally a mimeographed manuscript that he'd used for a seminar he gave to a graduate literature class one summer at Yale. That was in the introduction of the bound Hutter volume, plus a note adding that the author was grateful that his little effort had found a home and a fine leather coat. Professor Witherspoon was sort of quaint."

"The police checked," said Alex. "Fletcher was in graduate school at Yale then. I'll bet he was in that seminar."

"Cripes," said Mary. "Why didn't Professor Witherspoon yell 'Stop thief?'"

"Because," said Alex, "when Fletcher published his *Beowulf* masterpiece—his magnum opus—Professor Wigglesworth was in his nineties, was professor emeritus, and in a nursing home."

"Fletcher took a chance that no one else in the class would recognize it," said Mary.

"Plagiarists always take a chance. But how many seminar papers do you remember twenty or more years later?" said Sarah. "That was before everyone took tape recorders to class."

"And little Alice the Beaver did it all."

"'Left no stone unturned' should be on Alice's grave," said Sarah. "Alice saw that Fletcher's book—the whole first three chapters, the thesis, the conclusion—was pure Samuel D. Witherspoon. Fletcher expanded it, dressed it up with references, more quotes from *Beowulf*, but it was the same idea and it spells plagiarism with a capital *P.*"

Mary stretched herself and pulled a pillow under her head. "I don't think I have the strength for Mrs. Parker's murder. Capsulate it, Sarah, because I'm weary with skiing and fain would lie down."

"You are down," said Sarah. "And I don't think much of this is very funny."

"I'm not trying to be funny, not really. It's just past my bedtime. And don't you be stuffy. Bad enough to work in a department of stuffed shirts without finding you turning into a stuffed blouse. Anyway, Patrick Fletcher decided to murder Parker before she could squeeze him dry or ruin him. Or get herself a Ph.D."

"In a capsule, yes," said Sarah. "He must have found out that she often worked late learning to use the word processor, so he prepared a manuscript."

"Knew she just loved to type manuscripts," said Mary. "The secretary's road to glory."

"I'd guess he made up a manuscript just long enough for someone to finish on the word processor in, say, three hours.

That put her safe in the English Office with the covered door."

"Bided his time," said Mary. "Then the big snowstorm. English Department filled with murderous types. No one would know who came or went."

"Which they didn't," said Alex. "And Fletcher must have been pleased to see that Amos was again conveniently drunk, passed out in the waiting room, but, of course, he didn't figure on Mary and Sarah hiding out and the body being found so promptly. He arranged to turn down the heat, almost forcing Mrs. Parker to drink her hot cocoa and knowing that the cold office would have made the almond smell less noticeable. So he waited his chance and doctored her Thermos sometime that evening. Probably had her in a good mood by making encouraging noises about the honorary degree."

"Supposition, supposition," said Mary, from the end of the sofa. "Conclusions without a premise. Hypothesis without fact. Illogical scenario."

"Have you got a better one?" demanded Sarah, suddenly weary of the whole thing, yearning for bed, quilt, pillow, and Alex alone.

"I'm just a little Italian girl looking for Mr. Right. Red whiskers, red tail, pointed ears."

"And I hope he bites your nose off," said Sarah, "because you are *asking* for it. Not being a murderer doesn't turn Amos Larkin into a admirable character, and let me finish. Mrs. Parker works late, starts to word-process the manuscript that Fletcher gives to her after the department clears out. Ready and waiting is the printer with its new printing thimble. That's where I should have come to when Linda told me the printer didn't have its regular thimble. This was a special-language one with accent marks, the Greek alphabet, and the Old English symbols, the eth, the ash, and the thorn."

Mary nodded. "And Fletcher is the master of the eth and the ash and the thorn."

"Right. So Fletcher hides out in his office, waits for the body to crash, runs in, makes sure the plug is out of the computer and printer, grabs the disks and the manuscript. Leaves either by the regular door or, to be safe, out the back hall fire-escape window."

Alex revived. "That's what we gather Amos Larkin did. Woke up sometime that night and departed by fire escape . . . probably still half soused. Left a glove on the stairs. It's a wonder he didn't bump into Fletcher. Of course, George thought that the disturbed snow came only from Amos."

Mary heaved herself into a sitting position. "I suppose it's too late to make a formal call on Amos Larkin. Tell him all is forgiven."

"Much too late," said Alex. "I'll drive you home."

"That's what I want, a home. A sort of wrecked old farmhouse with a porch and maybe a ski run going past the back half acre. And don't you be a wet blanket, Ms. Deane. To each his own."

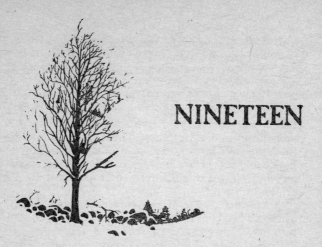

NINETEEN

T he next afternoon Alex and Sarah took advantage of an
unexpected display of sunshine to go on a long walk—
Alex in the hope of a reported short-eared owl or an early
spring migrant, Sarah, with Patsy on a short lead and wearing
his new choke collar, intending to make a start on the long
neglected matter of Patsy's obedience training. After a period
of leisurely sauntering along a country road, they met Vera
Pruczak with a fringed shawl, green leather boots, and a large
orange cat on a leash.

"Darlings. This is Ishtar. He belonged to Rosalind
Parker, who called him 'Bowmouth.' Too dreary. I've re-
named him and taken him in. And all this excitement. Better
than anything I could write. Think of Patrick Fletcher jumping
out of the library window into that pile of snow. So demean-
ing for him. But I'm using him in my next. Wicked Lord
Hamstead poisons Dame Moira's posset after she's retired to
her closet and everyone thinks he's gone to rescue Lady
Sarah."

"Does Lady Sarah get rescued?" asked Sarah, interested.

"Of course. But not until the last gasp. You shall have a
copy."

Alex and Sarah continued their walk, not caring much
about direction or progress or Patsy's failure to heel. Alex
revived the subject of marriage.

"Have you been thinking about it?"

"I'll start. As soon as I get my breath."

"A little country wedding, then true-blue New England summer peace and quiet."

"You mean like the winter peace and quiet we've just finished with? Never mind, I do love you and I'll think about that country wedding." Sarah smiled and pushed her hand more firmly under Alex's arm. Then, looking ahead down the road, she saw a man and a woman walking toward them: Amos Larkin and Mary Donelli. Mary, dark hair loose, cheeks glowing, looking in a long hooded scarlet wool coat like someone escaped from a Donizetti opera.

"Hi, there," said Mary. "How do you feel, Sarah? I had a hell of a head this morning. All that Pansit Tagalog and Alex with his whiskey One-Two-Three *and* brandy."

"Fortunately," said Amos Larkin, "she knew where to go for advice on morning heads."

With the appearance of small pale clumps of snowdrops and daffodils, spring came to Bowmouth College. The English Department, shaken to its roots by earlier events, began to regroup and reshape itself. Professor Fletcher's classes were divided up among the senior faculty; Howard Bello, with a sigh of relief, drew up plans to rotate out of his job as chairman and turn the department over to Joe Greenberg; and Linda Lacroix, now officially in place as the department secretary, showed symptoms of becoming a new despot.

As the temperature moved more reliably into the fifties and lower sixties, Professor Ivan Lacey appeared on the campus roads in a Mustang convertible and took to wearing yellow open-necked shirts and designer jeans for his classroom appearances; Professor Merlin-Smith faded further into the academic woodwork; Constance Garvey, following a luncheon and the presentation of a silver tray, retired; and as for Jakob Horst, he departed for either another teaching position or a drug rehabilitation center (campus opinion divided on this).

In the final weeks of May, Mary Donelli successfully defended her dissertation on the poetry of Jonathan Swift, and Vera Pruczak's production of *King Lear* (with Sarah Deane listed as understudy to Goneril) was pronounced a smash. Occasionally some members of the college community mentioned former Professor Fletcher, whose scheduled trial would no doubt enliven the Bowmouth summer term, but on the whole the interest of most people turned on the one hundred and eighty-second Bowmouth College commencement and the promise of a perfect June day.

Sarah, feeling rather frivolous in a new straw hat and a red-and-white striped dress, stood by Alex's side after the final speech had been made, the last degree awarded, the last photograph taken by the last of the proud families. Alex, she thought, looked remarkably distinguished in his black gown with the green velvet hood showing the doctor of medicine. He had complained mightily of having to parade in costume but said the medical school had turned the screws; the dean liked a faculty display.

Equally distinguished was Mary Donelli in her black cap with its gold tassel, her gown with its black velvet panels and bands and with its long hood lined in Bowmouth's crimson and blue and edged in white, showing the doctor of philosophy. Professor Amos Larkin, impressive in his Cambridge academic robes, joined them and shook Sarah and Alex's hands.

"I'll be staying here with my nose to the grindstone. Assistant Professor Donelli, here, and I are roughing in a new biography of Swift. *The Early Years.* You know how it is, publish or perish." He looked at Sarah and winked. "Have a good summer, Amanda Tibbs."

THE SARAH DEANE MYSTERIES BY

✿✿✿ J. S. BORTHWICK ✿✿✿

FROM ST. MARTIN'S PAPERBACKS
—COLLECT THEM ALL!